Governing Passions

Love in a Changing Climate

Book 2

Chris Cheek

2FM Limited

Consultancy and Analysis
Publishing & Communication

**83 Latimer Road, Eastbourne
East Sussex, BN22 7EL**

Tel: 01729 840756
e-mail: admin@two-fm.co.uk

Cover images: Shutterstock, David Burrell

A CIP catalogue record for this book is available
from the British Library

ISBN 978-1-9996479-4-0

"Three passions, simple but overwhelmingly strong, have governed my life: the longing for love, the search for knowledge, and unbearable pity for the suffering of mankind."

Bertrand Russell

Prologue

Luke

It's late and we've been drinking. It's the last Sunday night of term, all exams finished, results keenly awaited. After visiting a couple of pubs and eating in our favourite Italian, six of us have ended up back at the flat that Annie, Jackie and Jenny share with their friend Lauren. We've been drinking coffee and raiding Annie's drinks cupboard. The Spanish brandy has gone and we've moved on to liqueurs.

"We ought to move," says Dan, looking at me. "If we're going to get back to the campus without spending a fortune on a cab."

I nod slowly, reluctant to leave my comfortable place next to Jenny. "I know, Dan. The last bus beckons." There are six of us in the room – all friends from the university's debating society – political animals to our fingertips, but not affiliated to one party or another. We're either genuinely undecided or unwilling to declare yet.

Dan, Annie, Jackie, Robbie, Jenny and me. All close, and apparently three happy couples, enjoying a hedonistic few weeks at the end of term; in five cases, the end of their university careers, and in my case, waiting to see whether I can get beyond my freshman year. Judging by how little I actually knew when I sat down to do my first-year exams, it's going to be a close-run thing.

But we aren't actually three couples at all, in the true

sense of the word. True, Dan and Annie did have a fling at the start of the academic year, but something must have happened because they've been much more distant during the summer term – barely friends. Jackie and Robbie are certainly very close, and they're good together. Jenny is my girlfriend – except she doesn't know I am using her as cover.

She is blissfully ignorant of the fact that think I'm probably gay and that the only feelings I have for anybody in the room are for Dan. The sole inaccurate word in that last sentence is "probably". *Of course* I'm gay – I've known that since the age of thirteen but have never actually accepted it. At the start of my university career, I decided that it was only a phase and that I'd put it all behind me. I am now a nineteen-year-old adult, an undergraduate at university, not some pubescent kid in Year 10, and I'm jolly well going to behave like one. And being gay is definitely *not* part of that.

Except it hasn't gone at all according to plan, and here I am in love with the man who's become my closest friend. Instead of hanging out, doing stupid student stuff together, I am sitting here desperate to reach out and touch him, to run my hands through his soft brown hair, to kiss those pretty lips and bathe in affection from those gorgeous blue eyes...

I shake my head to clear it and smile at nobody in particular. *Of course* he isn't gay. And he's certainly not interested in me in *that* way. We've become close during the last twelve months, even though he's in his final year and I'm in my first, so much so that he's probably one of the best friends I've ever had. I really must try to get over this stupid crush.

We first met during the Freshers' Fair in my first week as a student. He was president of the Debating Society. As I wandered around the stands at the fair, I immediately felt attracted to his personality as well as his looks. It absolutely didn't matter that he struck me as one of the most beautiful men I'd ever seen – though, of course, I wasn't doing any of the gay stuff. That phase was so over. When I expressed interest in joining, he was charming, friendly and welcoming. In conversation he had this knack of focusing and making eye contact so that you felt that you were the only person in the world that he wanted to talk to at that moment. It made you feel so warm and secure. At least it did me.

Over the winter, we discovered shared tastes for music, sci-fi films (*Star Wars* in particular) and we loved many of the same books. We even followed the same football team, and went to a match together during the Christmas vac.

At the start of the summer term, our friendship was cemented when we worked closely together organising a series of debates during the General Election campaign that went on through May. Even though there had never been any doubt that Tony Blair would repeat his 1997 triumph, there were still plenty of things to talk about – not least the prospect of Britain joining the European single currency. Because the campaign coincided with Dan's finals I did most of the grunt work, but we consulted about the arrangements every day. I helped him revise for a couple of his papers, too, and saw him through a couple of bad nights when the stress almost got the better of him towards the end of the exams.

The prospect of Blair being elected for a second term as PM only seemed to bother those on the far left, who regarded him as some sort of closet Tory. Not that the Tories would agree with that, of course. But they were defeated, demoralised, and hardly seemed relevant to Britain in the second year of the twenty-first century. Right?

Yeah. Anyway, here we are at eleven-thirty on a Sunday night, feeling all comfortable and friendly, knowing that this is probably one of the last times we'll be together as a gang, if that's what we are. Dan and I are planning a holiday at the end of term. He's staying up for the week between before the graduation ceremony and I'm going to be here as well before I take up my summer vacation job. We're plotting some cool hiking trips.

It seems too much of an effort to move, all for the sake of a last bus home. "You could always stay here," Jackie says. "Lauren's away for another night, so two of you could borrow her bed." Lauren, the girls' fourth flatmate, has largely stuck to her own circle of friends and now that she's in a relationship she rarely sleeps at home.

I look up at Dan, who cocks an eyebrow. He could be flirting with me, seeking my assent to a night of unbridled passion. *In your dreams, Luke.*

"Thanks, Jackie. Terrific. Shame to break up the party."

Dan nods. "Cool, Jackie. Thanks. Now who's for another liqueur?"

It's six in the morning. Last night we had a few more

drinks and Dan and I were fairly sloshed when we fell into Lauren's big double bed. I'd been asleep in minutes, determined that nothing whatsoever would happen between us, and virtually clinging on to the edge of the mattress to prevent myself from bumping into any part of Dan's body. I could feel his heat under the bedclothes on that warm summer's evening.

My resolution that nothing would happen is still at the forefront of my mind. Now, though, lying awake at six in the morning, it feels a bit different. I turn onto my other side so that I am facing him. I watch him sleep in the dim, early-morning light.

God, but he looks so beautiful. I love him so much and we get on so well. How great it would be if we could spend the rest of our lives together. I squeeze my eyes shut but cannot prevent a tear from escaping and dropping on to my pillow. I've never felt like this about anybody before and it's torture not being able to do anything or say anything about it to anyone.

There's a sudden movement. Dan snuffles a little in his sleep and turns over, facing away from me, but the movement brings his whole body closer. I can feel the heat of his skin so near that I tremble slightly. Could it be? Is there a possibility that, after all, something might happen?

Then I make the fatal mistake. I ease myself forward as if to spoon him. I am, of course, rock hard by now. Gradually I move close enough for him to know that I am there, without actually touching him. Except that my erection brushes one of his arse cheeks.

I remain where I am, tense from making sure that I don't move, trying to enjoy the moment of closeness, absorbing

Dan's warmth through my every pore. But a moment is all it proves to be. Dan moves away, my proximity having awoken him. Abruptly, he gets out of bed and leaves the room.

Nothing is ever said. I get a short note from him to say that he's sorry but the hiking trip is off – something has come up and he has to go home. I avoid all of our friends during the last week of term and don't exchange another word with him before he leaves, complete with the First for which he had hoped and worked so hard. I don't even get to congratulate him.

Chapter 1

Fifteen Years Later, September 2017

Luke

"Ladies and gentlemen, please welcome your grooms for today, Joshua Ashcroft and Steve Frazer."

Predictably, the room erupted into applause. My boss, Steve, and his much-loved partner, Josh, were at long last tying the knot – formalising a relationship that all of us at Pearson Frazer had watched grow with increasing joy and admiration.

Even though they were fourteen years apart in age, they seemed made for each other. Watching the transformation that their love had wrought in my boss had been an astonishing experience. From a grumpy, humourless bear who seemed perpetually about to erupt into volcanic rage, Steve had become a gentle, witty man. He was still committed to everything that the consultancy firm he'd co-founded with Andy Pearson and our practice manager Barbara stood for and just as passionate about the quality of our work, but he was so much less tortured and more comfortable with himself.

Now, after three years together and two years after their engagement, Steve and Josh were at last formalising their relationship into a marriage. It was a moving moment for all of us at the firm – especially those, like me, who had first welcomed Josh as a young consultant with his new doctorate, a terrific sense of humour and a pronounced tendency to blush at the slightest provocation. As you can imagine, today being his wedding day, he was spending a great deal of time being rather red in the face.

We'd all watched with growing admiration how he had handled Steve, coaxing him out of his shell and forcing him to face up to the realities of whatever had happened in his past life. None of us had known the details, of course, until that awful day when Steve had been stabbed in the pub in his home village by the person responsible for the death of his boyhood sweetheart. I, for one, would never forget the terrible moment when Barbara emerged from her office having taken an urgent call from Josh to tell us about the assault.

In that year of astonishing stories, we also learned that not only was Josh a brilliant environmental consultant, he was also an accomplished jazz and swing performer. That was the career he'd been following with increasing success ever since; indeed, the Joshua Ashcroft Trio was now one of the biggest selling jazz combos in the UK market.

Talk about a roller-coaster ride!

Now that we'd formally welcomed the happy couple, we could move on to the speeches and then the food. The speeches involved much humour, a great deal of cheering

– especially from the Pearson Frazer contingent – and lots of references to music and Hollywood films. We had our suspicions confirmed that afternoon: Steve was the Scarlett O'Hara of the relationship, whilst Josh was the Rhett Butler.

Predictably, when it came to Josh's turn to make a speech he decided to do it in song instead of words. We got his signature tunes of "Fly Me to the Moon" and "Luck be a Lady", before surprising everybody – including Steve – with a rendition of a country song by the out-gay singer Billy Gilman. Called "I Will", it brought the house down and there wasn't a dry eye in the room.

I loved the whole day but couldn't help being reminded of my own situation in life. I had spent the last fifteen years flitting from one partner to another, mainly after a single night. My experiences over the years had taught me that getting sex and friendship muddled up into one concept called "a relationship" simply didn't work. Sex was sex and friendship was friendship and never the twain should meet, at least as far as I was concerned. That was my philosophy and it worked most of the time; I enjoyed myself and had some great sex – even spectacular on one or two occasions. But the truth was that the great moments were increasingly far in the past. At the age of thirty-four, the task of finding suitable and willing partners when I was in the mood was getting more difficult – not to say exhausting – and frequently dispiriting.

I was determined to avoid sliding back into the pit of depression that I'd suffered after the business with Dan at the end of my first year at university; that pit took a long time to climb out of, costing me a year of my life and a bundle of heartache. But I had emerged stronger for the experience, formed a plan, and by and large stuck to it. The trouble was that sometimes it was difficult to appreciate what my plan had brought me: as much loneliness as I'd suffered during my student days. I didn't have many friends since I tended to push them away with my standoffishness. True, I had achieved some material prosperity, particularly since joining Pearson Frazer, but what was the use of that without somebody to share it with?

I reached for the red wine, determined not to allow my bleak thoughts spoil the day, and made a dogged effort to join in the conversation with my colleagues at the table. The new lad, Matt Somerville, who had joined three months ago, was also sitting on his own. In many ways he reminded me of Josh when he'd first joined – bright and humorous but painfully shy. I spent the next hour trying to draw him out of his shell, with some success though it was hard work. Then Steve and Josh came to sit at our table, which prompted Matt to go even redder and flee in the direction of the gents.

"It's Steve's fault. He teases poor Matt something rotten, as a result of which the boy is even more terrified of him than we were," Josh confessed. "You'll have to train him better, Luke."

I grinned at him. "I thought training Steve was your job now, young Josh."

"I know, but there are limits, especially when I'm away. You'll have to join the rota with Barbara and Andy. It's called the KFUC committee – as in Keep Frazer Under Control."

Steve had been talking to his business partner, Andy

Pearson, but now turned to us and looked at Josh with a quizzical eye. "Are you fermenting rebellion amongst our staff again?"

Josh laughed. "No, no – busy engaging Luke as part of the committee to keep you under control."

Steve huffed. "Oh, is that all? But I'm just a little woolly lamb these days – always there to do as I'm bidden."

"What, chewing grass and growing wool?" Josh replied with an expression of mock horror. "That's not going to keep me in any sort of style. Should I start the divorce proceedings now, Luke, do you think?"

I put up my hands in surrender, laughing at their banter. "Don't involve me in any of this. I'm strictly neutral. But meanwhile, can I offer my congratulations to you both – and my thanks? It's been a lovely day."

Josh took me into a big hug and it was one of those moments that mean so much. We broke the embrace but he kept hold of my elbows and looked me in the eye. "I caught sight of you earlier looking very solemn. Are you okay?"

I smiled at him. "Yeah, fine, thanks. There are times, you know, when I miss having somebody in my life. I think today was one of them."

Josh nodded. "I can understand that, Luke. Been there. Just keep in touch, okay. Don't be a stranger – and I'll see if I can set you up with a hot drummer."

I laughed. "Why a drummer, Josh?"

"A great sense of rhythm, silly." He laughed and winked at me. "Keep up the pace all night."

I've always found September an unsettling month. I suppose that's because, for most schoolkids, it has always been the point of change – moving up a form, changing teachers or schools, later going to college. University careers start in late September or early October, too.

The result was that, even in my mid-thirties, the onset of autumn tended to make me fidgety. If no changes happened, as seemed likely this year, it made me wonder why. I started to worry that my life was so dull that nothing interesting was ever likely to happen again. I knew it was ridiculous but it reinforced the oddness of my mood.

Anyway, I was wrong. Things were about to change for me, and in a bigger way than I had expected.

It all started when Steve and Josh got back from their honeymoon. They'd been away for three weeks and would have stayed longer but for a big meeting with a major client that was set for the last week of the month. The Griffin House project was a government contract that Steve, together with Josh during his time with the firm, had won for us against all the odds three years earlier. Named after the building in Bristol from where it was run, the project was a partnership involving academics, civil servants and the private sector to administer a grant scheme for environmental projects. Evaluating applications, processing grants and then assessing the effectiveness of the projects had been the foundation of our current prosperity as a firm. The Griffin House project was important to us all, and there was no way that Steve would miss the engagement.

Steve got back to the office a few days before the meeting, which was scheduled for the following Monday. On the Thursday, he called us all in for intelligence gathering and a brainstorm on tactics. He asked whether any of our contacts had given us a heads-up as to what might be happening. We had a good session: everybody had heard hints that the project was regarded as a success for government and there was a desire in some quarters to renew and extend the scheme. Indeed, the whole approach we'd developed for the grant system was being touted as a template for the government's post-Brexit rural strategy –if they ever got round to thinking about one. There were some opponents, especially in the Treasury, but that was inevitable. The expected outcome was a round-table conference to discuss the future, to which Pearson Frazer would be invited to contribute.

We started to leave the room, ribbing Steve gently about the end of his honeymoon period and facing up to reality – stroppy clients and an English winter. As I reached the door, I heard his voice calling me back. "Luke, a word, please, if I may?"

"Sure, boss. What can I do for you?"

"Two things. First there's a message from Josh. I don't understand it, but he assures me that you will. He said, 'Tell Luke that I haven't forgotten his hot drummer.' What the fuck does that mean?"

I laughed and blushed at the same time. "Oh, it was your wedding day. Josh caught me looking a bit glum, so promised to set me up with a hot drummer. Something about keeping up a good rhythm."

Steve roared with laughter. "Now I get it. The only thing that worries me is how does he know?"

"I did wonder the same thing but decided the question was better left unasked."

"Hmm, I think you might be right there. Anyway, the second thing – and this is a question I do have to ask – how would you feel about stepping up to become an associate director?"

I sat there with my mouth open. That had taken me completely by surprise; I'd had no idea that they were thinking of promoting me. "I ... er. Gosh, that... Terrific. I mean... Yes." I stopped burbling and took control of myself. "That is to say, thank you, Steve. That would be brilliant! I would love to."

He beamed across the table. "Thought you might be pleased. Barbara will sort out all the details – you know, new contracts, etcetera. We thought a salary of a hundred thou would do for now. Is that okay?"

Considering that meant a twenty-five per cent increase on my existing package, it was more than satisfactory. "Yeah, that's more than okay, Steve. Thanks."

"Good. We aim to please," he said with a smile. "You've worked bloody hard since you joined us five years ago, Luke. We're lucky to have you. Congratulations." He got up and shook my hand.

Still in a state of shock, I wandered out of the room and into Barbara's office. As I sat down, she glanced up and gave me a smile. "Good start to the week, eh?" she asked.

"Yeah, I mean – wow. I never expected that. Terrific!"

"You deserve it, Luke, sweetie. You've done a lot for this place and I'm so proud of you."

Crikey, when would this "Buff-Up Luke's Ego-Fest" end? I beamed at Barbara and thanked her.

We sorted out the details – new contract of employment, holiday standards, revised pension arrangements, and so forth. After an hour, my mind was dizzy with all the details.

Suddenly, Steve put his head round the door. "Two things. We've been put on a warning about Monday's meeting. Apparently, they definitely want to hold a departmental conference – effectively a brainstorming session – on Griffin House. It's slated for the twenty-fourth and twenty-fifth of October, somewhere near Bristol. The main point of Monday's get together is to set the agenda and plan the programme. They're going to invite us to attend the conference and make a presentation. You okay for that, Luke? Can you keep your diary free?"

"Sure, no problem," I replied.

"Great." He moved to leave us.

"Steve?"

"Yeah?"

"What was the second thing?"

"Oh, yes. We have yet another new Environment Minister."

"Another one? But the present one's only been in place for a couple of months."

"I know – it's all to do with a reshuffle after one of the Cabinet resignations, I think."

"So who's the new Minister?"

"Some guy called Daniel Forrester."

Oh, bloody hell. Dan – my Dan – a Minister of the Crown.

Governing Passions

Chapter Two

Dan

I was over the moon, sitting in my plush new office, savouring the sweetness of victory in three General Elections and having the honour to serve as the Member of Parliament for Wessex South. Today, I'd achieved my lifelong ambition to become a Minister of the Crown – albeit at the lowest rank. My new formal title was Parliamentary Under-Secretary of State at the Department of Environment, Energy, Climate Change and Rural Affairs, DECRA for short.

This "super-green department" had been created a year earlier in attempt to convince people that the government was serious about environmental issues. In addition to saving money, the Prime Minister had hoped to end the semi-public rows that had frequently broken out between two separate ministries, Energy and Climate Change on the one hand and Environment, Food and Rural Affairs on the other. In reality, as I was about to find out in the weeks ahead, the old rivalries had simply "gone underground" within the new department, morphing into perpetual internal bickering and jostling for position.

Though delighted at having achieved ministerial office, I was not totally ecstatic about the job itself. To be frank, the whole idea of the green agenda bored me rigid. True, I'd never taken much of an interest, but now I faced at least a year of having to be pleasant and agreeable to whichever bunch of sandal-wearing weirdos were piloted through my door, not to mention dealing with a shoal of paperwork on a subject about which I knew little and cared less.

Then there was my newly appointed private secretary, Jeremy Cavendish. He was immaculately dressed, exuding the sort of effortless grace that only the truly beautiful can achieve. He was a delight to the eye and had already demonstrated that he had a mind like a razor blade. He stood just over six feet tall, I reckoned, and had the body of a swimmer: big shoulders and narrow hips. He had thick, flowing, dark-brown hair, which he wore down to his collar, and well-honed, almost sharp features, an attractive smile, a straight nose and penetrating grey eyes with a touch of green.

For a closeted young Minister like me, he would be a constant source of irritation. He would be the one people looked at when we entered a room. He would act as a constant temptation because he was so gorgeous. And he would be a constant reminder of all that I was missing by remaining so firmly in the closet.

Still, I'd get used to him, I supposed. I consoled myself with the thought that at least I'd got my foot on the ministerial ladder. Jim Hayden, my old boss in the Whips Office, had been kindness itself. "You're a bright lad and should go far, provided you keep your nose clean," he'd told me. "Play your cards right and you could be in the Cabinet in a couple of years."

I shuddered now at the memory of that conversation. Even though Jim had been very kind, I couldn't help wondering how being a closeted gay man was compatible with "keeping my nose clean".

"Minister?" Jeremy's voice called me back from my reverie.

"Yes, sorry. My mind wandered," I responded. "Just reflecting on how it feels to have achieved office."

He took my remark seriously and considered it for a moment. "Yes, it must feel good. Like hitting a really good drive on the golf course, or a perfect square cut when batting."

Without thinking, I went right back at him. "I hope you're not comparing the honour of ministerial office with a shot in an inconsequential sport."

His expression tightened and he lost his smile. "Of course I'm not comparing sport with the serious business of government, Minister." He paused and an awkward silence descended. "I was thinking of the feeling you get when everything comes together and you hit the shot – it feels as if you could conquer the world. I imagine you must have felt a bit like that when the job offer came through."

I realised that my response had been more than a little pompous. Anxious to lighten the mood, I spoke more gently. "I see what you mean. And yes, it did feel a bit like that."

"Rather like great sex, I suppose."

My eyebrows shot up. Was he flirting with me? "Yes, well. Jeremy, I'll let *you* go and tell the Prime Minister that being asked to serve in her government is like having an orgasm."

He shot me a wry look. "Sorry. I do get carried away with my analogies sometimes."

"No, no, that's okay. I can imagine the look on her face, that's all."

We looked at each other and burst out laughing. Maybe this was going be more fun than I'd expected.

Our laughter subsided and we turned to business. Jeremy explained the three enormous briefing documents that awaited my attention – one on climate change, one on air-quality and one on greenhouse gases. As we talked through some of the issues, I began to realise why he was considered to be a rising star in the department. His explanations were crisp, lucid and laced with the sort of everyday allusions that helped to make the complex questions more memorable.

After about an hour he said, "You know, the real fun of all this is that there is no single answer. Do something to address one issue and it has consequences that affect others. Like diesel cars – we encouraged people to buy diesel because it reduced greenhouse-gas emissions but without seeing what the consequences would be for NOx and what that would do to people's health."

"You mean the asthma problems in kids?"

"Yes. And the adult respiratory diseases that have worsened too."

"So what you're saying is that this is all about detail at a time when nobody does detail any more."

"Especially the media. Fun isn't it?" He gave a short laugh. "But you wanted the job, Minister."

"Yes, thank you, Sir Humphrey," I shot back, immediately understanding his allusion. "Surely we've got beyond eighties' TV sitcoms in the second decade of the twenty-first century?"

He shook his head. "Not really. Much of what they said and wrote still applies today. Some things have changed – twenty-four-hour news, social media, speed of communication, and so forth. But much of it is still relevant. I've watched and re-watched *Yes, Minister* and *Yes, Prime Minister* all my life and it's amazing how many time I hear Humphrey Appleby's words on somebody's lips." He smiled wryly at me. "Even my own."

I laughed. "Perhaps you'd be kind enough to warn me when I sound too much like the bloke who was the Minister. What was his name? Jim Hacker?"

"That's the one. I'll bear your request in mind. Maybe we should invent a code for when we're in meetings," he said, still smiling. "I could intervene and say the code word to warn you if you're fudging or becoming too Hacker-like."

"That sounds like a good scheme. What should we use?"

"How about 'much fruitful activity'? You remember how Sir Humphrey always loved working parties and reviews?"

"Oh, yes. Minutes, agendas, drafting and redrafting position papers, that sort of thing. Great. 'Much fruitful activity' it is."

"It's a deal." Jeremy looked at his watch and frowned. "Duty calls, Minister. You're due at the House for a vote in a quarter of an hour."

A Gilbert and Sullivan misquote popped into my head

and I sang quietly to myself, "*With parliamentary duties to be done, to be done.*"

Jeremy's surprisingly sweet tenor voice responded, "*A Minister's lot is not a happy one.*"

"*Happy one,*" I intoned in a deep bass voice. We left the office laughing. Maybe being a Minister would actually be fun.

Chapter Three

Luke

I'd followed Dan Forrester's career, of course. He'd been a successful journalist for a few years before entering Parliament at the 2010 General Election. After only a couple of years on the back benches, he went into the Whips Office and largely disappeared from view since, by tradition, Whips neither spoke in the House nor appeared in the media. Before his appointment, I'd listened to a couple of his radio interviews as a backbencher around the time of the London Olympics; he sounded competent and plausible – and you certainly couldn't say that about many politicians these days.

I liked many of his beliefs and he was surprisingly liberal on social issues – for a Tory. He was a "Remainer" as far as the EU was concerned, exactly in line with my own views. But I also couldn't help remembering the cold way he'd treated me after that Sunday night and the brush-off I'd received.

"Is he okay on green issues?" I asked Steve, who kept a close eye on the politics of environmental policy – it was, after all, the firm's lifeblood.

He shook his head. "Never uttered a word on the subject, as far as I can see. Not sure whether that's a good thing or not."

"I knew him for a while at university. He didn't strike me as the type to campaign on anything much, other than furthering his own career."

"It sounds as if you didn't like him much."

Too much for my own good. "No, no, he was fine. I was fairly close to him for a few months, but he was a couple of years older than me and he left at the end of my first year. We lost touch after that."

"You might get to meet him again at this Griffin House conference, if he comes."

"Good grief, I hadn't thought of that. Do you think he will?"

Steve shrugged. "He may do. It depends how interested he is."

"I think we can probably rule that out. Anyway, politicians don't like doing overnight conferences much, do they? Takes them too far away from Westminster."

"Spot on. Anyway, you two, must dash. I'll leave you to your negotiations."

Barbara and I quickly wrapped up our discussions about my new position and I returned to my office. I enjoyed the rest of the day, though it wasn't exactly productive. When people weren't popping their head in to congratulate me, I was staring out of the window with a goofy grin at the idea of being promoted. Eventually I gave up and set off home.

As with many of the staff at Pearson Frazer, I lived close to our office in Crystal Palace. I loved the area, with its majestic views over the Surrey hills to the south, and central London to the north. No matter how hot it got in the centre of the city, there was always that bit more air up here. I strolled down the hill to my home near the station, trying to work out how I actually felt about Dan Forrester after all these years – and the prospect that I might meet him again.

I knew that he'd never married. He always deflected questions about that by saying he hadn't met the right person yet and being an MP tended to rule out an active social life. That always made me smile; being an MP didn't stop some politicians from having a very active social life indeed. What if he was gay after all?

The thought hadn't crossed my mind before and now the possibility made me even crosser with him. To dump me unceremoniously as a friend because I'd made one small mistake was one thing, but to have been gay all along and still push me away would be almost unforgiveable.

I'd reached my own front door when I suddenly laughed out loud. After all these years, why on earth was I still obsessing about what had happened that morning so long ago? If we did meet, Dan probably wouldn't remember me, much less the whole bed incident. I should forget it and move on.

I pulled out my phone and opened up my dating app. Would there be anybody around tonight to provide a distraction? Yes, indeed there was. We arranged to hook up immediately. I went upstairs to shower before the guy arrived.

Governing Passions

Chapter Four

Dan

"We should talk about the Griffin House project, Minister," Jeremy remarked.

I groaned. "Must we? I still haven't waded my way through your briefs."

He chuckled. "I don't think I ever envisaged you going *there*, Minister. You're not exactly my type."

I adopted a shocked tone. "Jeremy! Whatever are you talking about? I meant those weighty tomes you greeted me with last week."

"Sorry, it just struck me. I've never considered underwear in the context of ministerial briefs."

"And, on the whole, I'd prefer it if you didn't now! Otherwise I won't be able to behave with due solemnity with the Permanent Secretary."

"My apologies, Minister," he intoned.

It was my second week in the job and I was having more fun than I'd had in politics for years – and that was almost solely due to my private secretary. Jeremy was a delight to work with; he was brisk, efficient, charming, and he had developed a way of keeping my nose to the grindstone without it all seeming too much. For some reason, and to my total surprise, I was finding the whole green agenda absolutely fascinating. I wondered why I'd taken no interest in it before.

"All right, tell me about Griffin House. What is it? An office block somewhere?"

He nodded. "It is – it's where we based our joint project unit for our environmental grant system. It's a co-partnership scheme that involves the private sector, the academic community and our department."

"Sounds like a copy-book example of partnership in action."

Jeremy nodded. "Correct. What's more, it's been run superbly for the last three years by this small consultancy business in South London. We'd be mad to lose it."

"And are we likely to?"

Jeremy shook his head sadly. "'Fraid so."

"Why?"

"Several reasons. First of all, the Secretary of State is under pressure from the Chancellor and the Cabinet to deliver more budget savings, so the Treasury guys have been crawling all over the scheme. You know the sort of thing – they've been asking whether it could be done cheaper in-house, and why we should pay others to do our own work. There's also another group in this department that's sceptical about the benefits delivered by the grants – the old Min of Ag and Fish gang, mainly. Brexit will give them back their power over farmers and they're anxious not to be forced into an arm's-length grant system that takes away their ability to tinker and micro-manage."

"So what's happening with this Griffin House project?" I asked, increasingly fascinated by Jeremy's story. I hadn't worked with him for long but I was coming to trust his judgement; if he thought the scheme was good, it probably was.

He looked out of the window for a moment and sighed. "It's like we said the other day – straight out of *Yes, Minister*. Casting doubt on the methodology used to calculate the benefit-to-cost ratios; challenging the evidence on the benefits of the projects we've grant-aided; drip-feeding small criticisms of previous decisions. Hints of nepotism or cronyism – never any specific allegations but enough smoke to get people looking for the fire. Whereas it's actually the best-run project I've seen in five years in government."

"We British are good at doubting our own success stories, aren't we?"

"Quite so, Minister," he responded, his voice becoming more formal as the Permanent Secretary knocked and entered the room.

Sir John Rainford was a tall, somewhat aesthetic man. It always struck me that he would have been happier as a don at a small Oxbridge college rather than a leading civil servant in one of the largest government departments. He gave me a watery smile. "Ah, Daniel."

"Good afternoon, Sir John. To what do I owe the pleasure?"

"A small matter only, I'm pleased to say. I was wondering whether you might have space in your diary to cover for the Secretary of State at a conference."

I frowned. Why on earth was the Permanent Secretary

getting involved in something as mundane as ministerial diaries? I caught Jeremy's eye and raised a questioning eyebrow. He gave the smallest of shrugs.

"In principle it's not a problem. What's the event and when?"

"We're convening a round-table conference on the future of this Griffin House thingy. You know, the grant scheme."

"Yes, Jeremy has been briefing me about it. Sounds a good scheme."

"Ah, indeed, indeed. That is to say, up to a point. I am aware that young Cavendish is rather keen on it." He turned and gave Jeremy a wintry smile, before resuming in his customary solemn tone. "We are convening a conference – what I believe they call a 'brainstorming' session – next month. The Secretary of State was scheduled to attend but I am, as ever, concerned about the multifarious demands on his time. I was wondering whether his attendance was critical to the success of the event or whether our collective brain could storm without him."

Jeremy cut across any reply I might have made and something about his face made me sit up and take notice. His cheeks were slightly redder than usual and there was the hint of a tick in his lower right jaw. "We had assumed that Mr Forrester would be attending as a matter of course, since he is the Minister responsible for the grant scheme."

Sir John frowned, as if trying to get head round the novel idea that the Minister responsible should attend a conference about one of the most important aspects of his job. "Ah, yes, I see," he intoned. "I must confess that had not occurred to me but you're right, young Cavendish.

That has eased my mind considerably. I will leave you gentlemen to your deliberations. Good afternoon."

Jeremy waited a couple of seconds before flinging his file down in disgust. "The wily old fox!" he exclaimed. "God, he's a smooth operator sometimes."

"Presumably that why he's Permanent Secretary?"

Jeremy laughed briefly and relaxed a little. "You're probably right. But that was classic Rainford."

"I'm still not with you, I'm afraid."

"And you an experienced politician, Dan?"

"Oh, ha-ha, Jeremy. Just explain what the fuck you're on about."

"Right, words of one syllable. Sir John has decided that the Griffin House project should be sacrificed on the altar of austerity and giving the Ag and Fish guys back their power. So, the first thing is to distance the Secretary of State from it. If *he* came to the conference and made enthusiastic noises, he'd be pinning his colours to the mast."

"I see what you're getting at. The Secretary of State pleads diary pressures, doesn't go to the conference, avoids endorsing the scheme and finally appears judicious and disappointed when they announce the scheme's closure."

"Got it in one," Jeremy responded. "See, I said you were an experienced politician."

"So how do we play it?"

"We could always force the Secretary of State's hand and plead an unbreakable constituency engagement. After all, you've only been in the job a couple of weeks and you're bound to have prior commitments."

"Yeah, but he could also issue me with a direct order."

Jeremy chuckled. "Can you imagine this Secretary of State ever issuing a direct instruction about *anything*? I'd be surprised if he's ever managed to order so much as a pint."

"No, I suppose you're right. But pleading a prior engagement would mean that I couldn't go the conference. And I think I'd quite like to."

"Okaaay," he responded, stretching the word as he deliberated. "Yes, I can see that. And I agree. It would be good to be there."

"So, if we've lost the Permanent Secretary and the Secretary of State, there's not much hope for the Griffin House project, is there?"

"Not much. But you never know – we can always have a good old-fashioned departmental fight about it."

"Count me in," I replied.

Jeremy handed me another substantial file. "You'll need to wrap your brain round all that."

"Another of your briefs to get into?"

"Yes, yes, I know. Ha bloody ha. You don't need to master it completely – especially not the detailed descriptions of assessment methodology and benefit calculation. But Part One looks at the history behind the scheme, and Part Two explains how and why it was implemented three years ago. Part Three contains a useful table showing how much was paid to whom and what we got for our money. It will give you a good grounding and probably a better grip on the detail than even Sir John has."

"And what then?"

"We'll head off to the conference at the end of next month and see what happens. There's a planning meeting here on Monday morning. It might be a good idea if you could look in at some point and meet some of the team."

"Fine. Come and fetch me when you think it's appropriate. Now, what's next?"

"Parliamentary duties again, I'm afraid. A series of votes in the House on the Brexit bill."

"Oh joy. Voting for a bill I don't believe in, designed to achieve an exit that I think is a huge historic mistake. Exactly the thing for a wet Wednesday evening. Lead on, Macduff."

Governing Passions

Chapter Five

Luke

The drive southwards out of London was slow and tedious. It was Sunday morning and I was on my way for lunch with my parents. Driving across London and down the A3 was definitely not my favourite way of spending a Sunday but it was my mother's birthday. I'd managed to put off seeing them for a whole six months so I'd swallowed my annoyance with them and accepted the invitation.

My father was Dean at Harchester Cathedral in Hampshire. The city was still the perfect setting for Anthony Trollope's Barchester novels, even though it was a hundred and fity years and more since they'd been written. Enclosed by its medieval (and in some cases Roman) walls, it was an oasis of peace in the winter. In the summer, though, it could be a hell on earth of tourists, coach parties and loud, teenage language students.

It also tended to be patrician and overly conscious of its own prettiness. It was run by a small group of incredibly snobbish middle-class residents who served on all the important committees, manned the magistrates' bench and ran the local authority. They were full of their own sense of importance and their sense of virtue in serving their community. I despised their stuffy complacency and hated the place.

The house I was visiting was not my childhood home. As the son of an ambitious cleric, I'd led a peripatetic existence. The only real sense of permanence I'd ever experienced was at boarding school. Leaving there and going to university had been my parents' choice for me as opposed to my own, and there'd been the most terrific row when initially I'd refused to go. Eventually a comprise was reached: I would study for a degree, but at a "plate-glass" institution founded in the 1960s, and my subject would be vocational – hence my career in environmental sciences. That didn't conform with Mummy's vision of playing the *grand dame* while visiting her son at an Oxbridge college but it was better than having a son working as a labourer, which was what I was threatening to do.

Father had got the job of Dean at Harchester three years earlier and my mother was delighted – "such nice people, darling". A comfortable, historic house in the Cathedral Close came with the job, and she was able to play out her fantasy of being chatelaine to her heart's content. The only black spot on the horizon was that, having reached the age of fifty-seven and still being a Dean, my father was in danger of missing out on the bishop's job that my mother so coveted for him. That would have put him on a par with her father, who had been a bishop when she was a girl, and with her best friend Pru, whose husband Geoffrey already wore a bishop's mitre. The real prize, of course, would have been one of the sees that still entitled the holder to

40

a seat in the House of Lords, but that was now looking increasingly unattainable.

Inevitably, the real reason for my distant relationship with them was my sexual orientation. My difficulties and depression after the fall-out with Dan had worried them greatly, but I had rebuffed their attempts to get me to explain my problem. At one point, I'd decided to drop out of university but that caused another huge row. Even so, coming out and coping with their reaction at that point was more than I could face.

After that, I'd never felt the time was right. I couldn't face the predictable row that would follow so the simplest thing was to avoid them as much as possible. Fortunately, with my mother's social ambitions and my father's clerical ones, there was little room for me in their lives. I had concluded long ago that there would be concern about my physical well-being and the state of my soul, but I was on my own emotionally.

On the outskirts of Harchester I pulled into a layby to make myself presentable for Sunday lunch at the Deanery. I put on my tie, which felt strange because I so rarely wore one, but I knew it would be expected here. I placed my suit jacket on the seat next to me, ready to grab when I got out of the car, pulled a comb through my hair and checked my appearance in the driving mirror. I would pass muster.

I pulled out of the layby and merged back into the stream of traffic, entering the city a few minutes later. After I parked in the Deanery drive, I remained in my seat for a few moments, eyes closed, breathing deeply.

Once I'd got myself together, I went to the boot for the parcel containing my mother's birthday present before I turned and walked towards the front door. Time to face the music.

The lunch party that day was every inch my mother. The bishop and his wife Pru were there, of course. He full of gentle Anglican bonhomie, honed from long practice in parochial gatherings. Pru, my mother's lifelong friend, was tall, elegant and detached. She was the best-dressed person in the room by a long way; her hair, trimmed in a page-boy style that framed her face perfectly, was immaculate as always. Her grey eyes were full of humour – as if she were observing the occasion for use as a future anecdote. She greeted me warmly: we had always been super close. Though we were not related, I'd always known her as Aunty P.

Other guests included the local MP and his wife, a thin, angular woman who looked completely humourless. Any *joie de vivre* she had ever experienced had probably been driven out by being married to her insufferably pompous, self-satisfied, boorish husband. *Bet he voted Brexit*, I thought as I was introduced.

Next came the leader of the County Council and her husband. Brenda Whiteman was an attractive woman with bouncy blonde curls, but she had a shrill voice and a laugh like a hyena. She was full of self-deprecating remarks and confidential little smiles that never reached her sharp little eyes. Her husband, George, was a retired academic; tall and thin, he had a slight stoop. He also had a ready smile and kind, gentle eyes. He was the only stranger in the room that I could possibly see myself liking.

The conversation flowed reasonably well during lunch. We all wished my mother many happy returns and she fluttered about like a little girl, pretending to be embarrassed by the attention which in reality she craved.

Toasts over, the conversation turned to politics. As I had foreseen, the MP, Edward Bickerstaff, was a Brexiteer and a militant one at that. Originally from Lancashire, he had moved south in the 1970s but had not entirely lost his accent, especially when roused as he was now. He'd been making free with the fine claret my father served with the roast beef and had gone steadily redder in the face.

I watched, fascinated, almost eager for the car crash that this lunch party was undoubtedly going to turn into. Sure enough, it unfolded before my eyes.

"And now she's had the nerve to appoint another Remainer to the government. No sense, that woman, no sense at all."

"I take it you're referring to our Prime Minister?" asked Pru, her grey eyes sparkling with humour.

"Certainly am," blustered Bickerstaff.

"Only I've always found her a most charming and intelligent woman," she continued.

"Never had much time for women in politics – always bossy and often shrill. She's one of 'em." He suddenly realised he'd gone too far and hastened to row back. "Present company excepted of course, my dear Brenda."

Pru, seated next to the Member, opened her eyes wide and addressed Brenda. "Surely we don't have a good old-fashioned male chauvinist pig in our company?" There was the slightest hint of emphasis on the word "pig".

43

"It would certainly seem to be the case," Brenda replied, letting out one of her barking laughs. "Edward, I'm shocked."

A blush spread upwards across the face of the MP's hitherto colourless wife, Jessie. She had hardly spoken; now she earned a glare from her husband by saying quietly, "You don't know the half of it."

"You sound like somebody out of the 1950s," said Pru, eyes alight with humour as she provoked Bickerstaff.

"Aye. I rather liked the 1950s, actually," he responded, his Lancashire accent strengthening. "Everybody knew where they stood."

"You didn't have to live through them," remarked George Whiteman. "It was an age of snobbery, smug self-satisfaction and intolerance."

The bishop intervened to change the subject, raising his voice slightly to smother Bickerstaff's attempted response. "What's the new ministerial appointment of which you clearly disapprove, Edward? There have been so many changes lately that I've lost track."

"Some whipper-snapper called Daniel Forrester. Been in the Whips' Office for a while."

My ears pricked up at the mention of Dan's name. Pru's eyes sought mine and she raised a quizzical eyebrow as she asked, "And what's his new job?"

"Oh, pandering to the weirdos and the Greens at DECRA."

George Whiteman snorted. "He's actually Minister for the Environment, Bishop. An important position, considering he's only thirty-six."

Bickerstaff harrumphed. "You don't *believe* all this

climate change nonsense, do you?"

The bishop headed off another rant about wind farms and bus lanes – he'd heard Bickerstaff on this subject before. Many times. "Ah, yes," he said, again raising his voice to cut the MP off in mid-sentence. "I think I've met young Forrester a couple of times in Parliament. A bright lad, so they tell me. Very ambitious."

Yep, that sounded like my Dan.

Bickerstaff blundered in again. "Queer as a nine-bob note, so they tell me."

His remark was greeted by a shocked silence before Pru intervened. "I beg your pardon?" she asked crisply.

"You know, a poofter. Likes the boys not the girls."

The atmosphere round the table chilled. Although I might not be out to her, my mother knew that this sort of bigotry would rile me. She shot me a pleading look; for her sake, I decided to hold my peace.

"And do you have any evidence for this astonishing statement?" Pru asked coldly.

"No, no. Like I said, only passing on the gossip."

"You should be aware, my dear, that my husband has never had a single original thought in his entire life. He therefore thrives on gossip," Jessie said.

Bickerstaff had evidently decided to ignore his wife's rapier-like jibe, merely remarking that gossip was the life-blood of politics and there was nothing wrong with a bit of harmless chatter. But Pru had not finished with him. There was a slight flush to her cheeks and the humour in her eyes had been replaced by anger. She was seriously pissed with Bickerstaff and boy, did it show.

"So you make unsubstantiated allegations against a

charming and intelligent young man using the most unpleasant, homophobic language and expect us to accept that this is simply a bit of 'harmless chatter'? Mr Bickerstaff, really."

Bickerstaff suddenly went very red. "Madam, I'll thank you not to put words into my mouth. I did not make any allegations, merely remarked on what has been said. After all, the man is thirty-six and unmarried, and he's seen about with lots of good-looking young men. I worry about this – I think there are too many of these people in public life. They're polluting our country."

I was so busy absorbing this fascinating information about Dan that I almost missed the next bit. My expectation that Mummy's birthday lunch would be the social disaster of the year was about to come true, but in a most unexpected way.

It was actually George Whiteman who unwittingly started things off. He couldn't keep the anger and scorn from his face as he addressed Mr Bickerstaff. "Presumably you'd lock them all up, like we did in the fifties?"

"I wouldn't go that far," the MP replied. "But I've observed that since we changed the law there seem to be an awful lot more people choosing to be queer. Seems a bit unhealthy to me."

There was an audible gasp – but the words that provoked the crash came from a most unexpected source: my father.

Chapter Six

Dan

Sundays had never been my favourite day and this one was proving to be no exception. I'd been able to plead the pressure of my new appointment and avoid visiting my constituency this weekend. I loved going down there normally, but I needed some time to come to terms with the changes that were happening in my life.

I decided to treat myself to a small celebration of my promotion by booking an escort for the night on Saturday. Doing this had been the outlet for my sexual drive for a number of years, pretty much since I'd been able to afford the fees. It was quick, uncomplicated and discreet. The boys were usually good looking and good at their jobs; best of all, it involved no complicated emotions and left me in control as a customer as opposed to a supplicant.

Adam was a pretty blond in his mid-twenties who did escort work on the side to support a fledgling acting career. He was good; we spent a pleasant evening over dinner followed by three rounds of boisterous sex.

My only trouble now was getting rid of him. He was

remarkably unwilling to get out of bed on Sunday morning and kept trying to drag me back for a fourth round. He pouted when I turned him down, pleading – truthfully – that I had a lot of work to do and needed my energy.

"But it's only another hundred and I could sooo do with the money. There's a seriously cool pair of jeans on offer at Harvey Nicks that'd do so much for my profile." He waggled his eyebrows suggestively and wiggled his cute backside.

I couldn't help it; he was adorable, especially when he was getting his own way. I reached for my wallet and pulled out some notes. "Get the jeans on me, darling boy," I suggested. "And remember that you owe me one."

He reached for me, still pouting a little, but I batted his hands away. "Go, baby boy. Much as I think you're the sexiest thing on this earth, I must do my red boxes. Otherwise Auntie PM will fire me and I'll be out of a job. There'll be no more sexy jeans for little Adam if that happens. Now go buy them, before I change my mind."

He left and I leant against my front door, breathing a sigh of relief before making myself some more coffee and sitting down to work. Somebody once remarked that writing was "ninety per cent perspiration and ten per cent inspiration". I was finding out that being a Minister was pretty similar: ninety-nine per cent perspiration and one per cent independent thinking.

Two hours later, I'd worked through the first of my three weekend boxes. The first one contained the routine correspondence and paperwork that are the lifeblood of any office – responses to complaints, letters of thanks, memos, draft position papers, three sets of minutes from working parties. The second box contained more long-term material, including the latest data from the various climate-change monitoring groups. Though some might seek to deny it, all the signs were that things were heating up – literally and figuratively. It made me realise what an important job this was and how I needed to buckle down and get things done. Which brought me to my third box containing the three basic briefing documents Jeremy had prepared for me and the Griffin House file. I had already worked through them carefully but they were my bible for the job I was going to do for the next few months, or even years. I needed to go through them again, annotating and highlighting, making my own notes, trying to fix the key issues in my mind.

By three o'clock, I'd worked solidly for five hours and needed a break. I rose from my desk and went into the kitchen. I could forage for lunch in the fridge, order something in or go out for a walk, buy a takeaway and eat it in the fresh air.

It was a beautiful late September day, warm and pleasant with a cloudless blue sky. The trees in the park were beginning to turn, so the colour of the leaves added to the golden light.

I was fortunate that my prominence in public life was not sufficiently great to warrant any form of security. I tended not to get recognised in the street, so I enjoyed my stroll in the sunshine and ate my sandwich in peace and quiet. Peace, except for the shouts of the children playing on the grass, and quiet apart from the constant underlying rumble of London traffic. The occasional wail of a siren pierced the air. This was the nearest to peaceful and quiet that the city ever got to.

I lived in a small mansion flat in Kensington, not far from the Royal Albert Hall. I'd bought it when I first moved to London fifteen years earlier, using a small inheritance from my grandmother and the bank of Mum and Dad to scrape together the deposit. The decision to buy had been a good one: the flat was now worth at least ten times what I'd paid for it.

I knew that I should probably move closer to Westminster; on the other hand, the place was comfortable, convenient and *me*. I could shut the front door on the world and be left to my own devices, to think, to write occasionally, or simply sit and dream. The only people who crossed the threshold were my parents on their occasional visits to London, my cleaning lady and my boys – the escorts I hired in when the need arose.

I left the bench I'd been sitting on and meandered through the park with no specific sense of direction.

I was still feeling out of sorts. The sense of detachment from the day-to day-maelstrom of modern politics had, if anything, grown since my appointment. I was away from Westminster for most of the time, so I missed the drama of the Whips Office, heightened now that the government had lost its majority at the last election. That was where the real horse-trading was done: quick chats with members or opposite numbers behind the Speaker's Chair; sorting out membership of the committees that were so crucial to getting the government's business through Parliament; shepherding MPs through the lobbies, and ensuring that they were there for crucial votes both in those committees and in the House itself.

The days had gone like the wind. The parliamentary recesses were essential to enable people to recover and recharge their batteries but they seemed so empty, leaving the Palace of Westminster an eerie, echoing sort of place, especially when the tourists had gone too.

For me, all that had been replaced by the equally demanding but less frenetic life of a junior minister. This entailed lots of meetings in reasonably elegant offices, discussions in the much more measured tones of the English civil service, and lots of reading. Above all, the reading. The paperwork was endless, despite the decades-old talk of the paperless office. That was a concept that was definitely not reaching government departments anytime soon.

Experience so far taught me that the biggest issue in a Minister's life was time management. For all Jeremy's calm efficiency and charm, we seemed to spend an inordinate part of our days running late and apologising for the fact. I supposed that it went with the territory; I'd never met a Minister yet who managed to be on time for everything – or indeed anything.

Aside from a vague feeling of disillusionment with the whole political process since the Brexit decision, my biggest problem was not having anybody to share all this with. Nobody to tell about my day, with whom to share my moments of triumph, or to help soothe away the awful bits.

Dammit. I realised I was lonely.

The realisation came as something of a shock: it was not something I'd allowed myself to feel before. The boys helped, of course they did. Sex was great for relieving stress but I couldn't afford to pay too often, especially the fees charged by the top escorts. But as for everything else ... there could be no sharing of jokes or angst or dreams or ambitions, at least not on my part. In fact, the one thing I couldn't talk about with them was my job. To do so would be to invite trouble with the Official Secrets Act, the House of Commons and, of course, the tabloids. Over the decades, many a disillusioned boy had sought fame or fortune by spilling the beans on his former clients.

Hooking up with escorts as stress relief was all very fine. But I needed more in my life now.

I want someone to love.

Christ, where had that come from? It must be tiredness, I decided. My feet had barely touched the ground for the last few weeks. Yes, that was it. Fatigue was turning me sentimental.

Such a thing as loving someone had not crossed my mind for years. The last time I'd felt anything like that was my friendship with a boy in the months leading up to my finals at university.

But that had got too heavy, especially when I realised that he might want more than friendship. I'd pushed him away pretty quickly, walking away and never looking back: that was much too dangerous and threatened my life plan. I'd not thought of him for years. What was his name? Keith? Kevin? Lance? No, Luke. Yes, that was it: Luke Carter. I wondered what had happened to him.

Suddenly, my mind took me back to a morning fifteen years earlier when he'd been so close to me. I'd only needed to move an inch or two – no need to reach. Just that tiny movement and my life could have been so different. It had been so dangerous, that incident, that I'd expunged it from my memory. Why did it have to surface again now, just when my life plan had begun to deliver?

I was almost overcome for a moment at the memory and sought another bench for a few moments. I took a couple of deep breaths and rubbed my hands over my face. I'd started to recover when I heard a voice calling my name. I looked up and there was Adam, dressed in a stunningly sexy pair of skinny jeans – presumably the ones I'd paid for earlier.

"Hey, Dan, are you okay? You looked so soulful sitting there."

I nodded, surprised for a moment that he'd noticed. "Yeah, fine, baby boy. Just a bit tired, that's all."

He smirked and raised his eyebrows. "Third round too much last night?"

"You did wear me out a little bit, but in a good way. I had a great time. But I did a lot of work after you left this morning. I was feeling a bit down, that's all." I looked up at him and smiled, striving to change the subject. "Are those the jeans, little one?"

He pouted. "Not little. That's not what you said last night."

I laughed out loud. "No, I agree. Nothing about you is remotely little, Adam – especially not in those jeans."

He giggled, "Yeah, they are a bit revealing, aren't they? Better not wear them to one of Mummy's dinner parties, eh?"

"How on earth do you get them off?"

"With great difficulty," he responded. "Want me to show you?"

I looked round anxiously.

"No, not here, silly," he teased, eyes wide and blond fringe flopping in the slight breeze. He threw back his head and laughed at his own joke. At that moment, I envied him his sense of freedom. He was bright and ambitious for his acting career – we'd discussed that a couple of times – but he, and his chosen profession, came with none of the constraints and contradictions that surrounded my own life.

What was even worse, I realised in that split second, was that the constraints on me could only get tighter if I continued to climb the career ladder. Cabinet Ministers with 24/7 protection and a staff of advisers had absolutely no time to themselves – no casual meetings with pretty escort boys on Sunday afternoons.

I looked into Adam's frank, open green eyes. "I'd love to see you taking them off – especially if I get to help."

We set off back to my flat. For a moment, I felt so happy and carefree in his company that I even thought about holding his hand.

Careful, Forrester. You're a customer not a supplicant. Don't get carried away.

Chapter Seven

Luke

Aside from proposing my mother's birthday toast, my father had been very quiet during lunch – uncharacteristically so, for he could almost always use his priestly skills to ease a social occasion.

Now, however, he spoke. He used a tone that I had rarely heard before: once with me, when I'd almost been expelled from school for some prank or other, and once with my mother following the receipt of a particularly hefty credit card bill.

"Mr Bickerstaff, there is something you should know before you continue your unpleasant rant."

There was undoubtedly something in that tone of voice that struck people. It was cold and hard, immediately demanding attention. In this case, fortunately, it struck the MP dumb. The bombast ceased and he looked at my father, swallowing nervously.

"I used to think like you. That homosexuals were somehow lacking in willpower to resist their unpleasant ... er ... tendencies. But I've come to realise that I was wrong, and so are you." He paused, glancing round the room but avoided looking at me. My eyes were wide with surprise ... shock, actually. Then he resumed.

"A couple of years ago, one of the members of the clergy team here, Gregory Allen, told me that he was gay. I am ashamed to say that I did not take it well. None of us in the Chapter was supportive in the way that we should have been. Indeed, I made what I now realise was a huge mistake: I insulted him by trying to pretend that I could pray the condition away."

I looked at my father in amazement. He gave me a small smile in return but quickly turned his attention back to Bickerstaff. "That night, Greg told me a few home truths about the religion that has been my life and about being chosen by God to love men rather than women."

That was almost too much for the bishop, but his attempted intervention was stilled by an angry gesture from his wife.

"I use the word 'chosen' advisedly," my father resumed. "Because the thing that Greg emphasised so strongly, and which hit home more than anything, was this question of choice. He assured me that he did not have a choice in the matter. He begged me to understand that if there was anything he could have done in his teenage years to change the way he felt, he would have done it. But there was nothing. His orientation had been set for him by nature or by God or fate – whatever you happen to believe in. Three weeks later, he resigned both his post here and the priesthood. He no longer found his orientation compatible with the Church's stance on homosexuality.

"His resignation saddened me deeply. Both his words and

his sincerity in uttering them made a deep impression on me. I have to tell you now that all the research I have done since – and that has been a great deal as I have wrestled with my conscience over this matter – has indicated the truth of Greg's words. Being gay is not a lifestyle choice, Mr Bickerstaff. I must ask that you respect Greg Allen – and the countless others – who struggle every day with being different."

Bickerstaff's colour turned even stronger – by now, he was almost purple in the face with anger. "That's bloody rubbish. Of course it's a choice. It has to be. The Bible says it's wrong. All the churches say so. If we don't adhere to that we'll be lost in …. a … a stinking pit of sin and debauchery. I hate them. I hate all queers – they're the devil's disciples, sent to undermine our Christian world." He spluttered to a halt, his anger and fear getting in the way of his ability to speak. He was sweating profusely.

My father remained icily calm and spoke again. "If you do not, or cannot, accept what I say, then I think it's better if you leave."

Bickerstaff opened his mouth to speak again but his wife intervened. "My husband is unwell, Dean." She rose from the table. "I shall take him home. Come along, Edward." She helped her husband to his feet, before turning to face my father. "Dean, I'd like to apologise for breaking up the party. Your story was most interesting, but I am afraid that neither of us can accept what you say. Your words are contrary to God's law."

I longed to speak out, but reluctantly decided to keep my counsel. This was not the time for a coming-out party. My father inclined his head but didn't speak. At a gesture from him, my mother remained in her place. The silence whilst Bickerstaff and his wife left was awkward, to say the least. As we heard the front door close, we all let our breath go. There was an audible sigh across the room.

I was still shaking, whether with anger at Bickerstaff or astonishment at my father, I wasn't sure. I realised, though, that it was typical of him that, when confronted with an issue such as this, his reaction would be to research carefully before wrestling with his conscience. What surprised me was that he had proved to be so open-minded.

"I am sorry that it happened like that," my father said to the bishop. "I had intended to talk to you in private before you left today, but sadly Mr Bickerstaff intervened and I couldn't let it pass."

"Quite right," said Pru vehemently. "What a truly awful man he is."

The bishop frowned slightly at her. "Now, Prudence. You know we must strive to see good in everyone."

She sighed and smiled gently at her husband. "I know, Geoffrey darling, I know. But I'm afraid that sometimes, with some people, the task is beyond me."

"My dear, 'Love the sinner, hate the sin'," her husband replied piously.

"I think I can manage 'Despise the sinner, deplore the sin' in this case. That will have to suffice on this occasion," she replied firmly, before turning to my mother as she rose from the table. "Muriel, my dear, I must thank you for an excellent lunch and some fascinating entertainment. But I think we should get out of your way now. Besides, we have to attend evensong in Basingstoke so we must get going soon."

My mother, who had remained mute in a state of shock throughout these proceedings, awoke as if from a coma. "Thank you, Pru. And you, Geoffrey. It was lovely to see you today. I'm only sorry that it didn't turn out to be the pleasant, relaxed occasion we all hoped for." She gave me a slightly irritated glance.

As this was happening, the bishop approached my father and me. "Richard, I was very struck by the hard work and research you've clearly done on this. I would love to talk it through with you. Can we do that? Can you talk to the office and set something up for a couple of hours?"

"Certainly, my dear chap," my father replied.

With that, we said our goodbyes to them, closely followed by the other guests. Before Pru left, she whispered something to her husband and drew me to one side. "Walk with me for a moment, my dear boy," she said.

We set off down the drive. "You're looking a bit gloomy today. Is everything okay?"

"Yeah, yeah, fine," I responded. "That ass Bickerstaff got to me, I'm afraid."

Pru looked at me kindly. "Yes, I'm sorry you had to endure that, Luke. I've known you all your life and better than you think. I understand why you've never told your parents, and your secret is safe with me – so long as you wish it to be a secret. Is that young Minister the same boy you loved, who hurt you so much at university?"

"Good Lord, Aunty P. How did you know?"

"A process of deduction. I knew you were close friends for several months. You brought him to lunch, if you remember, when we were at Lambeth. I watched the way you looked at each other and immediately knew that you were very close. Then suddenly you weren't. Within weeks, you were suffering from that terrible depression. Looking back, it seemed a logical progression. But I was wary of saying anything in case I was making two and two add up to five."

I sighed. "No, no. Definitely four. Yes, you're right, but it wasn't Dan's fault. We were extremely close but he never gave me any encouragement to believe that it was more than friendship. When I ... suggested it might be more, he pushed me away and cut off all contact. The worst you can accuse him of is moral cowardice – but which of us can plead not guilty to that offence?"

Pru laughed. "Certainly not me."

"The Dan business affected me at the time because it made me so fearful of the future. I concluded that I had lost his friendship because I was gay. How many others would feel the same? I was convinced that Dan would tell everybody at university about me whereas, of course, he told nobody. I began to feel that other people were watching me and talking about me behind my back. The fear of that stopped me going out. I cut lectures and goodness knows what. And the rest you know."

"Yes, my dear, I do. Look, I simply have to go, Geoffrey is tapping his watch. But do keep in touch. And if you want my advice, Luke, after today you should tell your parents. And sooner rather than later."

I nodded. "It's certainly given me a lot to think about." I kissed her goodbye and watched them leave before returning to the drawing room and my parents.

"Well, that was a bloody disaster," observed my mother.

"Not a triumph, Mum, I agree. But I found it hugely entertaining – as did Aunty P, I suspect."

"I can't see why you had to invite the Bickerstaffs, Muriel," my father remarked.

"I know he's an appalling old man, but he *is* our local member. And he's still an influence in the Tory Party. You need friends there, Richard, if we're ever going to get you a bishopric."

I couldn't help laughing at that point. "That didn't exactly go according to plan."

"No thanks to you," she snapped back at me.

"Me? What did I do? I kept my own counsel. It was Dad here who threw him out. And quite right, too."

"No, but you didn't help. You could have said something to rescue the moment."

That irritated the hell out of me. "What was I supposed to do? Agree with him?"

"That would have helped. Besides, it would have been polite."

I gawped at her in amazement. "Mother, why the hell should I have done that?"

"It was my birthday! I wanted everything to be nice, not to start talking about former priests who were a bit batty anyway."

My father intervened. "Muriel, that was only peripherally to do with young Greg Allen. Bickerstaff is an oaf and a bully. He was being rude to everybody, and he has hateful opinions about the place of women and the environment, not to mention being homophobic. If the price of being a bishop is to suck up to people like him, I'd prefer to stay where I am."

"Oh, Richard! It's all we've ever dreamt of."

"No, Muriel, it's all *you've* ever dreamt of. And if I may offer my humble opinion, you've sacrificed too much – including your son's affection – on the altar of that particular ambition."

My mother looked genuinely shocked for a moment before she dissolved into tears. "A fine birthday this has turned out to be," she exclaimed, and fled from the room.

Dad remained in his seat.

"Shouldn't you..."

He shook his head sadly. "She'll calm down after a while and then we'll talk. I've known your mother too long to spoil one of her big exits."

We changed the subject and talked more generally for a few minutes until it was time for my father to prepare for evensong and for me to leave. With the important DECRA meeting in the morning, staying overnight was not a possibility. However, an hour or so would not make much difference so, when my father asked if I was joining him for the service, I agreed but said that I would sit separately from the congregation and slip away at the end.

Though not a believer, I still loved the language and the music of the cathedral services I'd known for much of my life. In addition, I was always impressed and somehow comforted by the fact that daily worship had taken place within these walls for more than a thousand years. Evensong had always been my favourite service; its elegiac quality on a fading September evening was exactly what I needed.

My farewells to my mother were a little cursory. She was still cross, still coming to terms with the damage to her social ambitions and still, to an extent, blaming me. I was cross with her, too: I resented the blame and the fact that she obviously saw her own interests to be so far ahead of mine.

My father and I said goodbye before the service, leaving him free to greet colleagues and worshippers when it ended. The parting meant much more on this occasion. For a start he hugged me, something that had not happened for fifteen years. "Come again soon, dear boy. Don't avoid us, and please don't make assumptions about our feelings." That was a big surprise.

I was moved but managed to croak out a reply. "Thanks, Dad."

I took a seat in the nave of the church, away from the congregation which was concentrated in the choir stalls beyond the screen. Of all the buildings my father had worked in over the years, this was my favourite. It was a Romanesque church, dating mainly from the twelfth century. The plain curved arches had a stark simplicity that appealed to me, whereas I found some later Gothic buildings to be over-elaborate. In addition, I loved the sense of history that the building exuded from every stone block and every tomb, reinforcing the sense of continuity that seemed important in these uncertain and puzzling times.

The service was beautiful, with music by Handel and Stanford, whilst the choir and congregation sang "The Day Thou Gavest, Lord, Has Ended", a favourite hymn of mine since childhood.

The afternoon's events had certainly given me a lot to think about – the whole incident with Bickerstaff and his wife, and the pure delight of seeing my Aunty P with her sense of humour and sharp wit, not to mention her apparent ability to read me like a book. My father's sudden and astonishing conversion to the gay cause had taken me completely by surprise, as had his words to me as we parted.

And there was Dan and the possibility, hinted at by Bickerstaff, that he might be gay after all. I couldn't explain why that meant so much to me. Of all the things that had happened today, that was the most important. I didn't understand why, but it was. And it made me smile as I listened to my father's sermon. Appropriately enough, he preached on forgiveness.

It was late when I got back. The traffic was awful, the particular kind of awfulness that comes from weekend drivers: agonisingly slow for most of the time and speeding up in built-up areas, as if driving in open countryside were somehow intimidating. This was accompanied by unpredictable braking, crass overtaking and poor signalling decisions.

I went straight to bed, tired after a long and eventful day, thinking of the hymn we had sung earlier. "The sun that bids us rest" would indeed soon be waking, and I couldn't help wondering what Monday would bring.

Chapter Eight

Dan

When we got back to the flat, Adam stayed for one more round of vigorous sex. For some reason we were both in a good mood, and he did look so good in those jeans – which, as predicted, proved a devil to get off. Nevertheless, I stuck to the task manfully and was rewarded when Adam wrapped his long naked legs round me while I entered him. It was immense fun and made a pleasant memory to store up and sustain me through the week.

As we lay in bed recovering, I heard my mobile buzz a couple of times. I assumed they were social media notifications, so didn't bother with them. I felt relaxed and content; the dark moment that I had experienced in the park had passed completely, thanks to the romp with Adam. I noticed with amusement that he'd now drifted into a light doze – so much for the stamina of the young.

Suddenly I heard a noise, which had me sitting up abruptly. It was a key in my front door. Jeremy was the only person who had a key – we'd agreed that it would be sensible to allow him to drop off boxes and pick up papers when I was busy elsewhere.

Fuck. What's he doing here at this time on a Sunday evening?

I grabbed my dressing gown and made for the door. Adam, woken by my sudden exit, looked puzzled and not a little put out. "Stay there," I whispered. "Sorry, it's an unexpected visitor."

As I reached the bedroom door, Jeremy called out. "Hello? Anyone there?" He was about to enter the sitting room as I appeared.

"Jeremy. What on earth are you doing here?"

"Sorry, this is obviously a bad time. My apologies."

He looked at me with extreme embarrassment. It must have been obvious what had been going on – apart from my tousled state, there was a trail of discarded clothes leading into the bedroom. Then Jeremy's eyes opened wider and I glanced over my shoulder; an even bigger clue was the sight of Adam, naked apart from a pair of briefs, leaning against the door jamb and looking puzzled.

"Oh, hi, Jer. Thought I recognised your voice. How are you doing?"

Jeremy looked from one to the other of us, mouth working like a fish before responding, "Hi, Adam. How's things?"

"Good, thanks. Nice to see you." Adam disappeared into the bathroom and we heard the shower start.

"My cousin," Jeremy said, inclining his head towards the bathroom door. His face was a deep red colour; every part of it, right to the tips of his ears, was lit up by his embarrassed blush. "God, I'm sorry about this. I did text a couple of times and, when you didn't reply, I assumed you were out. I finished a couple of draft speeches and wanted you to have them ready for tomorrow. I thought I'd drop them off to save you having to print them. I was passing the door, and..." He ran his hand through his thick dark hair. "Christ, I am sorry."

I closed my eyes and took a deep breath. "I ... er ... had no idea that Adam was your cousin."

"Why would you? We're not that close, though I do know that he's been known to do ... um ... escort work to keep the wolf from the door. Presumably...?"

"Yes. I use escorts because it's simpler." I had to smile at the irony of that statement in the present circumstances. "At least, it's usually simpler."

Jeremy nodded. "I understand." There was silence for a moment as we looked at each other, neither certain what to say next.

"For what it's worth, Jeremy, I had planned to tell you. About all this, I mean..." I gestured towards the bedroom "...about being gay, when we got to know each other a bit better. I'm not out or anything – it's all a bit complicated – with my family, and one thing and another. This seems the best way to cope."

He shook his head and looked away, not meeting my eyes. He ran his right hand through his hair again before looking up. "I understand."

"Really?"

He nodded and gave me a small reassuring smile. "Really, Dan."

I sat down abruptly on the sofa. "Wow. I didn't see this one coming."

He laughed, releasing the tension in the room. "Nor me. Never even occurred to me."

Now it was my turn to be amused. "Oh, come on! Thirty-six years old, never married? Plus the odd whisper floating round the House."

"I can tell you that no rumours have ever reached me and my gaydar has never been at all strong. And I've never been one to pigeon-hole people – so, there we are."

"That's interesting. What about you? How does it work for you?"

"Out and proud. Married to a second violinist in one of the big London orchestras – we met at college and got married as soon as the law changed."

"Jeremy, that sounds wonderful. I do envy you."

"Yeah, we had a great time, got absolutely ratted at their expense." This was from Adam, who'd reappeared at the bathroom door, hair damp from the shower. He still wore nothing except the grin on his face and a skimpy pair of briefs as he leaned languidly against the door jamb for support again.

"We're still paying off the bar bill," Jeremy joked. "Ads, for fuck's sake go and put some clothes on."

"Oh right." He looked from one to the other of us, understanding dawning on his face. "Is he your boss, Jer?"

"Got it in one."

"Oh, shit. How embarrassing. Sorry." Now it was Adam's turn to blush. He looked even more appealing when he was that colour.

I gave him what I hoped would be a supportive look. "It's no problem, Adam. You weren't to know. It's nobody's fault."

"Bloody embarrassing, though," he muttered, gathering up his clothes before disappearing into the bedroom.

"I should go," said Jeremy. "I'm meeting Seb in a few minutes."

"Husband?"

"Yeah. Sorry. I didn't say, did I? Maybe we should talk about this sometime."

"I think so. And maybe I should promise to keep a closer eye on my phone."

"Possibly. Mind you, it can be a bit difficult if you're otherwise engaged."

"Exactly. Anyway, are we okay?"

"Of course. We're good. I'm glad, in a way – it'll make it easier to help."

"Thanks. See you in the morning."

"All being well." He called out goodbye to his cousin and left.

Adam emerged from the bedroom the moment Jeremy shut the front door. For some reason he was now mortified; it seemed more to do with the fact that I was Jeremy's boss than that he'd been seen doing escort work. I calmed him down eventually and took him out to supper. We ate pasta at a neighbourhood Italian, and several glasses of Chianti helped lift his mood.

Eventually Adam left me with a grin and a casual wave. He was such a sweet boy. I wandered back to the flat, put an internet classical station on my stereo and decided to work before turning in. The boxes needed doing, but it was also a welcome distraction from reliving the events of the afternoon. I suspected that it would be a long time before I forgot the sinking feeling I'd experienced when I realised that I was about to be outed to my private secretary.

It was time to read more about some of the big questions

facing the department over the coming years, particularly air quality. With research constantly finding new medical conditions that seemed to be affected by pollution, the political urgency to "do something" was growing and the issue was a rising concern, particularly amongst young families where parents were concerned for the deteriorating health of their children.

The problem for this government was that doing something meaningful almost certainly meant doing something about private motoring. The interests of motorists were almost sacrosanct in the eyes of most of the Parliamentary party, so the prospects of getting anything controversial through the Commons were slim to say the least. Up to now, this had been dealt with by devolving responsibility to local authorities and focusing on buses and lorries, which were much easier to regulate. However, they accounted for a relatively small and diminishing proportion of overall emissions as new regulations and technology made them cleaner. Pollution was not falling quickly enough, but air quality certainly was rising up the political agenda.

It would have been a difficult enough issue at the best of times but, as a government focusing almost exclusively on Brexit and its own survival, we were never going to do anything controversial or which remotely smacked of leadership.

By the time I'd finished reading the briefing paper, I certainly knew more about the issues; it was yet another impressive piece of work that carried Jeremy's hallmark. The trouble was that I was even more convinced of the hopelessness of actually doing anything about it – and of me personally influencing matters in any way, shape or form. Here was I, a Minister of the Crown in one of the oldest democracies in the world, administered by what was supposedly the best civil service in the world – but when confronted by an issue like this, we were largely powerless. It was immensely frustrating and profoundly depressing.

The good mood induced by Adam over the weekend had been sharply reduced by Jeremy's arrival at the flat. Now the mood had been destroyed completely by these fifteen pages of A4. I had worked hard and played hard but, by the time I lay my head on the pillow that Sunday night, it had availed me nothing. Not a good frame of mind in which to start the new week.

"Goodness me, you look as if you've lost a pound and found a penny," said Jeremy as I entered the office, followed by my driver with the red boxes.

"And a good morning to you too, Jeremy."

He looked concerned. "Bad night?"

"Not at all. I took Adam out to supper and calmed him down. For some reason, he was more agitated by your sudden appearance than I was."

"Again, I'm sorry that happened. I can't begin to tell you…"

I waved him away. "Then don't, Jeremy. I know how you feel about it, so let's regard the subject as closed."

He nodded. "Fine. Message received. What spoiled your mood?"

"I read your air quality briefing."

Jeremy gave a small smile. "I might praise your diligence, but I can't endorse your choice of Sunday evening entertainment."

"Me neither, in the end. I was informed, impressed and depressed all at the same time."

"Oh?"

"Yes, informed by a crisp summary and impressed by your mastery of the subject, depressed by my own sense of powerlessness."

"We must explore that further some time, Minister – but not now, I fear. We are summoned to the presence."

"Crikey, is he in this early?"

"Yes, the Secretary of State – our revered Permanent Secretary – wishes to discuss the Griffin House project and the planned conference. I gather he's recruited a new special adviser, so I expect he'll want to introduce us."

"Okay. What's this guy's name, do you know?"

Jeremy glanced at his phone. "I've got the e-mail somewhere. Here it is. Yes, he's called Sean Andrews."

"Bloody hell, not him. Christ! No need for introductions. He used to work for Jeffrey Speight, my neighbour in Portcullis House when I first got into the Commons. I can't stand the bloody man and the feeling is entirely mutual."

"What's he like?"

"A walking disaster area. Arch-Brexiteer, homophobe, climate-change sceptic – you name an unattractive right-wing policy and he supports it. I totally dislike the man." The prospect of having anything to do with Sean bloody Andrews completely ruined my Monday morning, He was sharp, devious, fanatical and slippery. An absolute shit.

Jeremy shrugged. "That doesn't bode well. Still, he'll no

doubt keep us on our toes."

"True enough. We'd better go upstairs. Presumably this is your Griffin House prediction about to come true?"

"That would be my guess. We should be done in about half an hour, so I suggest we drop into the planning meeting immediately afterwards."

"Sounds fine. Assuming we're spared."

The Right Honourable George Eckersley, MP, Her Majesty's Secretary of State for Environment, Energy, Climate Change and Rural Affairs was known in political circles a "safe pair of hands".

Generally speaking, Prime Ministers like safe pairs of hands because they can be relied on to steer their departments competently, keep them out of the headlines and strike consensual, non-controversial tones. "Uncontroversial" means largely listening to the civil servants in your department, sticking as far as possible to their advice and not falling out with anybody, especially not the Treasury. This is also regarded as "competent", though in some circles competence is defined as doing nothing. Harsher critics refer to such ministers as "uninspiring" and "boring" – especially when they do precisely what the Treasury tells them. Certainly, there is little chance of radical policies or major reforms originating from them; ministers who advance such things are referred to, with a curl of the lip, as "loose cannons".

George Eckersley was certainly uninspiring and boring, and uncontroversial to a fault largely because he almost never decided anything. By instinct, he was on the right of the Tory Party and certainly his utterances signalled that. However, since his natural inclination was to do absolutely nothing, his politics made little practical difference beyond setting the tone.

When we arrived in his spacious top-floor office, sure enough there was Sean Andrews sitting next to my ministerial boss and Sir John. Sean was now in his early thirties, prematurely balding, with dark skin that spoke of a Mediterranean background. His hair loss, which he attempted to disguise with a comb-over of sorts, combined with his long nose to accentuate the oval shape of his face. His most memorable feature, though, was his hooded eyes. They made him much more difficult to read. When you could see his eyes, they were a pale grey colour. He stood around six three, I estimated.

As we entered the room, he stood and we exchanged glances, neither of us looking exactly friendly. We shook hands when introduced but without warmth. His grip was strong, in an attempt to be intimidating. I ignored this and dropped his hand quickly.

The meeting was brief and to the point. George told us that Sir John had pointed out that the demands on our time were such that we could not justify two of us attending the conference. It was felt that, as the Minister directly responsible, I should attend and represent him.

I expressed my agreement, of course. As the political new boy, my job was to sit still and do as I was told. I was briefly reminded of the line from the Gilbert & Sullivan operetta *HMS Pinafore* about a politician who "always voted at his party's call and never thought of thinking for himself at all".

Partly as an attempt to smoke out their intentions, I added a line to my assent. "Jeremy has briefed me thoroughly on the project, and I'm looking forward to the event."

The Secretary of State's eyebrows shot up. "Ah, such enthusiasm, Daniel. Very commendable." His tone was anything but commending.

"Yes," I replied enthusiastically, prompting a small smile from Jeremy. "Great example of successful partnerships, offering potential for other similar schemes elsewhere. Real benefits to the taxpayer."

Sean snorted. "I fail to see how anything that helps the great global-warming myth could deliver any benefit to the taxpayer."

Sir John coughed before intervening. "I don't think we have time to debate the merits of the scientific case for global warming this morning." He turned to me. "I think what the Secretary of State means is that enthusiasm is all very well, but some restraint might be necessary until the department as a whole has come to a conclusion on the scheme's future." He glanced disapprovingly at Jeremy.

"I see, Sir John. I understand what you're saying." I nodded judiciously and tried to keep my tone neutral.

"What we actually need are not government handouts but deregulation," Sean said. "We can do that once we're out of Europe, of course – get rid of all this red tape – or should it be green tape in this case?" He laughed at his own joke but nobody else joined in.

"Also a discussion for another day, I think," said the Secretary of State, frowning at his new adviser. "We all understand each other on this conference business.

Singing off the same hymn sheet." He rubbed his hands together briskly and rose from his seat. "Splendid."

The meeting was clearly over. Jeremy and I left the office, carefully avoiding each other's eye. When we got downstairs, he started to laugh. "Something tells me that young Mr Andrews is going to be a pain in the proverbial."

"I did warn you. Interesting that George didn't seem exactly impressed, either. I wonder who foisted Sean onto him."

"Hmm. An interesting question. Meanwhile, well done, Dan. You got them to reveal much more of their hand than they intended to."

"Ever since I started in politics, I've always found that a display of boyish enthusiasm is extremely useful. How people react can be so revealing."

"It certainly was in that case."

"Absolutely. Mind you, your crystal-ball gazing skills are pretty good, Jeremy. As you said last week, it's pretty clear that distancing is going on. What's the next step?"

"Let's drop into the session on planning the conference. We can give them the good news about the Secretary of State not boring them rigid. And we can see how the land lies."

"Jeremy," I responded in a shocked tone. "Are you telling me that our lord and master's speeches are boring?"

He grinned at me. "Yes, Minister."

We were both laughing as he led me through to the suite of meeting rooms on the fifth floor. The rooms had deep glass partitions so that the participants in each meeting could be identified easily.

As we approached our room, I saw him. Sitting next to a

guy with longish hair and a ponytail, he was immediately recognisable. It was my friend from university days, Luke Carter.

Governing Passions

Chapter Nine

Luke

Steve and I met at the station before heading off to our meeting with the Griffin House guys about the planned conference. Fortunately they'd decided to hold it at the DECRA offices, saving us a trip to Bristol on a Monday morning.

We bumped into the Bristol-based staff in the reception area and chatted amiably whilst we waited to be taken upstairs to the meeting room. Like everywhere these days, security was intense so our bags were searched and we were issued with passes before being allowed anywhere. We were told to wait in reception for somebody to fetch us. Steve remarked that it was a bit like getting into Fort Knox.

When the meeting started, we were told that the Minister might look in to say hello if his schedule allowed it. I assumed they meant the boss man, the Secretary of State, so thought nothing more of it.

We started on the agenda and made good progress sorting out the programme for what we wanted to discuss and who would speak at each session. We had a short break and were preparing to resume when there was a noise outside our room.

I looked up to see two figures approaching along the corridor, chatting and laughing, looking relaxed and authoritative. One was Jeremy Cavendish. I'd met him before, in the early days of Griffin House; he'd recently joined the department at that stage, and worked with us for a while, but he'd been promoted rapidly and disappeared again. He looked as devastatingly handsome as ever, the more so today in a tight-fitting, well-cut, blue pinstripe suit. He gave us all a smile of recognition through the glass.

The other chap was instantly recognisable too, even though I hadn't seen him since I'd lain beside him on that Monday morning fifteen years earlier. It was Dan Forrester.

I closed my eyes, desperately trying to process his sudden reappearance in my life. My feelings were as conflicted as ever: disappointment at the way he had treated me; anger if – as now appeared to be the case – he had been gay all along. But there was also an overwhelming joy at seeing him again after all this time.

I opened my eyes and found myself looking directly into his through the partition. He had matured, obviously, but he was still easily recognisable. His reddish-brown hair was naturally curly, long on top but shorter at the sides and carefully styled to look modern while still seeming conventional. He'd grown a beard since I'd seen him, short and well-trimmed. It balanced his face beautifully.

Seeing him now reminded me that he had one of the most expressive foreheads I had ever known: two horizontal creases sat above five or six vertical ones, all ready to move together if he was puzzled, tense or upset. His dark eyebrows had always been one of his strongest features and they served to highlight his brilliant ice-blue eyes: they could sparkle with amusement or wonder but equally could turn cold and intimidating. If he was surprised or uncertain, his eyes opened wide and his eyebrows raised in the centre, something I'd always found adorable.

This gave me the clue to his reactions now. His eyes were wide open with surprise and his forehead was deeply creased. His eyebrows were at such a steep angle they almost resembled question marks. His eyes met mine briefly but quickly turned away. I managed to give him a small smile but I was unsure whether he'd seen it.

I closed my eyes. No wonder I'd fallen so hard for him as an eighteen-year-old undergraduate.

Jeremy ushered in the Minister and addressed the guy who was chairing the meeting. "So sorry to disturb your deliberations, Andrew, but the Minister thought this would be an ideal opportunity to meet the team ahead of next month's event."

He led Dan round the room, introducing him to everybody and coming to Steve and me last. "Minister, this is Steve Frazer and Luke Carter from Pearson Frazer, our trusted advisers on this project."

Dan shook hands with Steve before turning to me. He now managed something resembling a smile, The creases in his forehead reappeared and his eyes opened wide. As they met mine, I felt giddy and faint. He offered his hand for a shake, and when our hands touched a definite spark shot up my arm. We both withdrew quickly as if we'd received an electric shock,

"And Luke and I have met before," Dan said. "But it's been too long, hasn't it?"

I managed a mute nod, before finding a voice of sorts and murmuring, "Yeah, fifteen years, I think. Good to see you again, Minister."

"Oh, Dan. Dan, please. And you. To see you, I mean, after all this time." He was burbling and anxious, not at all the smooth-talking charmer I had expected. He was blushing slightly. Silence fell, and Dan and I continued to look into each other's eyes until there was a quiet cough to my left. I look up caught a puzzled look on Jeremy's face.

I stepped back, allowing Dan to turn and address the room. In moving, he appeared a little off balance for a moment and reached out to steady himself against the meeting table. Then he spoke. "Folks, I won't take up any more of your time this morning. It was good to drop in and meet you all. I'll look forward very much to discussing the Griffin House project and how we progress it with you next month."

So saying, he and Jeremy left the room. As they passed us in the corridor, Dan caught my eye and gave a small smile. I returned the look, then he turned and followed his private secretary towards the lift.

Wow.

Chapter Ten

Dan

I'd met and talked to literally thousands of people during my political career but nobody had achieved anywhere near the same impact on me as Luke. He'd reduced me to a burbling mess; I swear I almost swooned when he moved away from me.

He was still as handsome. Light brown hair brushed forwards on to his high forehead. Hazel eyes, one slightly darker than the other. And there was his bright, wide smile – and the beautiful way the skin round his eyes crinkled when he did so.

I managed to say something appropriate to the people in the room then allowed Jeremy to steer me out and back towards my office. I gave my head a quick shake as if to clear it as we walked towards the lift, and he regarded me curiously as we rode up to my office. "That was... quite a moment, Minister," he observed in a carefully neutral tone. "Is there anything you'd like to share with me?"

For a moment I thought about confiding in him. I was growing fond of Jeremy and starting to trust him – but I recognised that, if it came to it, his first loyalty would be to the Civil Service rather than me. He already knew I was gay – but could I trust him over this?

"Hmm. I think I have a Mars bar in my desk, if you'd like half."

He laughed. "Nice deflection, Minister. Worthy of a snick past the slips for a four, I think."

"You and your sporting analogies, Jeremy. How do you fare if people have never played cricket?"

"With great difficulty," he acknowledged. "But so few of one's friends have never played the game."

"I never have," I remarked.

"That is a surprise."

"I was never big on games – I managed to avoid them at school by studying all sorts of different things."

"So you were never much of a team player?"

"No. Always preferred to go solo. Still do, actually."

"Hmm. I'm beginning to realise that." He looked at me intently. "And is that okay? Truly?"

"Probably not. It's become a habit, though, pushing people away. Friendship has always been dangerous territory – it gives people knowledge about you. And that can make you vulnerable."

Jeremy opened his eyes wide, pausing to consider my remark. "I can see what you mean, of course – particularly in politics. Though ultimately I think we all need a friend, someone to confide in occasionally."

"You may be right. But we can't have everything. I got into Parliament and now I've got this job," I replied abruptly. "It's all I ever wanted and I've got it now, so I can't complain." Jeremy registered surprise at my tone, prompting me to add in a softer voice, "Even if I did miss out on a few things along the way."

He frowned. "Like what, for instance?"

I shrugged. "Love, friendship, leisure. I used to love live music and theatre but I never get time now."

There was silence for a moment. Then Jeremy spoke in a surprisingly tentative voice. "I could be your friend, if you wanted that. But you'd have to be honest with me about everything. Otherwise I don't think I could find it in me."

"That's good to know, Jeremy," I replied as we reached my office. "I'm touched. Thank you."

The shrill ring of the phone ended the conversation, so I was spared any immediate decision as to whether to accept his invitation and what I would say if I did. I was touched, though, and it made me smile. What an interesting morning I was having.

Governing Passions

Chapter Eleven

Luke

"Are you okay?" Steve asked anxiously. "You looked as if you'd seen a ghost."

We were on the train back to our office in Crystal Palace. "I'm good, thanks. It was a bit of a surprise, him appearing like that."

"You two – you were close?"

"For a few months. He was in his final year at university and I was a fresher. But he graduated and we lost touch."

"How close?"

"Not *that* close, Steve." I looked out of the window at the suburbs, watching the slate roofs and chimneys of the little Edwardian and Victorian villas slide past. "Friends for a few months, that's all. We could have been closer, but it wasn't to be. He – um – he graduated and that was it." I couldn't help it: my eyes filled again at the memory.

Steve saw and I noticed the concerned look in his eyes. "And it was important to you." It was a statement, rather than a question. "And still is, judging by this morning."

I nodded.

"Still, he wasn't exactly indifferent, was he?"

"But he's straight. I'm sure of it."

Steve shook his head. "And I'm a Dutchman."

I didn't reply. My heart was too full to say any more.

"Anyway," Steve continued. "You'll see him again at the Griffin House conference. We'll see what develops there."

"Indeed."

The train was in the tunnel approaching our station. We got up and went to the door. Steve placed his hand in the small of my back. "Whatever happens, Luke, don't try and handle it alone. Talk to Josh and me any time. All right?"

'Yeah. Thanks, Steve. I'm very grateful."

"Only we're pretty good at handling the past. We've had lots of practice."

I didn't have chance to think about the events of the morning until I got home that night. I had a couple of tasks to complete that week and forced my mind to focus on them instead of handsome thirty-something ministers.

It was a different matter later, though. The image of Dan's face and the look in his eyes when he greeted me were burned into my memory. And the feel of his skin when our hands had touched – I looked down at my right hand, almost expecting the spark that had passed between us to have left a mark.

I went upstairs to change before making some supper, and physical movement brought me to my senses. I had to stop behaving like a lovesick teenager; I was a grown man, thirty-four years old, newly promoted and confident.

Why should I melt into a puddle of goo simply because an old crush smiled at me?

It was nonsense, anyway. It couldn't go anywhere even if he was gay, which I still doubted despite Edward Bickerstaff's nasty innuendo the other day. Even if he was, he wouldn't be interested in me. The look of surprise on his face when he saw me had contained more than a hint of fear, so my presence hadn't been entirely welcome.

In any case, I certainly couldn't handle any sort of media attention if he came out. In any case, why would I want to? The way he'd treated me – the ruthless way he'd dumped our friendship – were pretty good indicators of his character. He was self-obsessed, ego-driven, ambitious and single-minded. All politicians were, it went with the territory. There would be no room for me in Dan's world, that was clear.

Then I recalled the small, almost secret smile he'd given me as he and Jeremy had walked away from the room. I could be as logical as I wanted, but that expression gave the lie to it all. And I couldn't deny my reaction either. Standing there in that meeting room, all the affection and attraction I'd felt for him fifteen years earlier had flooded my mind in one great wave, barrelling for the shore and submerging me.

Who was I kidding with all this logic? I'd take anything that Dan Forrester offered me – smiles, handshakes, distant acquaintance, friendship, love – and be grateful for it.

Governing Passions

Chapter Twelve

Dan

The next couple of weeks passed in a blur of meetings, visits and paperwork, followed by more votes in the House during the evening, always voting at my party's call.

As time went by, Jeremy and I grew closer. Professionally he continued to impress me, whilst personally I couldn't have asked for a better companion. He was kind, considerate and gentle. We did not refer again to his offer of friendship or to the encounter with Luke, which I resolutely refused to think about anyway. Nevertheless, both topics lurked in the background, as if we both knew that they'd have to be aired eventually. Neither of us was quite ready for that moment.

During the week before the Griffin House conference, however, that moment did arrive. It was mid-October and stormy outside, the wind doing its best to rip the dying leaves off the trees. We were back at the flat enjoying a nightcap after a particularly gruelling day. I realised that I should send the poor guy home to get some rest, but the day had left me feeling out of kilter and particularly lonely.

And what was the point of having a little power over people if you couldn't indulge yourself?

"You should go home, Jeremy," I said eventually.

"I know, but I don't think I have the energy to move."

"Today was a killer. I don't mind back-to-back meetings but when they all overrun and nobody makes any decisions..."

"In fairness, the air-quality working group did decide what sandwiches they wanted."

"Yes – and proceeded to eat the bloody lot before we arrived. I was absolutely starving by the time we got out of there."

"Still, the nice lady at the group in Islington did give us a cup of tea."

I huffed. "Tea? Is that what you call it? It tasted liked yesterday's washing-up water." I shuddered at the memory.

"I know what you mean. Still, it was at least wet and warm."

"I could name several other things that are wet and warm but I wouldn't want to drink them."

"I think we'd better change the subject away from things that are nice to swallow, Minister," Jeremy responded with a chuckle.

"What? Oh, er, yes. I see what you mean."

"Before I go, there was one topic I wanted to raise: next week's conference."

"Oh?"

"Yeah, and specifically the question of Luke Carter."

"Ah."

"I don't want to interfere with your private life, but I

think you ought to have some sort of plan as to how you're going to handle seeing him again."

"Why?" I asked, shifting uneasily in my seat.

"Several reasons. Firstly, we should avoid potentially awkward scenes like the other day in front of the other delegates. Secondly, Pearson Frazer are important to the department – to our hopes of saving the Griffin House project – and we don't want to jeopardise that. And thirdly, for your own sake. It's pretty clear that Luke is – or could be – important to you. If I'm reading the situation right, the event could be a useful way of starting to reconnect with him, if that's what you want."

I moved again in my chair: the airing of the topic had made me decidedly edgy particularly after a long day. I was on the brink of deflecting the subject to another time. Alternatively, I was severely tempted to deny any possibility of having feelings for Luke. Fifteen years on, I might be a little more relaxed about being gay, but a long-term relationship was still not part of the life plan. A job in the Cabinet beckoned – maybe even Number 10, who knew? Having a boyfriend would mean coming out, and all that entailed. It would generate media attention for all the wrong reasons. Absolutely not: it would seriously jeopardise everything, including my somewhat fragile relationship with my parents.

Jeremy took another sip of his drink and looked at me intently, awaiting my reaction. His reasoning was, of course, absolutely spot on. What was more, he wouldn't believe a word of any denial I might utter. He smiled at my hesitation. "Having a plan doesn't mean you're going to propose, you know."

I barked out a laugh. He was right. And in any case, who was I kidding? *Of course* I wanted to see him again.

"So is honesty your litmus paper?" I asked. "For friendship?"

"Yes. I value it in all aspects of life, but particularly in owning up to oneself and in personal relationships," Jeremy replied, getting my allusion to the discussion in the lift after the encounter with Luke.

"Yes, especially to one's self," I replied. My hesitation of the last two weeks had evaporated. I would tell Jeremy everything because his friendship was important to me. He already knew my closest secrets: that I was gay and occasionally paid for sex. Frankly, there wasn't much else to know – other than the shabby way I had treated Luke fifteen years earlier. That incident was the worst of me.

Suddenly I knew that I needed a friend in whom I could confide more than anything in the world – even more than my political career. That realisation came as a shock, but the feeling was real nonetheless. Telling him this might make me more vulnerable but on the other hand, if I was open and honest with everybody, it robbed bad people of their ability to do me harm.

Jeremy picked up on my tone of voice. His eyes were full of concern. "I take it that self-deceit is at the bottom of all this?" he asked.

I nodded. "Got it in one."

"I see. So, if I'm reading this right, this is about coping – or more precisely not coping – with your sexuality?"

I nodded again. "I've been running away from myself for at least twenty years, Jeremy. It seemed … necessary."

"I can understand that. Your chosen party hasn't exactly

been friendly to people of our sort over the years, has it?"

"No. I concluded aged sixteen that, if I was to have a political future, my true nature would have to be denied or suppressed. I've spent the time since doing just that. That's done nobody any harm in all that time, except me of course, with the one exception – the guy I met the other day for the first time since my graduation. I let him get too close fifteen years ago and I suspect that pushing him away hurt him deeply."

"Your reunion was very intense," Jeremy replied. "I'm sure only the most insensitive could have missed that. It was rather moving in its own way. I could tell that Steve Frazer was fascinated. I'm sure poor Luke was cross-examined closely all the way back to Crystal Palace."

"Maybe. But where does it leave me?"

"Judging by his reaction to you, you're in pole position," he responded. "I don't think you need have any worries on that score."

"But I can't take it for granted, Jeremy. I owe him a huge apology for what happened, for pretending that I didn't share his feelings. By running away and cutting him off completely, I lost a friend as well as someone I could – and probably did – love. If he shared my feelings, I must have hurt him so badly. I can't expect forgiveness for that."

"You may not expect it, but you might get it anyway. That's his decision, not yours. He gets the right to decide and you shouldn't make assumptions as to which way he'll jump."

"I certainly wouldn't forgive me, if I were him."

Jeremy laughed. "I don't think you actually believe that. Nothing is ever that simple. Few decisions we make in life are a binary choice because that allows no room for compromise. You did what you felt you had to do at the time and you've paid a price for that in loneliness and in depriving yourself of the balm of friendship and love."

"You're absolutely right, of course. It was... just necessary"

"That's the second time you've used that word, Dan. What was so important about a political career?"

"Because I had a sense that I'd been born to it. My entering Parliament was always taken for granted in our house, especially by my father."

"He was in the House for a long time, wasn't he?"

"For more than fifty years until he stepped down in 2010."

"And you were expected to follow in Daddy's footsteps?"

"Absolutely. It's what the Forresters do, public service. You're a Cavendish, you know how it goes."

He laughed. "Oh, but only a distant forty-ninth cousin, fifty-four times removed from the Chatsworth lot. We're the Coulsdon North branch of the family – decidedly suburban and not county at all."

"God, how absurd all those terms sound now."

"Yes, but they still have meaning even in the second decade of the twenty-first century. This is England, after all, snobbish, class-ridden England. It's been diluted a little over the last fifty years, that's all."

"I suppose you're right. Anyway, the weight of expectation was certainly on me as I was growing up."

"Only child, right?"

"And a late child, too, for my father especially. He was on his second marriage, you see, and the first one was childless. He was fifty when I was born. He's eighty-seven now. Still hale and hearty, but he hasn't changed many of his views since about 1958."

"That sounds hard."

"Not really. As a boy, I was content – it was a nice life and I was happy to conform. Still am, in some ways. My parents weren't particularly strict and they were loving and supportive. But it always felt conditional: I would be loved so long as I didn't disappoint. I first realised that at the age of twelve when I opted to play soccer and not rugby at school. My father had got his rugby blue at Oxford and I was expected to do the same. The atmosphere was fraught for a couple of weeks that autumn. My father still can't understand my interest in soccer, which he always describes as 'such a working-class game'."

Jeremy nodded. "I suppose it was, in the old days, before it became a branch of show business."

"Yes, but the key lesson for the teenage me was that being different from Daddy got me into trouble. When I got to the age of sixteen and realised that I liked boys rather than girls, I was terrified. It might have been 1997 with Cool Britannia and all that, but the subject was simply not discussed in the Forrester household."

"So you couldn't tell your parents?"

"No, nor anyone else for that matter. If I was going to follow my father's footsteps and become a Tory MP, those tendencies had to be suppressed." I paused, remembering the thinking I did late at night at school, recalling the pressure of looking at all those horny, good-looking teenage boys and being too scared to do anything about it.

"I understand. It must have been pretty awful."

"It was mostly okay because it became the norm. That was my life and I just got on with it. University was okay, too. I made a few good friends and had a nice life. Until my final year, when I met Luke." I paused again, remembering that day when we first met at the Freshers Fair.

"Go on," prompted Jeremy gently.

I shrugged. "There's not a lot to tell. We hit it off from that moment. I knew he was dangerous and that I was falling for him, but it didn't seem to matter. We were soul mates, so at ease in each other's company. I introduced him to my friends and he became a part of our group, helping to run the debating society. During the 2001 election campaign, he and I ran a series of debates on campus. We had such fun." The memory of that spring made me smile.

"What happened?"

"Largely by accident, we ended up sharing a bed one night towards the end of my last summer term. He hit on me, very gently and tentatively, and I was so tempted to respond. But I panicked and ran away. I didn't see him again from that night until the other day. God, I was such a fucking idiot."

Jeremy cocked his head at me. "You mustn't be too hard on yourself, Dan. You did what you felt was right at the time. You clearly weren't ready for any kind of sexual relationship. Dropping him like that might have been cruel, but who's to say that staying friends with him after that could have been possible?"

"I suppose you're right. But I still feel guilty, and I couldn't honestly blame him if he'd never forgiven me."

"And now? How do you feel about him now?"

"Like I'd risk anything – everything – to be with him."

I had no control over the words: they were instinctive. There had been no process of conscious thought. I was shocked when I realised that I'd said them but immediately recognised their truth.

Jeremy looked at me in surprise. "That strong, eh?"

"Yep."

"Which is why we need a plan."

"How do you mean? What sort of a plan?"

"How to greet him, whether to invite him for drink and a chat, that sort of thing. Fifteen years ago, you were so embarrassed that you didn't want to speak to him ever again. Now that has to happen, we need to work out how to handle it. Don't forget that I gave you three reasons why this was important. We've focused on you tonight, but we mustn't forget the other two."

"Yes, I see that. Sorry if I'm being a bit dense."

He grinned. "That's okay, you're a politician. It goes with the territory."

"Thanks," I laughed, welcoming the return of a little levity. The conversation had got rather heavy.

"I'll give it some more thought, but we need to create a space for you to spend some time alone with Luke. We're scheduled to arrive at two on the Wednesday in time for the afternoon session. There's a break around five until dinner, which is at seven. You're scheduled to speak at the end of dinner at about nine, nine-thirty. There's no time on the Thursday morning – you'll stay for the final session and the wrap-up, but that'll be it. You're due to visit Bristol to talk to the Mayor about air quality."

"Immediately before or after dinner sounds best, doesn't it?"

He nodded. "I think so. And before, preferably. You'll need to spend some time networking in the bar after dinner, so disappearing off too soon won't look good." He smirked slightly. "Besides, inviting somebody to your suite for a drink at eleven o'clock at night is a tad unsubtle, don't you think?"

I laughed. "That might happen anyway, if I got lucky."

"Sure, but not as a first date. What happened after that would be a different matter. Anyway, you – and Luke – might find my presence in the other bedroom in the suite a little awkward."

"Not if we managed to fix you up as well," I replied with a grin.

Jeremy pretended to look shocked. "Minister! Please remember that I am a happily married man. Quite what Sebastian would make of my boss fixing me up with a date, I don't know."

"Sorry, I didn't think. I'm not used to the idea of your being married yet."

"It never seemed relevant until last night." He smiled fondly. "As I said, we've been together since university. Because Seb's a musician, he's often away on tour. What with that and my job, we don't see a huge amount of each other, but it's fine."

I frowned. "Tonight? Am I keeping you from him tonight?"

"No, no. He's off playing Elgar in the Baltic States somewhere."

"Oh, okay. Baltic States, eh? Impressive."

"Yes, miss him terribly but only another week to go." He glanced at his watch. "But it is getting late. I should let you get some rest. We're on parade again with Sir John at eight-thirty."

I rolled my eyes. "Oh, joy."

"Could be worse – we could be back in Islington drinking tepid dishwater."

"Don't remind me."

"Anyway, about next week. We have a plan. Luke Carter will be invited for a drink with the Minister in his suite shortly before dinner. Okay?"

"Okay. And thanks, Jeremy."

"Only doing my job."

"You and I both know it's more than that. Seriously, thanks for listening."

"No problem," he responded as he reached the front door. "It's what friends are for."

I couldn't help the warm feeling that those words gave me. It was a long time since anybody had called me a friend. I could get used to that.

Governing Passions

Chapter Thirteen

Luke

Steve and I worked hard to prepare for the Griffin House conference. Allocated the first session on the Wednesday afternoon immediately after the introduction, we'd been asked to cover the overall administration and to talk specifically about the assessment methodology.

Steve said he'd do the introduction and the admin spiel and asked me to focus particularly on the assessment model.

"Can't you ask Josh to do it?" I asked, with a grin. "He wrote the model, after all." The memory made me smile; Josh had written the winning bid for Griffin House virtually single handed in his first few months with us. Working together on that project had brought Steve and him together.

Steve laughed. "'Fraid not, old son. He's singing that night – in Goole, of all places. He gets all the glamour these days. But he's already said to give him a shout if you want any help. He's home until the end of the week."

"Oh, terrific. Thanks."

We roughed out what we were going to say and then swapped drafts, batting ideas back and forth. Later, I arranged to visit Josh and go through some of the detail for a couple of hours; he still spent some time working at Pearson Frazer as a freelance associate between music engagements and, as author of the original bid, his insights would be incredibly valuable.

We sat in their big lounge with its spectacular view across London. As we finished, Josh made us some tea and we sat chatting. "Thanks so much for this afternoon, it's been brilliant, such a help," I said.

"I've enjoyed it, Luke," he replied, eyes sparkling with amusement. "A trip down memory lane."

"I'm sure it has been. Do you remember that night when you had to delete the file because it had been corrupted?"

"God, do I ever? And the monumental roasting I got from Steve the next morning. I thought he was going to have an apoplectic fit."

I laughed. "Still, it all turned out right in the end."

"Certainly did. Now what's this I hear from Steve about your hot minister?"

I felt myself blushing. "Oh, it's nothing. Only a short friendship long dead. It was good to see him, though."

"But Steve said there seemed to be a connection."

I shifted uneasily in my seat. "Yeah, well. But I'm sure he's straight. And in any case, the way the friendship ended..."

"Straight wasn't the impression Steve got," Josh said, a smirk playing round his lips. "Anyway, we'll see. I gather he's going to be at this conference thing next week?"

"That's right."

"If you get together with him, I expect a blow-by-blow account."

I raised my eyebrow. "That detailed, eh? I get a BJ from a Minister of the crown and I'm supposed to tell all?"

He threw back his head and laughed. "Absolutely."

"All I can say is that chance would be a fine thing."

The ministerial car was pulling away from the front of the hotel as Steve turned into the drive. I caught sight of Dan and Jeremy disappearing through the big front door of the Palladian mansion that was to be our home for the next twenty-four hours. The eighteenth-century country house had been converted into an hotel some years earlier and offered spectacular views across the Severn Valley from the top of the Cotswold Escarpment.

By the time we'd parked our car and walked into reception, Dan and Jeremy had already gone upstairs. As we checked in, the receptionist handed me an envelope. The paper was thick and I saw the House of Commons portcullis logo on the flap. When I turned it over, I recognised Dan's handwriting immediately. Even after all those years, I could remember it from that other envelope with the note he'd sent me cancelling our hiking trip. Was this another one asking me to keep clear?

I quickly stuffed it into my pocket. If it did contain a "keep clear" request, I wanted to be on my own when I read it. A few moments later, room keys in hand, Steve and I went across the hall toward the grand staircase.

"Aren't you going to open it?" Steve asked.

I tried to act casually. "Oh, er – I suppose so." I'd been on the point of snapping about it being my business, but it struck me that my knowing Dan was also the firm's business – another reason it was so complicated.

I put down my bags, took out the envelope and tore it open.

Luke

I'd love to use this opportunity to have a personal word. Would you be kind enough to join me for a drink in the Cotswold Suite before dinner this evening? Around six would be fine. Please let Jeremy know if that's okay.

Dan

I passed the note to Steve, who read it quickly. "You'll go, of course?"

I swallowed hard. "Yes, I think so. Not much choice, have I?"

We picked up our bags and walked towards the staircase once more as Jeremy appeared at the top and started heading down. We greeted him warmly; we'd enjoyed working with him until his promotion had taken him off the project.

After exchanging greetings, he asked, "Did you get the note?"

I nodded. "Thanks, I did."

"And?" he asked, his tone surprisingly anxious.

I adopted a formal tone but finished with a grin. "Please tell the Minister I'd be delighted to accept."

He beamed. "Excellent. The suite's on the first floor, opposite the top of the staircase."

"Terrific, Jeremy. Thanks."

"See you later. Excuse me now, I need a word with reception."

The opening session went extremely well. Steve was his usual eloquent self and he looked so distinguished with his ponytail neatly brushed and his smartly tailored suit. I detected Josh's influence there.

When it came to my turn, I was extremely nervous. During Steve's presentation I'd looked for Dan and seen him a few rows in front of me, seated on the front row of the left-hand side of the room, flanked by Jeremy and another guy from his private office. He was focusing intently on what was being said, looking down from the screen occasionally to make a quick note. His presence in the room added to my state of near panic, but I suddenly realised that I was far more nervous about going to his suite for a drink than talking about something that I knew backwards.

In the event, the hard work we'd put into preparing our slides paid off handsomely and I relaxed as I worked through the familiar material. I concentrated on the opposite side of the room, deliberately not looking at Dan. Instead I randomly picked two people who were clearly responsive, making eye contact occasionally and using them to make the talk more intimate and less like a lecture. It was a habit I had learned from my mentor at college and it always worked for me.

As I neared the end, I risked a quick look in Dan's direction but he was making a note at that moment. Instead my eyes met Jeremy's and he gave me an encouraging wink and a small smile. Almost before I knew it, I'd reached my peroration. I sat down to some applause, which came as something of a surprise. Steve patted me on the back as he joined me at the top table for a question-and-answer session.

After a slow start, that proved interesting. There were clearly two or three people from the department who were intent on damning the scheme with faint praise. One of them, a guy named Sean Andrews, asked a couple of questions that were distinctly hostile in tone. It turned out that he was a special adviser to the Secretary of State. Jeremy had seemed surprised when he arrived, slipping into the room shortly after Steve had started to speak.

The man's tone caused some embarrassment in the room and prompted a degree of coughing and shuffling of feet. Steve handled both Andrews' questions very capably, though, and I backed him up with supplementary points. Although we were well prepared on the detail of the scheme, neither of us had expected hostile questioning about the principle of environmental regulation or the need for intervention in the climate. Once again I was forcibly reminded that many people were antagonistic to the idea of global warming – primarily, I suspected, because they didn't like the measures that would be needed to manage it.

During the second exchange, I found the courage to look in Dan's direction again. He gave me an encouraging nod and a tight smile. It gave me a warm glow. The room and its occupants faded away as I focused on his smile. Then I noticed he was getting to his feet: the chairman had asked him to wrap up the session. I hadn't heard him give a formal speech since our days in the university debating society, but I could see immediately why he was so highly regarded as a politician. He gave a seriously impressive summary of what we'd been talking about, highlighted a couple of points by which he'd been impressed, and thanked Steve and I elegantly before closing with a small joke.

It was polished, eloquent and informal. It was also pitch perfect, so professional. Other than those few words in the conference room at the department, I'd not heard his voice since I'd seen him on TV just before the Olympics five years earlier.

He looked so handsome standing there in his immaculately tailored suit with not a hair out of place, clearly in his element. His voice was slightly more polished than I remembered from the days of our friendship. Then, his Derbyshire accent had been a little stronger; now you could barely hear it, though I could still hear the odd inflection, such as the short 'a' in bath or 'Newcastle'. The audience was left smiling at the end of a session which could have been tedious but ended up being, as Dan put it, "informative and stimulating".

Steve and I stayed at the top table, chatting to delegates. I was experiencing an adrenalin rush from the success of the afternoon and hardly noticed the next twenty minutes fly by. Then suddenly I realised that I needed to get showered and changed for dinner before I went for the drink with Dan, so I didn't have much time.

The lack of time in which to get ready was probably for the best; it gave me no opportunity to overthink this and get even more nervous about being alone with Dan. Seeing him in action this afternoon had definitely been hot; it had only served to confirm that my feelings for him were still there. That thought alone would normally have rendered me a gibbering wreck, but now I had to focus and make sure that I presented myself at his door dead on six.

I made it with thirty seconds to spare, so had time to stand in the long corridor outside his suite gathering myself together. I closed my eyes, took two deep breaths and raised my hand to knock. My hand shook slightly as I realised that, with any luck, the next few minutes might be fundamental to how I spent the rest of my life. If nothing else, I'd be able to close a door on that incident fifteen years ago and move on. But I so hoped for something else...

Jeremy opened the door and smiled broadly as he showed me into the sitting room. This first floor of the building had contained the state bedrooms in the house's heyday. The room was immensely tall and had two huge windows flanking a set of doors that led onto a small balcony formed from the portico covering the front door.

The house faced south-westwards so the sun, which had started to set on this late October evening, flooded the room with a golden light, making the chandeliers sparkle as if they were lit. There were two elegant sofas either side of a huge fireplace with a low coffee table in between, and there was a desk in one corner. It was impossible to see the colour of the décor because everything appeared in silhouette against the background of the spectacular sunset.

Also silhouetted against the light was a figure standing at the French doors, looking out at the view. Deep in thought, he had not heard us come in.

Jeremy cleared his throat and said quietly, "Luke Carter to see you, Minister." He paused then added, "I'll be downstairs in the bar if you need me," and left the room.

The figure turned to greet me. As he emerged from the shadows, his features became clearer and he gave me a huge welcoming smile.

"Dan," I said, hand outstretched.

Governing Passions

Chapter Fourteen

Dan

"Luke Carter to see you, Minister."

Jeremy's voice awoke me from my reverie as I stood at the French windows looking out across the Severn Valley. I don't know what was in my mind at that moment; for at least the previous half hour, I'd been trying to distract myself to avoid thinking too much about this meeting.

Seeing him during the conference session that afternoon had been an exquisite torture. He looked so sexy standing there in his suit, talking so eloquently about his work. His passion and commitment shone through and were seriously impressive, as well as totally adorable.

Fortunately he had avoided making eye contact with me, otherwise there was no way that I could have concentrated on his words. And I simply *had* to concentrate: firstly, because I was going to sum up and thank the speakers at the end of the session, and therefore had to know what had been said; secondly, the combination of my own instincts and Jeremy's advocacy had made me a fan of the Griffin House project, so I needed to get a grip on the subject.

I'd been distracted momentarily by the arrival of Sean Andrews, which had been unlooked for; certainly I had not expected him and neither had Jeremy, judging by the look on his face. I wrestled my mind away from the Andrews issue, because the real reason for needing to concentrate was Luke himself: his work was clearly immensely important to him. If he and I were going to have any sort of relationship, it was important that I at least understood what drove him.

Now here Luke was, in the room with me, all polished and scrubbed up for the conference dinner. I moved forward to greet him, a wide smile plastered across my face.

"Dan," he said, hand outstretched.

I took his hand in both of mine. I wanted to greet him with more than a handshake, but it was too soon for hugs. "Luke, thanks for coming – and congratulations on this afternoon. It was a great session and you were superb." Our hands remained joined for a few seconds. I was reluctant to let go but forced my myself to.

"Thanks. I think we were both pleased with how it went."

"What can I get you to drink?"

"Some water would be fine, thanks," he replied, his voice slightly strangled as if he were struggling to speak. He gave a small smile. "It might be a long night."

"Still or sparkling? Do sit down. Ice?"

I busied myself pouring him some sparkling water and a small Scotch for myself. He might be right about the evening stretching before us, but I was in immediate need of something to help me calm down.

I turned, drinks in hand, to find him on one of the sofas at the end furthest from the fireplace. I handed him his glass and our fingers touched. The warmth of contact, however brief, felt glorious. I sat at the other end of the sofa, unwilling to put the coffee table between us. "It's great to see you on our own, Luke. Been a long time."

"Yeah, as we said the other day, fifteen years. Gone quickly, though, hasn't it? Sometimes being a student seems like yesterday."

"I know what you mean. So, how have you been?"

"Okay, I guess. I love working with Steve – I've been with Pearson Frazer for around five years, since not long after they first started. I live about ten minutes' walk from the office in a nice little house."

"Still single, or do you have a partner?"

"No, still single. Never met the right person."

That's the good news.

"What about you? Congratulations, by the way, on the new job."

"Oh, thanks. I'm enjoying it. Jeremy keeps my nose to the grindstone, though, so I don't get much time for myself."

"Does that bother you?"

"No, I don't think so. It's what I always wanted. Why I came into politics." I paused, adding, "So I can't complain."

"And personally? Are you with anybody?"

I shook my head. "No time, Luke. And, like you, I've never met the right person." *Until now.*

There was a pause. Suddenly, Luke looked so young and tentative, like the boy I had first met. He took a sip of water and cleared his throat. "Are you still in touch with any of the old crowd?"

"No more than the odd Christmas card. We ... grew apart. You?"

He shook his head. "We lost touch completely after the end of that year." He paused and looked up, meeting my gaze.

God's he's shaking. Is this all so terrifying?

He took a deep breath. "So, here's the thing. About what happened at university. I feel I owe you an apology. For that last night, I mean ... I never intended..."

I was appalled. I hadn't expected this first meeting to get so intense so quickly, although I could see his logic. No point in fencing – get the whole subject aired. We had to if there was to be a future of any kind. I interrupted him. "Luke, please. You don't owe me anything. If anybody in this room should apologise it's me."

"Why, Dan?"

"For being spineless. I wanted to respond, to reach out, but I was so bloody frightened. God, what a fucking coward I was."

His eyes opened wide. "Do you mean? I... Does that mean you were...?"

"Gay? Yes, I was – am."

"Fuck, Dan,"

"I know. I'm sorry. You are gay, right?"

He nodded but remained silent, looking at me in surprise.

I carried on. "I remember how close you were, and how beautiful you looked when I watched you sleep."

"Christ."

There was a pause. I was at a loss but instinct told me that

I needed to say more. "Looking back now, what bothers me most is my cruelty to you. I shouldn't have pushed you away, or lacked the courage to see you again. Did it upset you very much?"

There was a pause. Luke took a sip of water and looked up at me. "Yes, actually it did."

"Eeh, lad, I'm sorry." The blow his words struck was almost physical, and my instinctive reaction took me instinctively back to the inflection of my youth.

"Going back for my second year was hard – I wasn't in a good place after ... you know, you left."

My heart sank. What had I done? I looked away from him and took a sip of my drink

Luke frowned. "I ... had a bit of a rough time for a while. I told myself that I'd lost you as a friend because I was gay – which was something I hadn't totally accepted anyway."

My feelings of guilt bubbled to the surface. "God, Luke, that must have been hard." I wanted to reach out and comfort him – another instinctive reaction that rocked me back a little. I had never been much of a hugger – we didn't go in for that sort of thing much in our family – it was all handshakes and kisses on or near the cheek.

"Yes, it was. I ... er ... had a bit of breakdown. Depression and things. Couldn't go back after the Christmas – had to repeat my second year in the end." He closed his eyes for a moment and I was sure he shuddered.

"Jesus, Luke. I really mucked things up, didn't I? You must hate me."

"You certainly weren't my favourite person for a while, but actually none of it was your fault. It was me, in my head, and I'm sure it would have happened eventually whether I'd met you or not. It was about being gay and facing up to it. You were the trigger, I suppose."

"Maybe. But..."

He cut me off. "No, Dan. Don't go there. What happened, happened. If you'd responded differently that morning, who knows how things would have turned out? But you weren't ready to cope with being gay either, and I don't suppose either of us was up to running a relationship. We can't know what we'd have done."

"You're right, of course. But it was easy with you. I've never felt as close to anybody since – nobody's ever got me like you did."

"I know what you mean," Luke replied. "Funnily enough, the sex bit has been easier than the friendship. It's quick and easy to hook up with a cute guy in a bar. Much more difficult to get to know somebody."

I gave a short laugh. "Heck, yes. Mind you, I don't get to many bars in this job."

"It's only been in the last couple of years, being friends with Steve and his husband Josh, that I've realised what I've been missing. Watching them get so close has been a real eye-opener."

"I can imagine. I've rather taken to Steve. He was seriously impressive this afternoon."

"He always is. Great to work with – since he met Josh, anyway. But you're lucky having Jeremy in your private office. We worked with him before he was promoted. He's a great guy."

"He definitely keeps me in order. We've become friends, I think. He's good for me. Stops me getting all pompous and ministerial."

Luke laughed. There was another pause as he gave me another intense look. "God, Dan, it's good to see you again."

"I know. It's been too long." I paused for a moment, gathering the courage to ask him the next question that would address the issue that lay between us. "So, Sky, can you forgive me?"

Governing Passions

Chapter Fifteen

Luke

"So, Sky, can you forgive me?"

That was almost too much. I hadn't heard Dan's nickname for me for fifteen years. Though my parents had named me for the Apostle and Gospel author, Dan had decided in the early days of our friendship that my father was a closet *Star Wars* fan and that I'd been named for Luke Skywalker. He'd started to call me Skywalker, but it had gradually been shortened to Sky. I'd almost completely forgotten about it.

My breath hitched on that ... then there was his question. I hadn't had time to process our discussion; he'd dealt three hammer blows to my composure in quick succession: that he didn't blame me for the events of that night fifteen years ago; that it was panic and fear, not revulsion, that had made him flee that morning, and the revelation that he was gay.

What the hell should I do? I reached for my water and swallowed it down, then rose from my seat. I needed to get away, to think. I was on the verge of panic and needed some air. Now. "I'm sorry, Dan. I can't answer you at the moment. I should probably go." I headed for the door of the suite.

"Is that a 'no' then, Luke?"

I shook my head. "I meant what I said, Dan. All that you've said tonight, all that I went through fifteen years ago. I just need some time to think and some fresh air. Sorry."

Dan's forehead was deeply furrowed as he struggled to respond. "I'm sorry I mucked it up, Luke. I never meant to hurt you. Perhaps we could have a nightcap later? Will that be time enough, do you think?"

I nodded, unable to speak. Anything to get out of there. I fled.

Leaving Dan's suite, I felt slightly unsteady as I descended the stairs. My emotions were still running on high. Reconnecting, the revelation about his feelings, his apology. I saw Jeremy in the hall, looking surprised at the shortness of my time with Dan. I nodded to him but kept moving. I'd be fine if I could have even a couple of minutes in the fresh air.

The sun had set after casting its spell over Dan's suite earlier, leaving behind a sky streaked with purples and pinks. Discreet lighting picked out the path into the hotel garden and I followed it round to the side of the house, finding a bench with another view across the valley.

I sat down and took a few deep breaths. Seeing him again at close quarters had been intense. The fact that he'd used my nickname, plus the totally unexpected apology and having my hand held in his two, even if only for a moment … it had all been truly awesome.

A fifteen-year-old memory had been robbed of its power to depress me. There had been times during the intervening years when, sleepless at two or three in the morning, I had squirmed with embarrassment at the memory of Dan being in the same bed with me, and particularly the curt note he'd sent me afterwards. But now…

Shame and regret at having made an apparently unwanted advance, however tentative, had been replaced by a measure of nostalgia for the people we had been. Inevitably it was tinged with regret at what our affection could have grown into if only we'd been honest with each other. But my overwhelming feeling was relief – as though a weight had been lifted from my shoulders. As I sat there in the gardens, I felt a lightness of being that I'd rarely experienced during my life.

But why hadn't I been able to forgive him there and then?

The answer was that, deep down, there was a part of me that still held him responsible for the miserable time I'd had during the rest of my academic career. If he'd been genuinely revolted by my tentative advances that morning, I could have understood and kept up the process of moving on that I'd begun all those years ago. In those circumstances, the apology I had offered tonight could have given me some closure.

But somehow the fact that his response had been born of fear – that he had actually wanted me that morning but had been too frightened to respond – made it seem much worse. And it made his subsequent behaviour more difficult to understand. He must have had some inkling about what I was going through after he'd left me that morning, but he'd still written me that curt note and cut me out of his life.

How could I trust him not to do the same thing again? Politics were his life; how would he react if all he'd worked for was threatened? The danger was that, confronted with choices over his career and his personal life, he would choose his career.

Even if I was prepared to forgive the heartlessness he'd meted out fifteen years ago, could I risk that he'd do exactly the same thing again?

I heard a rising volume of voices from inside the building, suggesting the pre-dinner reception was getting under way. I needed to pull myself together and get inside. I was, after all, on duty here. That had to be my priority now.

Chapter Sixteen

Dan

After Luke left my suite, I had a few minutes before I needed to go downstairs. I swallowed the rest of the whisky and stared into the glass, watching the play of the room lights as they were caught by the crystal.

I couldn't help but be disappointed by the outcome of my all-too-brief meeting with Luke, but I could hardly blame him for needing to get away. After all, he'd clearly felt somehow responsible for what had happened that night, then endured total silence for fifteen years. I had simply walked away after inflicting a wound on his soul that had obviously gone far deeper than I could ever have imagined. No, that wasn't true. I hadn't walked. I'd run so hard he couldn't see me for dust. The next thing he knows is that he's faced with an abrupt apology and a plea for forgiveness. It was hardly conducive to instant decision-making.

I took consolation from the fact that he hadn't flung my pleas back in my face – some people would have done. And he'd agreed to come back later for a nightcap. That had to be a good sign – always assuming that he turned up, of course.

Even if he did, it was still quite possible that he'd reject my peace offering. But, deep down, I knew that wasn't going to happen if he did make an appearance.

I gave my head a quick shake to try to clear it, and then did a last check before going downstairs for dinner. "Wallet, phone, speaking notes," I muttered, forcing myself to concentrate. They were all in place. I would have put on my brave face and cope with tonight's formalities whatever my trepidation about Luke. I pushed back my shoulders and opened the door of the suite.

Jeremy was pacing around the lounge as I descended the great staircase. He looked up when he heard my footsteps and raised an interrogative eyebrow. "All right?" he asked quickly, seeing the conference chairman hovering.

"Not a triumph," I replied. "But I didn't muck it up completely, so no outright rejection. He's coming up for a nightcap later to talk some more."

He nodded and squeezed my shoulder. "Probably the best you could expect. Better than nothing."

We started socialising and I managed to turn on the smile for the occasion.

By the time you added together the team from our department, the consultancy staff, the academics and several of the project's clients, there were about fifty people for dinner. I allowed Jeremy to steer me as we worked the room; it helped enormously that he'd worked on the project for a few months, so he already knew many of the people there. His judgement and timing were perfect; by the time dinner was announced, we'd managed to greet pretty much all the delegates. That would go down well.

Once again, I was impressed by the commitment and enthusiasm shown by those working on Griffin House. It confirmed the conclusion I'd already reached that there was something special about the scheme and its framework that shouldn't be lost, not least because it offered an important template for how government should deliver policies.

I managed to relax and even felt quite happy, particularly when we ended up talking to Luke and Steve shortly before dinner was announced. For form's sake, I greeted Luke as if we'd not been together twenty minutes earlier. His eyes showed a twinkle of amusement as we shook hands – though in other ways he seemed a little distracted. Not surprising, I reflected.

I congratulated them both on the success of their presentations and said how I envied their ability to use PowerPoint. "With me, people only get to listen – and it can be pretty tedious sometimes, especially if Jeremy has had an off day."

"Minister, I'm appalled," he said with mock indignation. "My speeches for you are always positively Churchillian."

"Yes, yes, Jeremy, of course. I marvel at your ability to make the opening of a sewage works in Scunthorpe the occasion for a morale-raising oration."

He grinned. "Have we opened a sewage works in Scunthorpe?"

"Not that I can recall. Mind you, I've been in the job

127

all of four weeks, so my memory may be getting faulty. All those meetings and visits tend to blend into one after a while."

Jeremy raised his eyebrows. "Is it really only four weeks? It seems like years."

"No, that's only when I have to stand up and deliver your speeches."

"If you two spend all this time sniping at each other, it's a wonder you ever get any work done," Steve remarked.

"We make such a great team, the work virtually does itself," I replied.

"What the Minister means, of course, is that I do all the work and he takes all the glory."

"Ah," I quoted solemnly. "'It's the same the whole world over...'"

Jeremy came back with the next line. "'It's the poor what gets the blame.' The poor private secretary, in this case."

I fixed him with a stare of mock severity. "Jeremy, you and I may be many things but poor isn't one of them."

He feigned a look of surprise. "Do you mean not everybody has to choose between caviar and smoked salmon for breakfast? How shocking."

"It's clear that you two make a great team," Steve remarked. "Maybe you should go on stage as the latest successors to Morecambe and Wise."

"Ah, yes," said Jeremy. "I can see it now. Up in lights ... Cavendish and Forrester, the Laurel and Hardy of modern government."

Dinner was announced so the four of us parted. As I joined the conference chair and we walked into the hotel's spectacular dining room, I felt more relaxed and happier than I had for many years.

Governing Passions

Chapter Seventeen

Luke

As Steve and I took our seats for dinner, we were still chuckling over Dan and Jeremy's banter. Our brief chat during the reception had helped enormously; it was if he'd been put back in his proper context and was no longer looming so large in my imagination.

The food at dinner was pleasant without being particularly memorable, but it was an enjoyable evening. After coffee had been served, the conference chair uttered a few platitudes and before handing over to Dan. He was commendably brief but, as during his vote of thanks earlier, he projected warmth and charisma. He made some kind comments about Pearson Frazer's contribution to Griffin House, which made Steve's night, and was enthusiastic about the whole project, making his own commitment to the project in a way which clearly surprised some of the older hands in the room.

"There are some I know in Whitehall who are sceptical about this project – the innovative way of working, the strong partnerships we've forged between government, academia and the private sector – something we've struggled to deliver effectively for decades. The success of Griffin House has nothing to do with whether and how we should be dealing with climate change, or how we regulate our environment."

He paused and looked straight at Sean Andrews, the hostile questioner from the afternoon. "What's important – and so good – is that it's using partnerships to deliver public policy objectives more effectively than the government can do on its own. Some suggest that profit should have no place in public administration or public services. My friends, I disagree. The risks and rewards available in business offer powerful incentives to managers and staff to deliver the best possible service to their customers – because that is the best route to survival and success.

"But private-sector companies work best when they have an informed and pro-active client who communicates effectively with them. That's what the civil servants working on this project have achieved with the support and advice of their academic colleagues. Teamwork and communication have been the hallmarks of Griffin House, so congratulations to you all on what you've achieved, and all the best for the future. You're a beacon of success in a difficult time for government, and long may that continue."

Dan's words were greeted with thunderous applause. Only one or two people were less enthusiastic, and I spotted Sean Andrews and a couple of his cronies sitting on their hands. Their reaction seemed churlish and ill-mannered; there was evidently something going on in the department about the next round of funding. I made a mental note to ask Steve about it.

Dan's speech marked the end of the formal part of the proceedings and people started moving to the bar, though others carried on talking at their tables. The time for my nightcap with Dan was approaching and my stomach clenched, partly with nerves but also with the anticipation of having more time in private with him and resuming our earlier discussion.

I looked up to see Steve watching me with a gentle smile on his face. "Good, isn't he, your Dan?"

"He's not mine, Steve. But yes, he is. Terrific."

"Knows his stuff, too. But I suppose we've got Jeremy to thank for that as much as young Mr Forrester."

"Yeah, I think you're right."

One of the academic team came over to our table and started chatting about benefit-to-cost ratios and assessment methodologies. It was useful because it distracted me from useless speculation about events to come, and I hardly noticed the passage of the next half hour. I was in the middle of a discussion about modelling when Jeremy touched my elbow. I excused myself and turned to him.

"The Minister and I are about to disappear. He's got some urgent red box papers to get through and some e-mails to do, but he should be clear in about an hour. He'll be more than ready for a nightcap by then. Is that okay?"

"Brilliant." I glanced at my watch. "So, I'll come up around eleven?"

He nodded and glided away, leaving me to resume my esoteric discussion on assessment methodologies and how to improve them.

Governing Passions

Chapter Eighteen

Dan

God, there were times when I hated this damned job. And this was one of them. Here I was, quarter to eleven on a Wednesday evening, stuck doing my boxes – reading some boring minute about the importance of some breed of toad to an obscure river valley in rural Devon. Ludicrous. But the draft order, which would hopefully prevent the extinction of the breed, needed to be signed and I refused to sign things without knowing what they meant.

Anyway, that was the last document in the box, and Jeremy and I had already cleared the urgent e-mails. The rest could wait for the journey back to London after tomorrow's mayoral visit.

I finished the document, appended my initials and put it back in the red box, closing it with a flourish. "There you are, oh slave driver mine. All done."

Jeremy looked up from his laptop and gave me a smile. "There's a good boy. Now you can have your reward. Luke should be on his way up in a minute. I shall make myself scarce."

"Not staying for a drink?"

"I may like fruit, Minister, but I'm not playing gooseberry for anyone."

That made me chuckle. "Understood," I replied. "And thanks."

"For what?"

"Your understanding. Your discretion. Your advice. Need I say more?"

"Always happy to listen to praise from my hot boss."

"Jeremy! Are you flirting with me?"

"Oh, perish the thought, Minister. No, no. Doing my job, part of which is to keep your morale high."

"If it's any consolation, you're certainly succeeding. Today was a good day."

He nodded. "I agree. There was some good stuff this afternoon and your little homily went down well tonight."

"Good. Pinned our colours firmly to the mast."

"Yes, enough to raise a few eyebrows in some quarters. Especially in George's private office – I can't get over him sending his SPAD to keep an eye on us."

"It's quite useful in a way. We intended to send a signal today – this means it'll get through a bit faster than we expected. It was the object of the exercise, after all."

"Quite so, Minister. Now I'm going to disappear. Breakfast at seven?"

"Fine."

"We need to be away from here by ten if we're going to make your appointment with Mr Mayor."

"Okay, I'll bear that in mind."

We were interrupted by a soft knock on the outer door of the suite.

"Right, good night," Jeremy said *sotto voce* as I moved towards the door.

I heard his bedroom door close as I opened the outer one.

"Perfect timing," I remarked to Luke as I let him in. He looked nervous as he walked past me into the room. I closed the door. "What's your poison?" I asked. "Still drinking single malt?"

"God, how on earth did you remember that?"

"Oh, there's a lot I remember about you, Sky."

He swallowed hard. "I didn't even know if you'd remember me at all."

"'Once seen, never forgotten'," I quoted, handing him his drink and pouring the same for myself. "But seriously, we had a good time that year – it was probably the best year of my life."

"Really?" Luke asked. "For you too? So why did you never..."

"I was still set on suppressing everything about being gay – it didn't fit into my life plan. End of." I closed my eyes. "But God, Luke. I missed you."

I sat next to him on the sofa, our knees almost touching. I could feel the warmth of his leg and it filled me with joy. I raised my glass to him. "Here's to old acquaintance."

"Which should never be forgot." We clinked glasses. "I missed you too, Dan. Thought of you pretty much every day. Feeling ashamed of what happened. Wondering how you were doing."

"That's amazing. Luke, I'm so sorry. Such a waste of our lives. Can you forgive me for what happened?" I gazed hopefully into his eyes, but still he hesitated. I found myself tugging my collar and pulling my earlobe with nerves. He saw my gestures, and something in his eyes melted.

"Of course, Dan. The past is the past – it's not what's gone that matters, but what's still to come."

I exhaled a huge sigh of relief and felt my body relax. I almost slumped with relief. "Thanks, Luke. Means a lot, that does."

His knee pressed into mine and stayed. He shifted closer and took my hand, intertwining his fingers with mine. "Maybe we could reconnect? Become friends again, maybe more. If that's what you want?"

Holding his hand like that almost took my breath away. The warmth, the soft skin of his palm. I could have sat there for hours like that. "That would be grand, Luke. I'd love us to be close again." I leaned into him, resting shoulder to shoulder. "In fact, I can't think of anything I'd rather do."

"Brilliant. That makes me so happy, you've no idea."

We lapsed into silence for a few moments, but it was comfortable rather than awkward. Then Luke spoke again. "I know we can't fix the past, Dan, but we can learn from it. Whatever else happens between us, the lesson is that we must talk. We could have fixed all that business fifteen years ago if we'd had the sense to talk to each other and be honest."

"That's certainly true." I snorted. "And the daft thing is that I found it easier to talk to you that year than anybody else before or since."

"I know, me too. We were crazy – just two frightened kids, I suppose."

"So not much has changed there, then," I replied, huffing another laugh. "I might not be a kid any more, but the whole thing still frightens me to death."

"Still not out?" he asked. I shook my head. "To anybody?"

"To Jeremy and now you, plus the boys I occasionally hook up with. But nobody else."

Luke widened his eyes for a moment. "Boys?"

I nodded. "No secrets, Luke. I occasionally meet up with a boy, to scratch an itch. They're ... paid to be discreet." I tensed, waiting for an adverse reaction, but none came.

"Yes, I see. That's probably sensible under the circumstances. No judgements from this Grindr user."

I breathed a small sigh of relief. "And how about you? Presumably you came out to your family?" My eyes widened in surprise when he shook his head.

"No, not yet," he said. "It seemed too complicated, with all the Church stuff and everything. I think they know, though."

"How would they react, do you think?"

"Interesting question, Dan. I'd always assumed badly. If the subject came up when I was younger, Dad very much took the line about it being a mortal sin and would talk about his duty to save people's immortal souls. But something happened recently which seems to have changed his mind. A bit of a Damascene moment."

"Heck! What happened?"

"It seems that a colleague at the Cathedral resigned the priesthood over the Church's attitude to his being gay. To cut a long story short, Dad now accepts that we're gay because we're made that way, not because we've made any sort of choice."

"That's good, isn't it?"

Luke nodded. "I think so – it certainly makes things a

bit different. Anyway, I've decided I'll tell them next time I go down and take it from there."

"That's grand. I wish I could find some of your courage."

"I'm sure you will when the time is right." Luke leaned into me more closely. His smile widened. "In the interests of the good communication we promised earlier, can I ask you a question, Dan?"

"Ask away."

"May I kiss you?"

"You most certainly may."

He turned his head and put his lips on mine. It was a chaste kiss, that first one. Only lips, no tongues, no open mouths. A gentle, loving, coming together. He pulled away after a moment and looked me in the eye. "All right?"

I nodded.

"Again?"

"Yes, please, Sky."

He put his glass down on the coffee table, never losing eye contact. He leaned in again, and there was nothing chaste about that second kiss. After a few minutes, we paused for breath and our eyes met again. We were both breathless and started to laugh at the magic of it all.

Chapter Nineteen

Luke

When I awoke, the wind was throwing the rain against the windows like showers of small pebbles. I glanced at the bedside clock: six-forty. Ten more minutes and I would have to get up. I needed to shower, dress, breakfast and check out of my room before the conference resumed at eight-thirty. I groaned slightly at the thought after no more than four hours' sleep.

It was gone two when I left Dan's room. I sighed with contentment as I recalled the events of the night. That first kiss had been magical, and what followed now seemed to take on the same quality. In reality it had been a very physical thing, involving hands and mouths and lots of holding each other.

I supposed that the magical quality came from a feeling of paradise postponed. I'd spent years yearning for what might have been. Our reunion was bound to feel special, and indeed it had.

I recalled how it had felt to embrace Dan, to kiss him and be held by him. Just as we had bonded as friends all those years ago, we now fitted together physically as well. Lying on that sofa in his arms felt like coming home. I drew strength from his embrace, a feeling I'd never experienced with anyone before.

I remembered his weight on top of me. I closed my eyes and felt again the perfection of lying there for what seemed hours, holding him as we kissed each other's lips, necks. Thrusting against each other, followed by minutes lying still, looking into each other's eyes. Every now and again, the embrace would turn into a vice-like grip as one of us responded to the joy of holding the other.

We had gone no further, both sensing that this was not the right place or time. Even so, such an intense and moving experience prompted me to shed a few tears. He tried to kiss them away but the gentleness of his actions only produced more.

Eventually, we heard the longcase clock in the hall downstairs strike two. Dan pulled back slightly, kissing me lightly on the end of my nose. "I'd ask you to stay, but it's probably not a good idea," he said.

"I was thinking the same thing. It's a shame – I could happily hold you for ever."

"Me too. In the words of the song, 'We don't want to lose you, but we think you ought to go'."

I chuckled. "Silly devil. So...?"

"'When shall we two meet again?' Soon. I'll be in touch in a day or so. I can't wait to see you, to be with you again." He looked up, uncertainty crossing his face. "That is, if..."

I smiled into his eyes. "Yes, Dan, I do want to see you again very much, and as soon as possible."

He tilted my chin for another kiss. After a while, he put

his mouth to my ear. "Thanks ... for tonight, I mean. This has been beyond words."

I tightened the embrace. "Me too."

I straightened my clothes and left Dan's suite, walking along the galleried landing towards the staircase and my second-floor room. A rumble of voices wafted up from the hall below where two delegates from the department were enjoying a nightcap. One of them looked up and I recognised Sean Andrews. He gave me a hostile stare. I was too tired to care and continued upstairs.

I was brought back to the present by the noise of my phone alarm. It was definitely time to move, no matter how tired I felt. I swung my legs over and stood, groaning at the stiffness in my muscles. It acted as a more tangible memory of the night's activities. I shivered with pleasure and moved towards the shower.

Twenty minutes later, I was downstairs for breakfast with Steve. As we entered the hotel dining room, we bumped into Dan and Jeremy on their way out. Dan greeted Steve with a handshake before giving me a shy smile and a wink, using the opportunity of a handshake to caress the back of my hand with his thumb. Our hands remained in contact for a heartbeat or two longer than was strictly necessary.

Jeremy's eyes were full of mischief. A small smile played round his lips as he greeted us. "I trust you slept well?" he asked.

"Very well, thanks," I responded, before turning to Dan to change the subject. "So you're off to Bristol, I gather."

"Yup. A visit and a couple of meetings. Back to town tonight, though."

"Yes," said Steve. "We're heading back to the Screaming Alice after lunch."

Dan looked mystified for a moment until Jeremy intervened. "Cockney rhyming slang. He means Crystal Palace."

Dan huffed a laugh as Jeremy stepped towards the exit.

"Have a safe journey, then. And thanks for all your kind words yesterday about our work ... and things," I stammered out.

Dan shook my hand again and repeated the gesture with his thumb. When he spoke, his voice was quiet, but his accent was strong again as his eyes twinkled. "Look after thissen, our Luke. We'll be in touch." He turned and followed Jeremy.

Steve and I turned to the maître d' to be seated for breakfast. Steve winked at me. "No need to ask whether you had a nice time with his nibs, I assume," he muttered.

I gave a small smirk. "Highly satisfactory, boss. Highly satisfactory."

He nodded. "Pleased to hear it, old son. That's good."

It was still stormy when we left the hotel. Steve drove us out of the main gates and turned the car towards London. The road was not too busy as we left the Cotswolds behind us and aimed for Swindon and the motorway to London. Steve was focussing on driving in the dreadful visibility caused by the rain, so neither of us spoke for a while. I listened to the beat of the windscreen wipers and stared out of the window.

My mind was buzzing, trying to process the events of the last twenty-four hours. I was still on an emotional high from my encounter with Dan. Being with him, holding him close, had been the fulfilment of a dream that I'd had for more than half my adult life. It was a lot to process – and the trouble was that the fantasies pretty much stopped there.

There was no plan "A" for our relationship, never mind a plan "B". How would it work? After all, neither of us was fully out – Dan hardly at all, other than malicious rumours like the one I'd heard at my mother's birthday lunch. It was obvious that I would have to tell my parents formally what they seemed to have already guessed and it was comforting that my father was likely to be less antagonistic than I'd feared previously.

But what of Dan? What would a public relationship do to his political career? There were more openly gay Members of Parliament – and indeed Ministers – now than there had ever been. But there were still risks, particularly for someone like Dan who represented a primarily rural seat. His constituency party was likely to be more right wing than in an urban area, and less forgiving. If he came out to them after several years as their MP, he would have to admit to having told lies – or at least having withheld the truth – about himself. How would that impact on the crucial relationship between the MP and his local party?

There was Dan's father, too. Now eighty-seven, and Dan being convinced that he was homophobic, how would he cope? Wouldn't it be kinder to wait? On the other hand, he seemed to be hale and hearty – he could live for another fifteen or even twenty years. We surely couldn't hide for that long, could we?

The chances of what we had going any further seemed impossibly remote. There was too much weighted against us, even before we considered how our lives could be made to fit together. And could I cope with the public scrutiny that would inevitably follow? Okay, so Dan was only a junior Minister so he was hardly Hollywood red-carpet material – but he was clearly on the way up and could reasonably hope to make it to the Cabinet in the next three or four years. Apart from the hard work and long hours such a promotion would involve, it would also lead to intense media scrutiny, social media exposure and constant pressure to conform to other people's expectations.

I sighed. If that were all true, what was the point of carrying on? I couldn't cope with feeling so intensely about somebody, only for it all to fall apart within a few weeks or months. Surely it was better not to take the risk?

But that was ridiculous, I told myself. After all, the man sitting next to me in the car had faced a similar choice a couple of years back. Steve and Josh had certainly taken some risks to get to where they were now. And in any case, I was already in too deep. It was inconceivable that I would voluntarily walk away from Dan – the man I'd dreamt of for all those years – right at the moment a good few of those dreams were being fulfilled.

Hearing my sigh, Steve broke our silence. "Penny for them?"

"Not worth it. Only staring vacantly into space," I responded.

"What did you make of the event?"

"It was good – very revealing. Especially watching the guys from the department fencing with each other."

"You noticed? Fascinating to watch, wasn't it? Especially during the discussion this morning."

The closing hour of the conference was a free-form discussion under the title "Where Next?", during which we were supposed to put forward ideas as to how we could steer the project during the next three-year funding round – always assuming that we got the money.

"The civil servants were obviously split pretty much down the middle," I said. "One faction is determined to take everything back in-house and get rid of us and the academics."

"I get the impression from something Jeremy said last night that it might be worse than that. He hinted that the grant scheme might be axed altogether. That seems to be the aim of that guy Sean Andrews. He's a SPAD for the Secretary of State."

I laughed. "Why does he need a Signal Passed at Danger?"

"Special adviser, silly sod. Mind you, it sounds as if he *is* a danger."

"Strong Brexiteer, right wing, anti-climate change, all that sort of thing."

"So I gather. Talking to a couple of the other delegates this morning, it appears that Andrews is pushing Eckersley to row back on all sorts of environmental policy – especially once we've left the EU. Cutting a grant scheme would be one in the eye for the green lobby and would please the Treasury no end. Even though Griffin House is seen as a success, Andrews has persuaded Eckersley to distance himself from it – hence his non-appearance at this event."

"Oh?"

"It was always intended that he should come, as well as your Dan. But he pulled out a fortnight ago at the instigation of the Permanent Secretary."

"Ah, I see. Distancing himself big time."

"Got it in one. Battle has yet to commence, I'm told. But Jeremy's on board and he's trying to make sure that Dan fights our corner."

"That's good."

"Yes, but we need to do some planning. We can't assume that the existing Griffin House contract will be renewed next spring. We need to consider how we could either slim down or replace that income."

"I see what you mean. The risk is that we'll have the staff to run the job but not the income to pay them – so we'd be back to the size we were when I joined."

"I wouldn't go that far, Luke. After all, we've won a lot of other work on the back of Griffin House. But we've always known that this was a risk. Of course, some of the guys are on fixed-term contracts linked to the expiry date on the contract – but they're a good bunch and I'd be reluctant to lose them if we could avoid it."

"It would be a shame to break up our team. But we might not have a choice, right?"

"Right. I don't think there's a lot we can do except support the Griffin House guys as much as possible – and make sure Dan and Jeremy have any information they need."

I liked the idea of feeding things to Dan, even if that

was not exactly Steve meant. But I couldn't help myself: prospective redundancies at Pearson Frazer would have to wait. I wanted to daydream about my sexy minister.

Sensing the shift, Steve fell silent again. After a few moments, he must have worked out where my mind had gone. "Nice chap, your Dan," he remarked. "Spoke well last night, I thought."

"Absolutely," I replied, dragging my mind back to the present. "He's good."

Steve laughed. "So you reconnected properly?"

I couldn't help it. I positively beamed. "Yes, we did," I said dreamily.

"Hmm. That good, eh? I'm glad."

We lapsed into a comfortable silence as we reached the M4. Steve turned up the music a little and we each focussed on our own thoughts pretty much all the way home. I dozed a little to make up for the sleep I'd missed the night before.

Steve dropped me at my door around seven. He winked at me as I got out of the car. "Hope it goes well, Luke. With your fella, I mean."

"Thanks, Steve. Love to Josh."

Governing Passions

Chapter Twenty

Dan

Jeremy and I sat in the back of the ministerial car, chatting amiably about nothing in particular. We'd completed our programme of meetings and visits and, by some miracle, had been on time for them all.

Much to my amusement after our conversation the previous evening, we visited a new sewage works on the outskirts of Bristol where I had to unveil a plaque. The speech Jeremy had written for me was a masterpiece of succinct drafting, even if it didn't scale the oratorical heights of a Gladstone or a Churchill. I relayed that thought to Jeremy.

"You can just imagine it, can't you?" he said. "We'll fight sewage on the beaches, in the streets and in our rivers. We shall never surrender."

"Superb!' I added. "Or how about: 'If our new sewage main lasts for a thousand years, men will still say, "This was their finest water.""'"

"Oh, I shall *so* use that. Do you think we could slip it into one of George's speeches?"

"That's a brilliant idea, Jeremy. Though we must remember that our beloved Secretary of State might be many things, but an orator is not one of them."

"Quite. Silly old sod, devious bastard, indecisive pillock … I could go on. But we could definitely transform his style and reputation. He'd need to work on his growl. Churchill always growled."

"You mean as opposed to whining, as Eckersley does at the moment?"

We continued in this vein for few miles up the M4 towards London, but eventually we ran out of jokes. The laughter had done me good after a tiring day and a short night.

At one point, I couldn't prevent a huge yawn. Jeremy smirked. "Tired, Minister?"

"A little. It's the way you run me round all day."

"Hmm, it was a hectic schedule, I suppose, especially if one did not have much sleep the night before."

"Indeed."

"Can I take it that everything was okay?"

"More than. In fact, reight good, as they'd say at home. Thanks for your help, by the way, in setting it all up."

He gave me a smile of genuine pleasure. "Any time. Do I take it that we'll be factoring Luke into our diary planning in future?"

"I certainly hope so. There's one issue I wanted to run by you, though. Does Luke's status as an employee of contractor to the department mean there's a potential conflict of interest?"

"Crikey. Hadn't thought of that one." Jeremy paused, then shook his head. "Can't see it myself. You are not in day-to-day contact with Luke or anybody else in Pearson Frazer, for that matter. Griffin House is a devolved project with a separate management team. You're not likely to be involved in any decision over contracts, since they'd be handled by the procurement people. In any case, Luke isn't currently a director or shareholder in Pearson Frazer. If anything of that nature did arise further down the line, we'd have to declare it and recuse you from any decision making. That's all."

I breathed a sigh of relief. "Thanks. It struck me that there might be a problem."

"Worry not, Dan. I'm sure you're in the clear."

"Great. I told Luke we'd be in touch about fixing up something next week, if that's okay." I was genuinely hesitant about entrusting Jeremy with this personal stuff, and I realised that it would not necessarily go down well with Luke if our dates were all arranged by my private secretary. But the professional parts of my life were so demanding and ate so comprehensively into my time that I didn't see any alternative. After a few moments' thought, I mentioned this to Jeremy, who waved it away.

"Pfft. You've got a schedule that would exhaust Hercules. My job is to help keep you and your life on an even keel so you can continue to function and serve Her Majesty properly. That's as much about getting you appropriate rest and relaxation as it is about marching you endlessly from one meeting to another."

"Point taken. Thanks," I responded. "Though perhaps we should avoid discussing queens in this context?" I added with a smirk.

He nodded sagely, adding piously, "I see what you mean,

Minister."

"Excellent. So we can try to fit Luke in sometime next week?"

Jeremy's eyes twinkled with amusement. "I think that's your job, Minister."

We laughed so hard that we got a glare from our driver. After that, we maintained poker faces and talked of safer topics for the rest of the journey.

"I'm worried about that guy Sean Andrews," said Jeremy.

It was the morning after our return from Bristol, and we'd spent a couple of hours on the paperwork that had accumulated during our two days away from the office. The final document in today's pile was the first draft of the conference notes. We were reading separate copies and we'd both reached the question-and-answer session that followed the Pearson Frazer presentation on the first afternoon.

"I did tell you he was an asshole."

"I know. His questioning of the Pearson Frazer guy was incredible. So bloody rude," Jeremy responded.

"*And* he sat on his hands at the end of my Jeremy-crafted speech."

Jeremy chuckled. "How like a politician to remember that."

"Oh, ha ha. Go on then, why are you worried?"

"My spies tell me that he's in a strong position at the moment. He's held in high regard by the Brexiteers in your party – they love him because he's right wing and also a total climate-change sceptic. He's pushing George to distance himself completely from green projects, even more than Sir John. So we've got an ideological conflict *and* the Treasury wanting to save money – that'll make it much more difficult to keep pushing on Griffin House."

"So it's a sort of pincer movement, you mean?"

"Exactly. And if some in the department are anti-private sector and push to take the work back in-house, that makes it a triple whammy. We stand little chance of arguing our way out of it."

"Is there anything we can do?"

"I'm not sure – at least, not about Sean Andrews. He's a lost cause unless we can force him out. We may get some supporters in the department if we can convince the young radicals that opposing the renewal of the project means they're playing the Treasury's game."

"The old 'my enemy's enemy is my friend' approach, you mean?"

"Something like that. Most departmental civil servants dislike the Treasury – unless they've worked there or hope to do so in future. It's such a spoilsport – always telling people to save money, or that their favourite project is unaffordable. If we can get staff here to see that they're playing the Treasury's game, it should be possible to change their minds."

"But if their main objection to the scheme is private-sector involvement, how will we counter that?"

"That's not a Treasury issue. The main thing about Griffin House is that it takes funding decisions away from politicians. Decisions are made on objective criteria, so the money goes to deserving projects instead of being scattered like confetti to win votes in the marginal constituencies. That should be a point in its favour."

"Jeremy, I'm shocked! As if such matters influence Ministers' decisions!" I stared at him long enough for him to start to believe that I meant what I said. Until I winked. "Which is why some people don't like the scheme and want to get rid of it. It's seen as dangerous."

"Exactly. What's the point of having an MP if he can't win you more money for your local pet project?"

"Oh, that's simple. So that they can act as unpaid social workers to pick up the pieces when local authorities fuck up."

"I'd forgotten that aspect. Dan, you're getting as cynical as I am."

I sighed. "I used not to be. It was that bloody referendum."

"I know what you mean. But to come back to Griffin House, is it okay with you if I approach some individuals and see if I can shift their view?"

"By all means. See what you can do."

"I'll keep you posted. Now, before I leave you in peace, I have a diary query. About Luke. Did you discuss any dates when you were with him?"

I looked away and shuffled uneasily in my seat. I was still uncomfortable about involving Jeremy. He noticed and was amused. "I know you're twitchy about this. I don't mean to interfere but, as I said last night, I think it's part of my job to help."

"I know. I've never had a personal life that needed managing before, so I'm having trouble getting used to the idea."

"I'd probably feel the same. But we've got to be realistic.

If you're going to see Luke, we've got to plan for it – even if nothing gets written down in the official diary. I'm not being bossy, it's just how it is."

"I understand – though it doesn't make it any easier. Thanks for helping. It somehow seems ... oh, I don't know ... a little bloodless."

"If we should give it a code name, we won't have to refer directly to it."

"That's a good idea. Why don't we call it Operation Solo?"

Jeremy frowned for a moment. "Is that a *Star Wars* connection, by any chance?"

I couldn't help but laugh. "Well done, Jeremy."

"May I ask why?"

"It's a long story, but Sky was Luke's nickname at college, short for Skywalker."

"I see. Solo was Luke's pal, wasn't he?"

"Got it in one."

"Fine, Solo it will be."

"So have I got any time free next week?"

Jeremy opened up the diary on his tablet. It was scary realising that he had my life planned to the nearest five minutes for weeks and possibly months to come, a little like a form of predestination. Though I could put my foot down and insist on changes on occasion, the effort was rarely worth it.

"Next week looks dreadful. The Whips have warned that there are likely to be major votes on Monday and Wednesday. You have a dinner on Tuesday at which you're speaking, and then you're down in the constituency for the weekend – a surgery on Friday afternoon and opening the Autumn Fayre on Saturday."

"Christ Almighty. Am I going to have time for a pee?"

He chuckled. "Possibly not – you might need to tie a knot in it."

"Remind me – what's the dinner?"

"The annual dinner of the Chartered Institute of Sanitation."

"Great. All big in drains, I assume. I suppose I should refrain from jokes about flushing away my career."

"Quite so, Minister. You could bowl them a few jokes, though, and pan your critics in the process."

I groaned. "Yes, though I suppose it would be better to avoid mentioning manholes."

"Totally inappropriate, in the circumstances. And sucking and blowing to remove blockages should on no account be mentioned." Suddenly his eyes caught mine and we burst out laughing. "Before we exhaust ourselves by thinking up yet more lavatory puns, can we return to the subject in hand?"

"Which was?"

"Luke."

"Only in hand? I was hoping for at least a BJ."

"Too much information, I think, Minister," Jeremy replied.

I put my hand to my mouth in mock horror. "I've no idea where that came from. It must be your dirty mind, Jeremy, steering me off course."

"I've only be working for you for four weeks! How could have I corrupted you in such a short time?"

"I was innocent and naïve when I arrived. And I've always been easily led."

"Oh, sure. Like Pooh Bear to a pot of honey. Try and keep him away."

"Interesting. I'd always thought of myself more as Eeyore. I have a gloomy outlook on the world, you know."

"In this government, I'm not surprised."

"Yes, I know and I wanted the job. Ha bloody ha. So are you going to let me have time off to spend two minutes with Luke?"

"We might manage something. There's always Thursday evening. If you stayed in town instead of going down to your cottage in Wessex, you could see him then."

These days, it was *de rigeur* for the local MP to have a house in the constituency and to be seen there frequently. I had bought a small cottage in a village in the heart of mine. I was very fond of it and, before becoming a Minister, I'd spent as much time there as possible. If I could, I'd travel down on a Thursday evening after the Commons had adjourned and return early on Monday morning. That gave me Fridays and Saturdays for surgeries and other engagements, and Sundays off unless there was a pressing need to attend church or accept a lunch invitation. Fortunately, everybody recognised that as a single man I couldn't be expected to offer hospitality except at the local hotel or pub.

Life had changed since my appointment as a Minister and now my visits had to be restricted to two a month. I couldn't get down until Friday evening and usually had to travel back on a Sunday evening. It so happened that I'd planned to go down on Thursday evening so I could have a bit of a rest on the Friday morning, since my first engagement wasn't until nearly lunchtime.

"That sounds good. What time's my first engagement on the Friday?"

"Not till 11.30."

"Oh, fine. Let's do that. I'll text him and see if he's free."

Chapter Twenty-One

Luke

I was about to go for lunch when Dan's text came through. I saw his name on my screen with mixed emotions – pleasure at hearing from him mixed with some trepidation at what the message might say. After a few moments, I plucked him the courage to open the text: he was inviting me to dinner at his place the following Thursday.

Brilliant!

Fuck, I'd cancel an audience with the bloody Queen to accept this invitation. But as she was already busy that night, I could go anyway. I laughed at my own stupid joke, but quickly took a hold of myself, clicking the reply option and accepting the invitation almost casually, avoiding the "fuck, yeah" sentiments that dominated my brain.

LUKE:>> Thanks, that would be great. What time and where?

Dan replied within two minutes, suggesting 8.30 and giving me the address of his flat in Kensington. I replied with several smiley emojis.

I felt like punching the air, I was so pleased. At long last, maybe he and I might get somewhere. I wasn't exactly surprised after our time together at the conference, but I hadn't been taking anything for granted. Now I could hardly wait for Thursday to come so that I could see him again.

Fortunately, work was so busy that the days flew by. Saturday and Sunday were more difficult because I had no plans. I thought about going to see my parents but, when I suggested it to my mother, she said somewhat frostily that they were away for the weekend. Clearly, I'd not been forgiven the train-crash lunch on her birthday, though I still didn't understand why she blamed me for it. I arranged to go for lunch the following Sunday, resolving to make it my big "coming out" moment.

I spent the weekend at home, equipped with a list of odd jobs to do round the house, expecting to enjoy pottering around. In fact, I was on edge and unable to relax. I achieved less than half what I'd planned because I kept breaking off to think about Dan.

Back to work, and fortunately the next four days sped by as we made yet more attempts to save the planet. Our current projects were developing an air-quality strategy for a local authority in northern England and a report on alternative fuels for a small independent bus operator. Neither was likely to set the world on fire but, as Steve kept saying, our work was about encouraging as many people as possible to take "baby steps". The next tranche of Griffin House funding was due to be announced soon – the last one unless the scheme was renewed – so we were in for a frantic few weeks.

I left work on time on the Thursday afternoon. That

raised a few eyebrows, as I almost never left the building before seven. But today I needed the time to nip home, get ready and get to Kensington for eight-thirty. I took a quick shower and dressed carefully. Another stressful element of the week had been worrying about what to wear. I wanted to wear clothes that were smart and modern, but at the same time I wanted to dress my age – I might still have a good figure and pass for twenty-nine in the right light, but I was no longer a twink and I couldn't expect to dress like one. Besides, I was going to dinner with a Minister of the Crown – I could hardly turn up in T-shirt and sweatpants.

In the end, I opted for a dark-blue button-down shirt which matched the colour of my eyes, together with some tight black chinos and a light grey blazer. I hadn't shaved since the conference but decided I ought to, so off came my week's stubble. My hair was freshly trimmed. As my ride arrived to take me to Dan's place, I was confident that I looked my best.

I'd judged the timing right – my phone said it was 8.27 when my driver dropped me at the rear steps of the Royal Albert Hall. After forcing myself to relax during the journey, I felt the tension returning as I approached the entrance to Dan's building. I found his doorbell and pressed it.

No response. I pressed it again. Surely…

At that point, I saw someone getting out of a cab and hurrying towards me, clutching a bundle of papers under his arm and looking harassed. "Jeremy! What are you doing here?" I couldn't keep the irritation out of my voice, so added hurriedly in the friendliest tone I could muster, "How nice to see you."

"It's all right. I know I'm the last person you wanted to see right now. But the Minister – Dan, I mean – thought that I would be better than leaving you standing out here like a lemon."

"Problems?"

"You could say that. Let's go inside and have a drink. Dan should be here in about an hour. Don't think I'm exaggerating when I say that he's seriously pissed off about this."

Jeremy used his key to let us into the building and we climbed the stairs to the first-floor flat. I was impressed that Dan trusted him enough to give him a key – though, when I thought about it, it was entirely logical that he should have one.

Jeremy took my coat with old-world courtesy and showed me into the sitting room. It was beautiful – a mid-Victorian mansion flat with views across the main road into Kensington Gardens and beyond to Hyde Park. High-ceilinged with tall windows, the room was furnished in a traditional style, not at all the bachelor's apartment I'd imagined with big leather sofas and big-screen televisions. No, this place had a couple of high-back winged chairs opposite a comfortable sofa covered with cushions. A large glass and steel coffee table offered a touch of the late twentieth century. There were tall lamps with Chinese-style bases and a cast-iron and marble fireplace. A polished original wooden floor glowed in the lamplight as Jeremy switched on the lights; there was a huge Persian rug in front of the fire. I fell for the place immediately.

"Wow," I said. "What a terrific room."

"Beautiful, isn't it? I'm jealous of him living here. No

wonder he doesn't want to move nearer to Westminster. I'm only sorry Dan couldn't welcome you himself."

"That's what happens when you get into politics, right?"

"Right. Especially as a Minister. Mind you, most of the time the so-called crises turn out to be northing of the sort. Mainly it's spin doctors panicking over the next headline on twenty-four-hour news."

"That bad?"

Jeremy shook his head. "Oh, absolutely. The whole political machine is now obsessed with the immediate – short-term fixes to avoid bad headlines or to repair the image after a bad social media posting. It drives me mad."

"It sounds appalling."

"It is. Tonight is a perfect example. Somebody leaked a document about what will happen to environmental regulations post-Brexit. Number one, it's an early draft of a position paper somebody wrote six months ago and, as such, it's no longer relevant. Number two, the media only got half of it. But that was the section that prognosticated getting rid of most of the regulations. The bit that wasn't leaked listed all the reasons why that's a seriously bad idea."

"What happened?"

"As you can imagine, all the environmental groups like Greenpeace and Friends of the Earth went ape. The Brexiteers loved it, so they went round for a couple of hours crowing about this being what they meant by taking back control, etcetera, etcetera. A message from Number Ten told us not to publish the whole paper because it might upset the Brexiteers too much – because, of course, the conclusion was that nothing could or would change."

"And then?"

"The usual. Crisis meetings. Secretary of State panicking. Sir John flapping round the building like an over-agitated owl. Ridiculous. Anyway, the upshot was that Dan was sent to the Commons to brief the lobby correspondents that it was all something and nothing. That's where he is now. We'd had a pig of a day already and this made him so cross."

"Maybe I'd better go."

Jeremy laughed. "Don't you dare – that would just about finish him off. He's been so looking forward to seeing you again. Now, let me get you that drink. Dan said you had a favourite malt and he'd got a new bottle specially." He held up the bottle. "This okay?"

I gave him a thumbs up. My throat was too constricted for me speak – I was incredibly touched that Dan should have gone to the trouble of getting the whisky he knew I loved. It made me feel special.

Jeremy poured both of us a large measure and we clinked glasses. "Cheers. To our mother's sons, God bless them."

"Thanks, Jeremy. I am sorry your evening's also ruined."

"No problem – I'm used to it. Dan'll text me when he's on his way and that's my cue to get the food organised. It's already ordered, we only need to confirm the time we want it. If we do that, it should be here almost at the same time as he is."

"Great. What about you?"

"Oh, I'll be fine. Sebastian has something *hot* waiting for me at home," he replied, eyes sparkling with mischief.

"Yes, fine. Apart from that, what about dinner?"

"No, it's fine. Problem is, the whole bandwagon starts

rolling again at seven tomorrow morning. Dan has to be in his constituency office by eleven thirty."

"Is it always like this?" I asked.

Jeremy nodded and sipped his drink. "Pretty much. Between Commons votes, paperwork, meetings and constituency business, he doesn't get much time for himself."

"Does he have help, apart from you?"

"Absolutely. He couldn't survive without it. He has a secretary and two interns in his office at the Commons, and Helena down in Wessex who runs his constituency office. Fortunately, they're all nice people and we get on really well. Believe me, that's not always the case. Dan's predecessor had terrible problems because his constituency secretary and Commons assistant fought like cat and dog. Keeping the peace took up a huge amount of his energy. It was a nightmare – especially when they tried to involve me."

"How did you cope with that?"

"By using my blandest tone of voice and smiling a lot. My e-mails were models of calm and discretion and I never once rose to the bait of their stroppiness. God, that was the difficult part. The woman in his constituency used to send vitriolic e-mails, but I simply ignored the vitriol and addressed whatever issue she was raising. If there wasn't a practical point to the message – you know, simply a rant – I'd ignore it."

"That must have been difficult at times. When you get a stroppy message, there's always a temptation to reply in kind."

"Absolutely. The adrenalin flows and before you know

it you've sent a horrible reply that makes things worse."

"Though it makes you feel better at the time."

"Indeed – but it's all so draining. And such a waste of bloody time. Anyway, fortunately Dan's team is all sweetness and light and I have to say he's a joy to work with."

At that point, both our phones buzzed with a text from the man himself; he was on his way. Jeremy telephoned the restaurant and they promised dinner in twenty minutes.

"Thanks for all this, Jeremy."

"A pleasure. My job is helping Dan to function properly as a Minister, and he can't do that if he's stressed out about his personal life."

"I can see that. Steve was like that before Josh came on the scene, stressed all the time about pretty much everything. And he could certainly write a stroppy e-mail. I got some gems in my early days."

"But he seems so pleasant and calm these days."

"Oh, he is now – most of the time. That's what Josh has done for him. The only time Steve's a bit frayed at the edges is when Josh is away on tour."

"He's a musician, isn't he?"

"That's right – jazz and swing. Bloody good, too – you can see him on YouTube."

Jeremy laughed. "I must talk to Steve about it some time. The joys of being married to a musician."

"You too?"

"Sebastian is a violinist in one of the London orchestras. He's based at the Festival Hall most of the time but goes on overseas tours a couple of times a year. For the first few days it's bliss having the flat to myself, but after that it's hell. I miss him terribly."

"Being on your own is fine for a while, but there are times when I wish that there was somebody else in the house. Sometimes living on your own sucks."

"Have you always been single?"

I nodded. "I had a couple of relationships which lasted a few months, but they never reached the stage of moving in. In both cases it never occurred to me that we should live together. I suppose that explains why they didn't last."

"And now? With Dan? Not that it's any of my business."

"It's early days. But I might have hopes."

"Here's hoping, because you're definitely good for him. But you must understand what you're getting into. It won't be all sweetness and light. Being a politician's partner is a shitty job."

I grimaced. "Thanks for that, Jeremy. Good to know."

"It seems important to say it. I'd hate for you to be under any illusions and get hurt as a result."

"I understand. I don't think you've said anything I hadn't already thought about. But even though there are aspects I'm not keen on, like publicity and attention, I think I could cope. I'm not going into this with my eyes shut. But I do worry about the pace of things – the lack of time."

"Rightly so, Luke. Ministers have an impossible life in many ways, and it gets worse the further up the ladder you go. Twenty-four-hour security, cameras always on you, even more pressure – and even less time to think."

"So why do they do it?"

He shook his head. "You tell me. In Dan's case, I think it was always taken for granted. As for the others,

I've no idea... A sense of duty? A feeling of power? Self-importance? I don't know. Maybe a combination of all those. But I worry that these days political life has become such a terrible job that the good people are avoiding it."

"Hence the lack of talent on all sides?"

Jeremy gave a short laugh. "To quote another piece of political fiction, 'You might say that, but I couldn't possibly comment'. Seriously, though, I think you're right. I can't imagine any of the three current party leaders rising to the top in any other era."

At that point, we heard Dan's key in the lock and the front door of the flat open.

"Honeys, I'm home!"

Chapter Twenty-Two

Dan

"Honeys, I'm home!' The greeting I gave as I arrived back at the flat was a damned sight more cheerful than I felt. I was tired, cross that I was late for my date with Luke, and irritated with the nonsense that I'd been forced to spend the evening dealing with. It was the perfect end to the shittiest week I'd had since taking this job.

The arguments about Brexit were getting worse. Media speculation about what was going to happen because of our decision to leave the European Union was reaching fever pitch as the negotiations neared their conclusion – and the government looked increasingly shaky.

Since everybody knew my views – that the whole exercise was a catastrophic mistake – I'd decided to keep my head down, say as little as possible, and get on with my job at DECRA. Today's row over post-Brexit environmental regulation had been doubly traumatic – I'd been obliged by my spineless boss to bat for the department with the press and Parliament, and this drew attention to the fact that I was a "Remainer".

Somebody – probably Sean bloody Andrews – had leaked an incomplete early draft of a paper on future environmental regulation. By appearing to suggest that we could abolish dozens of regulations, the document played into the Brexiteers' arguments that staying in the EU, or even the single market, would subject us to over-regulation from Brussels bureaucrats. In fact, around a third of the regulations reviewed pre-dated EU legislation and had been incorporated into it at the insistence of the UK government. Of the remaining regulation, ninety per cent was there for sound environmental reasons – much of it to do with air quality – and had nothing to do with our membership of the EU. Hence the severely critical reaction of the environmental lobby groups earlier. In fact, the final version of the leaked paper demonstrated that there could be no question of abolishing the laws – indeed, there were areas where we might seek to tighten them in future.

The simplest way to deal with the row would have been to publish the final version of the paper, but some idiot in the Downing Street press office vetoed the idea because it would upset too many Brexiteers in the Commons at a crucial moment in the negotiations. Instead, I'd been despatched to carry the same message via the lobby system – the tradition of government giving out information to the press and broadcasters via a series of unattributable briefings. I'd spent the last three hours doing that, endlessly repeating the same well-worn phrases in a series of off-the-record interviews to political and environmental correspondents.

I hoped that I'd sounded convincing because my heart had certainly not been in it. I was too busy worrying about being late to greet Luke and thinking about the relaxed evening I should be enjoying with him instead of answering inane questions from people focused on political games who knew little about the issues involved and cared even less.

Fortunately, Jeremy had stepped in and ensured that Luke was not left standing on the doorstep. Meanwhile I, by being curt almost to the point of rudeness during my last interview, had managed to be no more than half an hour late.

As I walked into my flat, it was wonderful to see the lights on, drinks poured and two friendly faces in the sitting room. It was a long time since somebody had welcomed me into my own home. Above all tonight, I needed some rest and relaxation. At least we had the next couple of hours, but I had to remember that I needed to leave early in the morning for a weekend of events in the constituency. Oh, joy.

I plastered a huge smile on my face and went in to greet them.

"Dan, that was fantastic," said Luke. "It's a long time since I tasted something so good."

Jeremy had left quickly after my arrival, anxious to get home to Seb. The food arrived a few minutes later and we sat down to eat it. I'd planned for us to sit in the rarely used dining room, but it had seemed cosier in the kitchen, so we sat side by side on stools at the breakfast bar. Despite its shaky start, the evening was going well; I felt relaxed and happy now, and was revelling in Luke's company.

"Glad you liked it. I've known the place since I first moved here but they only recently started to do deliveries. I thought it was perfect for tonight – or at least it would have been if I'd been on time."

"Hey, you mustn't worry about that. Jeremy looked after me – I do like him a lot."

"Good. I'm so lucky – we've become very close. And he thinks a lot of you."

"A good judge of character, then," Luke replied before breaking into a big grin.

"Absolutely." I paused. "So, if you're finished, we could move to somewhere more comfortable. Do you want coffee?"

"No, thanks. I haven't finished my wine."

We moved through to the sitting room. He went towards the sofa, and I joined him.

Our greeting earlier in Jeremy's presence had felt a little awkward, neither a handshake nor a full-on hug but something in between that ended with a slightly embarrassing pat on the back from me. There had been virtually no physical contact between us since and I craved it.

I lay my hand on the cushion between us, brushing Luke's thigh lightly.

He immediately moved closer and after a few seconds took my hand. "It's good to see you, Dan. I've been looking forward to tonight."

"Me too. That's why I was so cross earlier. Bloody idiots."

"Enough! Don't get all stressed again. Just relax."

He entwined our fingers and looked down at our hands. He sighed before drawing our joined hands to his lips. "I never thought we'd do this. All those years of dreaming, thinking of you pretty much every day…"

"Luke … I'm sorry."

"No. We've been through that. No more apologies. I was simply savouring the moment."

"I know. I missed you. There was never anybody – friend, family, anybody – that I felt as comfortable with. Even at the conference in that hotel suite, I felt like I was coming home when you were with me."

"So, am I like a cosy old pair of bedroom slippers?"

I wrapped my arm round his shoulder, drawing him in and kissing his temple. "You're certainly cosy," I replied. "But not old. Never that – especially when you look as handsome as you did tonight when I got home."

"Why, thank you."

"May I kiss you?"

"You most certainly may," he replied, a smile spreading across his face, showing his dimples to full effect. "In fact, it's compulsory – it says so in this statutory instrument I've got."

"Oh? That's all right then. I must have voted for it if it's a statutory instrument."

The last syllable was almost lost as our lips met in the gentlest, feather-like kisses I'd ever experienced. Luke pulled back for a moment, but quickly returned. This time, our mouths stayed together. I opened my lips slightly to lick his closed lips. He immediately let me in and we became steadily more passionate.

As Luke moved to straddle me, we broke the kiss for a

moment. I stared into his eyes, which were locked onto mine. If there had been any doubt before, at that moment I knew. He was my predestined partner. Whatever happened to the rest of my existence or my political career, Luke Carter would be at the centre of the rest of my life. I just had to pluck up the courage to tell him so.

Chapter Twenty-Three

Luke

When Dan got home to the flat that evening, I was horrified by his appearance. He was clearly exhausted: skin the colour of parchment, bags that would fill a car boot under his eyes, and the eyes themselves dull with fatigue. Was this what success in politics meant?

He revived after he'd eaten, and relaxed even more after we'd split a bottle of Montepulciano D'Abruzzo. Sitting on his large sofa and kissing clearly helped him to unwind – so much so that his expression when I climbed onto his lap and straddled him could only be described as blissed out. He tasted of red wine and cheese.

I needed to say something to him about how I felt, but it was too soon; he already had enough on his plate. I wondered if I ought to leave him alone to get some rest. He clearly needed it badly.

He forestalled me. "Sky? Will you do me a favour?"

"Of course. What?"

"Stay with me tonight? Not to do anything necessarily, but just to hold me? I don't want to be alone."

"Of course, I'll stay. I'd love to," I replied gently. "But are you sure?"

He nodded. "Absolutely sure. And by the way, are you doing anything this weekend?"

I shook my head. "I'm having lunch with my parents on Sunday but I can always put them off. I thought you were going down to your constituency?"

"I am. I wondered whether you'd like to come with me. I've got two or three engagements, but you wouldn't have to go to them. You could stay at the cottage while I do my duty. And you could still go to your parents – it's only about an hour from the cottage into Harchester – shorter than it is from here."

I was awestruck by the invitation. Here we were on what was effectively our first date, and he was inviting me to spend the weekend. Two or even three whole nights with Dan? How brilliant was that? Even if I'd had plans, which I hadn't, refusal would have been out of the question.

"Dan, that's terrific. I'd love to, if you're sure that's okay."

He beamed at me. "Good." He pulled me down for another kiss. "Now let's get ourselves to bed."

Reluctantly, I lifted myself from him and stood back, holding out a hand to haul him up. Once he stood, he reached for me again. We stood, toe to toe, every part of us touching.

Dan released my mouth. His lips moved round to my ear, kissing it, biting my lobe. He whispered, "I can't believe how lucky I am. To get a second chance with you. I hope I don't fuck it up this time."

I stroked his hair back from his forehead. "You won't,

Dan, Others might try to separate us, and we may pay a price somewhere along the line, but this is right. This is *us*, Dan." I kissed him again, plus another for luck. "Come on, let's get you to bed. You looked absolutely exhausted earlier, and you've got a long day tomorrow."

He guided me through to his bedroom and we got ready for bed; even something as mundane as cleaning our teeth seemed different. I couldn't believe my eyes when I saw his Star Wars electric toothbrush – I would definitely be taking the mickey out of him about that. He donned a pair of sleeping shorts and a fresh T-shirt and offered me the same. "They should fit you okay," he remarked. "We're about the same size."

He pulled the covers down and held them for me to get in. We curled round each other. He let out a small sigh and fell asleep within moments but I lay there for a while, thinking.

I'd enjoyed the evening, being with him. We were already well on the way to restoring the closeness and intimacy that we'd known as friends at university, but without the awkwardness about our sexuality that had constrained us. I was ecstatic about the invitation for the weekend and the very idea of it brought a smile to my face; it was clearly a spur of the moment decision but somehow more welcome for that. For somebody like Dan, whose life was so highly organised and regulated by others, spontaneity seemed all the more special.

I was determined not to put any pressure on him or to scare him away. The risk now was that outside events would drive a wedge between us. Dan's career, politics, the pressure of media attention – they could all push us apart if we let them. But we were going into this with our eyes open. We wouldn't let anything distract us, would we?

V

Chapter Twenty-Four

Dan

I found myself still wrapped in Luke's arms when I awoke the next morning a few minutes before the alarm sounded. It was a wonderful way to start the day. I had slept soundly right through the night, which was unusual especially after such a stressful time the previous day.

I lay there contemplating the evening's events. I had surprised myself when I asked him to stay the night, but I'd needed the comfort of his presence: it was primarily an emotional rather than a sexual thing – chatting, sharing jokes, frustrations and dreams.

Frankly, it was a bit of a shock. I'd spent years in solitude, telling myself that I was better off on my own, and trying to be strong enough to survive that way. Last night had given the lie to such tosh. I smiled: I was being transformed as if at the flick of a switch from a strong, independent loner to a slightly sentimental, slightly needy individual who craved the company of others and the affection of one man.

Asking Luke to spend the weekend was another big

shift. I'd never entertained a guest at the cottage before. It was very small, and I didn't have the sort of friends with whom I would spend intimate weekends. Besides, trips down there were mainly about work – surgeries, constituency events and my local party. Though I'd come to love the place, I wasn't there for leisure time – which was, in any case, a very scarce commodity now I'd joined the government.

If Luke was going to be in my life, that would have to change; I'd have to make time for him. And if I was going to come out and be myself, spending the weekend together at the cottage was a pretty good way to start.

Luke stirred, snuggling closer into my side. I closed my eyes to savour the moment. On rare occasions I had woken up in bed next to a man before, but it hadn't ever meant anything to me. Now it did.

The alarm broke my reverie and Luke stirred again in my arms. I reached out and killed the noise before wrapping my arms more firmly around him. "Good morning. Sleep well?"

He gave a contented sigh. "I did, thank you – not long enough, though. You?"

"Yes, right through. Most unusual for me. I liked having my own personal electric blanket. Thanks for staying."

He grinned up at me. "My pleasure."

I leant down and kissed him and shivered with pleasure as his body moved against mine. It was languid and sensual, and the kiss quickly deepened. Eventually, I broke away. "Sorry, need to pee – and I've really got to get moving. Are you okay there for a while?"

He looked up at me and smiled gently, "Definitely," he

said and curled up again under the duvet. I'd have given anything to re-join him.

It was a crisp autumn day. The constituency surgery was due to start at eleven-thirty but fortunately I'd managed to leave London on time, despite the distraction of having Luke with me. We'd started to snuggle together again when I came out of the shower; in the end, it had been his need to get to the office on time that had driven us out of each other's arms and into some clothes.

I was in a good mood, which not even the Friday morning traffic on the M3 could ruin. Sleeping together just for the joy and comfort of it had been amazing – another first in this week of revelations. We had parted reluctantly, he to go home and change before going to work, me to travel down to Wessex. He would drive down to my cottage in the afternoon, as soon as he could get away. I was to expect him about eight.

My only worry was that everything was going too swimmingly; I couldn't escape the feeling that something would force us apart again.

An incoming phone call interrupted my daydreaming. It was Jeremy. "Hi, Dan. Did you get away okay? How's the journey?"

"Fine, thanks, though I didn't get a chance to check the newspapers. How did yesterday's shit-show go down?"

"Not bad. There's the usual fluff about government in disarray, etcetera, etcetera, but we could hardly avoid that. Your work in the lobby undoubtedly calmed things down and the editorials are on board – the regulations are there for a good reason and need to stay. Job well done, I'd say."

"Fine. Any reaction in the department?"

"Supportive and positive. I gather the Secretary of State is content – though Sean Andrews is apparently spitting blood."

"Now there's a surprise. What did he expect – for everybody simply to roll over?"

"It's all part of the Whitehall conspiracy to keep us shackled to Europe, apparently. A betrayal of Brexit."

"Another one?"

"Quite. I'm still not sure what his game was."

"Me neither. Mainly trying to cause mayhem, I suppose."

"You could be right. Anyway, we live to fight another day. How was the rest of your evening?"

"Delightful. Thanks again for taking care of things. I'm very grateful."

"It was my pleasure – I enjoy Luke's company."

"It was much appreciated. He's joining me for the weekend."

"Oh. That's great, Dan. Hope you have a good time."

I could hear the slight smirk in his voice, but let it go. "Anything else for me?"

"Nothing from here – all under control. Your constituency office has been on the phone – they wanted to check if you'd be okay to have a word with your association chairman this afternoon. He wants to call in around five. I said that would be okay."

I frowned. I was already due to see him at an event the following afternoon – and in my book, one meeting was more than enough for one weekend. "That's fine. I wonder what that's about."

"Helena didn't say. She's a bit worried about some of the social media postings, though."

"Oh?"

"Yes, apparently, traffic on your accounts has suddenly gone up and a lot of it is distinctly unpleasant. It may be the start of a campaign of some sort. My spies tell me that you're not alone – two other Remainers are also getting some stick."

My presence on various social media sites was essential, even though I preferred to avoid the whole thing as much as possible. Helena, my constituency secretary, ran the accounts with a small team of part-timers plus some help from the department's PR staff. I rarely even looked at the sites; even if I'd had the inclination, I certainly didn't have the time.

"Thanks for letting me know. I'll have a word with her about it. Anything to worry about, do you think?"

"Not at this stage. The sites get their fair share of nutters and this is only just above that level. It's still mainly about policies more than you personally."

The queue on the motorway cleared in front of me so I brought the call to an end and concentrated on the road ahead.

Jeremy's call was disconcerting, and the chairman's request was a bit of a surprise. Our meetings were more akin to chats, usually taking place at events we were both attending. His request for a more formal session bothered me but there was no point in speculating; I'd have to wait and see what he wanted. The increase in social media traffic also made me uneasy. I preferred to stay below the radar, particularly so far as my private affairs were concerned. Especially now.

If my personal life was going to be the subject of scrutiny, I had to try to be in control of how and when things were said. The danger was that gossip would start and rumours would spread. The political atmosphere was so febrile currently that anything could happen.

I was convinced that Sean Andrews had been foisted on my boss by his pals on the right, who were determined to impose their vision of Brexit and a post-Brexit Britain on the government and the party. If yesterday's leak and subsequent events were anything to go by, they were prepared to engage in all sorts of mischief to sabotage departments in order to achieve their aims.

I found the whole business profoundly depressing. I wondered why those on the right of the party felt that they had to use intrigue and misinformation as a first line of defence rather than a last resort. It was almost as if they knew they were never going to carry the day by winning the intellectual argument. To them politics in general, and Brexit in particular, were matters of faith more than everyday policy. Practicality, pragmatism and the public interest could be sacrificed on the altar of an outdated form of nationalism.

As I crawled through one tailback after another, I knew that I would have to face the Brexit problem soon. At some point I would have to stop hiding behind the "respecting the referendum result" argument and make up my mind about what sort of future I wanted for our country – and then start fighting for it.

That begged the question of how much longer I could remain a member of the same political party as a large, and apparently growing, band of arch-Brexiteers. Any change of allegiance would mean quitting the government – and where could I go politically? The Lib Dems were a spent force for the time being, fatally wounded by their years in coalition with us Tories. Besides, I'd always felt mildly irritated by their "holier than thou" approach to politics. And though joining Labour under Blair might have been a possibility, under Corbyn it was out of the question.

If I had no political home, I'd have to give up my Commons seat and end the career I'd fought so hard to build over so many years. And what would I do? What else was I qualified for? I could try to go back to my old career in journalism, but that felt like such a retrograde step. Consultancy was also a possibility, though I knew little about how it worked – and cared even less. Besides, what expertise did I have to offer? A lifelong pursuit of political power was hardly a guarantee of knowledge and sound advice.

I had to face the fact that I wasn't qualified for anything but my present career. I was trapped; I needed to earn a living, and politics was what I did.

My stomach was gripped by momentary panic, and I found myself grasping the steering wheel until my knuckles turned white. Whatever was I thinking of? How could I even dream of giving it all up? I'd worked so hard to be where I was now. I'd wanted prestige, power and authority and now I'd got them. Walking away again was simply out of the question. I forced myself to relax and concentrate on the road, but I was still unsettled when I got to the constituency offices.

The journey had left me with a jumble of thoughts and fears swirling around like clothes in a washing machine, tangled together in a knot that would have to be unravelled at some point. It was all very scary, and my earlier good mood had certainly disappeared.

"Leave that with me, Mrs Walters. I'll get in touch with the housing trust and see what I can do."

My constituent expressed her thanks and got up to leave. She was my last visitor of the afternoon and I breathed a sigh of relief as she left the room. Constituency surgeries were a vital part of my work as an MP, and I genuinely enjoyed the interaction with the people I'd been elected to serve, but the sessions could be draining. The people who came to see me mostly did so because something was going wrong in their lives; their stories were usually harrowing and, on occasion, deeply upsetting.

Today had been no exception. The parents of a boy injured while serving with the army in Afghanistan were involved in a dispute with the Ministry of Defence about financial support for his care.

Next there was a case of bullying at school, which the authorities didn't seem to be taking seriously. This was very close to home: Ethan was a fifteen-year-old boy attending the local independent faith school who'd come out as gay and was suffering as a result. Painfully thin, with dark hair obscuring much of his face, he was clearly in a bad way. During the interview he'd shifted uneasily in his seat, clearly mortified by his mother's account. When we got to what his fellow pupils had done and said, his embarrassment was replaced by pain etched on his pinched, pale face. I asked him a couple of questions but he couldn't bring himself to look up, mumbling the answers in a monotone.

I longed to comfort him, reflecting how much it would help if I could tell him that I was also gay and he was not alone. I couldn't, of course, but I did manage to offer some words of comfort. As they left, I took Ethan's hand to shake it, which prompted him to look up and meet my eyes for the first time. I smiled and his eyes widened for a moment in recognition. He returned my smile and gave a small nod. It was a nice moment in an otherwise shitty afternoon.

It seemed to give him some form of boost because he spoke again, and his voice was stronger this time. "I don't feel safe at school being who I am, Mr Forrester," he told me. "They're not doing enough to prevent the bullying. I feel like whatever I do is worthless. Even if I do well, it wouldn't matter to anybody because all they can see is me being the gay sinner."

His words reinforced my sympathy for the boy, and my determination to help in any way I could.

Ethan and his mother were followed by three people with housing problems and one domestic violence case. Finally there was Mrs Walters, another housing case. There was a pattern emerging here, since all four cases concerned the same local housing trust that was chaired by one Andrew Kane, a leading member of my constituency association, pal of the chairman and one of my most vociferous critics.

Coming on top of yesterday's dramas and my earlier sense of unease, the surgery left me utterly exhausted.

Helena had sat in on the meetings to take notes. She looked at me with concern. "That was tough," she remarked. "I think we deserve a cuppa."

I ran my hand through my hair. "You're not kidding. The authorities do seem to make it tough for people, don't they?"

"Absolutely. It's a lack of empathy, I think. Cases become files, not people, and the easiest way to move a file on is to apply the rules rigidly and move the responsibility to somebody else. I'll go and put the kettle on." She returned a few minutes later with a tea tray, which she set down on the desk.

"Are those your home-made biscuits, by any chance?" I asked.

"I thought you deserved a treat."

"I love you for ever. Thanks so much," I responded as my hand shot out towards the plate.

I'd known Helena ever since I'd come to the Wessex South constituency nearly a decade earlier, firstly as a prospective parliamentary candidate and later as the MP. Throughout that time she'd been hard-working, efficient and loyal. I was very lucky. She'd formed a strong working relationship with Jeremy, and the liaison between my private and constituency offices was seamless. By all accounts this was somewhat unusual, and I counted myself so fortunate.

She was a lively fifty-five-year-old widow. Her husband, an Army officer, had been killed in Iraq, leaving her with three teenage kids. She'd taken the constituency job as a means of supplementing her pension but also to get out of the house, to "stop moping about" as she put it in her no-nonsense, clipped tones. She was always immaculately dressed with flawless make-up and not a hair out of place – elegant in an era when casual was the order of the day. Dressing smartly had restored her self-confidence after the loss of her husband, and it suited the constituency association members by creating a formal atmosphere in the office with which they were comfortable.

After she'd passed me a cup of tea, she spoke. "So, poor old Ethan."

"I felt so sorry for him. It struck me that he may well also have an eating disorder."

"I couldn't help thinking of my own boys and what it would have been like if they'd gone through the same experience."

"Me too. There but for the grace of God go I."

She was sipping her tea as I said this. She looked up with a frown. "Oh?"

I nodded. "Absolutely."

"Oh, I see," she said ruminatively. There was a pause before light suddenly dawned. "Oh, I do see."

"I know some of what he's going through, though I've never been out, of course."

"Until now?"

I nodded.

"Dan, is that wise? Here of all places?"

"Maybe not, but it's important. Jeremy knows, and it's suddenly more important because..."

"You've met somebody?"

"That's right. Ironically, somebody I was close to at

university but we ... er ... lost touch."

"Good man. I'm pleased for you. Be careful, though. The vultures are gathering over Brexit, and you could be about to give them a whole load of new ammunition."

"Understood. I'll think about it before I say anything to the chairman."

She nodded briskly. "Yes, you must. Now, what are we going to do about Ethan? A suicide risk, do you think?"

"Not yet, but he could be. I think he got the message from me that he's not alone. But we need to prove that by making a difference to his life."

"A word with the headmaster?"

"Do you think that'll make any difference?"

She wrinkled her nose. "I've met him a couple of times. He's a recognisable type – served in the army but only in the education corps. Never saw active service but likes you to think that he did. Bombastic, always wants to know which university you went to. Wears his religion too much on his sleeve for my taste."

I nodded. "Presumably that's why he's reluctant to act over Ethan?"

"Knowing him, he probably secretly agrees with the bullies but can't say so."

"But I have no status in this matter, do I? The school isn't even in the public sector."

"No, you don't – but if we genuinely believe that Ethan is at risk, you need to do something, I think. An informal approach might be best initially, perhaps over the phone. A friendly word. We could follow that up with a letter that makes it clear in the nicest possible way that the Head will be held responsible if anything should happen to the boy.

Chapter Twenty-Four

That should scare him into action."

"Helena, you're a marvel."

"Nonsense, just doing my job."

My discussion with Ethan's headmaster, Gerald Morris, went roughly along the lines that Helena had predicted – initially, he denied that there was a problem, but then changed tack and suggested that it was the boy's fault, brought on by his "lifestyle choices".

"We believe in Christian values in our school, Mr Forrester, which means that we don't accept the homosexual lifestyle as anything other than disordered. Our policy clearly states that homosexual acts go against the natural order. I'm sure, as a member of the Conservative Party, you'll understand our view."

"No, I don't, actually. Besides, whatever my personal views, I think your approach may be illegal under the Equality Act."

"I'm sorry, but that isn't true. Our policy has been drawn up to comply with the latest guidance. It clearly states that people with homosexual tendencies must be accepted with respect, compassion and sensitivity."

I gritted my teeth at both his tone and the content of his speech. "But then taught that they're disordered and any consummation of their love is a mortal sin."

"That is the teaching of the Church, Mr Forrester. God's word on the subject. Please don't shoot the messenger."

His tone irritated me: he managed to sound pious, slightly unctuous and smug all at the same time. But there was no point in losing my temper or expecting that any arguments I might make could change his views.

I continued the conversation, asking when he'd last interviewed Ethan. I was not surprised when he acknowledged that he had yet to do so, that he was relying on his head of year to deal with the matter. When told in the nicest possible way that both my secretary and I were concerned that the boy was a suicide risk, his first inclination was to question whether we were qualified to make such a judgement. That took my irritation with this stupid, pompous man to stratospheric levels. My voice took on an icy tone.

"I'm perfectly happy to acknowledge that I'm not an expert in these matters, Headmaster. However, I have been a Member of Parliament for seven years. In that time, my secretary and I have helped a great number of people and we do have considerable practical experience of these issues. You must do as you see fit, but my constituency secretary and I will be making written notes of our discussions this afternoon and of this telephone call, which we shall be sharing with you, for the record. I would urge you to consider the consequences if anything happens to Ethan and you were shown to have ignored our clear warnings."

He saw the threat. Having been too lazy or prejudiced to intervene before, he was now scared not to. By the end of the discussion, he was positively obsequious. Even so, I was shaking with anger when I put the phone down.

I needed some air, so I stuck my head into Helena's office to let her know that I was going for a walk. Once outside, I went into the municipal gardens opposite the office and took several deep breaths to calm myself down.

Eventually I returned to the office knowing that I had some hard thinking to do.

Governing Passions

Chapter Twenty-Five

Luke

When I got to the office that morning, it was eerily quiet. Steve and Andy were at separate client meetings, Barbara was on leave and a couple of people were working from home, with the result that our office had a ghostly feel.

The quiet gave me time to daydream about Dan and speculate about what the weekend would bring. I had so enjoyed our evening together, even if it had got off to a difficult start, and the memory of holding him and helping him to relax brought a smile to my lips. At that point, I closed my eyes for a moment to clear my thoughts and then made myself concentrate on some work. That lasted about ten minutes before something started me on a cycle of daydream, speculation and memory all over again.

One thing the evening had taught me was the pressure under which my boy was operating. Food and drink had revived him last night, and his skin had lost the colour of old putty it'd had when he reached the flat. However, the effect had not lasted and his tiredness had taken over again. I guessed that, despite his appearance of confidence and quiet competence, his mental reserves were pretty much exhausted and vulnerable to the pressure of events, like the fuss yesterday over the leak. A few more days like that, and I would be seriously worried for his health. I made a note to have a quiet word with Jeremy if the opportunity arose.

I recalled another aspect of the previous evening – that my presence had clearly helped to calm Dan and make him feel better. That feeling of being wanted, of being necessary to him, was a novel one and it was very special.

Eventually the morning passed although I only managed to write the odd paragraph in my report. I was about to go out for some food when Steve came back from his client meeting. He had a face like thunder; his demeanour was eerily reminiscent of the old Steve before Josh came on the scene.

"What's up, boss?" I asked. "Bad meeting?"

"No, the meeting was fine. It's this bloody article in *London Figaro*. Somebody's having a go at us."

I frowned. "What's *London Figaro*?"

"It's a satirical magazine, mainly online – a sort of posh *Private Eye*." He chucked his copy across to me, folded back to the offending article. Hedged round with the usual "alleged that" and other weasel words, the piece suggested that there was something fishy about the awarding of grants under the Griffin House scheme. Somebody had got hold of the fact that many of the projects that had been awarded funding had been advised by the same consultants – a firm called Low Carbon Promises. LCP had been set up by Freddie Angus, an ex-employee of Pearson Frazer. No specific allegation was made, more the usual brew of hints and questions, ending with a line of innuendo: *Do we smell collusion, or is LCP is very good at its job? We think we should be told.*

"I haven't spoken to Freddie for a couple of years," Steve said.

"Me neither."

"I mean, he's good – that's why we were sorry to lose him. All his clients' applications were strong because he knows what he's doing and reads the criteria properly. That's the whole bloody idea."

"Any idea where this has come from?"

Steve shook his head. "Not yet, but I've got my suspicions – and I can hopefully get them confirmed. An old pal of mine works on the magazine. That's the only reason I buy it."

As he spoke, his phone buzzed with a text message. Steve read it and nodded to himself. "That's from my mole at *London Figaro*," he told me. "Yep, I was right about the culprit. The bastard."

"Would this by any chance be to do with a certain bloke at DECRA?"

"Got it in one."

We said the name in unison. "Sean Andrews."

"He really is trying to put a spanner in the works, isn't he?"

"Yeah, he certainly is. I'm not sure whether he's after this firm, or Dan and Jeremy, or simply trying to destabilise everything."

"I'm told Andrews hates the Griffin House scheme, but I suspect it's also about Dan being a Remainer, and the Brexiteers wanting him out of the government."

"Fuck. I hadn't thought of that. What does that make us, I wonder? Collateral damage, I suppose."

"That's a good way to put it. That's politics for you."

"What do you think we should do? Ignore it?"

I nodded. "That might be the safest option. Why don't you talk to Jeremy? He can tell you what they're thinking at the department. Dan's on his way down to his constituency, so I shouldn't think he's even seen it yet."

"Good idea, Luke. I'll give him a buzz. Thanks."

I left him and resumed my mission to get something to eat. When I got back, Steve had already spoken to Jeremy. "As you thought, his advice is to lie low and keep quiet. He's keen to let this one die and the best way to do that is ignore it. I'm going to have a word along the same lines with Freddie."

I returned to my desk and managed to do a couple of hours of reasonable work by strictly rationing my daydreaming intervals. I left the office about three and went home to get ready for the weekend. An hour later, I was in the car and texting Dan to say I was on my way.

As anyone will tell you, Friday afternoon driving on London's orbital motorway is no joke; that day was no exception and, an hour after setting out, I was still only ten miles from home, having got caught up in a major jam after an accident near Reigate. My satnav kept telling me I was on the fastest route; I wondered what the slowest one would be like.

The hold-up gave me ample scope to resume my

daydreams. My weekend did have a down side: I was leaving Dan on Sunday morning to drive over to Harchester – my coming-out lunch with my parents.

The Bickerstaff incident a couple of weeks earlier had given me hope that it would not be nearly as bad as I'd always feared. It was clear that my father's attitude had undergone a major change after the experience with the young canon's resignation. Had I not heard it with my own ears, I wouldn't have believed it possible. I had to hope that his sympathy would extend to his own son.

My mother's reaction was much less predictable. Whatever else, I knew it would be dramatic and would probably involve tears. Whether their shedding would come from sympathy or disapproval was a moot point, but I knew from experience that her reaction would be about what was best for her.

Suddenly the traffic began to move. I needed to concentrate and it was not until I'd negotiated my section of the M25 and turned south westwards on the M3 that my thoughts returned to the weekend ahead.

Of course, I could postpone the big announcement at home and leave it for a more propitious time but I knew in my heart that there would never be a genuinely appropriate moment. Besides, postponement would be dangerous: the longer Dan and I carried on our relationship, the greater the risk of being outed by somebody – particularly with Sean Andrews on the lookout for material to undermine Dan's position. If my parents found out that I was gay from anyone other than me they'd be very hurt, and rightly so.

No, I had to grasp the nettle. At least, my mother would approve of the fact that Dan was an MP and a member of the government. She would immediately see the possibilities of him helping to get a bishop's mitre for my father.

God, I was getting cynical in my old age. I decided to think of something else, so spent the rest of the journey dreaming about Dan. What that did for my concentration or the quality of my driving, I wouldn't like to say.

Chapter Twenty-Six

Dan

As I was going back into the office, I got Luke's text to say he was on the way. Inside, my constituency chairman was waiting for me. I took a deep breath and pasted on my biggest smile.

"Anthony, how nice to see you. Do come in. Did Helena organise some tea for you?"

He blinked nervously, clearly discomfited by the warmth of my greeting. We had never been close, and I'd been wary of him since he'd taken over from his predecessor five years earlier.

Anthony Stewart was a large, florid individual, about fifty-five years old. Born locally, he was every inch a self-made man – as he reminded us frequently, particularly in front of the more patrician members from county areas of the constituency. He spoke with a West Country burr, but the rounded gentle sounds of the accent couldn't disguise the fact that he was a ruthless, self-opinionated bully.

Helena served him with tea. As we settled, I took a good look at him. He had surprisingly small eyes for the size of his face and the whites had a distinctly pinkish tinge. Piggy eyes, my mother had called them after meeting him once, and she was right. They swivelled a lot, too, constantly on the lookout for the next opportunity or the next person to intimidate. Now, the eyes settled on me. And it was clear that our Anthony was not a happy man.

"So, Anthony, what can I do for you?"

"It's more about what I can do for you," he replied, unsmiling. "About keeping your seat." He paused, no doubt for dramatic effect.

I wasn't surprised by his words. I maintained the benevolent, interested expression that I'd perfected for my constituency duties. "Go on," I said.

"It's about this Brexit thing. A few of the members are unhappy about you being opposed to it."

"I've never made any secret of the fact that I'd rather stay in the EU."

"We knew that, but now it seems to my pals that you're trying to stop us leaving."

"I don't know where you got that from, Anthony. I'm member of a government that is committed to honouring the verdict of the referendum and delivering the best possible outcome for us all." It sounded a little robotic, which it was; it almost sounded as if I agreed with it, which I didn't. But it would have to do.

"But all these stories about what they're demanding. Doesn't seem right to some of us."

"No, I can understand that, Anthony. But this is a negotiation and both sides have to reach an agreement. Some give and take is inevitable."

"I can understand that, but it seems to me – to a few of

us – that it's all them taking and us giving."

"I think you're being a little premature there, Anthony. None of us knows what the final deal is going to look like. And you've got to remember that it must be agreed by the other twenty-seven countries as well as us. I think you must be patient."

"Why? All we're asking for is having our rights back – things that should never have been given away in the first place."

"Anthony, what can I say? I know that the Prime Minister is doing her best to deliver the best deal she can. I support her in that, which is why I was so pleased to be asked to join the government a few weeks ago. I am fully behind what she's trying to do – which is deliver the best possible Brexit deal for all of us."

It sounded, and felt, like a party-political broadcast but that was inevitable. Since Anthony Stewart and his Brexiteer colleagues were looking for an excuse to be betrayed, there was nothing I could say to reassure him. There would be no meeting of minds over this, even within the same constituency association.

"And then there's this other business."

I looked up at him, genuinely puzzled. "What other business."

"About your personal life. There's rumours going round that you might be queer."

Christ. Where did that come from? "Oh, I see. And is the rumour a problem?"

"It'd be a problem for you if it was true."

"Only if it matters to people."

He frowned, clearly nonplussed by my response.

"You see, since you were kind enough to adopt me as your candidate back in 2009, I have – according to rumours – been engaged to three different women, had illegitimate children by two others, whilst one website had me down as a transsexual. So you'll forgive me if I seem unperturbed by the latest in a long line of intrusive drivel."

Again, he seemed nonplussed. I could almost hear the wheels turning in his brain. But he was not going to be diverted from his mission. "I understand all that, Dan. But this one's more serious. People are anxious."

"By people, I presume you mean you?"

"Not only me, but most of the Finance and General Purposes Committee."

This was the most important decision-making body in the association. Technically, its decisions could be overturned by the full executive or, *in extremis*, by a general meeting, but that was rare. If I ever lost the support of a majority of F&GP members, I was in serious trouble.

So here we were. Was this the crunch point? Was I going to come out now and get it over with? Something within me rebelled. When I did, it would be on my own terms and at a time and in a forum of my choosing. I was damned if I was going to say something to Anthony Stewart now and let him control both the agenda and the message.

Suddenly, the right words popped into my head. "Anthony, I'm grateful to you for bringing the matter to my attention. I wasn't aware that these rumours had begun to circulate locally. I need to give serious thought to the best way to respond to them. I'll let you know how I wish to proceed."

"So what do I tell my pals?"

"Exactly what I've just told you, Anthony. Give them my greetings and say that I'll be in touch as soon as I can. Now if you'll excuse me, I have to call my private office about some urgent government business. Nice to see you. Do give my best regards to Angelica and the children."

The line between ensuring a swift exit and throwing somebody out of your office is a fine one, but I thought I'd managed to stay on the right side of it as I escorted him from the building. The smile never left my lips, though it did not stretch to my eyes. Fortunately, Anthony Stewart was not very observant.

I closed the door behind him and leant against it. Helena popped her head out of her office door. "Has he gone?"

I nodded. "Thank the Lord. God, he really is an odious man."

"Tell me news, not history."

"He's up to something, Helena. Started on about Brexit but quickly moved on to my private life."

She cocked an eyebrow. "Oh? Along the lines we were discussing earlier?"

I nodded. "Apparently, 'there's rumours going round that you might be queer'," I said, quoting his words in his accent.

"You've got that accent off to a tee. Did he say any more?"

"Only that the members of the F&GP were worried."

"Interesting. Nobody's said anything to me." She frowned. "I know several of the committee very well. I'm sure Angela or Brian would have said if there was anything amiss. I think he's up to something."

"Possibly. It could have come from his Brexit pals –

there's a SPAD in the department called Sean Andrews who's causing all sorts of trouble."

"Yes, Jeremy mentioned him on the phone yesterday. He was spitting blood."

"Over the leaks, I expect. That all got a bit hairy."

"So I gather," she responded. "Is this against you personally, or to destabilise all the Remainers?"

"It could be all of us, though nobody else has said anything. I'll talk to the Whips Office when I get back – if there is something going on, they're bound to have got wind of it."

"Good idea. What did you say to him? Anthony, I mean."

"Oh, I reminded him about all the other rumours there've been about my private life over the years."

She chuckled. "Oh, you mean the illegitimate children and you being transsexual?"

I nodded. "I told him that I hadn't heard the new rumours but I'd give the matter serious thought and tell him what I proposed to do. I was damned if I was going to let him control the timing or the agenda."

"Quite right too. But what will you do?"

"In essence, I haven't got much choice. I need to be honest with them."

"Your decision, Dan. I'll back you whatever you decide. For what it's worth, I think you're right. Much better to be upfront and honest. I might not have heard much from the F&GP members, but I can see there's something amiss on the web."

"What sort of thing?"

"As you know, there've been mutterings for a while – nastiness about you voting remain, muttering about the government's green policies – especially since you became the Minister. But lately it's shifted again, become more personal. Little things – spiteful, petty, sarcastic. There was a debate on your Facebook page last week about whether you were handsome or not – one or two comments said you were too pretty to be straight."

Despite everything, I laughed out loud. "That's priceless, Helena. I must remember that one."

Her face turned serious again. "Some of it is funny, but it makes me uneasy. There's an undercurrent – as if somebody is orchestrating a campaign of nasty comments."

I shrugged. "Yes, Jeremy said something about that. He said you were worried. But there's not much we can do about it, is there?"

Helena shook her head.

"Which means that I still need to come out at the next available opportunity. There's an Executive Meeting in a couple of weeks' time, isn't there?"

"On the fifteenth, yes."

"Hmm. Better the full executive than the F&GP, don't you think?"

She nodded. "Yes, not as many of them are in Anthony's pocket."

"That's what I thought. I'll do the deed that night – it'll be a good opportunity to have a chat about Brexit too."

"Good scheme. Shall I let Anthony know?"

"Not until you have to. When do you send out the agendas?"

"These days, I e-mail everything a couple of days before the meeting."

"Good. Let's not say too much until we have to. I'm sure

you can slot me into the agenda somehow."

She nodded. "There's the Member's Report – you know, the one we normally do in writing."

"Fine. I'll liaise with Jeremy and make sure it's in his diary."

"And marked "not to be missed on any account.""

As I left the office for my cottage, a wave of tiredness hit me. The afternoon's events in the surgery alone would have been enough, but the confrontations with Gerald Morris and Anthony Stewart had completely drained my mental capacity.

Part of me wanted nothing more than to go home and hide under the duvet for the rest of the weekend, but that was not going to happen because Luke was on his way. A voice within me groaned at the thought of company. Entertaining here for the first time ever was bound to be a strain at the best of times, but my current downbeat mood and tiredness made it feel ten times worse. I had no idea how it would go. What if I hated having somebody else in the tiny cottage?

Then there was Luke himself. We hardly knew each other, really. We'd seen each other no more than three times since that first encounter in the department's conference room a few weeks earlier. True, we'd been close at university, but people changed a lot in fifteen years. Perhaps this invitation had been a mistake and I should slow things down.

We needed to spend at least part of the weekend talking

some of this through: what we were both hoping for, and how we could make things work. My mind quickly went back to the previous night. Holding Luke, and being held, had made me feel comfortable and secure, as if I'd come home for the first time in many years. My upbringing and all my years of loneliness, of pushing people away, meant that I'd never known the healing power of simple physical contact.

Another bonus was the relief I felt at being able to share my feelings and opinions with somebody who was likely to understand them. Triumphs and disasters were all very well, but there wasn't much difference between them if you couldn't share the elation or seek consolation.

The drive took about twenty minutes. My cottage was in the small seaside village of Monks Cheney, with stunning views of the coastline. It had been love at first sight with both the village and my small house when I'd been adopted for the seat ten years earlier. All the components were there: the green of the downs, the wide vistas of the limestone cliffs and the sea. The stone-built village had a rustic charm that would have been recognisable to Thomas Hardy a hundred years and more ago.

My cottage was a two-up, two-down, with a modern kitchen and bathroom in a small two-storey extension at the back. I loved the place deeply, especially the peace and relaxation it brought. One of the biggest downsides of my ministerial appointment was that I got to spend fewer weekends down here.

As I drew near, the tension of the afternoon dissipated and I started to focus on the weekend ahead. Despite my concerns, I was looking forward to what was to come.

Governing Passions

Chapter Twenty-Seven

Luke

I was a stranger to this part of the world, so was fascinated by the countryside through which I was driving. The road was narrow and twisting and I had to concentrate, but I loved the glimpses that I caught.

Rounding a bend, I passed through a line of trees, gnarled and bent from decades of the prevailing wind. A view of the English Channel opened up: I pulled to the side of the road and stopped the car to catch my breath and absorb the vista laid out in front of me.

The sun was setting through a sky dotted with small clouds, each of which was tinted pink. Across the horizon, a line of darker cloud had turned purple. This was all mirrored in a calm, almost glassy sea, with the sun's reflection causing a broad sweep of red light so vivid that the sea appeared to be on fire.

I grabbed my phone and took several pictures to try to capture the moment. Whatever happened this weekend, this sunset and the memory of this view would stay with me for ever.

I returned to the car and followed the road down the slope into Monks Cheney. It was a delightful village of historic cottages, all jumbled together and built of different materials, most in honey-coloured stone, others old-fashioned wattle and daub under a thatched roof, and some displaying a mixture of flint and red brick. Talk about chocolate-box England: I could immediately see why Dan had become so fond of the place. I followed my satnav's directions through the winding streets, and finally heard the magic words "You have reached your destination". Seven-thirty – slightly ahead of schedule.

Dan appeared at the door, smiling in welcome. Even though I'd been with him first thing that morning, the sight of him was still enough to set my heart racing. I got out of the car, beaming to myself. "Hi. Am okay to park here?"

"Perfect. Welcome to Monks Cheney."

He looked tired again, but otherwise seemed happy and relaxed. Dressed in an elegant red sweater and a pair of beautifully cut golden corduroy trousers, he looked every inch the country gentleman, even down to the brogues on his feet. It was a side of him I had not seen before and the look suited him.

I collected my bag from the back seat and we moved indoors: a welcome hug on the doorstep was clearly not advisable. Dan followed me through, shutting the door behind him. I dropped my bag and turned – and immediately found myself wrapped in his arms, his lips seeking mine.

It was a spectacular welcome, that kiss. It was like coming home: two loners discovering comfort and solace

214

in each other's arms.

Dan broke the kiss but still held me close. I pulled my head back and look him in the eye. "Bad day?"

He nodded. "I'm so glad you're here. It was a horrible afternoon. What about you?"

"I was a bit ... distracted this morning, thinking about this sexy man I know. But I did manage to get something done before I left. Bit of an odd conversation with Steve, though. I'll tell you about that later. Main priority at the moment is the bathroom."

"Oh, of course. Come this way. I'll bring your bag."

I glanced round as we made our way through the cottage and up the narrow stairs. The place was furnished in a modern, almost minimalist style, which blended surprisingly well with the historic fabric of the building. The furniture was light oak and the chairs and sofa upholstered in a grey fabric. There were differing shades of grey on some of the walls, complementing the bare stone on others. It was cool, elegant and beautiful.

Dan showed me into the master bedroom; the spare was set up as his office. He directed me to the bathroom. "I'll go and get supper organised, so take your time and relax."

"Mind if I take a shower? I feel a bit grubby after that drive."

"Please do. I've put you some towels out – the cream ones are yours. I'll get on with the supper. It should be ready in about half an hour. Okay?"

"Perfect."

215

"God, Dan, I'm absolutely stuffed. Can barely move."

"Me too. I'm devoted to Janet's Friday suppers, but there's always far too much."

It turned out that the famous Janet was a single mum from the other end of the village who looked after Dan's cottage for him. She always left him a meal to reheat on his first night. Asked to provide for two tonight, she'd made enough to feed a whole army – a steak-and-kidney pie with a vegetable bake, followed by the last of the season's strawberries with fresh cream. We'd washed all this down with a claret from Dan's small cellar.

We rose from the table and Dan gestured for me to take the armchair, whilst he sat on the sofa. I felt a frisson of disappointment but went with the flow – at least until I'd begun to digest my supper. "So how did you discover Janet?"

"It was Helena, my constituency secretary. Once I'd found this place, she asked around to see if anybody was up for the job. Janet was the friend of a friend. She's been an absolute treasure. She's a widow – her husband was killed in Iraq in 2008. She has two boys, both teenagers. They're great lads. I don't know what I'd do without her."

"This is a terrific place, Dan."

"Glad you like it. One of the downsides of getting the ministerial job is that I get to spend less time down here."

"That's a shame. You must miss it."

"It's a great place to chill out and have some time to myself. Even if it's only for a few hours around constituency business, I still go back up to town refreshed. I realised this morning that this is the first time I've ever shared it with anybody."

That rocked me back and I was touched. "That's brilliant, Dan. I feel very honoured. Thank you."

"My pleasure." He gave me a warm smile, but I noticed that it didn't reach his eyes, which seemed dull. I could read the tension on his forehead. There was something wrong.

"You said you'd had a shitty day. Want to tell me about it?"

"You don't want to hear about all that crap."

"Something upset you, didn't it? I can tell. I'm sure it'd help to talk about it."

"Are you sure?"

"That's part of what I'm here for. To help and support you."

"I suppose so. I hadn't thought of it like that. I simply wanted to lose myself with you and forget it all."

"But you clearly can't."

"No. It was such an odd afternoon. My surgery was difficult, and I'm worried about the number of cases arising from a housing trust that recently got a new chairman. He's a big donor to the constituency party and local bigwig, but he's a bully and seems to be causing mayhem amongst the tenants." He paused and sighed. "I haven't decided what to do about that, because it was pushed aside by a case that upset me a lot. It was a mother and son – the boy's sixteen and gay. He recently came out, so he's now being bullied at school and the authorities can't – or won't – do anything about it."

"That's awful."

"If you could have seen his face, Luke. I don't know – he looked defeated. Pitifully thin and so tired. Helena and I both thought he might be a suicide risk."

"Jesus. What can you do?"

"I spoke to the headmaster. Old school, ex-army and very religious, apparently. All he did was bang on about the boy's unfortunate lifestyle choices."

"You're kidding. I didn't think they were allowed to say things like that these days."

"Well, apparently he thinks they can. He told me that he ran his school on Christian principles."

"Yeah, like 'Love thy Neighbour as Thyself'". So what did you say?"

"I mentioned the Equality Act, but he claimed they were fully compliant, with all the right guidelines in place. He also said they had a right to assert the Church's teachings."

"Oh, that's bloody great, isn't it?"

"Yes, and the depressing thing is that he's absolutely right. I did a quick check tonight."

Luke shook his head.

"Anyway," I continued, "I warned him the boy might be a potential suicide risk, and said that Helena and I would record that in writing and send him a copy."

"What did he say to that?"

"That made him change his tune a little and promise to take action: he saw that he risked being held responsible if anything did go wrong."

"Did you believe him?"

Dan looked away and shook his head. "Frankly, no." He looked at me full in the face again and his eyes were so sad. "I dread to think what's going to happen next. You know what really makes me cross is that folk like him still think like that. Even in the second decade of the twenty-first century, they're in charge of young lives. It's terrifying."

I understood how he felt but couldn't help wondering what the real reason for the strength of his reaction was. "But we have made progress, Dan. You must see that."

"Of course. If you'd told me as a boy growing up in the days of Section 28 that a Tory government would legalise gay marriage, I'd have laughed at you. And yes, I know more of the public accepts same sex relationships than ever before. But that still leaves an awful lot of people who don't, according to the last research I saw."

I nodded. "About a third, isn't it?"

"Something like that. And they can still hurt vulnerable youngsters and cause them lasting harm. It's too easy to forget that when we live in our nice middle-class liberal bubble."

"I know what you mean, but you did all you could today, surely."

His eyes were suddenly sharp and full of passion. "No, I didn't, Luke. That's the point. I should have been able to say more to that lad, told him that I was gay too and understood what was going through. You know, been a bit of a role model. Instead I'm buried so deep in my own closet that I'm too bloody scared – so I stand on the sidelines, looking on and keeping my mouth shut while unspeakable things happen to other gay people, not only in my own country but also in the rest of the world."

He slumped back in his seat. The passion seemed to drain from him and was replaced by dejection. I moved to the sofa and put my arm round him. He tensed for a moment, evidently unused to such contact, then relaxed and put his head on my shoulder.

"Would it have made any difference with that headmaster fellow, though?" I asked. "Surely it would have undermined your position as the local MP in his eyes?"

"Possibly. I get that my ability to influence local people and organisations relies on my status..."

"But here's the thing: how would he have reacted if he'd known you were gay too? Something along the lines of 'you would say that, wouldn't you?', I bet."

"I tried that, Luke. But it won't wash – it simply plays into the hands of the bigots and the homophobes. If the only way somebody like me can get chosen and elected is to tell lies or avoid questions, then we haven't got very far at all, have we? If I can't do my job as an MP or a Minister without hiding the truth about who I am, it doesn't say much about other people, either. But if I then accept that and play their game, surely it proves that I'm ashamed of what I am."

"I understand that totally. It's bloody difficult, though, isn't it?"

"You're not kidding. I suddenly realised this afternoon that I fought three general elections hiding the truth – some would say lying – about who I am. And at a time when others are prepared to be open about it. So, at bottom, it's actually about me, about my cowardice."

"Dan, you're being too hard on yourself."

"Am I, though?" He shook his head. "My credibility and integrity are on the line until I come out and fight an election as an openly gay man. What's more, I don't think the lies will wash any more."

"What makes you say that?"

"After my surgery, the local party chairman came to

see me. He wanted to whinge on about me still being a Remainer, but he also said there were rumours about me 'being queer', as he put it. And there was a strong suggestion that his pals don't like it."

"Bloody hell, Dan. What are you going to do?"

"It doesn't leave me much alternative, to be honest. I think I've got to come out. But that means telling my parents, which I dread. There's also the possible effect on you."

"Me? Why me?"

"Because once the media latch on to the fact that I'm gay, they'll want to know about my relationships. Even if we didn't make a big thing of being together, it wouldn't take them long to cotton on to us."

"I see that. I'll have to get used to the idea."

"Are you sure, Luke? They can be a bloody pain."

"I know. But I've thought about this – about what it might mean getting lots of media exposure – and I'm okay with it, I think."

"I don't want your life to be made a misery."

"I know it's a risk but I'm sure it'll be fine. I'm out at work, and my family will know after Sunday so that shouldn't be an issue."

"True, but..."

"No buts, Dan. You must do what you need to for the sake of your career. That's the most important thing. Whatever develops between us can't be at the cost of everything you've worked for all these years." His expression softened. I'd obviously said the right thing – and I'd meant every word of it. "How will it play out?"

"There's a meeting of the party executive in a couple of

weeks. I'm thinking that I'll make an announcement that night and announce it on social media at the same time. Helena and I talked it through this afternoon and that seemed the best plan."

"Did she know already?"

"She'd guessed, I think."

"So you came out to her?"

"Yes – first time ever."

"Good for you! And what did she say?"

"Didn't bat an eyelid, bless her. Totally supportive."

"That's great. At least you've got somebody on your side down here."

"Indeed. Though I like to think there'll be others."

"I'm sure there will. I bet all the old ladies love you."

He laughed and some of the furrows in his forehead faded. It was a welcome sign. "Let's hope so." He raised his glass and clinked mine. "Anyway, here's to being out and proud."

"I'll drink to that. And to my own, very sexy member."

"Thanks for that," he responded with a laugh, but his face quickly turned serious again. "More importantly, though, thanks for being here tonight and putting up with me blathering on. You've no idea how wonderful it is to feel that somebody's got my back. Somebody I can talk to about all this."

If I'd been a cat I would have purred. "My pleasure."

Chapter Twenty-Eight

Dan

I took another swallow of wine. Luke had been right: discussing the events of the afternoon had helped to put them into perspective. The issues hadn't gone away, but talking them through gave me a better sense of proportion: suddenly they loomed less large and didn't seem as scary. It made what we'd been talking about seem possible, as opposed to a looming danger that needed to be pushed into the future.

"It's amazing," I told him. "I've been running away from my sexuality for so long, living in fear of it. The idea that I might turn and make a stand is scary, but it's exhilarating at the same time, you know?"

"I know. It's not easy for you – and I can hardly talk. I need to have my own little coming-out party on Sunday."

"God, yes. I hope that goes okay."

He shrugged. "What will be will be. You and I can't hope to build anything lasting together without being honest with ourselves and others."

I couldn't help but catch my breath at that. It was not

only the words themselves, but also the casual way Luke said them – as if our future together was a given. "And do you? Want to build something together?" I asked, unable to stop my tone from sounding nervous and tentative.

"Absolutely. As I told you the other week – I fell for you in Freshers' Week sixteen years ago this month. The more I see you, the more I realise that nothing's changed."

"Nobody's ever given me a reason to face up to being gay before. I know how absolutely daft I was to push you away, and I'm not going to muck it up twice. So yes, I'm in as well – wherever all this takes us."

As I lay with my head on his shoulder, Luke kissed me on the temple. It was a simple gesture but made me feel safe and relaxed. The trouble was that the combination of the relaxation and the warmth reminded me how exhausted I felt. I couldn't stifle the yawn that overtook me.

Luke laughed gently. "Somebody's still tired, I think."

I nodded. "Completely jiggered, *again*, I'm afraid."

He snorted at that. "Jiggered, eh? What a wonderful word. Where did that come from?"

"Our housekeeper at home in Derbyshire when I was growing up. She had a fund of amazing words and phrases. They just pop into my head sometimes."

"That's certainly a new one on me. I must remember that. Come on, oh jiggered one, let's get you to bed. Dr Luke prescribes more cuddles and lots of sleep. What time are you on parade tomorrow?"

"I'm due to open the Autumn Fayre at two so I should put in an appearance about one, to thank all the helpers and have a chat with some of the Exec members. I'll do my 'you've all done very well' spiel and tour the stalls. Should be clear by three-thirty or four at the latest."

"In which case, I'll alter my prescription to cuddles, sleep *and* a lie-in."

"Sounds good, Doctor Luke."

"Come on, then."

Thus it was that I spent my second successive night wrapped in Luke's arms. Once again, I was out for the count right through until my alarm woke us at nine. Nearly ten hours' continuous sleep was a near miracle for me. I reached out and turned off the alarm, turning over to face Luke and drawing him to me so that our heads lay on the same pillow.

The feel of his body moving against mine was delicious. I ran my hands gently down his sides, enjoying the feel of his skin, soft to the touch despite the bone and muscle that lay underneath. He shivered at my touch and moved his head slightly to brush my lips with his. "Good morning," he whispered.

"Hello, there," I responded. "Sleep well?"

"Like a log. You?"

"Same. A wonderful night. And all the better for not having to rush this morning."

"Absolutely." He moved his hand to down my tummy, rubbing there in gentle circles. I arched into his touch and stretched my legs out. His hand brushed my erection and I couldn't help but tremble. "Luke...'

His head had stayed close so I moved to return his kiss, but more firmly. My tongue brushed his lips and he parted them. We spent the next few minutes languorously exploring each other's mouths, our bodies moving against each other in a slow rhythm. It was blissful.

Eventually we broke the kiss, laughing as we both gasped for air. Resuming the connection, our movements became more urgent. Luke rolled us so that he was on top of me. I opened my legs to accommodate him then wrapped them round his hips. Our erections brushed together and he hissed at the touch.

I closed my eyes and hung on to him for dear life, suddenly full of joy at holding this beautiful man in my arms. I was determined to cherish the moment because it wouldn't last. He moved from my lips and buried his head in my shoulder.

He reached between us and aligned our cocks, then gripped them together, starting to thrust gently. The sensations were amazing, and I thrust back, quickly settling into a rhythm. I groaned at the sensations I was feeling. Sex had never ever been like this before. Then my senses blotted out conscious thought and I reached my climax, shouting Luke's name as I shot prodigiously across my body. Luke came after two more thrusts, letting out a long "ohhh" as his muscles spasmed.

We remained where we were for a moment or two before Luke lifted himself off me. We turned on to our sides, still gasping for breath and coming down from the highs we'd experienced. At length, I recovered enough to speak. "Luke, that was..."

"I know, Dan."

"Just so you know, it's never been like that before. I know I haven't had a huge amount of experience, but that was so special."

"Me too."

We lay there quietly, sated but happy. After a few minutes, Luke's breathing changed as he dozed off. I lay there with a smile on my face at the memory of what we'd done and how amazing it had felt.

I'd read in gay romance books about the supposed difference between having sex and making love. It was a distinction I'd never fully grasped and had tended to dismiss as sappy and sentimental. Not any longer. Now I understood.

The cold, analytical side of my brain kicked in. This was the part that had kept me in the closet for so long, always arguing that sex and emotion were worthless in contrast to the rewards to be had from achieving my goals. I dreaded what was to come but the analysis surprised me.

Having sex with another person for whom you had feelings obviously took things to a whole new level. Given that it truly did make that much difference, it changed lots of other things too. That had to be a factor in my decision making, in how I wanted to live my life in future.

Being with Luke gave me companionship and support. We had a lot in common, shared interests and tastes. Plus there was the simple affection I felt for him; if, on top of all that, there was totally awesome sex, it was a pretty compelling combination.

Happy with that conclusion, I forced the analyst in me to shut down for a while. A thought crossed my mind that prompted a smile. It occurred to me that, if you had to put a label on that mix, it would read "love".

Luke moved in his sleep, drawing me even closer. I

relished the sensation and relaxed into his embrace. Moments later, I also drifted into a doze.

Chapter Twenty-Nine

Luke

Dan's clock said ten-thirty when I awoke again. He was still fast asleep in my arms, and he looked so peaceful that I was reluctant to disturb him. However, nature was calling with increasing urgency, so I disentangled myself as gently as possible, although inevitably the movement woke him.

"Sorry, but I needed the bathroom."

"No problem. Probably time we were moving anyway. I could get used to lie-ins like this, though."

"Mm. Me too."

"Take the shower first if you like. I'll stay here and snuggle."

"Okay, fine. Won't be long."

I showered quickly and dressed as Dan took my place in the bathroom. Since he was on parade later, his grooming needed to be more extensive than my somewhat sketchy efforts. When he did emerge, his towel was round his waist, and his hair was dishevelled. It was all I could do not to grab him and start kissing him all over.

He gave me a wicked grin, as if knowing what was going

through my mind. "Did you by any chance just have thoughts of doing dishonourable things to this honourable gentleman?" he asked as he slipped into a T-shirt and a pair of sweatpants.

"God, yes. You looked so sexy coming out of the bathroom."

"I'd love to stay, but I've got this fair thing at lunchtime. Besides, I don't know about you, but I'm hungry. Best I can do is a definite promise for tonight."

"I can work with that, I suppose. And breakfast does sound a good idea."

"Come on, let's go and forage. Janet was going to leave us supplies."

Janet had indeed left Dan's fridge well stocked. He cooked us a full English breakfast, and we lingered over coffee for an hour or so, reading the paper and chatting about nothing in particular. At around twelve-fifteen, he disappeared to get changed and reappeared a few minutes later in another of his sharp suits.

"Hmm, look at you all togged up. Very smart ... and seriously hot."

"Have to do the suit thing, even at weekends. The natives expect it."

"I can imagine. My parents are the same – I've always hated having to put a suit on for church on Sundays, but my mother insists that I dress up 'for your father's sake, dear'. I'm sure I never look as sexy as you do. That pale grey really suits you, and the blue tie matches your eyes."

He blushed slightly, clearly unused to comments on his clothes, much less compliments. "Thanks. I'd better be off. You sure you'll be all right?"

"Honestly, I'll be fine. It'll be nice to chill for a couple of hours. What time should I expect you back?"

"Around three-thirty, maybe a bit later. I've got a red box to do, which should take me a couple of hours tops."

"No rest for the wicked."

"Absolutely not. But I'm sure I'll get my reward in heaven."

"I might arrange for one sooner than that," I replied.

"I'll look forward to that. Must go."

I got up to see him out. He gave me a farewell hug, ending it with a kiss. It felt wonderfully affectionate and domestic. I returned to the kitchen feeling a warm glow, and tackled the washing up.

I sat on an easy chair in Dan's sitting room, reading an old detective novel I'd found on his bookshelf. Classical music from an internet radio station played in the background. I felt relaxed and stretched luxuriantly.

It was shortly after two-thirty in the afternoon, and Dan was still at his local party's autumn fair. I suspected he was doing a lot of smiling – and flattering old ladies.

I couldn't have done it. Whatever interest I'd had in politics when I was younger had not stayed with me into adulthood: apart from anything else, I was put off by the realisation of what you had to do in order to succeed. Being nice to people all the time, even when you couldn't stand the sight of them, was beyond my capabilities. And you had to be incredibly thick-skinned, which I most certainly was not.

Dan, on the other hand, was a natural. He had a talent for switching into automatic mode, enabling him to charm the birds off the trees whilst thinking about something else entirely. As with most charismatic figures, he also had a knack of focusing on people during a conversation, making them feel that they were the only person in the world he wanted to talk to.

Judging by this morning's performance, being charming wasn't the only thing at which he was a natural. Waking up with him and making love had been an awesome way to start the day. Thrusting together without penetration had never been one of my favourite things, but with Dan it had been so much more special than with any of my previous partners. I'd loved watching him come – eyes wide open, eyebrows curved upwards and his forehead creased in wonder.

I started to get aroused at the memory, shifting in my seat as I tried to calm down. I resumed my reading but the book could not hold my attention. Instead I put my head back and thought nice thoughts about my sexy host.

I'd got used to the idea that the deep affection I'd felt for him all those years ago had been reawakened when we met at again, and the more time I spent with him, the deeper my feelings were growing.

Beneath that charming but slightly cold exterior, there was a warm, kind and considerate human being. I admired his strength, his single-mindedness in achieving his ambitions. But the price for that was loneliness. He was not a clubbable man at the best of times, and he admitted that he'd had been wary of friendship for fear of revealing his sexual orientation.

Having been starved of close affection for most of his life, he now seemed to be blossoming under my watch. The sudden discovery of this new side to his own character must have seemed pretty scary. If I was reading him right, he was revelling in this new experience, but it did make him vulnerable – having found such affection, he would always crave it. To lose it would be doubly distressing.

It struck me that I needed to remember this, to be patient and respect the fact that all this was so new to him. Not that I was a huge expert on the subject of running a relationship. There might very well be times when both us would be all at sea. And there was always a risk that we could fail.

I quickly dismissed this last thought, though. *Of course* it was going to work out. No question of it.

The music changed at that point and I recognised the *Adagietto* from Mahler's fifth: wonderful. I closed my eyes to listen. I thought again of Dan in my arms and sighed at the memory as I slipped into a light doze.

The light doze must have deepened, because the next thing I knew a car door was slamming outside heralding Dan's return. I looked at my watch: I'd slept for over an hour, so that it was now three thirty-five. He was bang on time.

Governing Passions

Chapter Thirty

Dan

I felt good on the drive back to the cottage. The autumn fair had been a happy occasion; everybody's mood seemed to have been lifted by the brilliant October sunshine, and the hall was full of chatter and laughter as I made my way round the stalls.

I switched into automatic charm mode on these occasions, but most of the time also genuinely enjoyed interacting with members of the association. With the possible exception of Anthony Stewart and a few of his cronies, they were a genuinely nice bunch of people, and had an enviable capacity to take pleasure from small, everyday things.

I gave a standard morale-boosting speech at the opening, trotting out the usual loyal tributes to the PM and brickbats to the Opposition; it went down well, as they always did on these occasions. I declared the fair open with the usual exhortation to spend generously in a good cause, and set off on a tour of the stalls accompanied by a little flock of followers, including Helena, a scowling Anthony Stewart

– who seemed to relish the title of Association Chairman far more than the duties that went with it – and the chair of the organising committee, a fluttery and fawning woman called Joan, who was dressed in bright yellow. "Not her colour, dear," I heard one stallholder say, rather cattily but with a certain cruel accuracy.

I bought two pots of home-made jam and a stuffed toy, a red squirrel with a fluffy tail. It was daft, I knew, but it had an expression on its face that reminded me of Luke. I explained to the lady who'd made it that it was for a friend's child. It was a casual fib, but better than admitting I'd bought it because it reminded me of my boyfriend.

I smiled again as I rounded the bend and the sea came into sight. The idea of having a boyfriend was a new and slightly frightening one. Being able to introduce him as such to people down here seemed an attractive idea. I was sure that most of this afternoon's participants would have been welcoming and friendly, not worried at all by my sexuality.

That reminded me of a stolen conversation with Helena during the afternoon, during which she'd told me that she'd been right: there were no rumours circulating about my sexuality and no discontent amongst the F&GP members – other than Anthony and his two Brexit cronies.

The conversation had improved my mood even further and the news seemed to bode well for my coming-out plans. I'd made a start with Helena yesterday afternoon; it was time to tell the rest of the world too. But that process would have to start with my father – a task which I dreaded. I wasn't going to think about that now. I had a lover to go home to.

I was brought up short by that thought. Words like *boyfriend* and *lover* were unfamiliar, alien. At the same time, I revelled in them. I, Dan Forrester, had a lover: not somebody who was with me because I paid them, but a person who was with me because he wanted to be – and for whom I felt affection. No: strong affection. Oh hell, I might as well admit it – somebody I was coming to love.

This was both unexpected and scary. It had never occurred to me that I might meet somebody and want to build a life with him. My dreams had not been of love, but of the Commons chamber and ministerial office.

It was the loss of self-sufficiency that was scaring me – the defensive shield that I had spent most of my life perfecting, but which was now crumbling. Once I'd known the feelings of comfort and joy that Luke was bringing into my life, it would never be the same again.

There was no element of personal choice here; I'd been lost from the moment I saw Luke again in the department's conference room. I was experiencing a lightness of being that I had never known before. The world seemed a happier, brighter place, a feeling that was reinforced when I arrived home to be greeted by a sleepy Luke. I wanted this, and I wanted it for ever.

We had a cup of tea whilst I told him about the events of the afternoon, and particularly the intelligence that Helena had passed on. I also introduced him to our small red squirrel, which he immediately named Duke because it combined letters from both our names. He thought it was adorable, though was he most definitely not flattered when I explained that I'd bought it because its expression reminded me of Luke. He frowned slightly and pursed his lips.

"There! That's exactly the expression I meant," I laughed. "You frown and purse your lips when you're upset about something or when you're concentrating hard."

Luke looked in the mirror and held Duke up next to his face. He frowned and pursed his lips as if about to kiss somebody. His expression cleared and he began to laugh. "Okay, okay, I can see a slight resemblance. And I am touched that you should be thinking of me when 'undertaking your constituency duties'." His voice took on a prim tone, which set me laughing too.

"Can't stop thinking about you most of the time at the moment."

"Me too. Should know better at our age."

"Love is love at any age," I responded. I brought myself up short: had I just used the "l-word"? Wasn't that far too soon?

Luke played it with a straight bat, responding with a simple, "True."

"And talking about behaviour, I'd better be a good Under-Secretary and do my box."

"Of course. Why don't I make us some dinner while you do your duty to Her Majesty?"

"Are you sure?"

"Of course. No problem."

"I feel a bit rotten asking you down for the weekend then making you cook."

"It's fine. I've had a lovely day lazing about. The least I

can do is cook some dinner while you work. Besides, I've got Duke to help me."

"Okay. There are some chicken breasts in the freezer. I thought we'd defrost those and roast them with some veggies, if that appeals."

"Sounds perfect. Leave it to Luke and Duke. Now shoo – the quicker you shift that box, the more time I get to spend with you."

Fortunately, the contents of the box were not too demanding and I finished the work in double-quick time. I was back downstairs making a gin and tonic within ninety minutes. Dinner was in the oven.

Luke looked slightly apprehensive. "While you're still in work mode, I wanted to ask you whether you'd seen this week's *London Figaro.*"

"No. Should I have?"

"There's a short bit in it about Griffin House – it doesn't mention the department specifically, but hints at collusion between Pearson Frazer and another consultancy over grant awards. Steve picked up on it on Friday morning – he was splitting blood."

"Crikey, Luke. I bet he was."

"An acquaintance of his works on the magazine. The story seems to have come from Sean Andrews."

"Fuck. I don't know what that guy is up to, but he's proving to be even more of a pain in the arse than I thought he would be."

"You've come across him before?"

"He started as an intern for a backbench colleague who had the office next door to me. That was a few years ago, before I went into the Whips Office. He was trouble in those days and obviously still is: totally right wing and a passionate Brexiteer. I think he was foisted on George as a SPAD by some of his ERG pals to cause trouble. If I'm right, he's certainly succeeding."

Luke frowned. "Remind me. ERG?"

"European Research Group – you know, the extreme Brexiteers – a party within a party, to all intents and purposes."

"Why would the ERG want to cause trouble?"

"Several reasons. Number one, to destabilise the government if it doesn't do as they want. Also, they want to damage the careers of people like me, the Remainers. They want us out of the government and, I suspect, the party too. I think they're trying to distract people so that the Brexit negotiations get held up, which boosts the chances of leaving without a deal because that's what they want."

"Bloody hell, Dan. That's awful."

"It's called modern politics, Luke. And I hate it. Everything's about the next tweet or grabbing a headline on the six o'clock news. Nobody stops to think any more. Tony Blair's government might not have 'done God'. This one doesn't do policy."

"We always knew politics could be a dirty game, even in our student union days. But this is crazy."

"I know – and one day it's all going to blow up in our faces. Anyway, let's change the subject. I get too agitated thinking about it."

"That's fine. I wanted to make sure you knew about *Figaro*. Steve talked to Jeremy about it on Friday afternoon, so they'll handle it."

"Great."

Luke sipped his drink and looked at me over the rim of his glass. "What did you want to talk about?"

"Us," I replied.

"Oh?"

"We've both said things in the last couple of days that suggest we're developing stronger feelings for each other. I thought we should explore what that means – what the end game might be."

"I'm happy to do that," he responded, a little warily, I thought.

I hastened to reassure him. "No regrets, Luke. I'm not pulling back. But I do feel that we ought to plan a bit. Over the last forty-eight hours, you've had a sample of what my life's like these days. I want to make room in it for you, if you want that – but it'll take some working out. I don't want you to feel upset or neglected. Above all, I don't want you to get hurt again because of me."

"I understand all that, Dan. And thank you. Yes, I definitely want to be part of your life. I know it's going to be difficult, and the media could be intrusive, but I'm confident I can handle it."

I managed to disguise my sigh of relief as a deep breath. "I hoped you'd say that." I sipped my drink and resumed. "I've been thinking about how it could work and looking at my diary for the next few weeks. If we try for a conventional date at a sensible time in the evenings, we wouldn't see each other for three weeks. Plus there's the risk of it all going wrong like it almost did on Thursday."

"Crikey."

"Yes, it's bloody impossible sometimes. I was thinking

that I should give you a key to the flat. That way you could come and go as you please, and we could spend some weekday nights together. It was so magical on Thursday night, coming into the flat and finding you there. I loved being welcomed home."

Luke's eyes widened. He clearly hadn't been expecting that. He broke into a big smile. "That sounds a great idea. Are you sure?"

"As sure as I've ever been about anything. While I'm doing this crazy job in these crazy times, it's the only way I can see us getting to know each other properly."

"Like we already know each other improperly?"

"Maybe," I replied through my laughter. "Though probably not improperly enough."

"True. Anyway, you can count me in."

"At weekends, I thought we'd come down here together as often as we could."

"Fabulous. And if you're stuck in London but want a change, you could come over to mine."

"Sounds perfect. I'll get a key for the flat organised on Monday."

Luke opened his mouth to speak again but was interrupted by the timer on the cooker. He moved towards the oven. "One thing, though: it seems to me that this will only work if we're both fully out."

"Absolutely. It's going to be difficult enough without skulking around trying to keep secrets."

As it turned out, Luke was a much better cook than I could

ever have hoped to be. He produced a stunning meal, which we washed down with a bottle of New Zealand pinot noir.

"That was fantastic, Luke. Thanks."

"Glad you enjoyed it. I love cooking but it's often a bit of a chore for one so I don't bother, especially during the week. It's great to have somebody to cook for."

"You can cook for me anytime. I'm pretty hopeless. I have a small repertoire of dishes I can manage, but that's it. But I've never had anybody to cook for before."

We made some coffee and returned to the sitting room. Luke joined me on the sofa. "Let's start the 'getting to know you' process. Favourite film?" His eyes were twinkling. "Still *Some Like it Hot*?"

"You remembered! I'm seriously impressed." I thought for a moment. "Yes, I think it's still my all-time favourite. Though *When Harry Met Sally* runs close."

"Oho, a romcom man. That's new. So, *You've Got Mail* or *Sleepless in Seattle*?"

"Both," I replied firmly. "I love *Sleepless* but *You've Got Mail* has a slightly more plausible plot."

Luke nodded. "Yeah, I can see that. You've not disqualified yourself so far."

"What about you? I seem to remember that you were gone on old musicals."

"Absolutely. Still am. If I had to name one, I suppose it would be *Holiday Inn*."

I frowned. "Wasn't Fred Astaire in that?"

"Yeah, Fred Astaire and Bing Crosby. Irving Berlin did the music – it's the film that first featured 'White Christmas'."

"I remember now – I haven't seen that in years, probably since you made me watch it at college. But weren't you also into *High Society* in a big way?

"Oh, definitely. It's brilliant – great story, fantastic songs and a cast to die for: Crosby and Sinatra, Grace Kelly, Louis Armstrong – not to mention the amazing Celeste Holm. What's not to like?"

I loved his enthusiasm for these old films, which had obviously lasted well beyond his student days. "Dan, do you ever watch anything made after 1970?"

"Oh, sure. I loved *Moulin Rouge* and *LaLa Land.*"

"I've not seen that, though I heard all the fuss about it at the time. Is it as good as everybody says?"

"Absolutely – the opening sequence is amazing, the score fantastic, and I loved the fact that they had the courage not to give it a storybook ending. I cried buckets."

He laughed but I could see his eyes filling with tears as he talked about it. It was adorable.

"Right. So we've both burnished our gay credentials with old Hollywood films and musicals. What about colours?"

"Hmm. That's a difficult one. It would have to be Lincoln green, I think."

"Ho-ho! So specific. Robin Hood's colour. All about men in tights."

"Of course. All that dashing about in Sherwood Forest firing bows and arrows. How butch."

"So a sort of leaf green, is it?"

"A bit darker, I think. It's a rich shade – that's why I like it. What about you?"

"As a loyal Tory MP, I suppose I ought to say blue. But like you, I'm keen on rich colours, so I'd go for purple."

"Nice. Very regal."

"If you make a joke about queens liking it, I shall hit you."

"Perish the thought, ma'am," he said with a real glint in his eye. Then he burst out laughing. It was a silly joke – but Luke's laughter was strong, full-throated and infectious. I couldn't help but join in.

As we both recovered, I realised how long it was since I'd had somebody to share silly jokes with. It gave me a feeling of deep contentment.

Governing Passions

Chapter Thirty-One

Luke

We swapped favourite books, theatre and music that night. At some point we moved into each other's arms, and the conversation slowed, was punctuated by small kisses on lips, temples, ears and even the ends of noses. I had discovered that the area of Dan's neck immediately below his ears was extremely sensitive and started to take full advantage of the knowledge. Eventually the conversation petered out altogether and the kissing took over.

After a few minutes, Dan whispered, "Time for bed." I nodded enthusiastically, and we made our way upstairs. It had been a great evening – the best Saturday night ever.

Our union that night was slow and gentle – and, for me at least, an opportunity to express my growing feelings for him. As we lay there and explored each other's bodies with hands, lips and tongues, it became clear that we both wanted to take our love-making to the next level. Thus it was that I felt Dan inside me for the first time. It was several years since I'd done this, and it had been a rare occurrence. The fact that I very much wanted it to happen added yet another dimension to our relationship. As he entered me, as gently and carefully as he could, I once again felt the rightness of what we were doing. After my body had adjusted to his presence and he started to move, I felt sure that we belonged together and that this physical union was the first of many in a lifelong partnership. It was a magical feeling. We reached our climaxes virtually simultaneously, our eyes locked together. Dan's forehead was creased in wonder as he came, shouting my name.

Sated, we cleaned ourselves up and fell asleep. In a matter of moments, it seemed, I awoke to see that daylight streaming through the window. The birds were singing in Dan's small garden. It was Sunday morning.

Dan had moved out of my arms at some point during the night but was still sufficiently close that I could fell his body heat. I lifted myself onto one elbow and looked down, watching him sleep. In repose, the creases on his forehead were smoothed out and his questioning eyebrows were at rest. His lips were curled upwards a little in a slight smile.

Tears pricked the back of my eyes. "God, I love you so much," I whispered, mainly to myself. In a flash, Dan had turned over to face me, eyes wide. "And I you, my love. More than I can say."

We embraced and sealed our declarations with a long kiss. I rested my chin on his shoulder, looking across toward the window. The tears returned and leaked out. Despite trying to hide it, a sob escaped.

Dan pulled his head back to look at me. "Hey. What is it, Luke?"

I sniffed and laughed. "Nothing. I feel so happy with you. In your life and in your arms. It feels as if this is what

I've been waiting for all my life."

"I know what you mean. Lying here now with you, it's as if I've come home for the first time since I was a small boy. I never want it to end."

There was nothing else to say, so we simply lay there, wrapped in the tightest of hugs.

Eventually, Dan spoke. "I've just noticed what time it is – we need to be moving if you're to get some breakfast before you set off to Harchester."

I groaned. "Don't remind me, please."

"Still dreading it?"

"A little, but the real reason is that I don't want to leave you, to break this magical spell."

"I know what you mean," Dan sighed. He quickly brightened though. "Hey, I've got an idea. I've got to drive back this afternoon and I can be home by seven – what time can you get away from your parents?"

"I usually leave after Evensong – say half five."

"Come straight to me. We can have another evening together and you can stay over, if you like."

I nodded vigorously. "Oh, I'd like. Very definitely."

"Great. That's a plan. You can tell me how things went and give me lessons in how to come out to your parents."

"I'd forgotten about that! When are you going to do it?"

"Whenever I can persuade Jeremy to let me off to go up to Derbyshire."

"Can you fit it in before next Friday week?"

"I shall have to, Luke. I can't say anything down here without telling my parents first."

"I understand. For them to find out from the media would be awful."

"Indeed. Anyway, that's a discussion for tomorrow. I'll send Jeremy an e-mail when you've gone and he and I can talk about it first thing in the morning. Now hop in the shower while I rustle up some breakfast."

I got away from Dan's cottage around ten-thirty. Unless there was a problem en route, I'd be at the Deanery by twelve and that would hopefully give me time for a word with my parents before any lunch guests arrived. Guests for my mother's Sunday lunch parties were usually summoned for a quarter to one.

I drew into the drive at exactly eleven forty-five. The ride up from the coast had been a delight as the low autumn sun bathed the countryside in a golden light. The colours of the leaves were deep and rich, as if I were moving through a fifties' Technicolor film. I played Elgar, Holst and Vaughan Williams and sang along, reflecting on my joy at the events since Thursday evening.

It had been an extraordinary few days – alternately gentle and passionate, friendly and loving. If I'd ever visualised what a lasting relationship would be like, this was it. It wouldn't always be like this: the realities of two busy careers were bound to intrude. But I was sure we could work everything out.

The Deanery looked beautiful in the sunshine; I understood why my mother loved the house so much. Of the many houses she had lived in during her marriage, this was by far her favourite and I could see why. There was something about the sense of proportion that early eighteenth-century builders had – but houses like this one, built in Queen Anne's reign, also had a flamboyance that later Georgian designs lacked.

I parked the car, reached for my jacket and tie, and entered the house. My mother greeted me effusively: she'd returned from morning service in the cathedral, but dad was still there. She explained that the only guests for lunch would be my godparents, Pru and George. I breathed a sigh of relief; at least Auntie P would be on my side if all this went wrong.

"You're looking a bit tired, Luke. Is everything okay?"

"Absolutely fine, Mum. I've been down on the Dorset coast for a couple of days, staying with a friend."

"Oh, lovely! Anybody I know?"

"You met him once a long time ago when we were at university together. Dan Forrester."

Her eyebrows shot up. "The Minister? Gosh, Luke, how exciting."

I was amused by her enthusiasm – her eyes positively glittered with the possibility of social advantage. "Yes, we met again recently through work. He's the Minister in charge of a big contract that our firm runs."

"I didn't know you moved in such exalted company, darling."

She had never understood my career. Along with many of her generation, she still associated environmentalism with sandal-wearing hippies and tree-hugging anti-road protestors. True, there was still some of that on the fringes, but firms like ours were solidly professional in our approach, and used the latest technology and analytical techniques to help our clients become "clean and green".

I had tried to get that across to her but the subject bored her, so she failed to take it in.

"There you are, you see, I do have my uses after all."

She laughed somewhat uneasily, suggesting that my little barb had hit home. At that point, my father entered the room. "Luke's been staying in exalted company, Richard."

"Oh?" He greeted me with a brief hug.

"Yes, a Minister of the Crown, no less."

My father gave me a questioning glance.

"Dan Forrester," I explained. "He was a friend from university – we met up again recently. He invited me down to his cottage in Dorset for the weekend."

"And did you have a good time?"

"Great, thanks. It's a lovely part of the world. I didn't know it before." I paused; this seemed a good opening, so I took a deep breath. "Actually, about that. The thing is that ... since we met up again, Dan and I have become ... very close." My head was spinning as I tried to get the words out. "As I think you may have suspected, the point is that I'm ... er ... gay. And um ... Dan and I are ... together."

There was silence in the room. Predictably, it was my mother who spoke first. As I'd stumbled through the sentence, her expression had changed from one of benign interest to faint disgust, as if she had a nasty smell under her nose.

"Oh, Luke, how could you?" It was more as if I had committed some social solecism than revealed an important aspect of myself. There was a pause. "Oh my God, I'll never live this down." It was if I'd turned gay deliberately to thwart her social aspirations.

I closed my eyes, braced for a ratcheting up of the tension, but my father forestalled her. "Muriel, calm down. This is our son's life, not a tea party that's gone wrong." He turned to me. "Thanks, Luke, for telling us..."

He was interrupted by my mother. "I might have known that I couldn't look to you for support, Richard. My son announces that he's ruining his life and you tell me to calm down!"

"Mum, I'm not ruining my life. God or fate or whatever has decreed that I like men rather than women. It's not something I chose, it just *is*. That's all. This isn't the 1950s: I'm not going to get castrated or locked up."

"Yes, but ... but it's not what people like us do."

I was getting angrier. "Oh, really, Mother? And what do people like us do? Contract loveless marriages to disguise our true selves? Live a life of constant lies and deceit so as to satisfy some cultural norm?"

"That's not what I meant and you know it," she snapped back. Her eyes filled with tears. "It's not what I wanted for you, Luke. That's all. I thought you'd meet a nice girl, have a family and live a nice life."

"These days I might have a husband and a family and a nice life," I retorted. "Dan and I haven't got as far as talking about children yet, but it's certainly a possibility."

My father intervened. "Muriel, Luke is still your – our – son. Surely you recognise that? He didn't choose this, it's what he is. Gregory Allen made me understand that. This is about us giving him our love and support, not judgement."

"Thanks, Dad. I know what a big shift that has been for you."

"Yes, it has, my boy. But it had to be done. Greg's

struggles and revelations made me see that."

"What finally convinced you?"

"As I said the other week, his strongest point was always this business of the lack of choice. Once you accept that homosexuality is a state of being and not a state of mind, you have to accept that gay people are also part of God's purpose."

"I understand that. But what about mortal sin?"

"If you continue to believe, as sadly many people do, that homosexuality is the result of conscious choice, then the fact that it is condemned in the Bible provides the sin. If you're told something is wrong but still do it, that counts as defiance of God's word. Once you accept that there is no choice in the matter, as all my research shows me, I would argue that the question of sin falls away."

"How so?"

"When all these rules were drawn up two thousand and more years ago, they applied to tribes of nomads wandering the deserts of Israel and Palestine. Of course they were worried about people who didn't procreate – child mortality rates were high, you needed younger people to look after you in old age."

"Yes, I see that – having a bunch of guys into each other would reduce the population and make survival more difficult. In the same way as eating pork or shellfish was dangerous in the heat of the desert."

"Indeed. But life has changed a bit in the interim. I suppose that I've concluded that the rules need to be re-written every now and again."

My mother looked genuinely shocked at that. "But it's the word of God."

I shook my head. "No, Mum, it was the word of God two or three thousand years ago. Has anybody asked Him what He thinks lately?"

She looked at me blankly. Clearly the thought had never occurred to her.

"I know it's difficult for you to accept, but you have to understand that my being gay is not a choice I've made. Do you think I would willingly have put myself through all the heartbreak and fear I suffered when I was younger if there'd been a way out? God made me this way, Mum, and so, as Dad says, I simply can't accept that expressing my sexuality is in any way a sin."

She looked at us both doubtfully but didn't argue. We knew from experience that this meant we'd probably won the argument. "I'm sorry, but I think it's a shame. And I bet that bloody Alice Reeves makes hay out of it for weeks. Now I'd better go and see to the lunch if we're to eat this side of Christmas."

My father winked at me. Alice Reeves was the wife of the Archdeacon at the Cathedral and my mother's sworn enemy – though nobody could remember the precise cause. The ladies of the Chapter seemed to regard her as the arbiter of taste in the Cathedral Close community and the wider diocese. This enraged my mother, who felt that role should properly fall to her. Since Alice had lived here for many years, whereas Mum and Dad were comparative newcomers, the woman retained her leadership role, and a sort of armed truce existed between them. From experience, though, my father and I knew that invoking Alice's name meant that my mother didn't have anything else to grumble about, which was tantamount to acceptance.

"I'm sorry if she upset you," my father said as she flounced out of the room.

"Don't worry. It wasn't as bad as I'd expected. I knew she'd throw a bit of a wobbly." I grinned at him. "It's what she does."

"She loves you very much and she's extremely proud of you, you know, in her own way. She'll be worried that it is all somehow her fault."

"Her fault? Why on earth would she think that?"

"Because I suspect it's what every parent of a gay son or daughter worries about. Always wondering whether there was something they did or didn't do, or could have done differently."

"That had never occurred to me."

"The other thing is that she'll worry that people will think less of you."

I snorted. "That's certainly a fear I'm familiar with."

"I can imagine," he replied with a sigh. "Especially me?"

"Honestly? Yes. I've kept quiet all this time because I was convinced that you'd hate it – throw me out, even."

He looked horrified. "Never that, Luke. I certainly wouldn't have approved, and I'd have prayed for you, for your immortal soul, because I'd have thought it in jeopardy. But throw you out? Never."

"Anyway, it doesn't arise now. Thanks for your support."

"I suppose you should thank Gregory Allen," he responded.

"What's happened to him? Do you know?"

"Yes, he's back at his old college in Oxford, living with a partner and working on a PhD. We've become friends.

Chapter Thirty-One

He's very happy, I think."

We were interrupted by the doorbell announcing our guests. We heard my mother saying "I'll go" from the kitchen.

"By the way, Aunty P knows about me. She guessed."

My father stood up to go and greet the visitors. His eyes twinkled with amusement. "Hmm. Very perceptive, our Pru."

I sat for a moment or two, letting out a huge sigh of relief. It had all gone reasonably well. My mother had been as difficult as I had imagined, my father less so. I was glad it was over. I didn't expect everything to be all sweetness and light – we were too different for that – but at least I wouldn't fear the disappointment about the lack of a wife and children that I had dreaded every time I visited. I could relax in future without the small lies and omissions that had been necessary to maintain my disguise. One comparatively short conversation had eliminated the fear and uneasiness that had dominated our relationship since my teenage years.

It was a relief, and a lightness spread through me. When added to the good mood I was already in after my weekend with Dan, it put me in ebullient form.

Governing Passions

Chapter Thirty-Two

Dan

The cottage seemed empty after I'd waved Luke off. I had about three hours before I needed to be on the move if I was to get back to London ahead of the congestion from returning day trippers and weekenders.

At least this week, I had something to look forward to on my journey home. Luke's visit tonight would round the weekend off nicely. I hoped that I would avoid that slightly uneasy, "what will the week bring?" feeling that so often dominated my Sunday evenings.

Today I was oppressed by the peace and quiet that I normally craved at the cottage. The walls seemed to press in on me, so I decided to go for a walk and set off towards the shore. The wind had sprung up and, when I reached the cliffs and looked out over the Channel, the line of an approaching front was clearly visible amongst the clouds. The sea was grey, though flecked with cream and off-white as the gusty breeze whipped the surface of the water.

I shivered slightly; somehow this felt very much like the onset of winter. It would be November next week, and the golden autumn would be swallowed by storms and fog. The thought disturbed my mood for a moment, but then I remembered that winter had its consolations, especially the run-up to the Christmas and New Year holiday.

I followed the path down from the cliffs, reached the cove at the bottom of the hill and turned onto the beach. The tide was ebbing, making me safe from any Canute-like encroachments. I stood and breathed deeply, watching the turbulent waters and listening to the sound of the waves hitting the beach followed by the roar as the water retreated over the pebbles.

It was as if somebody had thrown a switch and turned off my brain. I closed my eyes and simply existed, sucking in deep lungfuls of the air. It was a moment of true peace that I had rarely, if ever, experienced. I could feel the wind tugging at my hair and moisture on my cheek as the spray from a particularly large wave enveloped me. I retreated quickly, laughing to myself, and resumed my vigil from a safer spot.

Looking ahead, there was a great deal to do. In addition to the day-to-day routine, which was enough in itself, I had to put all the pieces in place for coming out and work with Jeremy on trying to save the Griffin House project. We had crucial meeting about that during the week, ahead of a final decision as to what should go into the department's budget submission to the Treasury. Plus I had to cope with all the Brexit nonsense, including the machinations of Sean Andrews and his paymasters. At least life would not be dull, I reflected with a smile. It was easy to understand why the phrase "may you live in interesting times" might be considered a curse in China.

A few weeks earlier I would have been in danger of being overwhelmed by it all, but having Luke in my life made everything less difficult. I had begun to see these things as challenges to be overcome, not as a threat to my future. He gave me a more balanced sense of proportion – and something outside politics and work that made life worth living.

I felt happy as I turned for home. Having something or somebody to live for was certainly novel and would require some pretty big changes in my approach and way of thinking. Needing to consider somebody else, to accommodate their needs and wants, to give and receive affection all the time – these were all aspects of life that were second nature to most people but completely alien to me. It was slightly terrifying, but I was hugely grateful for the opportunity to do it. I just hoped that I wouldn't fuck it up completely.

I returned to the cottage with a clear head and a renewed sense of purpose, something I'd been lacking for a good few months. As I zipped up my bag, my phone rang. It was somebody from home.

"Hello, Dan Forrester."

"Dan, darling, it's Mum. How are you, dear?" I frowned. To get a call at this time of day was unusual; they were usually both having a nap now.

"I'm fine, Mum. How are you? Is everything okay?"

"Yes, yes, we're both fine. But I wanted a quick word while your father's asleep. We're coming up to town this week – he's determined to vote on the third reading on some Bill or other about Brexit on Wednesday. I tried to persuade him not to because travelling makes him so tired these days, but he's adamant."

My father had been made a life peer when he'd retired from the Commons in 2010, but his appearances in the House of Lords had grown more infrequent in recent months as he'd started to feel his age. A long-standing and convinced Europhile since the late fifties, he had been appalled by recent events and clearly wanted to make his mark. I could hardly blame him for that.

"I can well understand, though. It's pretty awful in Parliament at the moment, and it would be great if he made a stand."

"Oh, he will. But I know he'd like to see you, darling. I know it's short notice, and you don't get on terribly well sometimes, but he is mellowing and often talks about you. Is there any chance you could meet us for dinner on Wednesday night?"

I groaned inwardly. Two hours of disapproval and being made to feel inadequate were not what I needed at the moment. On the other hand, if I used the opportunity to get my announcement out of the way, it would save a trip home which would be difficult to fit in anyway.

"Hang on a sec, Mum. Let's check my diary." I quickly scrolled though the week's engagements. "That should be all right, provided we stay inside the precincts. We're on warning for a series of votes late evening, so if the division bell goes off, I'll have to disappear. But otherwise it should be fine."

"That would be lovely, darling. I'll book the Peers Dining Room for us – about seven?"

"Yes, I should be clear by then. If not, I'll have to get my private secretary to let me out early."

She laughed, knowing from her own experience that private secretaries could be very demanding in ensuring their Ministers did their jobs properly. We chatted until I heard my father's voice in the background and ended the call.

I didn't have time to reflect on the conversation; I need to set off if I was going to beat the evening rush back into London. I finished zipping my bag, locked up the cottage and got in the car. The drive back was incident-free and the traffic kept moving reasonably freely. It left me free to contemplate the conversation with my mother and Wednesday night's dinner. That was the first time she had ever acknowledged that my dad and I did not get on.

It was difficult to pinpoint a time or an occasion when things had gone seriously wrong. I'd told Jeremy the story of my choosing to play soccer instead of rugby at school, and the paternal disapproval I'd incurred – but it wasn't about that. I'd been truthful when I said that I'd learned a lesson: namely to keep quiet and conform for the sake of a peaceful life. That had been the start of it, I supposed.

Though quietly spoken and superficially charming, my father liked to get his own way and was a bit of a bully. As with most bullies, the more you gave way and bent to his will, the less he thought of you. I realised now that he might have held me in higher esteem if I had fought back more, particularly as a teenager. As it was, he tended to be dismissive of me, to brush aside my – admittedly moderate – academic achievements. Despite my love of soccer, I was more enthusiastic than skilled, and he made no secret of his disappointment at my lack of interest in other sports.

As a young teenager, I had realised that I liked boys

and somehow was convinced, without asking, that he would disapprove. As a sixteen-year-old, I had looked up the debates on the 1967 Act which had decriminalised homosexuality and discovered that he had voted against the Bill during its passage through the Commons, though admittedly without speaking against it. I think that had been the moment when my resentment against him had properly taken root. I never tackled him about it because doing so would have risked revealing too much. The question lay there between us, festering away for twenty years.

Later we had argued over Tony Blair's decision to invade Iraq, me naively in favour, him defying the stereotype and voting against. Things were said that day that couldn't be unsaid, since when our fairly infrequent encounters had been icily polite, our conversations limited to formal enquiries about health and well-being. It was a shame, and I did sometimes wonder whether, like me, he occasionally regretted our distance. My mother's words this afternoon had been the first sign of this.

My decision to come out to them and finally reveal the person I had grown into would be a make-or-break moment. If he was accepting, we might rebuild some sort of a relationship. If not, our ways would probably part irrevocably. It was a daunting prospect – and it was far from ideal that it was now going to take place in a restaurant at the House of Lords. At least that meant that we couldn't engage in a shouting match; surely that was a good thing.

Chapter Thirty-Three

Luke

My mother had recovered her composure by the time she ushered Aunty P and Bishop George into the drawing room. She was chattering away to Pru, who sought my eyes and raised one eyebrow in a silent question. I nodded and she winked. As she embraced me, she whispered in my ear, "All right?"

"Yes, thanks. Fine."

"Good."

She turned to greet my father whilst I shook hands with the bishop. Judging by the wink he gave me, he had been clued in as to what was afoot.

The atmosphere was relaxed and there was an air of conviviality that I had not experienced in my parents' company for many a long year. Conversation over lunch was conventional, but during dessert it was enlivened by some diocesan gossip. One of the local vicars and a GP had been having an affair, prompting the vicar to leave her husband and move in with her lover. The situation was made more complicated by the fact that the doctor's wife was one of the church wardens in the parish. The situation had scandalised the local parochial church council, which was demanding the vicar's resignation. Users of social media in the village were having a field day, and the local newspapers and radio stations had now got involved following the exchange of some vituperative and possibly libellous posts.

It struck me as a classic 'aga-saga' story of middle-class infidelity. I was tempted to remark that, if violence had been involved, it might even have made a good *Midsomer Murders* plot. But I held my counsel, aware that this situation was difficult for my father and the bishop. Judging by George's expression, he felt deeply uncomfortable about the whole thing.

His wife was much more sanguine. "I keep telling him that he mustn't lose any sleep over it, that it will sort itself out. But he doesn't take any notice and continues to worry away at it like a terrier," Pru said to my mother.

"That's all very well, my dear," replied her husband. "But I have a member of the clergy who has broken the seventh commandment and some parishioners therefore feel that she's unfit to give them communion. If I ignore them, I'm afraid that the PCC will resign *en masse.* The congregation is so small that there's nobody who could replace them, so we'd cease to have a functioning parish."

"I understand that, but I still think the best idea is to get everybody to calm down and look at things rationally. They need to stop throwing things at each other, to come out from behind the barricades and talk. If you go in there heavy-handedly and try to knock heads together next week, you'll simply antagonise everybody."

My father joined in. "Pru has a point, George."

George looked glum, but after a moment his face relaxed into a rueful smile. "I know, and when hasn't she?"

Pru polished her nails on the lapel of her jacket. She winked at me.

My father laughed. "I certainly can't remember a time, George. I think I'd plead a full diary and agree to meet them in a month's time. With luck, that'll give them all time to calm down."

"I suppose you're both right," he said with a sigh. "Of course, if they really do calm down, I might not need to go at all."

Pru clapped her hands. "Oh, good, we can talk about something else now. I want to know all about Luke's Dan."

There was a silence for a moment. My father counted his shirt buttons and looked embarrassed. I started to blush. To my surprise, my mother joined in the ritual mortification. "Yes, come on Luke, what's he like?"

I realised that it would be easier to respond. "So, you already know from the telly that he's good looking, well-dressed and charming. He's also gentle, kind and considerate. His staff think the world of him and ... and...' I paused, hesitating for a moment over the words I had been about to say next.

Oh, what the hell.

"And I love him to bits."

My mother inhaled a little sharply. Aunty P, on the other hand, beamed at me. "Goodness me, Luke, that's quite a testimonial."

"It certainly is," added my father.

"When do we get to meet him?" chimed in my mother,

recovering her composure.

"We'll try to fix something up," I replied noncommittally. "As you can imagine, life's a bit hectic, what with Brexit and everything. Also, we have to be bit careful at the moment because he hasn't come out yet – he's preparing to do so later this month." I decided to omit mention of our plans for us to spend weeknights together.

"That must be hard," Pru said, her eyes full of concern.

I nodded. "Yes, I think being a politician is a pretty dreadful job these days. I don't actually know why they do it. I don't think Dan does either, sometimes."

Her husband interjected, "It's always been a fairly precarious life, though."

"I think it's got a lot nastier in recent years, especially since the referendum."

"Why?" asked Pru. "Surely it's not only the referendum?"

"Oh, no, I don't think so – that simply created a huge new reason for people to be discontented. Fundamentally, I think it's because it's too easy to be unkind at the push of a button. When you're interacting with somebody, even if it's on the phone, you're naturally more cautious, reticent – and most of us are taught to be polite. But if you're typing at a keyboard, it's too easy to forget the other human beings who are involved."

"You sound as if you speak from experience, Luke," George remarked. "Have you suffered from abuse?"

I shook my head. "Not directly, no. But I do see it at work, with online consultations. We also monitor comments on news reports about our work. If you say something that implies people might have take actions they don't like –

such as reducing car use, for instance – it doesn't take long for the comments to become nasty. If they disagree with you, they can't leave it there; they have to question your motives or accuse you of lying. The next step is to call you names."

"How depressing," remarked my mother.

"Precisely, Mum. And when you're somebody like Dan, who's on the receiving end of it all the time, it must get to you in the end. Fortunately, he doesn't look at it all that often – his staff run his social media sites for him."

George nodded. "It's the same for me," he said. "I realised that social media can be a very useful way of communicating, but I couldn't possibly do it myself. I'd never get anything else done."

The discussion had at least steered the conversation away from Dan and me, for which I was extremely grateful. Soon afterwards the party broke up to prepare for Evensong. I pleaded an evening engagement in London and left Harchester shortly before four o'clock.

My intention was to call home, change and grab some clothes for several days, so I could commute directly to and from Dan's flat when necessary. I drove into London feeling relaxed, confident and excited about the future: it was an unfamiliar feeling. If I had ever felt like this before, it was so long ago that I could not remember.

Governing Passions

Chapter Thirty-Four

Dan

"Good morning, Jeremy, and what a lovely morning it is."
It was eight o'clock on Monday morning, and here I was,
all bright-eyed and bushy-tailed.

"And good morning to you too. I trust you spent a pleasant
weekend, Minister?" Jeremy's eyes were twinkling with
humour as he adopted his best civil service voice and
formal manner.

I couldn't help but smile. "Yes, indeed, Jeremy, it was
most pleasant, thank you."

"Oh, *most* pleasant," he parroted. "That *is* good news."

I burst out laughing. "What's with all the formality?" I
asked.

"I thought it was more polite and restrained than
pinning you against the wall and demanding a blow-by-
blow account of how it went with Luke."

I raised an eyebrow "Blow by blow, eh? Not sure
I'm prepared to share that sort of detail, especially on a
Monday morning. You might be shocked."

"I promise you that I am unshockable," he replied with

a deadpan expression.

"I'll take your word for that," I responded.

He pouted. "Spoilsport. I was looking to you to brighten my otherwise humdrum morning with lurid details of your fun weekend. But if you must keep it all to yourself..."

"It went really well, Jeremy. We had a lovely time, honestly. And that's all I'm saying."

"Good," he replied firmly. "I'm delighted to hear that. And does it mean you managed to relax a bit?"

I nodded. "Yes, thanks. Though looking back on everything, I'm not exactly sure how. Decisions and dates galore for you to sort out."

He groaned. "Go on, tell me the worst."

"I need to be in the constituency for a meeting of the Association's executive on Friday week."

"Oh? That's new isn't it?"

"Yep. That's my day for coming out."

"Crikey, Dan! Is this what happens when I let you out on your own?"

I explained the reason, filling him in on the events of Friday afternoon – particularly the surgery and my delightful chat with my chairman. "Helena and I think that somebody here – Sean Andrews, probably – is feeding gossip to this man Stewart and his cronies. It's mainly about Brexit but I think calling me a liar over the gay thing would be another stick to beat me with. The only way to deal with that is to come out, and the sooner the better."

Jeremy frowned. For a second I thought he was going to try to talk me out of it. "Do you not approve?" I asked.

"Oh, of course I do. This must be your decision, Dan – and I'm the last person to say you shouldn't. But to be honest, it seems a shame that you should take such an important step as part of a political manoeuvre. I hope you don't feel that you've been forced into it, that it's something you actually want to do."

"I get that. But it's not the step itself that's political – I want and need to do it. The political bit is in the timing. Does that make sense?"

He nodded slowly, still deep in thought. There was silence in the room for a moment or two before he spoke again. "Sorry, I was trying to think through the implications." He ticked off a list on his fingers. "We'll have to warn Sir John and George that this is going to happen. As Secretary of State and your immediate boss, he's entitled to know, but the timing is delicate because you also need to let the Chief Whip and possibly the PM know as well – and it ought to come directly from you, as opposed to your boss. We'll have to work out a timetable for that."

I frowned. This was becoming complicated.

Jeremy resumed. "We don't want to do it too soon, because the earlier you tell them, the greater risk of leaks to the press – especially once Andrews gets a whiff of it. Once he finds out, he'll tell people in the constituency, so they'd find out ahead of the meeting and rob you of any tactical surprise."

"I see what you mean."

"We'll have to set something up with the press office here so that they can deal with any enquiries they get. The social media people will need to know too – and they'll need to liaise with Helena over what you're going to say."

I groaned. "Christ, Jeremy, I think I'll stay in the closet."

He grimaced. "I don't think that's what you want, is it?"

"No," I replied resignedly. "I've been telling lies for too long."

"Besides, it's only a matter of planning. That's what you've got me for."

"I'm sure this is all above and beyond, etcetera."

"I've told you before, my job is to keep you healthy, happy and functioning. Now, two more questions. One: what about your parents?"

"Wednesday."

He grabbed the diary. "I'm not sure we can get you up to Derbyshire for that."

"No, it's okay, they're coming down. Dad wants to vote on Wednesday night, so they're coming down specially – I'm summoned for dinner at the Lords."

"That's fortunate ... I think." He paused and frowned again. "Are you sure, Dan? Is coming out to your parents in a Parliamentary dining room entirely wise?"

"I know it's risky but it's heaven sent. You said yourself, the chances of me getting to see them at home before Friday week are virtually nil. Besides, being in public will at least prevent him from going off the deep end."

"True. I only wanted to make sure that you'd thought it through."

"I have. It's not ideal, but I think it'll be okay. Now, what's your second question?"

"Luke. How does he fit into all this?"

"For a start, he's in on the plan. He came out to his parents yesterday and that seems to have gone well. He recognises that he'll be identified as my partner fairly quickly, and he says he's all right with that."

Jeremy cocked an eyebrow at me.

"I know. It's a big risk. If he can't cope with being in the public eye, that could be the end of it – of us. It's the one aspect of all this that I'm most frightened of. I could cope with losing this job – even losing my seat – but coping with that shit show without Luke?" I shook my head. "I don't think so."

Jeremy smiled. "But you would. Cope, I mean. Anyway, I'm sure it's not going to come to that. Again, we need to think about it, to have a plan. Maybe even manage that part through you giving a joint interview – do it on your terms, so to speak."

"That's a thought. It would help keep us on the front foot."

"I've made a note. We'll think about that. Now, anything else you want to throw into my Monday morning mix?"

"Yes – I need to arrange a key for Luke. I realised that giving him access to the flat was the only way we'd ever see each other."

"I can see what you mean. It's a good idea. Leave it with me and I'll sort it out."

"Thanks. So, to business. What joys have you got in store for me this week?"

"You have three meetings this afternoon about air quality – a delegation from the local authority associations, the engine manufacturers, and three campaigning groups. I've e-mailed you the briefing notes but I've also got a hard copy here."

I took the proffered notes. "Thanks. I'll go through those. Nothing new or exceptional, I assume?"

"No, nothing at all. As you know, we have environment questions in the House on Thursday. The preliminary meeting about those is tomorrow morning with the full ministerial team and Sir John. You're in the House for the rest of the day – two of our statutory instruments are going through and you've got a three-line whip on a transport bill. Wednesday, you're visiting a vehicle-testing centre in Streatham – mainly photo-ops associated with plans to tighten up the emissions' testing in the annual MoT test. During the afternoon, we have a session on the preliminary work for the spending review submission to the Treasury – that's with Sir John again, though the Secretary of State won't be there: summoned to the presence at Chequers, I am told."

"Another Brexit crisis, I suppose."

He nodded. "And talking of Brexit, you're due in the House to vote on Wednesday evening – plus now your dinner. Thursday, you'll be preparing all morning then in the House until around four. You're addressing the dinner at a European climate change conference in Brighton on Thursday evening. Friday you're in the West Midlands – two visits in the morning, meeting the Local Enterprise Partnerships during the afternoon, addressing local university students at six, before the local association's annual dinner at eight, with a speech around nine-thirty. You should be clear of there by eleven and I've booked you into an hotel nearby for the night."

"Jesus. Obviously a fun-packed week. Still, as you never tire of pointing out, I wanted the job."

"Me also, in fairness. I'll be with you every step of the way – except Friday night, of course. I get to go home while you frolic with the party bigwigs."

I rolled my eyes. "And you can just imagine how much

Chapter Thirty-Four

I'm looking forward to that. So do I get any time at the weekend?"

"I think the local area guys have got you lined up for some photo-ops with shoppers on Saturday morning, and a fete immediately after lunch. Central Office is sorting that out and will give you the final details later. As I understand it, you should be free from mid-afternoon on Saturday and you've nothing on Sunday."

"Thank goodness for small mercies."

Jeremy looked concerned. "Are you okay with all this?"

"Me? Yes, fine. But it does seem a bit relentless sometimes – especially on a Monday morning." I smiled, seeking to give him a reassurance I didn't feel. "I'll be fine – and the weekend will be here before I know it."

"Right – so why don't I give you time to look at those briefs for this afternoon? I'll pop back in an hour or so and we can throw around some ideas about the coming-out strategy."

"Sounds like a plan," I responded, reaching for the documents he'd handed me.

Jeremy left the room and I sat back. The programme he'd outlined was fairly typical – and if anything slightly less hectic than some weeks I'd endured since arriving at the department. Why did its relentless pace suddenly seem so formidable? How come I was starting to resent the lack of "me time" in the schedule? The answer was obvious: for the first time in my life, I had something else I'd prefer be doing than practising politics. I wanted to spend time with Luke, to relax with him and to get to know him better, to have fun and pursue our shared interests. But I couldn't see how that was going to be possible with my life as it was now, and for the first time I resented it.

I put the question firmly on my "think about it tomorrow" list and turned to the briefings for the afternoon meetings.

Chapter Thirty-Five

Luke

It was Tuesday evening. I was sitting reading on the sofa in Dan's flat, legs curled up beneath me, waiting for him to get home. He'd been in the Commons all afternoon and had texted me to say he was on his way.

I'd prepared a meal and popped it in the oven to finish off after I received his text. Including the two nights in Dorset, this would be our fifth successive night together. We were moving fast, much more quickly than I'd expected, yet it didn't feel as if we were rushing things.

On this, the second evening of our new "getting to know you" arrangement, I was still a newcomer to the flat, yet I felt completely at home. No wonder Dan loved it. The high ceilings and large room sizes gave it a sense of space, and the view towards Kensington Gardens was beautiful, provided you could ignore the traffic rushing back and forth immediately in front of the windows.

When I'd arrived the previous evening, Dan had immediately presented me with my key. I'd been immensely touched that he'd followed up on that so quickly, despite all the other pressures on him; it was another token, if I needed one, of his commitment to what we were doing.

Now, the sound of Dan's key in the door had me on my feet with a big smile on my face. Within seconds I was enveloped in a hug. "Welcome home, Minister," I said into his ear.

"Great to be back – especially to a welcome like this after a day like today. First of all there's you, plus the sensational smell coming from the kitchen."

"I thought it would be nice to cook rather than get more takeaway. Nothing fancy, but I thought a lamb casserole would be good."

"Fantastic. I'll get out of my suit, if that's okay."

"It'll be ready in ten minutes so there's time for a quick shower, if you like."

"That sounds fun. You coming too?"

I laughed and shook my head. "If we go down that route, the dinner'll be burnt to a cinder."

Dan pushed out his bottom lip, pretending to pout, but quickly moved towards his bedroom. "Message received and understood. Anyway, I'm starving."

"Off you go. It'll be on the table when you're done."

"You said 'after a day like today' earlier. Was it so awful?"

We were on the sofa; I was at one end and Dan lay with head in my lap, eyes closed whilst I stroked his hair. His forehead, which had been creased with tiredness and worry when he arrived, was now smooth. His eyes were closed. Gentle jazz was playing in the background.

He didn't reply for a moment, and his eyes stayed closed.

I started to speak again. "Sorry, Dan, I shouldn't have asked. Don't want to stop you from relaxing."

He opened his eyes. "Don't worry – it does me good to talk about these things, specially to you. I was just trying to work out where to begin." He sat up but didn't move away, instead he wrapped an arm around me and put his head on my shoulder.

"That bad, eh?"

He gave a long sigh. "I think so. Not with the department or anything. I can do the job, even if it is bloody hard work. Jeremy is a godsend and keeps me focused. He says I'm doing very well. But it's the whole atmosphere around the place. It's poisonous."

"How do you mean?"

"To give you an example, I was in the Commons tonight. There were a couple of votes with a three-line whip, so I went down about five, spent some time in the chamber. After that I popped into the Strangers Bar. As you know, I did two years in the Whips Office and got to know fair number of members from both the government and opposition. We used to get on well, have a laugh and a joke, poke fun at each other – you know the sort of thing. But now..." He paused, shaking his head. "People from our own side won't even acknowledge me because I'm a Remainer. Those who do give me a curt nod and nothing more. It seems that anybody who gets into a discussion about virtually anything ends up having a row. Plus the fact that the Corbynistas hate us with a passion, so the whole atmosphere of the place is toxic."

"It sounds hellish, Dan."

He shook his head. "What's even worse is that I don't see us recovering from this. The arguments are so bitter and the divisions so deep."

"What'll you do?"

"In the short term keep my head down, do my job and hope for the best."

"And then?"

Dan laughed bitterly. "That's the sixty-four-thousand-dollar question, isn't it?" He sat up and turned to face me. "Looking back, I can now see how much I've given up over the years to get to this position – friendships, not least with you, leisure time, doing things like going to concerts and the theatre. All sacrificed on the altar of political ambition. And can I tell you the most disturbing thing of all? I'm not sure now that it was worth it."

I reached for his hand and intertwined our fingers. I sensed that this was a really big moment for him, and I wanted him to know that he was not alone in facing it. "How so?"

"Whatever I was after in seeking a political career all those years ago, whether it was power, influence or glory, I'm coming to realise that the price I paid may have been too high."

"So are you saying that you don't want it any more?"

"Politics? This life? I'm really not sure that I do."

"What do you *want* to do?"

He laughed again. "There's the rub, as they say. I don't know, my love. I was thinking about it on Friday on the way down to the cottage. If not this, what?"

"I'm sure you could do anything you want to, Dan."

"Thank you, my Skywalker. Trouble is, this is all I've

ever wanted, ever known. This was my destiny – follow in Daddy's footsteps to Westminster and get as high as I could. I never challenged it. It never occurred to me that I would do anything else. And here I am now, aged thirty-six, moderately successful, could go further – but...' He faltered, lifted his head from my shoulder and looked at me. The creases in his forehead were back and his eyes glistened with unshed tears. "What the fuck am I going to do, Sky?"

I pulled him into a hug, wrapping him securely in my arms as I spoke quietly in his ear. "We'll work something out, never fear. You're clever, charming, *very* good-looking and successful. Never forget that. Your experience over the last seven years is solid gold. Public affairs, writing, consultancy, the City – they'll all be open for you if you give up politics. Above all, you mustn't be frightened. You've got me now, and the rest of your life lies ahead of you."

He gave a short laugh and pulled back slightly from the hug. "You're right, I know. And I do feel like that most of the time, but every now and again it gets to me. Some small incident reminds me of what a total shit-show this is. It frightens me."

"It can't be easy, any of it."

"It isn't. Former allies are fighting each other tooth and nail. Friends of mine are now enemies. This'll go on for years."

I held him again to try to ease his fear and trepidation. It was difficult to reassure him, because I shared his worries about the future. In a world where we all needed to work together, to have friendships and alliances, we were pushing people away – our fellow Europeans and now each other in a vicious political civil war.

By comparison, my professional life was an oasis of calm. We had our moments in the office, but there were some weeks when the biggest drama was running out of Digestive biscuits.

Being involved romantically with Dan meant that things could change at any moment and I could be thrust into the limelight. I kept telling myself that I was aware of the challenges and could face them. In the meantime, my role was to support him in any way I could.

Chapter Thirty-Six

Dan

"So, how do we play this afternoon?"

It was Wednesday lunchtime. Jeremy and I were in the back of the car, returning to Westminster after our visit to Streatham. It had been a routine affair, greeting the staff, chatting with them and some customers before being photographed multiple times from every possible angle. It had gone smoothly – and for once nobody mentioned Brexit. Our next session was with Sir John and the department's management team over our submission to the Comprehensive Spending Review, known as CSR for short.

This was where we bid for our spending plans for the next three to five years. Today's meeting would set the tone for the remaining discussions on the draft, both internally and later with the Treasury officials. Amongst other things, this process could determine whether or not the Griffin House project had a future. If abolition was proposed and agreed today, the whole scheme would fall at the first hurdle. If, on the other hand, we could stay Sir

John's hand, it could survive, at least for the time being.

Jeremy thought for a moment before replying. "By ear, mainly. We don't actually know what's going to be said today because it's supposedly a scoping exercise. I think I've done enough work on the others to prevent outright abolition – but you never know. And Sir John is such a devious bastard."

We arrived back at the office and went straight to the meeting room. An hour later, we were still in the middle of a crowded agenda and had yet to reach our topic. There had already been several acrimonious exchanges about different aspects of the sprawling department's work, as if the Brexit poison were permeating every aspect of government.

Sir John looked discomfited, to put it mildly. His policy of appeasing the Treasury by offering voluntary cuts and axing whole programmes had been met with fierce resistance from his civil service team, rightly so in my view. Jeremy's behind-the-scenes work in preparing for this had been well worth it.

At last, the meeting turned to Griffin House. As we'd suspected, the draft outline submission suggested the scheme was dropped in favour of a heavily reduced, centrally run environmental innovation fund. All the progress made over the last four years in governance, assessment and administration would be thrown away.

I opened my mouth to speak but was forestalled by the briefest shake of the head from Jeremy. One of the other divisional heads started the discussion and weighed in against the line of Treasury appeasement. Jeremy winked at me as the official concerned, Arthur Ryder, summed up.

"It seems to me," he said, "that if, as a Department and a management team, we believe in what we're trying to do with the environment, we need to make the argument within the wider government sphere – not once, but many times. Offering our core policies for sacrifice on the altar of austerity seems fundamentally wrong."

There was a chorus of agreement from around the room and the Permanent Secretary's expression turned from mild irritation to deep anger. He glared at Jeremy, clearly holding him at least partly responsible for the string of defeats he'd suffered during the afternoon. Word of Jeremy's lobbying activities had obviously reached the Permanent Secretary's office.

But the man wasn't done yet: he turned to me. "In the Secretary of State's absence, perhaps our Under-Secretary of State could give us his thoughts on how we're supposed to deliver a submission within the government's own guidelines on future spending?" The sarcasm in his tone was plain to hear.

I paused for a moment before responding then put on my most amiable expression. "Forgive me, Sir John, but I thought today's exercise was only indicative? I'm sure I can speak for the Secretary of State when I say that the ministerial team values greatly the advice and guidance supplied to us by you and your Civil Service colleagues. It's surely too early for us politicians to pre-empt the advice that you might give us when it comes to finalising the submission and signing it off. Speaking personally, I would incline to Mr Ryder's view: we need to make the case for having the resources available to do our job properly. It is surely for others to determine whether we should have those resources or not. If not, we can ask our masters to change our remit."

I thought that was the politest rebuff I could deliver and, judging by the look on Jeremy's face, I had done a good job. Sir John glared at me and let out a deep sigh before proposing that we should refer the matter to a small committee to reconsider. That saved his face in the short term and might even allow him to regain control of the agenda. From our point of view, it did at least mean that we lived to fight another day.

Sir John's proposal was quickly agreed. After making some closing remarks that were brief to the point of curtness, he closed the meeting half an hour earlier than scheduled. Clearly angry at finding his own senior team virtually in open rebellion against him, he stalked out of the room.

"Game, set and match?" I asked.

Jeremy followed me into my office. Judging by the look of joy on his face, I guessed I was right. "I think you could say that," he responded. "I knew my informal conversations with people had been well-received, but I didn't expect that level of resistance."

"I was more than a little surprised, I must say. Everybody gave Sir John a hard time right from the start. That appeared to be pretty much unprecedented."

Jeremy nodded. "It is – and I was astounded when Arthur Ryder spoke. He's never been a fan of Griffin House and yet he said all that."

"Judging by the look on Sir John's face, I wouldn't fancy Arthur's chances of promotion any time soon."

"I wouldn't put mine very high, either. You should have seen the glare he gave me as he left the room."

"Yes, I assume word of your little chats with people must have reached him."

"Inevitable, I suppose. Anyway, that's round one to us. The threat to Griffin House hasn't gone away by any means, but at least we're still in the fight. And thank you for your support at the end there, Dan. It was extremely useful."

"My pleasure. Anyway, I meant what I said: what's the point of having advisers if you hem them in and second-guess them all the time?"

Jeremy laughed. "You won't find me disagreeing with that." He was about to continue when the phone rang. He took the call and listened for a few moments before saying in a neutral tone, "I'll check whether the Minister is available." He put the phone on mute and turned to me. "Somebody called Glyn Pargiter. Says he used to work with you. Are you here?"

"Oh, sure. Let me have a quick word."

I'd worked with Glyn for a couple of years in my time as a journalist. He'd started off as a colleague before he was promoted, spending a few months as my boss shortly before I was adopted in Wessex South and put in my resignation. He was a couple of years older than me and we'd lost touch recently. He'd left the paper not long after me and started his own on-line media business, which was going great guns. He was running a political intelligence website and YouTube channel – and was becoming increasingly influential.

Glyn was one of the few people I'd ever come out to; I'd been more or less bounced into it by his exuberant lifestyle and relaxed approach to his own sexuality. As I understood it, he now spent most of his time in the north, living with his husband Matt in a vast and expensive mansion near York.

"So, young Mr Pargiter, to what do I owe this pleasure?"

"Hi, there, Danny boy. How's life?"

"Shitty, thanks. What about you?"

"About the same. I shall be stuck in London all next week, missing Matt like hell and worrying about the future."

"That sounds fun ... not."

"I wondered whether we could get together, Dan. I've got something I want to run by you."

"That would be good. Let me check the diary."

"I know you Ministers have no time to yourselves, but I wondered about next Tuesday evening?"

Jeremy opened his diary app and passed his phone to me. "Yes, I could do that – about nine? Do you want to come to the Commons? Or did you have somewhere less reputable in mind?"

He laughed. "Dan, surely you know that the Commons is about the most disreputable place in London?" He named a members' club in Soho and I arranged to meet him there at nine-thirty. We said our goodbyes and I replaced the receiver.

I looked at it for a moment, before lifting my gaze towards Jeremy. "Glyn was my boss when I was a journalist," I explained. "Now he runs a politics website."

"Ah, I see. Any idea what he wants?"

I shook my head. "Glyn doesn't do small talk or much networking these days – he has staff to do that. He must be after something, though."

"Intriguing," he agreed, glancing at his watch. "You'll no doubt find out on Tuesday. Now, you're due at the House shortly and, of course, staying for your dinner engagement. I hope it all goes okay."

"No rest for the wicked. Thanks. I'm not looking forward to the dinner – but I suspect it's a bit like having a tooth out: it'll feel better afterwards."

He laughed. "That's a new image for coming out to one's parents. Anyway, good luck."

Governing Passions

Chapter Thirty-Seven

Luke

The days seemed to be speeding past. Admittedly, I'd spent most of it with a grin on my face; the evenings and nights spent with Dan were feeding my soul. The years of living alone punctuated by the occasional hook-up had suddenly receded in favour of evenings of close companionship, domesticity, and a feeling of deep contentment that was completely new to me.

The sexual chemistry between us was amazing but our relationship was much deeper than that. I couldn't hold Dan in my arms without experiencing the sensation of having come home. He felt right in my arms, as if we'd been made to measure. I smiled at that but moved uneasily in my chair as I recalled the previous night's lovemaking – the feel of Dan's body moving against me, the movement of his hips, the feel of his skin, the taste of his lips on mine. I closed my eyes and breathed deeply, only to be awoken from my reverie by the opening of my office door.

It was my boss Steve, with a face like thunder again. "Can you spare a minute, Luke? We need a quick confab."

I dragged my thoughts away from Dan. "Sure, boss. Anything up?"

"Press again. This *London Figaro* business – I'll give you the lowdown when we meet."

So that was why he was in a foul mood. The suggestion of collusion and corruption in the Griffin House grant awards had not gone away. Shit.

Five minutes later, I entered Steve's room, joining Andy and Barbara. All three of them had looked grim. Steve handed me a sheet of paper. I got to the end of the first paragraph. "Christ almighty! What is this?"

"It's an advance copy of a story in this week's issue of *London Figaro.* My mate e-mailed it to me this morning."

"Can we stop it?"

Steve shook his head. "There's nothing actionable in there – in fact, the story is only obliquely about us at all. The name Pearson Frazer is only mentioned once, referring to last week's article."

I turned back to the paper and read the whole story. It wasn't too long, but it had the potential to be hugely damaging. The headline read: *The mystery of the missing guidelines.*

I moved on to the substance of the article.

> *The mystery behind the government's environmental grant schemes deepened this week when a leading local authority claimed not have been sent a key document in the grant application process – adding fuel to the fire in the row about who got the money and why.*
>
> *Lonsdale Borough Council made an unsuccessful application last year under the scheme, known in gov-*

ernment circles as the Griffin House project. A member of Lonsdale's project team told us this week that the officials drafting the application had not been issued with a key guidance document, and the lack of this had caused their bid to fail.

The complaint followed last week's suggestion that money had been funnelled unfairly to authorities that had used one consultancy firm, Low Carbon Promises (LCP). Regular Figaro readers may recall from last week's issue that LCP's founder, Freddie Angus, used to work for Pearson Frazer, another consultancy in the field. Guess who Pearson Frazer works for? Yes, none other than DECRA, the government department that hands out money under the Griffin House scheme.

Responding to last week's story, DECRA told us that all applicants had received identical documentation, including detailed guidance on how to make a grant application. "All applicants received the same treatment," a DECRA spokesman told us, "and were assessed by independent experts. The process is transparent and fully independent."

Well, yes. But, as our source at Lonsdale says, "If the full guidelines are only sent to Freddie Angus's clients, no wonder they're the ones that keep winning. DECRA left us to our own devices and then said that our application didn't meet criteria we didn't know about. The whole process stinks."

So, come on, DECRA. Who was responsible for issuing the guidelines? And why didn't Lonsdale get theirs? Could it be that they weren't employing the right advisers?

I finished reading and looked up. "What a load of bloody rubbish. Of course they got the guidelines – they're in the same file as the application form."

"Exactly," said Steve. "But somebody's clearly got it in for the two consultancies."

"What was the Lonsdale application like, Luke?" asked Andy.

"It was crap. They completely ignored the guidelines, didn't answer half the questions and basically said 'we're a deprived area so we deserve the money'."

"I remember – we awarded it the prize for the worst application of the whole project," added Steve.

"But if they weren't actually given the guidelines..." said Barbara.

"You're right, of course. Except that the form is the last page in a PDF document that contains all the guidance notes and the whole description of the project."

"I suppose somebody could have printed out the form and ignored the rest," Steve remarked with a sigh. "You can only do so much to make things idiot-proof."

"But why go whingeing to *London Figaro*?"

"Left-wing council, virulently anti-government, think the world owes them a living," remarked Andy. "Why not use every opportunity to stir things up?"

The room was silent for a moment except for the click of Steve's mouse as he searched the internet. After a few moments, he blew out a breath. "Especially if the council officer concerned worked on the QuitEU campaign with Sean fucking Andrews."

"You're kidding!" I said.

"Nope. The interim CEO at Lonsdale Council is Kevin

Rook, put in by a consultancy firm after the leader sacked the previous CEO. One of Mr Rook's earlier jobs was head of administration at QuitEU campaign for a year in the run up to the referendum."

My mouth dropped open. "Bloody hell. So Andrews *again*?"

"Certainly looks like it," Steve replied. "Is it us he's after, or is he trying to destabilise the whole department?"

I closed my eyes and sighed deeply at the thought that crossed my mind at that moment. "It could be Dan he's after – getting at him through me."

"But Dan's only been there five minutes!' said Barbara. "He couldn't possibly be involved with Griffin House."

"Not directly, no. But how about 'unscrupulous consultant gets into a relationship with a Minister in order to exercise undue influence'?"

Steve looked at me in horror. "Nobody could possibly think that, Luke. At least nobody with an ounce of common sense."

"I agree," said Andy. "That's absolutely crazy."

Barbara looked thoughtful. "I can see where Luke's coming from. The thing about the Web is that you don't have to prove anything – you only need to drop enough hints and people start thinking 'there's no smoke without fire' and you're away. You've created a public perception that something is fishy or someone is corrupt. People make up their minds up accordingly."

I nodded. "She's right. And since most people think that politicians are crooks anyway, chances are they'll brand them guilty without another thought."

"Christ, who'd want to be a politician?" Andy remarked,

shaking his head.

"Not me, for a start," Steve replied with a laugh. "But where do we stand in all this? Is Pearson Frazer's reputation at risk here?"

"I would say it is, Steve," I responded with another sigh. "Andrews can't lose. He can spread this shit through his links with the magazine. Every time we try to defend ourselves, they simply put up the Mandy Rice-Davies line – 'they would say that, wouldn't they?'. It's a double win, too, because if Dan puts up too much of a fight over the future of Griffin House, they'll say we've got at him, using me as the conduit."

"Mandy who?" asked Andy

"One of the girls involved in the Profumo affair in the sixties," replied Barbara. "It was a classic example of a gossip-driven crisis made worse when everybody panicked and tried to lie their way out of it."

Steve frowned. "Come on, we need solutions, not history lessons."

"Okay," I said. "First thing we should do is check our records. I assume the pack was sent to Lonsdale by e-mail, in which case we should have a read receipt and the copy of what exactly was sent. That way, we can see immediately if all the correct documentation was provided – and prove it."

"Good thinking, Batman. Leave that to me," Barbara said.

"Second question." I was on a roll now. "Did anybody here check on the submission when it arrived? Ideally, someone will have looked at it and followed up with Lonsdale, asking them why the form wasn't complete."

"You can also leave that to me," Barbara said. "I'll check the servers and make sure that all the Griffin House correspondence is secured and separately backed up."

"Great," said Steve. "I'll check with the DECRA guys as to how they want to handle this. I'm going to push them hard to issue a statement this time. All keeping quiet does is make us look guilty."

Andy nodded. "I'll second that, Steve. We've got to get on the front foot or these guys will crucify us. Our integrity and reputation are paramount – we can't sit back and allow them to be undermined like this."

"What about Dan?" I asked with trepidation.

"You need to warn him, Luke," Steve replied. "And you should both talk it through with Jeremy. As I said earlier, I don't see a problem but you do need to be careful, both of you." He looked at my expression and his face softened into a gentle smile. "I know it's hard, but you mustn't let him sleepwalk into trouble because of you."

Although my heart sank at his words, I instantly recognised the truth of what he was saying. If anything I did or said could jeopardise Dan's position, he had to know about it. Keeping secrets from him was the quickest way to wreck whatever we were building.

I nodded. "Thanks, Steve. I knew everything was going too smoothly."

"I understand. But you've waited fifteen years for all this – don't jeopardise what you've got."

A few clicks of Barbara's mouse and we had our answers. "Yes, they did get the full package, and we have a read receipt."

Governing Passions

Chapter Thirty-Eight

Dan

The Central Lobby was buzzing with people as I walked across it, moving from the Commons chamber towards the Peers Dining Room and my dinner date with my parents. Even though I was thirty-six years old, a Member of Parliament and a Minister in Her Majesty's government, I felt as though I were nine or ten again, summoned by my father for a dressing down – probably for some sin of omission or commission or other shortcoming.

I supposed that I was about to confess to the biggest sin I could achieve in my father's eyes. Being gay, not carrying on the Forrester line, being somehow less than a man. This meant that I wouldn't be producing a son and heir to carry on the family's traditions of public service. Okay, modern medicine might mean that technically I could produce a son – but for my father and his generation, I had the feeling that wouldn't count somehow.

I went down from the lobby towards the Lower Waiting Hall and from there turned into the southern section of the Library Corridor. This led into the part of the Palace devoted to the House of Lords.

Of course, it wasn't too late: I was not absolutely committed to telling them tonight. I could put it off again, as I had been doing for the last twenty-five years – hiding my true self for fear of incurring my father's displeasure, or possibly even his wrath.

In my heart, though, I knew that the time for prevarication was over. If my relationship with Luke was to mean anything, I had to be honest with myself, with my family and, ultimately, the electorate and the whole world. Here I was, Daniel Forrester MP, gay man and proud partner of the man I loved. And if my parents or other people didn't like it, I was sorry but they could lump it. And if it cost me my relationship with my parents, my job or my whole political career, so be it. I could no longer build my life on the shifting sands of lies and deceit – especially self-deceit.

All too quickly, I reached the door into the Peers Dining Room. I'd only been in there once before and had forgotten how impressive a room it was: a perfect example of the Victorian elegance that Barry and Pugin, architects of the rebuilt Palace of Westminster, had been seeking to achieve. A high, elaborately carved, wooden ceiling topped panelled walls – each panel inset was richly decorated with yellow wallpaper patterned with a stylised thistle motif in red and green. The tables were set formally with stiff white linen. The chairs were upholstered in the same red leather as the benches in the Lords' Chamber, and each bore Parliament's portcullis motif in gold. A red carpet with a geometric pattern of green and gold completed the sumptuous picture.

I looked round, taking in the surroundings but also

searching for my parents. The maître d' greeted me; I knew him from his days in the Commons' dining room, and he smiled in recognition. I told him that I was a guest of Lord Forrester and he took me over to them, tucked away at a discreet table in a corner of the room near the fireplace. As I approached, I crossed my fingers, hoping against hope that tonight would be all right.

My mother greeted me with a hug and her usual warmth. My father stuck to his formal handshake, though there was more feeling in it than I expected. What with ministerial duties and the deepening political crisis, not to mention Luke, it was several months since I had seen them. My mother bore her seventy-five years very well, retaining a slim, elegant figure. Her clothes were stylish and her hair as immaculate as ever.

My father, on the other hand, seemed a little frailer than I remembered and struggled slightly to rise from his chair to greet me. He had lost weight so that his cheeks seemed hollow, and the remnants of his double chin hung in flaps below his jaw. In all respects, he seemed to have shrunk compared to the intimidating figure of my youth.

We exchanged pleasantries while we looked at the menu and ordered. An unhappy few minutes followed on the current political situation. Dad had been shocked by the levels of bitterness and recrimination pervading Westminster, much worse, he said, than on his last visit in the spring.

"I've seen nothing like it, Dan, in all my sixty years around this place. It frightens me – no spirit of compromise, no attempt to bring people together, no leadership. It wasn't this bad even in the depths of the IMF crisis in the seventies. I'm glad that I probably won't live to see the consequences."

"I know exactly what you mean. I've started to dread coming over to the House. Somebody is always arguing with somebody else – it's almost as if everybody's lost their temper at the same time. People I worked closely with in the Whips Office six months ago won't even speak to me because I voted remain."

The arrival of our first course prompted a change of subject. I asked after people I knew in the Derbyshire village where I'd grown up and my parents still lived. I felt myself relaxing, enjoying their company for the first time in many years. Eventually, though, the subject turned to my welfare: how was I coping with being a minister, whether I'd met any nice girls yet. I felt my jaw tense and I looked round the room. Fortunately, it was still early and there were not many diners. We would not be overheard, even if things got a bit heated.

"I have met someone, actually."

My mother brightened.

"An old friend from university days. Luke Carter. You may remember, he came to stay one weekend."

"I think I remember him," said my father. "He was a bright lad – some sort of scientist, wasn't he?"

"That's him. He's now an associate director of an environmental consultancy working for the department. I ran into him again at a conference the other week."

"That's nice, dear. He seems to have done well," my mother remarked. "You were good friends for a while, weren't you?"

I nodded. "Yes, but we lost touch – I hadn't seen him

for about fifteen years." There was a pause. I wondered how to put it. I ploughed on, and then the words came rushing out. "Anyway, Luke and I have become ... er ... very close. You see, I'm gay and so is he. And ... um ... we've got together."

There was silence for a moment. I closed my eyes, waiting for some onslaught. Instead, I felt my mother's hand lying on top of mine. "Thank you for telling us. We often wondered."

"Quite so," harrumphed my father. "Good man. Takes a lot of courage. I'm glad."

I nearly fell off my chair with surprise. "But ... I thought you'd hate the idea – you always seemed so anti, especially during the sixties. I looked up the voting records, you see."

My father looked wistful for a moment. "Yes, I'm sorry to say that I did oppose the Bill – both Humphrey Berkeley's attempt in '65 and the one they passed in '67. But that was the last time, Dan. I came under such pressure from the old guard in the association – there's a big Catholic community in the valley, you see. The local Anglican bishop was also apoplectic about it all. It seemed easier to cave in. I'd only been in the House a few years when the issue arose, and my majority fell to a few hundred after the '66 election. I had to be so careful. And I didn't know any better. I didn't understand the issues properly – so I accepted what I'd been told." He laughed. "I got such a roasting from Archie. He wouldn't speak to me for months afterwards."

"Archie?" I asked. "Uncle Archie?"

"Do you remember him at all?" asked my mother.

"Vaguely," I replied. "I liked him and he was always

very cheerful when we met. But I was only twelve when he... Oh!"

My father smiled sadly. "Yes, AIDS got him. He was fifty-four, but always seemed so much younger."

"He had a zest for life," added my mother. "More than anybody else I've ever known. And his partner was a lovely man, too."

"Peter went the year before Archie," my father explained. "Same thing. It was terrible."

"I had no idea. Why didn't you tell me?"

"It was still something you didn't talk about, even in 1992, AIDS was surrounded by taboos, especially for a Tory MP. You were away at school and didn't know him all that well. It was simpler to get it over with." He shook his head. "It was terrible, watching him die. He came home for the last few weeks. I just wanted it to be over."

"We realised quite early on that you might be like Archie," mother continued. "I was so frightened for you, that you'd catch that dreadful disease and suffer like he did. It was easier to push the whole thing away. And when you didn't say anything, I ... we ... began to hope that we'd been wrong."

"I was so scared, growing up," I replied, trying to keep the anger out of my voice. "I was convinced that being gay would ruin everything – I'd lose you both, wreck my prospects, pretty much destroy my life. I tried to suppress it for so long. Pushed Luke away, even. If only you'd said something about Uncle Archie, told me what had happened, it would have made such a difference. I wouldn't have been so terrified of saying something to you."

Tears welled up – whether of sadness or anger, I didn't

know. How could they have kept this from me? They'd never even given me a hint that being gay might be anything other than totally unacceptable, not something the Forresters did. And yet my own *uncle*. Christ!

"I'm sorry, Dan," my mother said, reaching for my hand again.

I sat for a moment, uncertain what to do. I needed to get away from them, to process all they'd told me, but running away risked causing another breach and I wanted to avoid that.

I conquered my desire to flee and glanced at my mother. I was wondering what to say next, when I was saved by the bell, literally. The harsh sound of the signal that members of the House of Commons were about to vote rang through the building, prompting MPs from all sides to drop whatever they were doing and head towards the division lobbies to cast their votes.

I rose from the table. "Sorry, got to go. I'll be as quick as I can."

My mother reassured me. "Don't worry, we knew it was likely to happen."

"Seems like old times. See you later, my boy," Dad said.

I left the room and went back towards the Central Lobby and the Commons chamber, still struggling to cope with what I'd heard. A gay uncle. He and his partner dying from AIDS. My parents sharing none of this with me, suspecting I was gay but saying nothing. It was unbelievable. I felt angry and grateful all at the same time, giddy with relief but furious about the pain and distress that could have been avoided if they had been honest with me.

I calmed down by the time I reached the chamber and

made for the "aye" lobby to cast my vote. As usual, there was a lot of standing about before we could pass the tellers and be counted. I took the opportunity to send a quick text to Luke.

Dan >>: Hey. Are you about later? Dinner going OK. Lots to share.

Luke>>: Sure – shall I come over?

Dan>>: That would be great. See you around 10.30?

We'd deliberately left our overnight arrangements flexible. Luke had said he didn't want to crowd me and that I might need some space after dinner with my parents. I thought it more likely that I'd need his help and support, so we'd left it open.

As I'd suspected, I wanted to see him as soon as possible, to share my news with him and to feel the comfort of his arms. Now that was arranged, I relaxed. I could go back and finish dinner calmly and without a meltdown ... I hoped.

I didn't stick around for the result of the vote but set off back to the Peers' Dining Room.

"Tell me about Luke," said my mother.

We had left the dining room and moved to the bar. It was getting on for nine-thirty, so I knew my parents would want to leave soon. They had kept their own flat in London, near Smith Square, so it was only a few minutes' walk for them. I'd see them home and get a cab from there back to Kensington.

I thought for a moment. "In many ways, he hasn't

changed from our days at university. Funny, clever, charming. He works for a firm called Pearson Frazer – they're specialist environmental consultants based in South London. They're doing extremely well, and he got promoted recently. He has a small house near his office. We have huge amounts in common – music, food, books – and he's still as kind and gentle as he ever was."

"I don't remember much about him from that one visit, but I can remember he seemed a nice boy," my mother responded.

"You'll like him, I think."

"What are you going to do about going public?" asked my father, ever the practical politician.

"Sooner rather than later. I'm planning to attend the next meeting of the association's executive on Friday week and I'll announce it then. I'm working with my private office on the media stuff. There's been the odd rumour already, so I'd best get on with it."

"How do you think it'll go down?"

"Not as badly as me voting Remain," I replied, laughing.

Dad joined in the laughter but quickly turned serious again, shaking his head sadly. "God," he breathed. "What a mess."

"I know, Dad. The serious answer is I don't know – there's a growing faction of militant Brexiteers in the association who may use it as an excuse to try to get rid of me. Others will be more supportive, I suspect. The big worry is that they'll think I've lied to them for the last nine years."

"That is a risk. How would you feel? If you had to quit politics?"

I sighed. "To be honest, I don't know. I've lived, breathed and eaten all this since I was fifteen. Loved every minute of it. When the PM offered me this job three months ago, I was over the moon."

"Rightly so, Dan. You've done very well," my mother interjected.

"I sense a 'but' coming," Dad remarked

"Certainly all the Brexit arguments have taken the fun out of politics, at least for me. I hate the atmosphere. I don't think the Tory Party will ever recover and, even if it did, I'm not sure I want to stay a member of what it may become."

"I can understand that, but I hope you don't think it's all been a waste of time."

"Part of me does, to be honest. Particularly since I got to DECRA, I've come to realise just how little true influence politicians have any more."

"Hasn't that always been the case, though?" he asked. "After all, Rab Butler said it was 'the art of the possible'."

"I think it's become the art of the impossible. Between the tabloid press, the focus groups, the spin doctors and social media, everybody seems to be frozen in the headlights. It's all about what you can get away with, not what's good for the country." I paused and sighed. "Trouble is, I don't know what else I'd do."

"Nonsense," replied my father. "You're jolly talented. You can write – you were a bloody good journalist – you've been a Minister of the Crown and you've got charm and personality. You can do anything."

I sat there open-mouthed listening to this catalogue of my talents. I'd never realised that my father had even read my articles during my time in journalism, much less thought them any good. We hadn't communicated for so long, and I was coming to recognise that it was at least partly my fault.

"Thanks for the vote of confidence," I said. "I thought about going back into journalism, but it seemed like a retrograde step somehow. I'll think some more – but I'll carry on for the time being."

"Talk to Luke too, Dan," my mother said. "I know you – you'll go all quiet and agonise about it all on your own. You've always done that, ever since you were little. You were such a serious little boy. That's where you get your furrowed brow from, I think."

"And there was me thinking it was all intelligence and film-star good looks!"

They laughed, and I couldn't help joining in. I couldn't recall a time when the three of us had been so relaxed together.

"Well," said my father. "It's past this old man's bedtime. Thanks for joining us tonight, Dan. And for taking us into your confidence."

"At last, I suppose," I responded.

"In your own time, Dan. In your own time. It had to be like that – we always knew that," added my mother.

I didn't know how or whether to respond to that, so just smiled briefly. "Come on. I'll walk you back to the flat. You've certainly given me a lot to think about tonight."

Governing Passions

Chapter Thirty-Nine

Luke

I'd been a little surprised to get Dan's text asking me to join him. I'd assumed that he would need some time to himself after his dinner with his parents, and I didn't want him to feel obliged to share everything with me immediately afterwards.

On the other hand, I wanted to be available if he needed me, so I hadn't made any other arrangements for the evening. I set off for his flat as soon as I got his text. I arrived shortly before ten-thirty and was paying off my cab when another one drew up and Dan got out. "That's good timing," I remarked.

"Brilliant," he said, pulling me in for a hug.

I raised my eyebrows at this public display of affection but said nothing. Once inside Dan's flat, he kissed me passionately. "Thanks for coming over, Sky. I needed to see you so much."

"Was it bad? Your parents?"

He shook his head. "No, not in the way I expected. In fact, I still can't get my head round it." He got out the whisky, pouring one for himself and lifting the bottle in invitation. I nodded.

"So, I found out tonight that I had a gay uncle who died of AIDS when I was twelve. He had a long-term partner, who also died of the disease. And my parents thought I was like my uncle, but have been waiting twenty years for me to tell them."

"Bloody hell, Dan. That's a bit of a stunner."

"You're not kidding." He went on to explain his evening in more detail.

"So they weren't bothered about you being gay?"

"Apparently not. That's why I was so torn. I was relieved and angry at the same time."

"I get that, absolutely. If only they'd spoken..."

He shook his head. "All that heartache and worry. All unnecessary. I can't help feeling that I've been robbed." His eyes filled with tears. "I've been so fucking *scared*, Luke, for all those years."

I threw my arm round his shoulders. "Tell me about it..." I paused, wondering how I could make it better for him. The furrows on his brow were running deep and I could see the unshed tears in his eyes.

"I'm sorry," he said. "I'm forgetting that you went through all this shit too."

"We all find our path," I replied. "What matters is that you and I are here together."

"But we wasted fifteen years, Luke. And I hurt you so badly."

"We've been through all that. No regrets, no recriminations. Remember?"

"But something like this, it brings it all back. If only

they'd said." He shook his head again and turned to look at me, eyes still full of hurt.

"Is it all on them, Dan?"

"No, of course not. And that makes it worse, too. I made so many bloody assumptions. I was sixteen, and certain I liked boys. I wondered how it would go down if I told my parents. And then it struck me: I could find out. So I went into the library one day and got out Dad's copies of Hansard. I looked up the debates in 1967. I saw his name in the 'noes' column every time – second reading, third reading, report stage. I thought that's what he believed, so assumed he would think of me as a criminal as well. I was an idiot."

"No, Dan! You weren't. It was perfectly understandable – it was a good way to check out his views before saying anything."

"That's what I thought, but I should have carried on. Because it turns out that was the last time he voted that way. He rebelled over Section 28 and opposed it, then went on to vote for every single liberalisation measure brought before Parliament until he retired. I only looked at the first one."

"Not top marks for comprehensive research, I grant you – but you were sixteen and scared. It's hardly surprising."

"I suppose you're right." He sat and stared at his hands for a moment or two, before lifting his head and looking at me. "Thanks, Luke. I'm so glad you could come over. I don't know what I'd have done without you tonight."

"And the seriously good news is that you're out to your parents and they're cool about it. That has to be a positive."

"It was that thought that enabled me to cope with the

rest of tonight. And by the way, they want to meet you – they both remembered when I took you to stay for the weekend."

I laughed. "You're kidding. I must have made a good impression."

"You were fairly gorgeous."

"Only 'fairly'? I'm insulted."

His features relaxed as he laughed. The tension drained from him; his face cleared, and I knew we were through the worst.

"English understatement, you dork. I thought you were absolutely the bees' knees – how I kept my hands off you all that year, I'll never know."

"You've certainly made up for that over the last month... And long may it continue."

We moved back into each other's arms. He kissed me, lifting one hand to cup the back of my head. I closed my eyes, lost in the sensations of his touch, tasting his lips and inhaling his distinctive scent. He broke the kiss and rested his chin on my shoulder. "Bed?" he asked.

"Oh, definitely," I replied, but neither of us moved. Sitting there, holding each other close, seemed sufficient for the moment. I closed my eyes and hung on. Unbidden, tears sprang to my eyes at the sheer joy of holding this man in my arms, this incredible guy who was brave enough to peel away layers of secrecy, deception and fear going back deep into his childhood. I was so lucky.

In the same way as the tension had left his face a few moments earlier, I now felt it leave the rest of his body: the tautness of his muscles as he held me gradually diminished and I felt him subside into me. We stayed like that, drawing comfort from each other.

After a few moments, Dan shifted slightly and I felt his arousal brush against me through his clothes. The mood shifted from gentle comfort to physical need. We rose from the sofa and moved towards the bedroom, fingers entwined. I glanced up. His eyes were wide open and his brow was furrowed – not in fear or worry but in wonder and love. He wrapped his arm round my waist and I realised that he felt it too. Something had shifted tonight. Whatever was happening between us had just got even deeper.

We made it into the bedroom and Dan pushed the door shut with his foot. I closed my eyes and relaxed again as I felt him lift me onto the bed.

Governing Passions

Chapter Forty

Dan

Something changed within me that night. Whether it was the act of coming out to my parents or their sad tale of my uncle Archie, I didn't know. A combination of the two, I suspected. But at the core of it was the fact that, for the first time since my childhood, I would not have to live in anticipation of my father's disapproval. A weight had been lifted off my shoulders.

It was an extraordinary sensation. With one conversation, I had been freed from the bondage of fear under which I'd lived for more than twenty years. There would be no more stomach-wrenching horror at the thought of being rejected and unloved by my family, of losing my career. I could now get on with my life, with loving and being loved.

And here I was, locked in the arms of the man who had wrought this change in me. He'd given me both the courage to say what I had tonight, and a reason to stop hiding. He'd made it all seem worth the risk. And here he was holding me, helping me to relax, to recover my balance. I was so lucky.

I needed to express my love and gratitude to him, not with words and glib phrases, but by making love to him, worshipping his body and making him feel loved, wanted, needed. I still hated what I must have done to him fifteen years earlier and I despised myself for the stupidity and self-loathing which had made me act in the way I had. I had been given a chance to redeem myself and to right that wrong.

The feelings of elation and freedom that I was suddenly experiencing were almost overwhelming, but with a supreme effort I overcame them and poured my mental and physical energies into making love.

I started by undressing Luke slowly and sensually, batting away his hands when he tried to help. Once I had him naked, I stripped off my own clothes and lay on the bed beside him, drawing him into my arms once again. Our mouths met in long, languid kisses as our bodies moved together.

We lay on our sides but after a while, I rolled on top of him, at the same time lifting myself clear with my elbows to look down into his eyes. His blissful expression and gentle smile were perfect. I shifted and started kissing him all over, moving steadily downwards from his collarbone and nipples to his stomach, placing feather-light kisses wherever I moved. I used my tongue on is tummy, following his happy trail down to his cock. Fully erect and leaking pre-cum, it was too inviting to bypass or tease. I kissed the tip, then licked from root to tip before taking him fully into my mouth. I hummed with pleasure at the taste, and at the complex combination of softness coming from the silky-smooth skin and the hardness of his erection. Keeping him in my mouth, I looked up and met his eyes, revelling once more in the sheer pleasure I saw in them.

Suddenly I was seized with a new desire – one that I had never felt with my escorts. I needed to feel Luke inside me: it would be a first, a new experience and one I would only ever have shared with him. In some ways I was reluctant to lose the feel of him in my mouth, but once I had conceived the desire, I needed to fulfil it. I pulled off him moved back up to lie next to him and kiss him once more.

After a while, I rolled us so that he was on top, enabling me to wrap my legs round his waist as we thrust gently together, our mouths still locked. "Luke, can we reverse things tonight? I need you inside me. Will you fuck me, please?"

He looked surprised – we had not discussed our roles but, so far, we had both somehow expected that I would do the entering. "Of course, if that's what you want, Dan. Are you sure?"

I nodded. "I'm sure. You'd be my first, so it might be a bit difficult. But I need it, Sky. I need to express who I am tonight, and this feels right. I'd prefer it be you than anybody in the whole world."

His eyes filled with tears at that, but he managed to croak some words in reply. "I'd be honoured, Dan. I'd love to be your first."

We made no immediate move but continued to hold each other. Gradually, though, Luke took control of our movements. I felt his hand slide down my back and into my crack. Using a gentle circular motion, he rubbed the pad of his finger over my hole before pushing it in a little way. I loved the feeling that gave me and pushed back.

He withdrew for a moment and reached for the lube on the bedside table, coating his fingers. He kissed me once more before turning me over onto my stomach. His hand went south again and one finger resumed its probing, sliding in more easily now. I revelled in the sensation, trembling uncontrollably with pleasure when he located and massaged my prostate.

One finger was joined by a second and then a third, massaging and stretching gently. It felt as if every nerve in my body was energised by the sensations Luke was giving me. My enjoyment of these alternated with the gentle, caring way in which he was looking after me, using his other hand to stroke my back and my thighs in long, calming motions, all the while whispering gentle words into my ear.

"That's it, my love. Let yourself go and enjoy this. I'll look after you. There's my lovely Dan. Ooohhh, that's my boy."

All too soon, though, his fingers were gone and I knew they were about to be replaced by his cock. I closed my eyes and breathed deeply, treasuring these moments but at the same time slightly fearful of what was about to happen.

Then it happened. I felt the tip followed by the push and the stretch. A sting of pain prompted a sharp intake of breath, but Luke soothed me again with his strokes and his gentle words. Then he was past the ring of muscle and the pain passed, replaced by a feeling of fullness; now this felt seriously good. I let out a small moan of pleasure.

He pushed in gently, slowly, allowing me to adjust. Finally, he was fully there and I felt his pelvis pressing against my body. He lay still, holding my hips and gently rubbing my skin.

Suddenly, the import of what was happening crashed into my brain, almost taking my breath away. Luke Carter, the man who had never truly left my thoughts since the day I'd met him, was here with me, our bodies joined in an act of love. Somebody was inside me. No, more important than that – *he* was inside me in a penetration I'd never wanted or permitted before. For the first time ever, I felt like the person I truly was and was always meant to be.

Then Luke moved, slowly at first, with the slightest undulation of his hips across my back. He withdrew almost completely before thrusting back in, gradually building into a rhythm that had me groaning with pleasure. When, on one deep thrust, he brushed my prostate again the groan turned into a shout. Without warning, he stopped and pulled out. I was about to ask what was wrong when he spoke. "Turn over, Dan, I have to see you for this."

I spread my legs and lifted them towards my chest, anxious to feel him back inside me. He re-entered me, more swiftly than before. Looking into his eyes, I could see the gentleness, the concern in his eyes. He sighed as he bottomed out once more, pausing before he began to move. The change of angle heightened my sensations. He bent down to kiss me and his stomach rubbed against my already throbbing cock, heightening everything even more.

After breaking the kiss, he sat up, shifting the angle once more and grazing my magic spot again. As I looked into his eyes, I realised that he'd been right to change positions; seeing his face, watching the movement of his jaw and mouth, made what was already special into something extraordinary. I lay back on the pillow for a moment and closed my eyes. I was in danger of sensory overload and my heart was so full it felt as if it could burst.

Chapter Forty-One

Luke

This joining, this act of love, was like nothing I had ever experienced before. True, I'd had my moments as a player on the scene, but to be able to look down and see *Dan* there. Somebody I knew, to whom I was close – dammit, whom I loved with every fibre of my being. That seriously was something else.

After turning him over and entering him once more, I leaned down and kissed him long and hard. Now I sat back up and looked down at him.

He lay back on the pillow, eyes closed, head turning slowly from side to side. His forehead was creased but in joy rather than fear or annoyance. I picked up speed and reached for his erection.

"Open your eyes, my love," I said. "I'm not going to last much longer, and I want to look at you when I come."

He obeyed. At the same time, a wide smile broke across his face. "Hi, Sky. Give me what you've got, my love. I want to take it all."

That certainly sent me well on the way to orgasm. I

increased my pace, and Dan matched my thrusts, our momentum combining as he thrust in and out of my fist.

"That's it. Oh yeah. Brilliant. Come for me, Dan."

"Coming, Sky. Oh, my love. Oh yeah." He shouted my name even louder as he came, spraying both our bodies with his release, his body spasming uncontrollably as he did so. The sight of this, and the feel of him clamping down on me, was enough to push me over the edge. I babbled and called out as I thrust into him, my brain almost overwhelmed by the ecstasy I felt as I filled the condom inside him.

I leant forward and kissed him, trying to recover my breath. I reached down and dealt with the condom before lying on my side next to him, tracing patterns with my finger in the cum on his stomach and chest. He shivered at my touch and turned to face me.

"Thank you, Sky. That was… indescribable."

"Thanks. And yes, it was. Indescribable, I mean. I've never…' I paused, groping for the right words. "I've never felt anything like that ever before, Dan. Being inside you was … awesome. And to be your first, well…"

"Thank you for being my first," he replied with a smile. "And for being so gentle and patient with me."

"My pleasure, Dan. Any time… And I mean that most sincerely, folks."

He laughed at my cod-American accent. "Idiot."

"Seriously, though, are you okay? Not too sore or anything?"

He was amused by my concern. "I'm very okay." He turned on his back and gave an enormous yawn. "Sorry, I'm fading fast here."

"No problem. Let's get you cleaned up a bit and then we can sleep."

I hopped out of bed and went into the bathroom, giving myself a quick wash down before wetting a facecloth with warm water and grabbing a towel. When I returned to the bedroom, Dan was already three-quarters asleep. I wiped him down as gently as I could and patted him dry.

He opened one eye and gave me a tiny smile. "Thanks, Sky," he whispered. "By the way, have I told you yet that I love you? Cos I do."

"And I you, Dan. Love you so much."

Almost overwhelmed by the events of the evening and the depth of my feelings, I dropped the facecloth and the towel on the floor beside the bed and climbed back in.

Dan snuggled up against me. "G'night, my love," he whispered. "My Sky." His breathing changed almost immediately, and he was away.

Lying there holding him, my eyelids quickly grew heavy. But I fought off sleep for a few minutes more, determined to fix these moments in my memory, to revel in the feelings of deep contentment and happiness. My lips to turn upwards in a small smile. It was still there as I succumbed and drifted off in the arms of my own personal Morpheus.

The other side of the bed was empty when I awoke next morning. As I lay there, I became dimly aware of a figure at the end of the bed smiling down at me.

"Morning, sleepyhead," Dan said. He was already fully dressed and clearly about to leave.

I registered the fact that it was still dark outside. "What time is it?" I asked, blinking the sleep out of my eyes and sitting up.

"Six-thirty. Don't worry, you've got plenty of time. There are some things I need to get on with today, so I thought I'd go in a bit earlier."

"Are you okay? After last night, I mean."

His lips curled upwards. "If you mean what we did, the answer is 'a little sore' but in a nice way." He waggled his hips. His small smile grew larger and his eyes sparkled with humour. He paused, then his expression became more serious. "As to the rest, I suppose I'm still coming to terms with it all – both about Uncle Archie and the AIDS thing and what it means for me, you know?"

I nodded. "Of course. That's inevitable. It's a lot to take in."

His phone buzzed with a text and he glanced at the screen. "That's my car. Must go. Don't forget I'm away for a couple of nights. See you Saturday?"

"Try and keep me away."

"Wouldn't dream of it," he replied leaning over for a quick kiss. "Should be back around teatime."

I nodded. "Whenever. I'll be here."

With that, he turned and went. I lay back in bed for a few moments, luxuriating in the warmth both of the duvet and Dan's affection. I thought of our lovemaking and remembered how it had felt to be inside him, but also the intensity of our feelings. It was almost as if, after years of struggling about our sexuality and who we were, we'd given ourselves permission to love.

I roused myself and got ready to leave for the office. It

was getting light as I let myself out of the flat and started my commute back to Crystal Palace. It was a grim day, cold and gloomy as I began my half-mile walk to the station. But I had a smile on my face and sunshine in my heart.

I had just reached the office an hour later when my mobile rang. I saw Dan's picture and picked up immediately. It was rare for him to ring during the day, so I wondered what was wrong.

"Hi, Dan. Everything OK?"

"Yeah, fine. Just needed to run something by you about next weekend."

"Oh?"

"Yes, slight change of plan, actually. As you know, I had to pull out of an engagement in order to get to the executive meeting."

"Was that not okay, then?"

"Well, Party HQ weren't very pleased, but they're used to it. Anyway, Jeremy has done a deal with them and they've managed to find a substitute for the dinner I'm pulling out of in Bedford."

"Good. But...?"

"Yeah ... the bad news is that their price is for me to cover a regional AGM on the Saturday afternoon."

"Oh, hell. Where?"

"Sutton Coldfield."

"Ah. So we won't be able to spend the weekend at the cottage."

"No. It's a bloody nuisance, I know. Jeremy tried to

trade for something later in the month, but they were in serious trouble over this engagement so they insisted. The Foreign Secretary was due to go, but he's had to pull out to attend a meeting in Geneva."

"Oh, that's a shame." We'd been looking forward to spending a couple of nights at the cottage in the weekend after Dan's coming-out speech. If he now had to travel up to the Midlands for a Saturday afternoon speaking engagement, I might as well not go at all – but I passionately wanted to be with him for the Friday. "You could have done with the rest, Dan."

"I know. But there is one consolation. They'd booked a suite for the Foreign Secretary at a luxury country-house hotel in the area. Part of it is a moated medieval manor house, apparently. Jeremy says it's a terrific place with wonderful gardens and a superb restaurant."

"Oh, very posh."

"So I believe. Anyway, the thing is that we could take over the booking. Do you fancy the idea?"

"Sounds terrific, Dan. And it means I could help with the driving on Saturday morning – stop you getting too tired."

"Thanks – I hadn't thought of that. It would be a big help."

"Brilliant."

We ended the call quickly, not least because the weekly management meeting at Pearson Frazer was about to start. But the thought of a romantic night away in a luxury hotel put another smile on my face – even if the price would be a flog up the A34, not my favourite way to spend a Saturday morning.

Chapter Forty-Two

Dan

Having sorted out the speaking engagement and taken over the hotel booking, I had a morning in the office then went over to the Commons for a debate and a couple of votes before setting off for Brighton and my evening engagement. On Friday it was an early start for the journey to the West Midlands and a full day of engagements, culminating in another evening engagement for a local constituency association. Saturday morning saw me out campaigning with them in a local high street before going off to a lunch in neighbouring marginal constituency.

The Brighton dinner proved to be enjoyable, and the delegates at the climate change conference were fascinating to talk to. Though Jeremy and others in the department had drafted my speech, I spent some time before dinner going through it and adding some personal touches, including an emphasis on my personal commitment to the government's policies. This was a new feeling, and I reflected on my change of attitude since getting this job two months ago.

The speech was well-received. I went upstairs happy and spent the next hour Face Timing Luke back in London. Later, as I climbed into bed, I realised just how integral to my life he had become. Here was another aspect that had changed radically since September.

The two days in the West Midlands were also fascinating. On Friday, I had some intensive discussions with local authorities over air quality and three fascinating visits to businesses engaged in the search for technological solutions to our environmental problems. I had no doubt that this was where the answer lay, not in some unrealistic harking back to a so-called simpler life that the more extreme campaigners argued for.

I respected their position and their sincerity, but I was a politician and needed a keen sense of what the electorate would and would not stomach. Expecting or persuading the bulk of the population to accept a backward step in their standard and style of living was simply not going to happen.

The constituency dinner was a less jolly occasion; there were clearly simmering tensions between members of the Association along Remainer and Brexit lines. My carefully crafted, Central Office inspired speech satisfied neither side. After the formal proceedings ended, I pleaded extreme tiredness and begged off as soon as I could. Fortunately, the association members were so busy arguing that they barely noticed my departure.

The Saturday morning jaunt proved to be an enjoyable occasion, with lots of smiles and handshakes, until another argument over the EU referendum developed just as we were packing up. I didn't get involved but listened closely as party members and local people argued it out. Depressingly, it followed the usual pattern of initial disagreement becoming heated argument, followed by insult swapping. We were just at the point where fists might start to fly when a policeman intervened and asked us to disperse.

There had been few issues during my lifetime that had provoked as much deeply felt disagreement as this one. It was this, as much as the uncertainties of life outside the EU, that made me nervous about the future of the country.

I travelled south on my own, feeling dispirited and out of sorts. I tried to dismiss the feelings as pure tiredness but somewhere inside me I knew there was more at work than fatigue. Fortunately, I managed to switch my brain off and dozed for the rest of the journey into Euston station.

To my intense disappointment, the flat was empty when I got home. I'd hoped to find Luke there, but instead got an apologetic text saying he was on his way after a shopping trip with Josh that had overrun. I unpacked, then sat down on the sofa to wait for him, only then realising just how tired I was. The sheer pace of the week, alongside the stunning nature of my parents' revelations and the depth of feelings they had unleashed in me, had drained me completely.

I awoke half an hour later to a kiss on the forehead from a deeply penitent boyfriend. I smiled up at him before tackling him down to my level on the sofa and giving him a proper hello kiss. I ended it and hugged him even closer, tucking my chin onto his shoulder. "God, you've no idea how much I missed you," I said.

"If it's anything like the amount I've missed you, I've got

a very good idea," he replied, laughing. "Sorry I was so late. I wanted to be here when you got back but I couldn't get Josh out of a boutique I'd recommended. In the end, I left him to it. He was waiting for Steve to come and collect him ... and all his carrier bags."

I glanced across the room. "Did you get anything?" I asked, noticing the large carrier he'd dropped by the door.

He gave a smirk. "I may just have bought the odd shirt or two. There's one for you in there as well – thought it would suit you."

The idea of a present from Luke made me smile. I found the fact that he'd been thinking about me, even when he was out shopping with his friend, surprising and oddly touching. Nobody had ever done that before; it was another addition to the list of firsts in a week already full of them.

We spent the evening cuddled together watching old Agatha Christie adaptations on the TV after ordering food in from our neighbourhood Italian. It was magical.

Reality came crashing back in on Sunday morning with a couple of urgent red boxes. Jeremy had arranged for them to be dropped off at the flat, and I sat in my study working on them, while Luke lay on the sofa reading and classical music played quietly in the background. In the afternoon we walked through Kensington Gardens, enjoying a burst of winter sunshine and chatting about nothing in particular.

It had been a perfect day but, as we got back from our

walk, I felt myself tense up. It felt like Sunday evenings of old, a sense that the weekend or holiday was coming to an end, feeling anxious about the week to come.

We made tea but our easy chatter had stalled, and we were silent. Luke made several attempts to start a conversation but quickly caught on to my change of mood. After one particularly long silence, he spoke softly, his voice full of concern. "Hey, Dan. Are you okay? Talk to me."

"What? Oh, yes. Sorry. Just thinking about this week – specially Friday night."

"Ah, the coming out. Are you still sure about that?"

"No," I replied, offering a thin smile.

He cocked an eyebrow but waited for me to continue.

"Number one, I'm worried about how it will go. Number two, I don't really see why I should have to stand up and talk about who I sleep with. And number three, the idea of answering questions about it seems preposterous."

"Entirely understandable, Dan. But?"

"But I know in my heart of hearts that I've got to do it for the sake of my sanity, to present the real me to the electorate. For you, too. I can't hide who I am and I'm tired of feeling threatened by aspects of my own life."

"Sounds pretty compelling to me."

I nodded. "It is. And after Wednesday night, I know how liberating honesty can be."

"How do you mean?"

"I've felt different since the dinner with my parents. I feel free, as if it's okay to be me. No more lies, no more holding back on who I am. Above all, no more fear about what Mummy and Daddy might think."

Luke chuckled gently. "Oh, I get that. Absolutely. The

fear that people will think less of you when you tell them. Despise you, even. I went through all that too, especially in my early twenties. Having a father who thought an eternity of fire and brimstone awaited all gays didn't help, either."

"Seriously? Was he that bad?"

"Well, I may be exaggerating a bit but that's how it felt sometimes. Anyway, that's all over now. And for you too, Dan. You've got through the most difficult part. Friday night should be a breeze."

"You're right, of course – but I can't get over the feeling that I'll be judged at that meeting and somehow found wanting."

"I'm sure that's not true. There may be a few who think like that, but sod 'em. You're a great MP and a superb Minister – and they know it."

I beamed at him and thanked him, taking comfort from his confidence. But it didn't still the small voice deep within me. And I suspected that nothing aside from the meeting itself would do so.

Chapter Forty-Three

Luke

"Morning, all." Steve's voice sounded grim as he gave his customary greeting at the beginning of Pearson Frazer's regular Monday management meeting.

This morning, the mood was markedly less ebullient. The reason was simple: the attacks on the firm in the satirical magazine *London Figaro* had now been joined by a campaign by trolls on social media. It had started on the firm's Facebook account but quickly spread to Twitter and LinkedIn. Regular posts about the firm's activities and a blog post from Steve were all being targeted by hostile comments. They ranged from repeating the allegations made in the magazine, via attacks on the firm's whole existence in the debate about climate change, to personal attacks on the directors, particularly Steve.

These had badly upset everybody in the firm, especially when the attacks raised the subject of Steve's earlier prison sentence for under-age sex with his then-boyfriend when they were twenty-one and nineteen years old. In fact, he'd been formally pardoned and the conviction removed from his record a couple of years earlier, but that didn't stop people from mentioning the subject. In a couple of cases, the comments had gone as far as equating the prosecution twenty-three years earlier with child sex abuse.

Barbara and Steve's husband, Josh – on a break between tours – had spent hours the previous day removing hostile comments where they could and reporting others. But it was an uphill task; more seriously, it was taking them away from other essential work.

"It's clear that we can't simply take the 'no comment' route any more," said Steve. "Our reputation is being trashed and we're not doing anything do about it."

"I agree totally," said Andy. "We've got to get some legal advice and get these *Figaro* people stopped if we can."

"That may be easier said than done," said Barbara. "They've worded their stories carefully, as always – it's all reported speech and innuendo. As such, they have a very strong public interest claim, especially since taxpayers' money is involved."

"Has anyone spoken to a lawyer yet?" asked Josh.

Steve shook his head. "No. Since the department had asked us to play it down, we didn't think there was any point in incurring the fees."

"So that worked really well," remarked Andy bitterly. "It's particularly bloody ironic since we know that the source of the stories is a member of their staff."

"Special adviser," I interrupted. "That's half the problem. If he was a civil servant, they could make him shut up but, as he's a SPAD, he's probably doing what he's told by somebody who's got an agenda."

"And is that what's going on?" asked Josh.

"That's what Dan and Jeremy think," I replied"

Steve nodded, "I remember you mentioned this when it first blew up."

"Yeah, it was only a suspicion then, but it seems more certain now." I replied. "The arch-Brexiteers are out to make as much trouble as possible – to destabilise the government and get rid of ministers who voted Remain."

"Christ," remarked Andy bitterly. "So we're simply pawns in somebody else's game?"

"That's pretty much it," I replied.

"Does that mean that we're completely powerless?"

"Not necessarily," Barbara intervened. "I agree with Steve that we need to get some good legal advice and start to defend ourselves as robustly as possible. It should help we can prove absolutely that last week's allegations about not sending the guidelines to some applicants are untrue."

"Okay," said Steve. "That's a plan – we'll get the lawyers in and start throwing some writs about the place. We'll need to tell the department, I suppose. But what about the web?"

"I suggest we go quiet for a while," said Josh. "Suspend the social media accounts and disable comments on the website. If we're not putting ourselves forward, people can't use our own sites to attack us."

"What about the blog, though?" asked Steve.

"Keep posting for our loyal followers, but try to be non-controversial for a while," Josh replied, grinning at his husband. "If you could possibly do that. Above all, keep those comments turned off. It strikes me that if we can disappear for a while, people will get fed up and move on to something else."

"Great, isn't it?" remarked Andy. "We're the ones falsely accused, and it's our business that has to suffer. I don't know how people put up with it. All that attention and bitchiness. Do you get all this too, Josh, from your fans?"

Josh laughed. "Yes, indeed. But you get used to it – part of the price of fame, I suppose. Social media is such a powerful tool that a small amount of nastiness seems a small price to pay."

Andy shrugged. "Maybe, maybe. But I still don't like it."

"Neither do I, Andy, believe me," Steve responded. "But we can't make the argument about climate change and green policies by staying out of the limelight all the time."

"I suppose you're right," he grumbled. "Sorry to be grumpy, but we founded this business to help the environment. I don't see how spending hours defending ourselves on social media helps us to achieve that."

"The short answer is that it doesn't," I said, intervening for the first time. "But what it does do is keep our name out there. Steve's blogs and our other postings keep the Pearson Frazer name in people's minds as having something relevant to say and knowing what we're talking about. You know, the people who know with a capital 'K'."

"Luke's right," said Barbara. "We've got to keep at it – even if it's a pain sometimes."

The meeting broke up shortly afterwards. Everybody's mood was grim; we didn't like what was happening but were powerless to prevent it. For a bunch of people in a successful small business to feel impotent was an unfamiliar and uncomfortable sensation.

The meeting and its outcome affected the atmosphere in the office for the rest of the day. Barbara had to field a couple of calls from journalists, but otherwise it was quiet. Steve and Andy went off about four for a meeting with some prospective lawyers who might agree to represent the firm.

Meanwhile, the social media comments and attacks kept on coming: insulting and demeaning us as a firm, as individual professionals and, worst of all, disparaging our personal lives. Steve was not the only victim of the attacks. They had spread – initially to Andy and then to me. The degree of personal information that the trolls had about us was unnerving. Information from Companies House and news items from the trade press were to be expected, but other material was downright creepy: data on likes recorded on some sites; the fact that we'd supported Remain in the referendum, and my profile on a couple of dating sites.

By four o'clock, I'd had enough: I suspended all my social media accounts. I'd also deleted my profiles from the two dating apps – I hadn't used them for weeks and I saw little need for them in the immediate future, if ever. Within the space of half an hour, I'd become invisible.

I felt better for having taken the action to protect myself, but it still left me edgy and depressed. I consoled myself with the thought that, once the meeting on Friday was out of the way, much of the anxiety that had formed the backdrop to our lives over the last few weeks would disappear.

Chapter Forty-Four

Dan

The week got off to a fairly calm start by our standards. There was the usual round of meetings about various projects on Monday, but Jeremy and I got the time to make progress on a number of fronts, not least in preparing for our defence of the Griffin House project for Sir John's review committee. We finished that off on Tuesday morning, after which I was due in the Commons.

Knowing I'd be at the House, I had also arranged a meeting with a fellow Tory MP who'd come out not so long before to pick his brains. Our quick drink had turned into an early dinner. Greg Randall was a couple of years older than me, and had already been in the Commons for five years when I was first elected. We weren't exactly bosom buddies, but we'd always got on well. He had stayed on the back benches and was an influential member of a couple of powerful committees, including the one shadowing my own department.

When Greg had decided to come out a couple of years earlier, he'd had a hard time with some members of his constituency association who'd tried to deselect him ahead of the 2017 election. They'd been roundly defeated by the rest of the membership, with the active support of the national party officers. I'd offered him as much moral support as I could and told him of my own situation. At that time, his strong advice had been to keep quiet, at least until Brexit was out of the way.

Now it was his turn to be supportive. I explained about how I'd met somebody and that rumours had begun circulating about my orientation. He said he'd heard them too, but had kept quiet. He thought I'd made the right decision. "It's important for you to control the agenda, Dan, and do it in your own time."

We spent some time on politics, also touching on departmental matters. As we parted, he wished me good luck and volunteered to send me the notes he'd made for his coming-out speech. I was grateful for the reassurance he'd given me; I set off for my meeting with Greg feeling better about my forthcoming ordeal than I had since I'd made the decision to come out.

I may have spent longer than planned with Greg, but I was still in plenty of time for my nine-thirty appointment in Soho. The club Glyn had suggested was situated in two of the surviving original eighteenth-century town houses a street off the square. They had been knocked together to form a single building. On the ground floor there were a series of small rooms, linked together with both the original doorways and some additional arched openings. The furnishings were eclectic, with lots of different designs of chairs and sofas in various states of dilapidation, all put together in a riot of different colours and fabrics. The place had a definite feel of the louche, and I was captivated from the moment I walked through the door. I paused only to reflect with a smile how I would have panicked even a few weeks earlier at the idea of going to a gay members' club and running the risk of being seen.

My host greeted me warmly and we ordered drinks. We sat down on one of the sofas. It was covered in velour fabric that was a particularly lurid shade of green.

"It's good to see you, Glyn. Been a long time."

"You too. Yes, too long, Dan. It's been so insane since we went live with the website and everything. Matt and I barely knew what day it was most of the time."

"Is it still like that?"

"No, thank the Lord. It's calmed down a bit, but we've also recruited some more people, which means we can take a bit more of a back seat. And what about you?" He grinned broadly. "It takes two to maintain radio silence, you know."

"Ah, yes. True. Politics has always been a crazy business, as you know. And it seems to be getting worse. I haven't led anything remotely resembling a 'normal' life since I joined the Whips Office. And being a minister? I tell you, Glyn, it's incredible."

We broke off our conversation as our drinks arrived, pausing while the waiter opened, and Glyn tasted the bottle of wine he'd ordered. As the attractive young waiter moved away, Glyn resumed. "Is it really that bad?"

"Endless meetings, going to the Commons for votes, at least two red boxes a night and three at weekends ... plus the constituency work – the surgeries and the follow-ups and the flag-waving visits. My majority isn't that big that

I can afford to neglect the seat – the Lib Dems aren't that far behind."

"Shit, Dan."

I nodded. "Plus there's Facebook and all the rest of the social media. I have to fund a small team that looks after all that. I try not to look at all the abuse, but I do have to take an interest in what's being said about me and to me."

"You sound like a one-man media show."

"I suppose that's a good analogy. Keep smiling, you're 'on' all the time."

"So, tell me: how has it all turned out?"

"How do you mean?"

"When we worked together, your whole life was about getting into politics – finding a seat, watching what was happening, making sure you were known at Central Office. It seemed to occupy almost every waking hour. Now you're almost there – next job in the Cabinet, and with the current turnover of ministers, that can't be long. Has the career lived up to your expectations?"

I took a swig of wine while I thought about my answer. I could lie and say it was all "absolutely marvellous, darling", but Glyn was too shrewd a cookie to swallow that: he'd see through the lie. And in any case, he was my friend: telling the truth was important.

"Honestly? No."

"How come?"

"My party has changed almost beyond recognition, and the Commons has become a much nastier place. That's partly about Brexit, but also because Labour has fallen apart under Corbyn. I'm coming to believe that good government is impossible: we don't have policy-making any more, we have government by Tweet."

"That's interesting. It certainly looks that way from the outside – but you're the first insider to admit it to me."

"Glyn, you've been watching all this for as long as I have – longer, in fact. The question for me is, what do I do about it?"

"Politics or the rest of your life?"

"Both, really. But it's the rest of my life that concerns me now. It didn't matter until recently but now it does."

"You've met somebody."

"Yep."

"Hey, Dan, that's good news. Anybody I know?"

"No, it's a guy I met originally at university. He's an environmental consultant."

"Fantastic! I'm delighted for you."

"Thanks. But you can see why it changes everything."

"Oh, absolutely. As soon as I met Matt, my whole perspective changed. It's an old cliché, I know, but I really did shift from living to work to working to live. He's my world now – hence the decision to get out of print media and start our own business."

Not for the first time in our friendship, I envied Glyn's assurance and sense of purpose. I could also see what a difference his new life had made to him: he looked at least five years younger than when we'd worked together – he looked healthy, and was dressed fashionably but casually in clothes that fitted him superbly. Such a contrast with my dull, safe suit, ordered online because I didn't have time to shop for decent clothes. Above all, he looked relaxed and happy. I envied him that too.

"Meeting Luke again has certainly changed my

perspective. And I think I'm going to have to make a choice."

"What, love versus ambition?"

"No, I already know the answer to that one; if it came to that decision, I'd choose Luke every time. But he knows me, that politics are in my blood and have been since I was a teenager. He's already told me that doesn't want me to change – as he put it, to throw away all I've worked for over the years."

"If he gets all that, he does sound special."

"Yes, he is. This is about me, though, what I want to do with the rest of my life, whether Luke is in it or not. I'd always assumed that I'd keep ploughing on to see how far up the ladder I could get. But I'm not sure that I want it any more – especially at Cabinet rank. That strikes me as even more of an impossible job than the one I've got now – with the added bonus of twenty-four-hour security and the total loss of privacy."

Glyn nodded. "I can see all that. Government does seem pretty impossible these days."

"So here I am, starting to wonder whether I should strike out and do something different. Maybe I should recognise that being a politician might no longer the be all and end all of my life. I got a fairly powerful nudge from my father last week."

"He was always keen for you to follow him into the Commons, wasn't he?"

"Absolutely. Long story short, I had dinner with him and my mother last night, and came out to them. That was okay – bit of a shock, actually. I'll tell you the full story some time. Anyway, he asked if I wanted to give up politics."

"Good grief, Dan. That's a big shift."

"Certainly is. He told me he'd understand entirely if I did."

"And do you? Want to give up, I mean."

I shrugged. "I'm more tempted now than I've ever been. There are things that I'd miss, aspects of being a Minister, being in the Commons chamber, meeting and talking to all sorts of people, sometimes being able to help them. But not the rest – the media, the plots, the manoeuvring for position."

"Any idea what you'd do?"

"Not really. I could start writing again, I suppose. Dad seemed to think there'd be plenty of opportunities."

"And he's right. Writing is certainly a possibility. You were a bloody good journalist, and I certainly missed you when you'd gone. And this is where I may be able to help you."

I frowned. "How?"

"As I said earlier, we've got things moving very nicely and the team has settled down superbly. Matt and I have been able to step back from day-to-day work and do some thinking about where we go next and how we want to approach things. We need to keep moving, keep expanding, doing new things. Our journalism and blogging are fine, and we've tons of users and our advertising revenue is flowing nicely. We now need to move into video – comments, discussions, possibly investigative stuff eventually. Build our own online channels but eventually sell programmes to broadcasters."

"That's seriously ambitious!"

Glyn nodded. "Sure is, but that's the way to go. We're sure of it. It doesn't need to cost a fortune these days – Christ, my smartphone can record video of sufficient quality. The art lies in the calibre of the presenters and in the editing. We can do that, but we need a front man. Which is where you come in."

"Me?" I could not hide my astonishment. "I'm no broadcaster!"

"That's where you're wrong, old son. I've been watching some recordings of you on *Question Time* before you went into the Whips' Office. You're a natural, Dan."

I stared at him for moment, incredulous. "Christ, it'd never even occurred to me. I thought if I went back into journalism, I might pick up the odd appearance on the telly, but no more than that."

"Perhaps you should think about it now. You're good looking and personable – and eight years in the House with ministerial experience could put you on a par with the Portillos of this world. Mind you, I couldn't pay you much, at least in the early days. I could probably match your MP's pay, but not the ministerial bit."

"That's not a problem. I own my flat outright anyway and don't have many other outgoings – I never have time to spend money. But I still can't see myself in the role, Glyn."

"You'd be fine. You can write, so your scripts wouldn't be a problem." He paused and grinned at me. "Plus, you were a bloody good journalist ten years ago, in case you'd forgotten. But believe me, the future is online, not in print."

"That's as may be. But..."

"Tell you what, come and do a test with us. Didn't I read somewhere that you're coming up north soon?"

"Yeah, week after next. I shall be up there from Sunday night until Thursday, I think."

"And what are you doing that weekend?"

"Nothing, as far as I know. I was hoping to spend it with Luke."

"How about you stay up north and come to us for the weekend? Bring Luke too, if you like. We could play about in our studio for a couple of hours and see how you get on. How does that sound?"

In fact, it sounded too good to be true. I still had my doubts, but Glyn's proposal might represent a plan where before there had been none. "Sounds great," I replied enthusiastically. "I'll look forward to that."

We chatted for a few more minutes before I left for home. We agreed to ask Glyn's PA and Jeremy to sort out the details, but it seemed that I would be spending a weekend in Yorkshire in two weeks' time, playing at being a TV host.

Governing Passions

Chapter Forty-Five

Luke

Dan got back to the flat around eleven and found me curled up on the sofa, listening to music and reading with my glasses perched on my nose.

"I love your preppy look with those specs," he remarked with a soppy look on his face. I immediately put my book aside and rose to greet him, wrapping him in my arms and kissing his cheek.

"Hey, Mr Bigshot Minister."

"Hey yourself, Sky. What's with calling me a bigshot.?"

"Whizzing me about the countryside giving 'important speeches' and taking me to posh hotels. Sounds pretty bigshot to me." I laughed.

"I suppose, when you put it like that," he replied, huffing on his nails and polishing them on his lapel. "What sort of day has the bigshot's boyfriend had?"

"Pretty good. Finished a project early, which was pretty awesome since it got me a pat on the head from Barbara and earned thousands of brownie points with Steve. I started writing a proposal for a big job in Wessex, but got distracted by dreaming of a nice man I know who owns a cottage down there. Just a routine day for a kickass consultant like me."

"Sounds pretty impressive to me, Mr Kickass Consultant."

"Do you want any supper? I know you said you'd eat at the House, but I bet you forgot."

"Actually, I didn't. My meeting with Greg Randall ran longer than planned. I was picking his brains about coming out following his experience a couple of years ago. He took me for an early dinner to talk about it. After that I went for a drink with another old pal, who also had lots of interesting things to say."

"You have had a bigshot day. What sort of interesting things?"

"Sit down and I'll tell you all about it."

I resumed my seat on the sofa. Dan poured a couple of drinks before joining me, snuggling close and putting my arm round his shoulder.

"Hmm. This is nice," I said dreamily.

"What?"

"This. Snuggling up with you on the sofa."

"I know. I still can't get used to how lucky I am." He sipped his whisky.

"Come on, then, spill. Who's this mysterious friend of yours? Should I be jealous?"

Dan gave a bark of laughter. "Of Glyn? Certainly not. We're just friends, nothing more. He's gay, but we never hooked up or anything."

"Who is he?"

"My old boss. We worked together for a couple of years,

then he got promoted and was my line manager for a few months before I left to fight the 2010 election. He's now got his own online business. It's going great guns and becoming one of the most influential political blog sites around."

"Wow. Sounds impressive. I don't suppose he offered you a job, did he?"

"Actually, yes."

I pulled out of his embrace and sat up to face him. "Dan, that's fantastic! This is what you've been looking for, isn't it? A possible route out of the Commons? What's he offering?"

"It's early days yet, but he wants me to front his new video show."

"Good grief!"

"My sentiments exactly. I told him I had pretty much zero experience of broadcasting."

"And what did he say?"

"That he'd been watching old tapes of me on *Question Time* and I was a natural."

"Bloody hell, Dan."

"Yeah, I know. I'm very sceptical but a bit excited."

I felt full of joy and excitement. "I think you'd be brilliant. What happens next?"

"I've agreed to go and see him and his husband Matt the weekend after next. They live near York, so I can go at the end of my ministerial visit. Do some screen tests, play around with formats and so on."

"That sounds fun."

Dan laughed at my enthusiasm. "It does, doesn't it? You're invited too, by the way."

"Bloody hell, I can't. It's my parents' wedding anniversary that weekend and I've promised to go down for the weekend. I'd actually planned to see if you could come as well, at least for Sunday lunch, but this is much more exciting."

"Oh, that's a double shame! We ought to try to shift Glyn's date."

"No way. With your crazy diary, the chances of finding another slot this side of the apocalypse are virtually zero. Go on your own and get this under way while you can!"

Dan had to acknowledge that I was right. He finished his drink and stood up, holding his hand out to help me up. "Time for bed, I think, don't you?"

I grinned up at him from the sofa. "Always happy to join you in bed," I responded.

"And it's my role in life to keep you happy. Come on." He took my hand and led me into the bedroom. Once there, we undressed and brushed our teeth, taking turns to use the electric toothbrush.

"There's something intimate about sharing an electric toothbrush, don't you think?" I asked.

"Except that we're not truly sharing – we have separate brush heads."

"I know, but still... Anyway, I like what your motor does to my mouth."

"Luke Carter, go and wash your mouth out. Such filth."

I chuckled. "Sorry, just have. See what using your motor does to my mind?"

Dan was back in the bedroom now, drawing the duvet back for us to get into bed. "Silly devil. Come on. Hop in and show me what your motor can do for me."

I climbed in beside him but immediately moved to straddle him. "Vroom, vroom." I whispered, before biting his earlobe. He grabbed my head and returned the compliment, sending shives of pleasure through me, waggling his hips so that our erections brushed against each other.

He grinned. "Gives the words 'power bottom' a whole new meaning, doesn't it?" he asked as he thrust upwards to boost the contact between us.

I smiled dreamily as I continued to move and make the occasional car engine noises. However, they became more sporadic as my movements became slower and more sensuous.

Dan lay back, clearing enjoying my gyrations. Suddenly he reached for me and hauled me down into a kiss, before whispering in his ear "You've certainly got me revved up now."

But "Vroom vroom" was the only reply he got.

Governing Passions

Chapter Forty-Six

Dan

After a day packed with meetings on the Wednesday, I was back in the office all day on Thursday. It was just as well, since I had to prepare for the constituency association meeting the following night. There was a speech to write, and a press statement to prepare and get cleared. Plus there were conversations – potentially embarrassing ones, too – to be had with my Secretary of State, the Chief Whip and, if necessary, the PM.

I was not particularly looking forward to the next thirty-six hours, but I knew they had to be faced and that they would be worth it. Though my discussions with my parents had not gone the way I'd expected, I was keenly aware of the sense of liberation I had felt in the wake of our dinner. For such frankness and openness to spread across the rest of my life would be a huge step forward.

In fact, between the coming out, spending more time with Luke and managing to keep the Griffin House project in play, life seemed to be going pretty well. I couldn't help feeling that it had all been a little too easy.

I glanced at my watch. I was seeing my immediate boss at four and the Chief Whip shortly afterwards. Time to get on with working out what to say on Friday night. Sorting that out would also make the afternoon a whole lot easier.

I was putting the final touches to it when Jeremy popped his head round the door. "All done?" he asked.

"Almost. I've stuck very much to the line we talked about. I think it should work well, and Luke's happy with it, too."

"Great stuff," he replied. "I'm sure it'll be fine."

"Thanks. Was there something you wanted?"

Jeremy shook his head. "Just checking – you're seeing George at the House, aren't you? We'll need to get going soon."

"That's fine," I replied. Except that Jeremy was definitely not fine. He was frowning slightly and clearly puzzled about something. I met his eye. "Are you sure you're okay?"

There was a pause. "What? Oh, yes. Sorry. Slightly baffled, that's all. I had a call from Adam a few minutes ago."

"Oh? Your cousin Adam?"

"Yeah. He's lost his mobile – but he's convinced that somebody has stolen it deliberately. He was a bit panicky. It seems there are some quite important numbers on there. And I don't think he's been all that careful to delete some of the texts."

"Including mine, presumably?"

"Yup. He wanted me to let you know. I don't think it's a problem – he probably left it somewhere. He's a bit of a scatterbrain, as you know."

"Certainly is," I replied with a short laugh. I had been fond of Adam when I'd used his services, but he certainly wasn't the sharpest knife in the drawer. He'd mislaid his phone three times in one evening at my flat. I was sure there wouldn't be a problem. "Thank him next time you're talking to him. Give him my best."

"Will do," replied Jeremy. "Now, let's get you over to the House."

In the event, the discussions with both my own immediate boss and with the Chief Whip were unremarkable. George Eckersley was supportive and expressed no surprise at my revelation. We weren't close politically or personally, but he wished me luck with my constituency association meeting.

The Chief Whip was more concerned about my future intentions than anything else. Jim Hayden had been my boss when I was in the Whips Office; we'd become close, and I counted him as one of my few political friends. He didn't bat an eyelid when I told him the reason for my visit. "Christ, Dan. You're not going to resign your seat, are you?" he asked, running his hand through his hair for the tenth time during our brief conversation.

"No, no," I replied with a smile. "I decided to be honest. That's all."

"Hmm. I'm not sure that the best policy in politics," he replied. "But there we are. So long as we don't have to face a by-election, I don't mind. The arithmetic's bad enough already in this place without losing anybody."

"That bad, eh?"

"Bloody dreadful, Dan. At least when you were here with me in the Whips Office, we knew what side we were on and who the opposition was. With this poisonous bloody atmosphere over Brexit, I don't know who my friends are any more."

"I didn't think Chief Whips had any friends."

"Fuck off, Forrester," he replied with a laugh. "You know what I mean."

"Oh, I do indeed. Never known anything like it – neither has my dad. Still, at least you haven't got a SPAD in your department busy stirring up all sorts of trouble."

"Oh? Who's that?"

"A guy called Sean Andrews. He's George's economics adviser."

"That little squirt? Christ! I thought we'd got rid of him."

"No, he's still around. In fact, I wondered whether somebody in the ERG had forced him on poor old George."

"That would figure. He's poison, that bastard. You leave him to me – I'll have words and see if we can't get rid."

"That would be very helpful, Jim. He's seriously bad news for the whole government, not only me."

"I'm on it. About your news, I'll let Number Ten know what's happening, so don't worry about the PM. She'll be supportive. Now, you get off down to the back of beyond and charm all those old ladies with tales about your boyfriend. I want you fully fit and voting next week."

"Thanks, Chief. I'm grateful."

"No problem, Dan. Seriously, lad, I hope it all goes okay," he responded.

I left the Chief Whip's room at the Commons and walked

back into the central Lobby. I couldn't help but smile to myself; all the fear and trepidation I'd felt at the beginning of the week had melted away. My parents, my immediate boss and now the Chief Whip had all been very supportive. But it wasn't over yet, by any means. The verdict of the constituency association tomorrow night might be totally different. After that, there was the court of public opinion. However, there was little I could do to affect what other people said about me, so I was determined not to worry about it.

I dialled Jeremy's number to let him know that all was well with the Whips Office. Jim had been happy with the line we were planning to take in the media, and Jeremy would brief the department's press office tomorrow afternoon on what I was about to say and how they should react to any questions. As I was not going into the office in the morning, we went over this again and agreed that everything was in place.

"So, have you finished writing your speech for tomorrow?" Jeremy asked.

"Pretty much. Funnily enough, the Brexit section has been more difficult to draft than my coming-out bit. Trying to keep them all on side is getting increasingly difficult. I think people are getting more anti-EU rather than less."

"I think everybody's getting more entrenched. Moderate Brexiteers are now becoming more militant, and friends who wanted to remain are getting steadily more exasperated. God knows where it's all going to end."

I sighed. "All I can do is toe the party line. We promised to deliver on the referendum result and are determined to do so, etcetera, etcetera. The PM and her team are the best people to do this and are focused on getting on with it."

"That's the line," he replied. "You'll just have to hope they'll believe you."

"Hmm. I think coming out might be easier."

Jeremy laughed down the phone. "I think you're probably right," he said. "But seriously, good luck. I shall be rooting for you. Give Luke my best."

"I will," I promised. "And thanks for all your help, Jeremy. It's been above and beyond – I am so grateful."

Chapter Forty-Seven

Luke

Friday morning saw Dan and I heading south westwards towards his constituency home in Monks Cheney and that night's meeting. It was a typical late-autumn morning – grey and dripping. By now, the leaves had all gone from the trees but stayed hanging about in gutters and on footpaths, soggy and slippery, a sad reminder of the summer now gone.

The morning was misty. As we left the London suburbs and drove into the countryside, visibility fell. The atmosphere felt damp; it was the sort of day when, if you were outside for any length of time, the cold seemed to penetrate your very being. Looking out of the car window, the fields lost their boundaries and seemed to dissolve into the mist. Distant trees took on a ghostly appearance, their newly bare branches pointing into the air like spectral fingers.

Dan had started a classical playlist on his phone, which he routed through the car's stereo system, and we sat in companionable silence for most of the time. It was one of the things I liked most about spending time with him – there was no compulsion to talk. We could simply exist in the same space, and I drew comfort from his presence.

We stopped for a coffee on the motorway but avoided any possibility of public attention by using the drive-through counter and staying in the car, only stepping outside to use the gents.

"We seem to be making good time," I remarked as we returned to the car.

Dan nodded. "We are. It was a good run out of London. I've known it take twice as long on some days."

"Me, too. I often come this way to Harchester. It can be a nightmare."

"That reminds me, have you warned your parents? About tonight?"

"Yes. I said that we didn't expect my name to be mentioned, but it might crop up."

"Good to avoid surprises."

"Do you think it'll happen? Tagging on to me?"

Dan shook his head. "I don't think so – not immediately, anyway. I didn't plan to name you in my speech, if that's okay."

"No, no, that's fine. As we said the other day, this is about you and your relationship with them. It's not about us."

"That's true, but ... I don't know. I'd have loved to take you along tonight to introduce you, at least to my friends in the association. You know, show them how awesome you are."

I snorted in response. "This isn't the right occasion, though, is it?"

"No. Too posh and formal. Anyway, there's all the other business they've got to get through. And, of course, half of them only want bitch about Brexit."

"Sounds fun... Not."

"I wanted the job, as Jeremy never tires of pointing out. Still, things might calm down once the PM has got her deal."

"Do you think so?"

"Bloody hope so. If she can't get it through the Commons, there'll be hell to pay. It'll probably finish her – and the party."

"Really?"

"Oh, yes. At some point we'll split between Brexiteers and Remainers – it's almost bound to happen. And that could be the end of the Tory Party as we've known it."

Knowing Dan, knowing how politics and his career had been his life for more than twenty years, I understood how difficult things were. "Whatever happens from now on, Dan, you won't be alone. I'll be with you all the way, whatever happens."

"Thanks, that means a lot. The next few months will be scary, especially for somebody like me who's always known what he wanted to do. Facing the prospect of that being turned upside down is terrifying. It'd be good to know that you'd got my back."

"Always, my love. And you mustn't worry. The skills you've learned will always be in demand. Who knows – you might find a job that has the fun without the stress."

Dan laughed, lightening the mood. "If you can find that for me, I'd give all this up tomorrow. Maybe if this thing with Glyn Pargiter comes off that could be the start of something."

After that we stuck to lighter subjects. We got to Dan's cottage about four in the afternoon, in time to unwind for an hour before he had to drive into Dorchester for the meeting.

It was good to be back there; whatever happened from now on, this place would always have happy memories from that first weekend. I hoped that Dan would keep the place, even if he no longer needed a constituency home.

Janet had left us a snack to eat before the meeting and a pasta bake to reheat for supper. We discussed whether I should stay at home or go to the pub across the road from the meeting venue. In the end, we decided that I should stay at the cottage. Dan promised to text me to let me know how things were going. He left around six-thirty after a long and lingering cuddle.

"Off you go and slay the dragons," I told him.

"That's no way to talk of my constituency ladies! I'm sure they love little children and are kind to animals."

"Yes, but will they be kind to my boyfriend? That's the question."

"I'm sure they will be. You mustn't worry. They're much more worried about the EU than whether I kiss boys."

"Boys?" I asked. "Do you mean more than one? Mr Forrester!"

Another peck on the cheek and he was gone. As soon I heard his car drive off, I realised that staying at the cottage was a mistake. I was never going to relax until I knew the outcome of the meeting; I should have insisted that I should be on hand in case things went south. Still, it was too late now. I would just have to sit and wait.

Chapter Forty-Eight

Dan

I couldn't remember being as nervous about a constituency event since my original adoption meeting almost ten years earlier. I tried to get a grip as I parked the car; I was here now and simply had to get on with it. Besides, facing this audience was nothing compared to dealing with the House of Commons when it was feeling cross or boisterous.

As luck would have it, the first person I saw when I walked through the door was Anthony Stewart, the chairman. To say that he wasn't pleased would have been an understatement. True, he was not expecting me to be there, because the member's report to the executive committee was a routine matter, usually given in writing and often taken as read. I was not expected to attend regularly, especially now I was a government minister.

"Dan, what are you doing here?"

"Anthony, nice to see you too. I thought it was important to show my face after our chat the other week." I switched on my blandest smile.

He had the grace to be discomfited by my sarcasm. "Yes,

well. I suppose..."

I nodded briskly. "Good. I shan't keep the meeting long but I have a couple of things to say, which I felt needed to be said in person."

We stood at the door of the meeting room and I gestured for him to go first. "After you, Anthony. I insist."

I maintained my smile as we entered the room. It was ironic; walking into the room together presented an image of amity and unity. The picture was a completely false one, of course: I felt neither friendship nor any sense of solidarity with him. But appearing to do so could have its uses.

Unbeknown to Anthony, Helena had set a place for me at the top table so I was able to take my seat immediately. He, on the other hand, was fussing about whether I had a seat, which made him look a little flustered. Then he bustled over to a corner of the room where he clearly had a little coterie of friends and admirers. I recognised some faces but others were completely new to me.

Helena noticed my uncertainty at the new faces and whispered, "New ward committee members from Anthony's ward. At least two of them joined last month after leaving UKIP."

"Entryism, do you think?" I asked.

She nodded. "We need to watch them – and not only over Brexit. They're likely to be to the right on other matters."

"Got you," I responded. "It'll be good to get this over with while I've still got some friends in the room."

"You've got loads, Dan. Don't worry."

I hoped she was right. I tried to pay attention to the opening formalities, but found it difficult to focus on such mundane matters as the minutes of the last meeting and the Treasurer's Report. My item came next.

The chairman's introduction was a clever combination of icy politeness and hostility. He welcomed the fact that I had "made time in my busy schedule" to attend in person, but also made it clear that my presence was not entirely welcome on a night "when there was a good deal of important business to get through". No doubt, he added, I would heed the busy agenda and keep my remarks brief.

I managed to smile while he spoke, then rose and thanked him. "I wanted to come in person tonight for three reasons. First and foremost, it's always good to spend time with my friends in the South Wessex Conservative Association. You have always given me a warm welcome over the last ten years. Secondly, there have been some changes in my personal life in the last few weeks that I want to share with you. And thirdly, I want to update you on the Brexit process and how we in the government, under the leadership of our Prime Minister, are working hard to deliver on the referendum result."

As I feared, the very mention of the "B" word sent a rumble through the audience. It might get a little heated later, which was why I wanted to tackle my personal agenda first.

"If I may, I'll deal with my circumstances first. Ten years ago, when I first became your prospective parliamentary candidate, I told you that I was still single because I had yet to meet the right partner. That was true in 2009, and has remained the case throughout my time as your Member of Parliament until the last few weeks.

"What I didn't tell you ten years ago, because it didn't

371

seem relevant at the time, was that when I did meet somebody whom I wanted to make my life partner it would probably be a man. Tonight, I think it right to let you know that the situation has changed. I've met somebody with whom I hope to spend the rest of my life. And he is a man."

I paused for a moment and glanced round the room. My words had been received in silence; there wasn't the instant reaction that the mention of Brexit had prompted. I received a couple of encouraging smile.

I carried on. "Alongside my announcement to you this evening, I've made a statement in the press and on social media. Earlier today, I let the Prime Minister know that I am gay and that my new partner and I have entered what we both hope will be a committed and long-term relationship.

"As you know, I am by no means the first openly gay MP on the Conservative benches. Some of you may be wondering why this was ever an issue. I can only say that coming to terms with one's sexuality, especially when it doesn't conform with the majority in society, is an intensely personal matter. People cope with it, and with the sense of otherness and isolation that it can bring, in their own way. I've struggled with the issue for too long, but I'm glad of this opportunity to be frank with you all. I want to reassure you that this won't impact in any way on my determination to be the best possible Member of Parliament and to continue to serve the voters of South Wessex for as long as possible."

"Hear, hear," said a voice from the back of the room. Somebody else joined in and there was a sprinkling of applause, quickly taken up by the majority of the people there. Inwardly I breathed a sigh of relief.

And that was it. Done. No gasps in the room, nobody getting up and walking out. A small knot of people grouped round one of Anthony's cronies had sour faces and failed to join in with the applause, but they were mainly older members who had been cold towards me ever since my adoption. Ominously, though, Anthony's new recruits to the executive also sat on their hands.

I acknowledged the applause and prepared to resume my speech. "Now, to more pressing matters and our progress on exiting the European Union..."

As had been clear at the start, the controversy over leaving the EU loomed much larger during the meeting than the revelations about my personal life. Passions were running high about the negotiations over the exit agreement, with several members arguing strongly for walking away – what the media were calling a "No-deal Brexit". I stuck doggedly to the line that the government was doing all it could to respect the referendum result whilst minimising the damage to our economy and our future relationship with our nearest neighbours.

At one point the discussion became heated, with one of the new ex-UKIP branch committee members accusing the government of treachery. He concluded his remarks by looking directly at me and saying, "We shouldn't be surprised – queers in this country have a habit of being traitors."

That was too much even for the chairman. Anthony might not have been my biggest fan, but we'd never actually fallen out. He told the man to moderate his language or leave the room. "There's no need for personal abuse," he snapped. "We're supposed to find common ground in political parties, not abuse each other."

The man glared at the chairman. "I thought you were one of us. But you're not actually – you're all Quislings intent on betraying us to Brussels. I quit." He got up and left the room, leaving an embarrassed silence apart from the sound of feet shuffling awkwardly.

After a few moments, the chairman broke the silence. "I'm sorry about that, ladies and gentlemen. I hope you'll agree that such language is totally uncalled for here and we shouldn't tolerate insults to our friends and colleagues." There were one or two muttered "hear, hears", before he carried on. "I think we'd better leave the discussion there. I had considered asking for an emergency motion on Brexit from the meeting that we could send to the PM, but I think we'd better leave that for tonight."

Suddenly everything clicked. That was the reason he'd been so put out when I'd arrived: he knew I would argue against him. He'd have more trouble stirring things up if I was in the room giving people chapter and verse on the latest position.

Now it seemed obvious what the game was: drive a wedge between me and the association, highlighting and emphasising the differences between us. In the end the members would be persuaded to deselect me, and another troublesome Remainer would be gone. In that sense, my coming out had been a bonus to him and his pals; there would always be at least one or two who would disapprove of my being gay, and that would rob me of their support.

The awful thing was that I no longer cared. This was not the party I'd been a member of since my boyhood. Before my eyes, this association – and hundreds of others round the country – was morphing into petty-minded, ultra-right-wing nationalism. The members had no interest in the centre ground or in appealing to the wider electorate; they were focused on getting out of the EU and recreating some post-imperial version of 1950s' England. All I could say was good luck to them but I wanted no part of their crazy project.

The Brexit discussion done with, the rest of the meeting was concluded rapidly. There was nothing else controversial: a discussion about fund-raising events in the New Year; arrangements for a policy forum for local councillors and prospective candidates for next year's council elections, and quick reports from each of the ward committees.

I allowed the routine business to wash over me. Fortunately, I was not expected to contribute, so I became lost in random thoughts about my future. It came as surprise to realise that Anthony was making his closing remarks and thanking me for coming down. I donned my most amiable face and nodded in acknowledgement, glad it was over. By now the room was warm and airless; I needed some fresh air and craved the sharpness of the cold winter's evening. But I would have to stay awhile and chat. It was expected.

"That was good, I thought," Helena's voice said in my ear.

I nodded. "About as good as we could have hoped for. At least nobody walked out in disgust."

"Aside from the UKIP nutter," she reminded me.

"Yes, but the people who really matter seemed okay. I'll circulate a bit, try and read the vibes."

"Good idea. Meanwhile, I'll keep my ear to the ground. The social media posts all went up on time, by the way."

"Oh, great. We can expect some hostile reactions on there, no doubt."

"Probably no more than the usual. But I'll let you know. Now go and be charming, Dan."

"Yes, ma'am." I grinned at her. "Thanks for your support tonight. It was very welcome."

It was another half hour before I could get away; it was often difficult to exit gracefully from a room after a meeting like that. There was always one more person who wanted a word or needed to express their opinion. We might no longer live in an age of deference, but MPs and Ministers were still celebrities to an extent, especially in a semi-rural constituency like this, so a kind word, a handshake or a smile made a difference. That was especially true in this gathering – these people were the core party activists, giving up time and money to get me and our councillors elected.

I texted Luke to say I was on my way as I left the hall. The chill air was welcome, but it was misty again and felt damp. Not a night to be out for long, and the drive home might be challenging if the mist worsened near the sea.

My mood fluctuated between relief, pleasure and gut-wrenching fear: relief that my big announcement was done; pleasure at its reception, and fear of the future, which for some reason loomed large tonight. Sure, opportunities were opening up and, as my father had reminded me, I had a range of talents that I could use. But losing the certainties that had governed my life for the last ten years felt like falling into an abyss on this dark and foggy night..

My trepidation intensified as I got nearer home. For the first time since Luke and I had got together, I felt the need for solitude. I knew that I should talk things through with him and that I'd probably feel better for it, but I wasn't ready. As my mother had reminded me, I had always had this tendency to retreat into myself ever since I was little. I needed time on my own to think things through. I couldn't do that when we were both ensconced in the cottage, or crammed for several hours in the car for the drive to Sutton Coldfield the next day.

Governing Passions

Chapter Forty-Nine

Luke

Settling down and relaxing didn't get any easier as the evening passed. I kept conjuring up scenes, ranging from an actual car crash on the way to the meeting to a virtual car crash once Dan got inside.

I tried to read but found myself going over the same sentence again and again. I thought an audio book might be a distraction, but I was wrong. I tried the television and channel hopped for several minutes. Eventually I gave up and put on some music, letting it form the background to my fretting.

Dan had said to expect him around ten, so I went into the kitchen around half-past nine to get the supper out of the fridge. It could go in the oven as soon as I got a text to say he was on the way.

When the text arrived a few minutes later, my stomach knotted again with anxiety. I ignored it and distracted myself with a flurry of activity: putting the food in the oven; laying the table; opening a bottle of wine; plumping the cushions; checking my phone every thirty seconds in case he sent another message.

Eventually I ran out of tasks, but Dan was still several minutes away. I sat down again, replaying his message in my mind. It was terse: *Meeting OK. On my way.* What did OK mean? Was it shorthand for "it went really well"? Or did it mean that it had been acceptable, in line with expectations? Or "not very good but survivable"? I'd never realised before that two letters could have so many nuances.

Finally I heard a car. He was back. Instinctively, I leapt up to open the front door. He was there facing me, eyes blinking in the sudden light cast from the hall, grim-faced and pale with exhaustion. My dreams of a hug and a celebratory drink evaporated as he greeted me with a nod and a brief half smile.

I stood back to let him through and followed him into the sitting room. "Did it not go well?"

"It was fine, Luke, honestly. Only one bad reaction, and that was because of Brexit as much as me coming out. I'm just so exhausted – the drive home and the fog."

"And the release of the tension, I suspect."

"Yeah, that too. I'm sorry…" His words were interrupted by the beeping of the oven timer.

"Never mind," I said brightly. "That's supper ready. You might feel better after some food."

He shook his head. "No, Luke. Thanks but I couldn't eat a thing. If you'll excuse me, I'm going to head straight for bed. Sorry." He looked away as he spoke, and his tone was terse. His arms were folded tightly, defensively. He moved past me to the stairs, pausing to give me a peck on the cheek. "Sorry."

"I'll come too, if you like."

"No, have your supper. Come up when you're ready. I'll probably be asleep and I'm sure you won't wake me." That was me told.

He climbed the stairs and went into the bedroom. I remembered the supper and dashed into the kitchen to retrieve it before it burned. Dammit, I was hungry. Once again I covered my anxiety by activity, eating, drinking a glass of wine, tidying up and dealing with the leftovers.

I sat in the sitting room for a few minutes, trying to unwind. It was no good going upstairs if all I did was toss and turn all night and keep Dan awake. He clearly needed his sleep – and some more to follow, ideally. A quiet weekend here would have done him the world of good, but that was not going to happen; we had a long drive in the morning and his speech in the afternoon. At least, with luck, Sunday should be quiet and relaxing aside from the drive back to London.

I felt hurt by his manner but, more importantly, I was perturbed by this new side of him: closed off, almost secretive. In all time we'd known each other, he had always been frank and open; we both had been, except for the one topic of our sexuality.

As I mulled it over, I realised that I shouldn't be surprised by his reaction. After all, he'd been on his own for the last fifteen years, with nobody he trusted enough to confide in. He was used to coping on his own, and was doing so again now, retreating into himself. My task tomorrow would be to coax him out again.

Governing Passions

Chapter Fifty

Luke

Driving up the A34 – the main trunk road linking southern England with the Midlands – wasn't my favourite way of spending a Saturday, but I'd promised that I'd do this for Dan to give him time to work, both on his speech this afternoon and his weekend red boxes.

He sat in the back of the car so that he could spread out his papers. The first hour and a half of the four-hour journey passed in almost total silence. That was hardly any different from breakfast time in the cottage. Though Dan had slept solidly through the night (unlike me), the rest had done little to improve his mood. During breakfast we'd barely exchanged more than a few grunts and monosyllables.

I remembered from our student days that Dan had always been capable of intense concentration for long periods, and I saw it again during the journey. After about three-quarters of an hour, he declared himself satisfied with his speech and e-mailed it to HQ so that it could be issued to the press later in the afternoon. After that, he worked on his boxes.

As we neared Newbury, I glanced in the mirror. Dan had lifted his head from his work, and was staring out of the window. "Fancy a break?" I asked.

"Have we got time?"

"Should be okay, provided we're not too long."

"That would be good," he said, smiling into the mirror, before dropping his head and resuming his reading. It was the first time I had seen him anywhere near relaxed since he'd left the cottage at teatime yesterday. I breathed a small sigh of relief.

We reached Newbury services a few minutes later. I visited the toilets and got two takeout coffees; as yesterday, it was simpler for Dan to stay in the car to avoid being recognised.

"You feeling better now?" I asked as I got back into the car.

He gave a sheepish grin. "A bit."

"Good. I was worried about you last night."

"Yeah, sorry about that. I was absolutely exhausted."

"But something had upset you too, hadn't it?"

"One remark comparing all gay people to Guy Burgess wasn't calculated to improve my mood."

"What, the 'all gays are traitors' line? Surely not?"

"Yep. Absolutely what he said. Oh, and I think the word Quisling came into it at some point as well."

"Fuck, Dan That's dreadful. I hope nobody supported him."

"No, they didn't. Even our beloved chairman was on my side, and that's a rare enough event."

"No wonder you were upset."

"It wasn't that so much. I looked round the room last

night and realised how little I had in common with them."

"But you've known them for ten years, haven't you?"

"True, but we've grown apart. The people there now have grown older – some have died or retired, but they haven't been replaced. It's a party of old fogies. At thirty-seven, I was the youngest person in the room by about twenty years. People have got harder and nastier since the referendum – and I realised last night that I don't think it can go on like this much longer."

"No wonder you were in a bad mood." I glanced at my watch. "Time we were on the move again. Have you got more work?"

"'Fraid so."

"We'll talk some more about this tonight. Okay?"

Dan gave me a proper Forrester beam, and I relaxed some more. I'd get to the bottom of all this tonight.

We made good time for the rest of the journey and Dan finished his last box as we approached our junction. I dropped him at the venue for his speech in time for him to do some meeting and greeting with his hosts while I headed for the hotel. I would return at five to collect him.

Our hotel was about ten minutes' drive away, through pleasant streets of prosperous 1930s' semi-detached and detached houses; it was clearly a prosperous area. My destination lay down a narrow lane set in an area of parkland sufficiently large that you quickly forgot the suburban setting. There was a fascinating jumble of buildings dating from different periods, and at their heart a magnificent medieval house. I checked in for us both – Jeremy had warned the hotel in advance that this would happen – and was whisked upstairs to our room overlooking the garden.

It was huge, dominated by a floor-to-ceiling bay window, in front of which stood a three-piece suite. The king-sized bed was laden with cushions and looked insanely comfortable. Now this sort of luxury I could get used to.

The porter brought our overnight bags and showed me round the room, pointing out the lighting, showing me the TV controls and explaining how the complicated shower worked. After he'd left, it was blissfully quiet. I glanced at my watch – still only two-thirty. I had a couple of hours before I needed to leave to collect Dan.

I showered first, while I still remembered how to use the controls. It was blissful to wash away the grime of a long car journey and I could feel the tension in my shoulders draining away. My only regret was that Dan wasn't there to share it with me. Still, there would be plenty of time later...

Refreshed, I dressed and rang down for some tea before settling on the sofa to read for an hour. I'd always loved reading and an afternoon such as this, with nothing to do but sit and lose myself in a fictional world, was sheer bliss.

Chapter Fifty-One

Dan

As I sat on the platform waiting to give my speech, I speculated on all the ways I could be spending a November Saturday afternoon. At a football match, perhaps, or relaxing with some favourite music. Best of all would be cuddled up with Luke in front of the fire.

I'd spent the afternoon listening to a series of diatribes about the sins of the European Commission and the failings of the government in the Brexit negotiations. It was ironic that the Opposition barely got a mention. Although one or two speakers did manage some invective towards Jeremy Corbyn, that was almost as an afterthought. For a body that was supposed to be making policy for the future, it was paying an inordinate amount of attention to the past. The spirits of Winston Churchill and Margaret Thatcher were invoked so often that I was surprised they didn't put in a joint manifestation in the hall.

This lot made the audience at my constituency meeting the previous night look positively moderate. It made me even more depressed, consigning me to a form of political homelessness that I'd never experienced before. The feeling of being apart, not part of the tribe, was akin to the feeling I'd got as a teenager about being gay – alone, nervous about my place and frightened of the future.

I was jerked out of my reverie by hearing my name. The chairman was starting his introduction, thanking me for accepting the invitation at short notice because the Foreign Secretary had been called away on urgent business. Flatteringly, he referred to me as a rising star of the government and – rather to my surprise – welcomed me to my first party occasion as an out gay MP, noting that I'd come out as recently as last night. The West Midlands was proud to have an openly gay Mayor, and the Conservative Party should be proud that both Andy Street and I were members. I detected a few mutterings and noted where they came from in the hall. There might be trouble later.

Meanwhile, the applause which greeted me when I rose to speak was warm and most of the audience were smiling. In the front row, one elderly lady turned to her companion and said, "Isn't he handsome?" She blushed when she realised I'd heard her. I gave her a dazzling smile, then moved to the lectern.

I'd agreed with Party HQ that I should start off with a good slug of opponent bashing. Some jokes about the Opposition Front Bench always went down well with party audiences, and today was no exception. Five minutes in, and the audience was eating out of my hand. Whether it would be enough to get me through the rougher waters of Brexit remained to be seen.

On Brexit, I was under strict instructions to toe the line: government was determined to stick to its manifesto commitments; it was respecting the verdict of the referendum, and working towards the deadline of 29 March 2019. I was to end with a call for unity in the face of differences between us. These were, after all, differences of nuance more than principle.

I'd been nervous about this line as soon as I'd seen the draft because it wasn't true. Our differences were far wider, and everybody in the room knew it. But I'd been told that the words had been crafted inside Number Ten, and woe betide me if I didn't deliver them as scripted.

I did – and they very much not appreciated. There were cries of "Rubbish" from round the room. The magic word "betrayal" crossed several lips – and "traitor" and "Quisling" were also bouncing round the room – a painful reminder of the previous night's jibes.

I ploughed on, reaching my peroration about this government and this Prime Minister being the only people who could be trusted to deliver Brexit successfully. In another line that had come straight from Number Ten, I had to say that the successful delivery of the policy would be in the great tradition of Tory government – confident, prudent, and in the interests of all the people.

I nearly choked on the words, but managed to get them out in what I hoped was a convincing tone. The hollow laughter from various corners of the room suggested otherwise. I sat down, relieved to get it over with. There was polite applause, but no enthusiasm and little of the warmth with which I'd been greeted at the start. I glanced quickly at my watch and saw that the meeting had overrun.

Luke would be waiting for me. I murmured in the chairman's ear that unfortunately I couldn't stay to take any questions as I had another engagement. Bugger it, I thought, I was damned if I was going to submit to another half hour of hostility over the bloody EU. I was tired and I wanted to rest. I needed Luke, if he would forgive me for last night. The chairman looked disappointed but was well-mannered enough not to protest.

The applause died down. I stayed in my seat as he rose to thank me for my "excellent" speech and uttered similarly meaningless platitudes about the need for unity. That over, I made my escape.

Chapter Fifty-Two

Luke

I arrived in plenty of time to collect Dan at four-thirty, and strolled towards the entrance. I heard the applause at the end of his speech; it didn't sound exactly enthusiastic.

A few people drifted out, exchanging comments about the afternoon. Several people, mainly women, were supportive, saying that Dan looked handsome and spoke well. Others were less so; I heard the words "traitor" and "betrayal".

One elderly married couple were busy disagreeing, the wife saying he looked "very nice", but the husband harrumphing and saying "they always look good, the poofs".

"Can't stand 'em myself. If I had my way, they'd never be in the party, much less the government." He paused for breath. "Bloody queers," he added, as they disappeared into the street.

I could have hit the nasty bastard. Was this the modern Tory party in action? If so, no wonder Dan had been upset last night. He clearly had no future with them.

I was getting my head round that when he appeared through the doors, pausing to shake hands with several members as he left, laughing with one who had cracked a joke. Once again, I marvelled when I saw Dan the politician in action – he was so easy with people, exuding an effortless charm.

His face lit up as he saw me waiting. To my surprise – and that of a good few party members – he drew me into a hug and kissed me on the cheek. "Thanks for coming, Luke. Have you been waiting long?"

"Er, no. A couple of minutes, no more," I stammered, still shocked by his tactile approach in public. "The car's right outside."

"Great. I'm dying for a cuppa. How's the hotel?"

"Fabulous," I replied enthusiastically as I regained my composure. "You'll love it."

"Good. Jeremy did promise me a night of luxury."

"And he's certainly delivered – so far, at least. So, what's with the big hug, Dan? In public?"

"Did I embarrass you? Sorry."

"No, I was a bit surprised, that's all."

He laughed. "What's the point in coming out if I can't be myself?"

"It somehow seemed a bit ... sudden. Judging by some of the comments I heard, there are those in the party who don't approve, however supportive people are in Westminster."

Dan nodded. "That's inevitable, I'm afraid. We might pay lip service to the Equality Act, but I'm sure the diehards on the right will never change – especially the Christian right. All the more reason to ram it down their fucking throats."

"Whoa. Where did that come from? Did something happen in there?"

"Nothing specific, but the more time I spend with the activists, the more I realise I no longer have anything in common with them. As I said this morning, I'm a stranger in my own party."

We reached the car. Dan settled in the front seat and we stole a kiss across the centre console. He was reluctant to lose his hold on me, even for a short drive, so he left his hand on my thigh. It felt wonderfully warm and comfortable, and it made me smile.

When we got back to the hotel he asked for some fresh air before we went up to our room, so I took him through the garden. We strolled for a few minutes before stopping by the moat, catching sight of a heron perched high on the wall of what had probably been the kitchen garden.

Dan reached for my hand; he was fascinated. The bird didn't move for three or four minutes as it perched high above the water. We were at the point of agreeing that it had to be a piece of sculpture when it lifted its wings and swooped down, the picture of grace, before scooping a fish into its long bill.

I felt Dan shudder. "That quick, eh?" he asked. "A life snuffed out. Makes you think, doesn't it?"

"That's a bit philosophical for a Saturday afternoon."

He shook his head. "Sorry. I'm in an odd mood. All our lives can end like that – snuffed out by a car crash or struck down by illness. So why do we spend all that time planning for the future and dreaming about achieving our ambition?"

"Ah, *carpe diem* and all that. Yeah, I know what you mean. But why now?"

"It's another aspect of the politics, I suppose. I've spent my entire adult life planning for the future. I knew that if I wanted to achieve my ambitions, I had to plot and scheme. I've spent years pretending to be something I wasn't in order to please people who could help me get on. It was bloody hard, Luke – and I didn't worry about pushing people aside who threatened my position. That included you, of course, fifteen years ago.

"I've come to realise over the past few weeks that I was wasting my time. Meanwhile, I've missed out on so much. I have no friends to speak of, no social life. It's years since I've been to the theatre or cinema, much less a concert. All to be able to put the letters 'MP' after my name. I must have been mad."

"Oh, Dan. I'm so sorry about all this. I still feel responsible, though, for distracting you and taking you away from your dreams."

"No, no, that's not true at all. I'd started to feel like this before we met up again. What you've shown me is that there can be an alternative. That there is life outside politics, and that it's something I crave. You're not a distraction, Luke, you're my escape route."

I was about to reply when his mobile started to ring.

"Who the hell..." He glanced at the screen. "Oh, it's Jeremy. I'd better take it."

He took the call and greeted his private secretary in a jokey tone. "Thought you were having a weekend off, old son. What's all this about?"

I moved away slightly, not wanting to appear nosey. Dan

began to pace up and down the path.

"How on earth? Oh, his phone. I'd forgotten, of course. Christ, Jeremy, is he all right?" There was a pause. "Oh, good. So, what happens now? … Half an hour? They want a response in half an hour? … Fuck, Jeremy what am I going to say? … Right, okay. Yeah, that sounds fine…. He wants to see me?" He sighed deeply. "All right, I'll come back. Not much choice, is there? … I suppose we can set off by…' he glanced at his watch "… sixish. I need a shower and then we'll need to check out. It'll take at least a couple of hours from here… Yeah, tell him I'll be there around half eight."

I had no idea what was going on, but it was clear that our romantic evening was off, and we were driving straight back to London. Dan had finished the call but was standing still, staring at the screen. The colour had drained from his face. He reached up to tug his ear lobe – a sure sign of stress – then ran his hand through his hair.

He turned to me, his face a picture of despair. "It's one of the Sundays – they've got hold of a story about me using an escort. *Green Minister in Rent Boy Scandal* is their headline, apparently. I'm sorry, Luke. We've got to go back to London. The story's going on their website at eight tonight."

Governing Passions

Chapter Fifty-Three

Dan

It was inevitable that my coming out would prompt some comment in the national press, but I hadn't expected any of the papers to go down this route and try to dig some dirt. God knows, there had been little enough of that in my deeply closeted existence.

We drove fast down the outside lane of the M40, heading for London as quickly as we could. The most I'd seen of our room at the hotel had been ten minutes in the shower. Luke had been right: it was indeed charming, and I'd have given anything to stay there.

Instead we were heading for a meeting at the Chief Whip's office in Downing Street, summoned to discuss this bloody story about my personal life. I'd offered to drive; Luke had already been behind the wheel for nearly five hours. But he'd insisted. I had enough stress to cope with, he said, without the strain of two hours on the motorway.

We'd passed the journey in almost total silence, each lost in our own thoughts. Eventually, as we neared the Oxford turn off, Luke asked, "Are you okay?"

"Think so. Bit numb. It hasn't hit me yet, to be honest."

"Will you have to resign?"

I shook my head. "I don't think so. It's not as if I've cheated on anybody or lied about anything. It's lies and covering things up that get people into trouble."

"Like Profumo, you mean?"

"Yes. It was lying to the Commons that did for him. Same with Nixon and Watergate – it wasn't so much the original robbery as the things he did to cover it up."

"So a couple of flings with an escort hardly signify?"

"Exactly. At least, I think that's what the Chief Whip will say."

"How well do you know him?"

"Pretty well. I worked in the Whips Office for four years before I got this job. He was always very friendly."

"Did he know, do you think?"

"That I was gay? Probably. Chief Whips usually know everything there is to know about their MPs, and I can't imagine that I was an exception. And he was very supportive the other day, when I told him about coming out."

"Will it all blow over?"

"I certainly hope so. I'm sorry you've got involved in all this, though. It won't be very pleasant. But I want you to know that I haven't … er … been with anybody since we met up again. Sorry, that sounds a bit crass, but I wanted to say it, in case … you know."

"Don't be silly," Luke replied, laughing. "You'd already told me that you used escorts occasionally, and I told you that I understood why. You had to manage as best you could."

"It was easier and safer to be in control – and paying seemed the best way of doing that. Once I met you again and decided to come out, it didn't matter any more."

"Don't worry, Dan. We'll get through it."

"I know, but I hate that you get caught up in the backwash. Fuck knows what your friends and family will think."

"They can think what they like. We love each other. That's the only thing that matters."

"Thanks for that, Luke. I'm so grateful."

We drifted into silence again, but I felt much more relaxed after that conversation.

My phone rang again: it was Jeremy, with the latest update. Apparently, we weren't going to Downing Street now. They'd decided that there was too much risk of being ambushed by the media. We were to head for Jeremy's place; the media were neither aware of, nor interested in, where my private secretary lived.

We got through that and then Jeremy said, "You know, this whole thing puzzles me. It's difficult to see why the papers would bother."

"They're always happy to get a salacious story – especially the Sundays. And especially about a Tory minister."

"All the same, it strikes me as a bit odd. To go to all the trouble to steal Adam's mobile and all the risks that entails, especially after the row after the phone-hacking scandal a couple of years ago."

Thinking about it, Jeremy was right; there was definitely something off about this. "We knew that Adam's phone had disappeared because he warned you earlier in the week," I said.

"And we thought he'd just lost it."

"Right."

"Now it looks like deliberate theft, to get data from his phone."

"Do you think so?"

"Yep. Somebody was after information about his clients, including you," Jeremy said. He paused briefly before adding, "So, I'm thinking it was more likely to be a sting aimed specifically at you."

"What makes you think that?"

"Whoever got hold of the phone has used it as a source for this story, but nothing else. There's been no attempt to blackmail Adam or bribe him to spill the beans."

"I see what you're getting at."

"So why are you the only victim? I think Adam has a pretty upmarket client list."

"I can imagine. You're saying that somebody stole the phone to order for the gen on me?"

"Exactly. I'm told that the paper was *offered* the information – they didn't seek it. And it was only about you. Nothing else was on offer. Whoever stole Adam's phone did it for one reason – to damage you, and maybe finish your career."

"Fuck, Jeremy. Who?"

"Security services? Special Branch? The Whips Office, maybe? The chief usually knows everything."

I pondered that for a moment. "We're saying Sean bloody Andrews *again* then..."

"That's the way it looks, Dan."

A wave if depression washed over me. As if government wasn't difficult enough without all this factional fighting.

"Shit. When is all this going to end? I suppose they'll be online again tonight, throwing more hatred at me."

"At a guess, yes. I'll warn Helena and her team."

We discussed the logistics for a few moments. Just before I ended the call, I told Jeremy to expect us in about three-quarters of an hour. I stared out miserably into the gathering dusk.

"I picked up most of that," remarked Luke. "Sounds pretty shitty to me. What do you want me to do when we get there? Make myself scarce?"

"No, no, Luke. This concerns you, too. If they know enough about me to pinpoint a few hook-ups with Adam, they're bound to know about our relationship."

"Jesus. I hadn't thought about that. I suppose I'll be next – Minister's boyfriend and all that."

"Reckon so. I suspect it's only a matter of time. Though why they should think that'll cause a problem, I don't know."

"Understood. But you mustn't worry about me, about my name getting dragged in. I'm prepared for this, Dan. Eyes fully open, love."

I found Luke's words oddly comforting. There was no doubt that having somebody else in my life, somebody to share my thoughts with, felt good. "You know the real irony of this situation?" I said. "This is the first weekend of my life when I've been open and honest with everyone. I went into that hall this afternoon completely relaxed, no fear about anything. And now all this shitstorm blows up."

Governing Passions

Chapter Fifty-Four

Luke

By the time we got into London, my eyes felt as if somebody had thrown sand into them. They were scratchy after the intense concentration of the driving. I felt light-headed with fatigue – though at least I'd had the opportunity to rest during the afternoon.

Dan, on the other hand, had worked solidly during our journey from Dorset, gone on to deliver an important speech, and had to endure all the meeting and greeting that went with such an occasion. He now had to face the stress of being in the forefront of a major story in the Sunday papers. As we entered Jeremy's block, I noticed how tired he was.

He took the opportunity of a slow ride in the elderly and creaky lift to give me a hug and a quick kiss. "Thanks for doing the driving, Sky. I'm so grateful," he said into my ear

"My pleasure. Tired now, though."

"Me too. I hope this doesn't go on for hours."

"Might it, do you think?"

Dan shrugged. "Dunno. I don't think so – we need to agree the line and draft of a statement. They may want me to do some interviews to clear the air, or else hide me away until the storm blows over. We'll have to wait and see."

Jeremy's flat was in an elegant mansion block immediately to the south of the river overlooking Battersea Park. It was spacious, elegantly decorated and furnished. Our host greeted us warmly at his front door, immediately wanting to know from Dan how his speech had gone down in the afternoon. They chatted about the meeting for a few minutes, before turning to the subject in hand.

"Thanks for hosting this, Jeremy," Dan said. "It's a great flat."

Jeremy grinned, "Yes. I was very fortunate. I inherited it from my grandmother. Seb and I love the place."

As we moved into the large drawing room, it seemed crowded. In addition to Jeremy and the Chief Whip, there were two others, Darren and Crispin, who were part of the communications team at Number Ten. Darren was in his late thirties, I thought, dark-haired and built like the rugby player he had once been. His speaking style was a little abrupt, but he seemed friendly enough. His colleague Crispin certainly had my gaydar pinging. He looked me up and down before shaking hands in a way that would have been more appropriate in a West End club than a high-level political meeting. He was short, no more than five foot four, with scruffy blond hair that fell over one eye, prompting him to toss his head every few minutes. When he spoke, he talked quickly in a vaguely mid-Atlantic accent.

I turned to the others in the room and, to my surprise,

saw my boss Steve and his husband Josh. Christ, were Pearson Frazer going to get tied up with all this? Shit.

The exchange of greetings was muted. There was silence for a moment, before Jeremy said, "We're only waiting for one more. The Chief Whip and I thought it would be a good idea if Adam were also here."

As he spoke, the doorbell rang and he ushered in a young man. Tall, blond and elegant, he was one of the most attractive boys I'd ever seen. He was dressed in skinny jeans and an cream cashmere sweater. He smiled and said, "Hi, everybody, sorry I'm late. My mobile is still away, so Uber was no-go and I couldn't find a taxi anywhere."

Jeremy quickly told him who everybody was. He blushed when I was introduced as Dan's boyfriend, stammering a brief, somewhat sheepish greeting to us both. I'd been prepared to dislike him on sight, but his embarrassment was much to his credit – the paid escort being introduced to his client's boyfriend was not an ideal situation.

As the senior man there, Jim Hayden started off proceedings. As I'd feared, *London Figaro* was running another story this week, so Dan was being named for using paid escort services in one paper and accused of using his position to further his boyfriend's interests in another. "It's decidedly thin, to say the least, Dan," remarked his old boss. "But I have to ask whether there's any remote possibility of it being true."

"None whatever," Dan snapped back furiously.

"Hey, I'm only the messenger," Jim Hayden replied, clearly stung by Dan's fury and lifting his hands in a gesture of surrender.

"Sorry, Jim. Didn't mean to snap. But really? As far as I

can recall, we've barely even discussed the project."

"Noted," he replied, before turning to me. "And Luke, you can confirm that you've never sought to influence Dan over this matter?"

"Absolutely," I replied.

"And you can confirm that you didn't pursue an acquaintanceship with Dan simply to further the ends of your employer?"

I could feel Dan moving uneasily next to me on the sofa, getting angrier at the line Jim seemed to be taking, but I recognised that these questions had to be asked. I had nothing to hide. "Certainly not. We'd been friends at university and met again at the Cotswold conference about Griffin House. We wanted to reconnect, that's all."

"Thanks. And Mr Frazer – Steve, isn't it?"

Steve nodded curtly, his jaw set and eyes like gimlets. I recognised that look from the office, usually seen before Steve had one of his explosions. I noticed Josh holding his hand firmly, trying to keep his husband's obvious displeasure under control.

"Fine. Again, apologies for asking. Can you confirm that, as Luke's boss, you've never asked him to seek to influence Dan about Griffin House or your firm's contract with DECRA?"

Steve's eyes flashed briefly again. When he spoke, he seemed to grind out his answer through clenched teeth. "I can confirm that."

"Good. Thanks. Sorry, but I had to ask. There's nothing in any of these hints about corruption – it's just mischief-making. Right?"

"And Jeremy and I think we know who the culprit is,"

Chapter Fifty-Four

Dan interjected.

"Don't tell me, Dan. Let me guess – Geoffrey's SPAD."

Jeremy nodded. "Dan and I also think he may be behind the story about Adam."

That certainly got Jim Hayden's attention. "Really? I thought that was standard tabloid scandal-mongering."

Jeremy explained the gist of his telephone conversation with Dan, then Adam quickly confirmed that he had not been approached by anybody, either to blackmail him or to offer money for a bigger story.

"So, what we're saying is that a government special adviser deliberately stole, or caused somebody to steal, Adam's mobile phone in order ... to do what?"

"Destabilise Dan's career?" suggested Steve.

"Seems a bit far-fetched, doesn't it?" asked the Chief Whip. "We're talking about criminal offences here, as well as breach of privacy. There's theft and conspiracy, at the very least."

Dan shrugged. "I know it seems that way, Jim. But the Brexiteer ultras do seem to be going after me because I've made no secret of my beliefs – I'm a Remainer and always will be. There was the chaos over the leaked report about regulation, all the *London Figaro* stories about Steve here, and now this. My local party membership has suddenly swelled, and most of the new members have been recognised as former members of UKIP. And it's all happened since the PM appointed me to this job at DECRA."

"There does seems to be a pattern," Jeremy added. "Most of it is low level, just making mischief and keeping us on our toes. But it's getting nastier each time – and this is clearly designed to ruin the reputation of both Dan and

Pearson Frazer."

"They may well be succeeding," added Steve. "We had to turn off our social media presence on Thursday to stem the tide of hostile comment."

Jim shifted in his seat. "The question is, what can we do about it? Number Ten wants all this shut down and quickly. The PM doesn't want any form of scandal overshadowing the Brexit agreement when it's finalised."

"The quickest answer is to get Andrews out of DECRA," Dan remarked. "At least then he won't have access to any more papers."

"Or the shelter of official status," added Jeremy.

Darren spoke next. "I think Dan has got to say something to the press, otherwise they'll only keep speculating and start making things up."

"Okay," responded Dan. "So what do I say? What's the line?"

"Any others?" Crispin asked. "Was Adam the only escort you used, luvvie?"

Dan shook his head. "There were a couple of others I saw on a fairly regular basis for the last couple of years."

"But not recently?"

"Not since I met up with Luke again in October."

"Serious, is it?" asked Crispin. "You and Luke?"

"Yep. Meeting him has changed everything. Hence coming out on Friday."

"There's your answer, duckie, isn't it? Classic deflection – give 'em the romance and they'll go with that – bet ya."

I swallowed nervously. Dan turned to look at me. I tried to smile. "Told you," I whispered to him. "I'm up for this."

He turned to the others. "Do you think that'll work?"

Darren replied, "I'd bet on it. The line would be something like 'Using escorts helped me come to terms with my sexuality. Now I'm in a committed relationship with my boyfriend Luke and here he is.' A couple of nice pics and you should be away."

"Okay," Dan responded, though the doubt was clear in his voice.

"What about this Griffin House business, though?" Jim asked, clearly anxious to move on. "Isn't that potentially more serious? Do we need to get the Standards Committee or Cabinet Secretary to investigate?"

"That's one possibility, certainly," Darren mused. "It would certainly defuse it. Kill the story for a few weeks. Then later we dribble out the news in a few months' time that there was no case to answer. Everybody will have forgotten about the story by then, anyway."

"Isn't that a bit drastic at this stage?" asked Jeremy, clearly foreseeing the fuss it would cause to have people crawling over the department's work.

"Depends what you want to achieve, luvvie," responded Crispin.

I didn't know about anybody else, but his combination of camp and cynicism was starting to grate on me. I tried to focus on his words as opposed to my irritation.

"You could always just issue a flat denial," he continued. "You know, unfounded allegations, no impropriety whatsoever. Trouble is, it probably won't wash, especially if the story is being drip fed for other reasons. This sort of campaign relies on innuendo but also on a constant drip, drip of new material. They've already had three bites of the cherry, and they'll want a fourth or fifth. No matter how many rebuttals you issue, they'll keep banging away. They only need one Opposition MP to take it up in the Commons and ask lots of questions for the story to get out of control."

"I agree with Crispin," Darren added. "Announce a full investigation now and you could bury the story."

"I'm a bit concerned about our reputation," said Steve, echoing my thoughts. "It's all very well burying the story, but it doesn't stop people wondering about our integrity. If there's an investigation, it looks as if there's something in it."

Dan weighed in. "I see what Steve means. People will see a few puffs of smoke and assume there's a fire."

"But everybody knows that governments investigate allegations like this in order not to find anything," replied Darren.

"Bloody great," Steve grumbled, his Yorkshire accent becoming more pronounced as his irritation grew. "Then everybody'll assume that we're guilty anyway. I'm not happy about that."

Crispin shrugged. "I understand Steve's concerns, but we're trying to make the best of a bad job. Trust me, this is the best way to handle it."

"I agree," said Jim firmly. As Chief Whip, he had the right to draw the matter to a close, but I could see that Steve was still unhappy. As was I. After all, I was the one at the centre of the latest allegation; it was me who was being accused of using sex with Dan to benefit the firm.

Steve still had a face like thunder. It was time for me to say something. "I understand where Crispin's coming from, but I'm the one effectively being accused of corruption.

Trying to bury the story by announcing an enquiry might be all right, but it makes it look as if you all think I'm guilty."

Dan looked horrified. "I'm sure it doesn't mean any such thing. Does it, Crispin?"

There was a long pause before Crispin answered. "Hmm... I do see where Luke is coming from. Nobody likes having allegations hanging over them, but it goes with the territory, boys, doesn't it?"

"Not with mine, it doesn't," I snapped back. "I'm a consultant, focused on doing the best job I can for my clients."

Crispin turned to me with a penetrating stare. "If you're going to try that line, darling, I suggest you don't fuck a Minister of the Crown."

Dan intervened. "What the hell, Crispin?" he snapped. "There's no need for that."

But Crispin wasn't easily intimidated and immediately bit back – hard. "Look, Dan, you know this game and you've got to be realistic. We're not playing pat-a-cake here. We're in the middle of the biggest foreign policy crisis this country has known in more than two hundred years. And frankly, that's much more important than the reputation of some small consultancy firm, or a middle-aged twink who's concerned about her reputation."

Steve moved to the edge of his chair and would have stood up but for Josh's restraining arm. "How dare you talk to me and my staff like that? I don't care how fucking important you are, or how big this so-called crisis is. You'll show some respect or we're out of here. We'll take whatever steps are necessary to protect our reputation with or without your input. Understood?"

Faced with hostile stares from Steve, Josh, Dan and me, Crispin realised that he'd gone too far. "Look, I'm sorry. I didn't mean to be rude, but you must understand that this is politics. Shit happens."

I couldn't help but intervene. "You should know."

"Believe me, sunshine, I do." The stare was still there, but suddenly it melted into a look of encouragement. "I do understand how you're feeling, Luke, and I know it's not comfortable. But I still think this is the best way out. And, after all, that's what these people pay me for."

I moved uneasily in my seat. If the people in this room were prepared to hang me out to dry, what chance did I stand of clearing my name? But what could I do? Flouncing out or having a tantrum wouldn't make the story go away. I felt powerless and scared. Dan must have understood because I suddenly felt his hand move along the sofa and onto the small of my back. I glanced at his face; it was full of sympathy and concern.

Eventually Darren spoke. "I'm sure we can come up with a form of words that says something about the allegations not being believed for one moment, but that asking somebody to look into the matter would offer reassurance."

"I think that's probably the best we can do," Crispin replied.

"Okay," I responded, feeling a bit lame in giving way.

Jim Hayden stood and rubbed his hands together. "Right, I'll talk to the PM tonight and tell her that's what we recommend." He glanced across at Steve and Dan. "Okay?"

They both nodded. As we all prepared to leave, Dan spoke. "Crispin, how do you want to play the stuff about Luke and me?"

"Let me think about that and talk to you tomorrow. A photo session would be good, I think, plus a couple of joint interviews – maybe even a daytime chat show."

I wondered how that chimed with trying to kill the corruption story. "Won't that simply draw attention to the allegations about me?"

It was clear from the lack of response that Crispin hadn't thought that one through. After a moment, he spoke. "Two things, I suppose: one, it gives you another opportunity to deny it all; and secondly, the more you're seen in public with Dan, the more people will realise that your relationship is serious. That can only be a good thing, can't it?"

"Yeah, I suppose so."

He gave a small laugh. "We'll see. Meanwhile we'll have to do social media postings too, of course."

"Naturally," Dan responded. "I'll put you in touch with my constituency team." He raised an eyebrow at me and I nodded back, nervous at the thought of media attention. But I'd promised him I would go through with it.

Adam, who'd been sitting quietly in the corner clearly fascinated by what was going on, asked, "Anything you want me to do?"

Crispin grinned at him. "I can think of several, darling, but they're not suitable for the here and now."

Jim Hayden huffed disapprovingly but Crispin only grinned at him, undeterred. "Seriously, though, love. I think that keeping as low a profile as possible would be your best bet. At the moment, you're very much the victim because your phone was stolen. But draw attention to yourself and they could go after you – after all, the guy who's got your phone has a good idea of your client list, presumably?"

Adam blushed again. "Yeah, afraid so."

"And you don't want that to be all over the front pages?"

"Fuck, no. Jesus."

"Then keep out of harm's way – abroad, ideally, for a few weeks. Who knows? If this Andrews bloke *was* behind it, we might even get your phone back for you."

The meeting broke up quickly. Jim, Crispin and Darren went back to Downing Street, and the rest of us stayed on Jeremy's sofas, shell-shocked by the speed of their thinking and the firmness of their resolve. Neither of them was exactly empathetic, but I realised there wasn't much room for empathy at the top of the political ladder.

Declining Jeremy's offer of a nightcap, Dan and I got ready to leave.

"We'll talk on Monday, Luke," Steve said quietly. "Don't worry. We'll be fine."

Josh wished me good night with a wink and a smile.

As we got into the lift, Dan reached for my hand. "My place, I think?"

"Certainly nearer. I don't think I could drive all the way back to Norwood tonight."

"That's what I was thinking. In the morning I can show you how grateful I am for all your support."

"That definitely sounds like an offer I can't refuse."

Chapter Fifty-Five

Dan

I don't think I'd ever felt so tired as I did when we left Jeremy's flat and returned to the car. The meeting had been pretty bloody in many ways; nobody in the room had either the time or the inclination to show any sympathy for Luke or Steve as they got caught up in this increasingly bitter political game.

Not that I could blame them because it went with the territory. Like any professional sports players, Jim, Darren and Crispin were totally caught up in the game itself – the next move, how to spook the opposition, winning attention for their point of view. They had no time for the human consequences; they were all out for victory at any price.

I recognised it for what it was because for years I'd been a player too, just as keen, just as focused on winning. Tonight, for the first time, I'd felt like an outsider and it had seemed empty to me. The thrill of the chase had become too exhausting; the victories were all pyrrhic. Like drugs when used too frequently, the highs became less effective each time.

"God, that was intense." Luke's remark brought me back to the present.

"Welcome to my world," I responded with a chuckle.

"Is it always like that?"

"Pretty much – especially when there's a panic on. Trouble is, there are so many panics these days that nobody has much time for other things, like governing the country."

"Thanks for supporting Steve and me. It was a great help."

"I didn't achieve much."

"Maybe not, but you had my back – literally and metaphorically. And you helped Josh keep Steve in check. I thought he was going to explode at one point."

"He certainly didn't look happy." We reached the car. Luke had kept the keys and had kept alcohol-free at Jeremy's, so would do the final stage of the day's driving marathon to my flat. "Are you sure you're okay with all of this?"

Luke puffed out his cheeks. "To be honest, Dan, I don't know. I'm shit scared, but I've said I'll do it so I will."

That wasn't the most convincing answer, but I was too exhausted to worry about it. To the extent that I could focus at that moment, I needed to make him comfortable. To anybody not used to being a media presence, the pressure of being named as a Minister's boyfriend would have been difficult enough without the added pressure of professional and personal allegations, no matter how far-fetched and delusional they were.

We drove the short distance home in silence and parked in the garage I rented in a mews round the corner from the flat. I leaned into Luke as we walked along the silent alleyway back to the main road. "Love you, Sky," I said.

"Love you too. But I don't think we're destined to live a quiet and boring life, do you?"

I shook my head. "No, you're right, there. Much as I might want to sometimes ... like now. I could sleep for a week but there's a mountain of things to do tomorrow, plus a ministerial visit in the North for four bloody days this week. We start at some ungodly hour on Monday morning, so Jeremy and I are flying up tomorrow night."

"Still, we've got tonight," Luke responded, reaching for my hand. "Let's make the most of that."

As we reached the corner and turned towards the entrance to my block I frowned. There seemed to be some commotion on the other side of the road. There was a hubbub of voices, and then I noticed a couple of big external microphones held aloft, their furry exteriors instantly recognisable.

Realisation dawned: they were waiting for me. A posse of reporters, photographers and camera crews were gathered like vultures, ready to pounce as soon as I put in an appearance, snapping pictures in a volley of flashes, shouting absurd questions trying to get a reaction, and tracking my every move and facial expression on camera. Those images would be analysed to death to spot a weakness or a hint of emotion. Fuck my life.

Luke and I stopped walking a few yards short of a streetlight. We were still in shadow, but it was only matter of time before we were spotted. He dropped my hand and turned to face me. It might have been the quality of the light, but it struck me that whatever colour had been left in his face when we left Jeremy's flat had completely drained away. "Christ, Dan, are they waiting for us?"

"Afraid so. Stay close to me and keep moving, Luke. Don't let them separate us and keep smiling. Above all, don't say a bloody word." I reached for his hand again but he kept it away, his eyes widening in horror.

There was a shout. "There he is!"

Even though I was still fifty yards away, the chorus of questions had already begun. The night was suddenly full of flashes going off. There was nothing for it but to face them and get through to the flat.

I started to move but Luke stood his ground, wide-eyed and clearly terrified. Suddenly the light levels on the street were transformed as powerful TV lights were switched on. The flashes kept going as the stills photographers took their shots, and the air filled with the noise of shutters opening and closing.

At last Luke moved, but not in the direction I expected. "Sorry, Dan, I can't do this." He turned and ran.

I watched him go, horrified. I closed my eyes. What could I do? I couldn't follow him – the media scrum would only give chase and that would make things worse. Besides, I didn't know what his panic meant for us.

There was only one thing to do. I opened my eyes, even though they were filling with tears, and turned to face my fate. I pinned on my bravest smile, pulled back my shoulders, and buttoned my jacket as I walked towards my front door. Years of training and preparation had schooled me for this moment. I shielded my eyes from the flashes, shut my ears to the facile questions and simply kept moving, pushing firmly through the scrum but careful not to shove anybody too hard. The last thing we wanted was an assault charge on top of everything else.

Eventually, shaking like a leaf, I reached the entrance to the building thanks to some help from some newly arrived policemen. The porter had already summoned the lift so it was waiting, doors open. I thanked him as he returned to his task of keeping the media out of the building, and strode into the lift, head still held high. I kept it together until I reached the sanctuary of my own front door and forced my shaking hands to insert the key.

Closing the door behind me, I leant against it then slid down to the floor and brought my hands to my face. The horror of the evening's events – from the news of the story through to Luke's flight – flashed before me. I stared blankly into space for what seemed like hours. Eventually, my exhaustion overwhelmed me, and the tears started to flow.

Governing Passions

Chapter Fifty-Six

Luke

Bind panic carried me away from Dan. I ran past the Albert Hall onto Kensington Gore and hailed a cab to take me home to south London. It would probably cost a fortune, but I needed to get away and the sanctuary of my own house seemed to be the best place.

As I sat in the back of the taxi, I tried to come to terms with what had just happened. My heart was still pounding as I took deep breaths, trying to recover from what I realised must have been something akin to a panic attack.

I rubbed my hands over my face, trying to calm down and focus. In my panic, I'd betrayed Dan and broken my promise, freely given, to stand by him. As a result, I'd almost certainly ruined my relationship with him and wrecked pretty much every aspect of my life. And all because I'd given way to irrational fear. What an idiot!

As we crossed the river, ironically by the same bridge that we'd used on the way back from Jeremy's barely half an hour ago, I tried to understand what had made me react that way.

The first thing was that I was dog tired – we both were – after an incredibly long day. I replayed scenes from the events in my mind: driving up the A34 with Dan working in the back seat; chatting over coffee; the garden of the hotel, watching Dan's face as he got the news of the breaking news story. I saw us driving together down the M40 before moving to Jeremy's flat. Then, without warning, my mind moved to the street outside Dan's flat. I felt my heart rate pick up again. My breathing quickened as my panic returned.

What a fucking mess! Suddenly our professional and personal lives were being stirred into a toxic mix. Dan's coming out, the press story about him and Adam, the attacks on Pearson Frazer and the whole row over the future of Griffin House were swirling around together. It was all fraught with danger for our careers, our relationship and our future reputations. It was a shitstorm into which had strode Darren and Crispin, media advisers who saw the thing purely from the government's point of view regardless of the human consequences. God, how I hated it all.

The cab reached Crystal Palace. I thanked the driver, paid my fare and stumbled into the street. It was late and bitterly cold. I was absolutely wrung out and shivering, so much that I could barely insert my key into the lock. My phone vibrated with a message as I opened the door. I flicked on the lights, moved into the kitchen and slumped down on a stool at the breakfast bar, head in hands.

I started to warm up after a few minutes and stopped shivering. I needed food and a hot drink, or to go to bed. The latter seemed easier so I slowly climbed the stairs.

Mesmerised by the sight of the bed, I fell into it fully clothed and fell asleep immediately.

When I awoke some hours later, it was still dark; the heating had yet to switch on, so the room was cold. Though still fully clothed, I shivered again. I pulled off my shoes and crawled under the covers. I pulled out my phone and looked at the time: a few minutes after five.

I desperately needed to sleep, but my mind had other ideas. My brain was a carousel, flashing pictures of the events of the previous few days before my eyes. As time passed, those images distilled into one figure. I was driving with him, sitting in the cottage with him, watching him charm the party members yesterday afternoon, sleeping with him wrapped in my arms, making love to him... Dan Forrester, once again the focus of my life after a fifteen-year gap. And I'd betrayed him, let him down when he needed me most.

What a useless idiot I was! How could I possibly face him after doing that? He'd put his life on the line for me by coming out and risking everything he'd striven for all his adult life so that we could build a life together, honestly and openly. And what had I done with that precious gift? Flung it away *within twenty-four hours.*

I turned over in bed. All I wanted to do was go to sleep. *Please, brain, shut up and give me some rest.* But the thoughts quickly returned. Dan deserved more. He was handsome, charismatic, clever and charming. He could do much better for himself than me. I'd been deluding myself in thinking that I could ever measure up to him and be worthy of his love.

Even if he didn't realise that, I did. I had to be strong for him, walk away, force him to look for somebody else like Adam, or even Jeremy. I constructed an elaborate fantasy in which Seb fell for a fellow orchestral player. They'd divorce and Jeremy would be free to marry Dan, giving him the love and support he needed. Jeremy wouldn't run away from anything: he was strong and brave and clever, not like me. Yes, that would be it. I could do something useful – keep out of the way and let them realise they loved each other.

Then sanity prevailed. If I had to leave Dan alone for his own good, I'd have to distract myself, keep myself so busy that I never had time to think of him. There was always work – losing myself in my job, coupled with an occasion hook-up via Grindr. They had kept me going for years until this autumn and could do so again. But they wouldn't want me at work now, would they? Steve and Josh would know what a coward I'd been and wouldn't want me as a friend. Who would, given the cowardly, useless shit that I was? The allegations would keep coming in *London Figaro*; Pearson Frazer's credibility with DECRA would be ruined and my integrity would be in shreds. We'd lose the contract. End of Griffin House, end of my career. Associate director? I'd be lucky if they'd give me a job cleaning the toilets.

I turned onto my stomach and beat my fists into the pillows in frustration. Why wouldn't my brain shut up and leave me alone? Why did it have to torture me with all these poisonous thoughts? I was so tired and just wanted to let go, so why couldn't I?

Then it all started again – but we were back to Dan. Gentle, loving Dan holding me in his arms. Smiling at me across the sitting room in his cottage. Laughing and joking as we walked on the beach, not quite brave enough to hold hands but walking close and occasionally bumping shoulders. Lying with him on the sofa in the flat, kissing gently and idling an afternoon away, simply enjoying being in love.

Now the tears were of misery rather than frustration; they filled my eyes, overflowed and ran down my cheeks. All those beautiful moments that I thought I'd have for ever. All gone. Never again to hold him. No hearing him call my Sky. Not another kiss from those lips. Ever.

My tears turned into sobs that wracked my whole body until my mind was emptied of all thought. Completely drained, I slept again.

Governing Passions

Chapter Fifty-Seven

Dan

When I awoke on Sunday morning, I was immediately conscious of being on my own. I tried to remember why Luke wasn't there. Then the horror of the previous evening washed over me again.

I'd recovered from my despair in the immediate aftermath of Luke's sudden panic, but only enough to move from the front door into my bedroom and discard my clothes. After that, I'd crawled between the covers and fallen asleep.

The fact that I'd slept through until eight o'clock was more a tribute to exhaustion than peace of mind. I barely had the energy to drag myself out of bed. I drew the curtains and peered out into the late November gloom. It was one of those foggy, damp London mornings where it barely got light. Certainly not the sort of day to lift my mood.

I rested my head against the cold glass. There was so much to do: talk to my parents; speak to Helena in the constituency; see how the social media accounts were doing; do the rest of my red boxes; prepare for this week's visit to the North East. Then there was the follow-up from last night's discussion. Presumably I'd have to do whatever media interviews they advised later in the week. But surely that was impossible now? How could I make positive noises about being in a committed relationship when I didn't know if I was still in one?

What the fuck was I going to do about it all? Tears welled up again – but this time of frustration. I picked up my phone. There were at least ten missed calls, five voicemail messages and enough texts to write a novel.

As I stared at the screen, the phone vibrated with an incoming call. It was Jeremy. Thank God for that. I could do what all sensible ministers do: leave it to the private office.

I pressed the button to take the call. "Morning," I said gruffly.

"Hi. I know you probably don't want to hear from me this morning, but I could probably help, if you'd let me."

"Do you know? About what happened outside last night?"

"Dan, I'm afraid the whole world knows, thanks to an alert cameraman who filmed the whole thing. After the speed at which he ran away, Luke's probably being courted to join the Olympic relay team."

"Fuck, Jeremy."

"I'm afraid the sight of your boyfriend fleeing has been all over the internet since one o'clock this morning."

"Oh, Jesus wept."

"Yes, He probably would have done. Anyway, I'm calling to say that I'm on my way and I'll pick up breakfast. Any requests?"

"Yes, a large slice of humble pie, please."

Jeremy gave a brief laugh. "Sorry, I shouldn't laugh, but the whole situation is so ... bizarre."

"I know what you mean. And don't worry – talking to you helps. As for breakfast, a greasy bacon sandwich would suit me down to the ground. I'll get the coffee on."

"Great. See you in a few minutes. Oh, and Dan?"

"Yeah?"

"Don't do anything or talk to anybody until I get there. All right?"

"Absolutely."

By the time he arrived, I was feeling a little better. I'd showered and shaved was beginning to feel human again. A glance out of the window told me that the media pack that had spooked Luke was still opposite my front door.

Jeremy arrived bearing gifts – bacon and sausage sandwiches, bottles of orange juice and two of the largest, flakiest Danish pastries I'd ever seen – comfort food *par excellence.*

While I ate, he scrolled through the messages on my phone, dealing with those he could, deleting the majority and making quick notes on his pad. As I finished, he looked up me. "So, parents first, then Helena. Meanwhile, I'll see how the land lies down in Crystal Palace and we can talk to Crispin about what to do."

"How will you do that?"

"I spoke to Josh before I rang you this morning. He was already on his way round to Luke's place. He and Steve had come to the same conclusion as me, that he shouldn't be left on his own."

I was immensely relieved that somebody would try to look after him, and touched by their concern. Surely, we'd be able to get through this. My parents were also very supportive when I spoke to them. Dad had been used to media storms during his own political career and he counselled calm and patience. The main subject of the story was not mentioned. "Smile a lot and for God's sake don't tell any lies. They're bound to catch up with you if you do."

Helena proved equally helpful. Her social media team had come in specially to help out, and they were coping, if only by the skin of their teeth. From what she said, there was some pretty horrific material around. Homophobic abuse, anti-EU sentiment and anti-gay self-righteousness from religious zealots made a pretty toxic combination, unleashing all the bile, prejudice and hatred that the internet could provide. Sifting through it all, deleting the comments and blocking the serial abusers was time-consuming and distressing, and I was immensely grateful for what the girls were doing.

"And how are you coping?" Helena asked as we neared the end of our conversation. Her voice was full of concern.

"Okay, I think. To be honest, I haven't had chance to get my head round it. Last night was pretty bloody though." My voice wavered a little.

"And Luke?"

"Friends are looking after him. Beyond that, I don't know. I'll try to talk to him later, I suppose."

"Good. Make sure you do, darling. Don't let it fester while you're away this week."

"I'll try not to. And Jeremy sends his love." I ended the call as he came back into the room. "Helena sends hugs."

"How are they coping?"

"With great difficulty. She says that some of the language is gross."

Jeremy shook his head. "I can't understand why people feel it necessary to spew all this hatred round the world."

"Me neither. I wonder what happened to it all before the internet."

"I suppose that's why we had so many wars... Did you get hold of Josh?" I asked.

"Yeah. Luke's okay. He let Josh in, then went back to sleep, apparently. Didn't want to talk."

"I'm glad that at least he's got the peace of mind to sleep. It'll do him good."

"The same is probably true for you."

"But we both know that's not going to happen, don't we?"

Jeremy gave a sad smile. "We do. But I think a little talk might help. At least we might get you in a better frame of mind."

"Hmm. That's true, I suppose. But what we are going to talk about? The weather? Intimations of mortality? The first half-hour of the Renaissance?"

"Oh, ha ha, Dan. Nice deflection, as usual. How about telling me how you feel?"

"Honestly? Like shit. Last night was awful. That meeting, Darren and Crispin's unfeeling attitude, poor Luke feeling miserable, and that shit-show outside here. No wonder he ran away, poor love."

"So, what now?"

"That's the million-dollar question. I can't expect any partner of mine to live under a spotlight that he doesn't want, to be a victim of lies and innuendo, constant criticism and bitchiness. Who'd want that? All they'd get in return is a relationship with a man who's so busy that they rarely see him and too tired to live properly when they do." I couldn't prevent the bitter laugh that followed.

"Doesn't he get a say in that?"

"He did, last night. And we know what the answer was."

"Maybe, but I think you're being a little unfair. Surely Luke's reaction was the product of exhaustion and panic. After all, neither of you was exactly prepared for the ambush."

I sighed. "No, that's true. But in a sense what Luke thinks is almost irrelevant. I've got to make a choice. Do I want to stay in politics and go further, when I know that would jeopardise my prospects of a future with Luke ... or indeed with anybody?"

"I understand that, Dan. I really do. But I'm worried that without talking to him you're setting yourself a false choice."

"I know what you mean, and in most circumstances I'd agree with you. But I'm convinced that the onus is on me before I try to talk to him. I've got to be clear in my own mind about my choices. I couldn't go in there offering him a choice, only to walk away if he gives the wrong answer."

"Yeah, I see what you mean. So, what *do* you want?"

I couldn't help laughing. "Back to the million-dollar question." I ran my hand through my hair, wondering what to say.

I took a deep breath. "Do you remember, not long after

we met, we talked about achieving ambitions?"

"I do indeed."

"You said then that achieving an ambition of your own would feel different from achieving one that had been thrust upon you by someone else."

"Yes, that's a crucially important distinction. I learned that through Seb. Not long after we met, he went through a bit of a crisis about his musical career. He wasn't sure whether he was in it for him, or his mum. It had been part of his life for so long, always taken for granted, but he'd begun to wonder whether he truly wanted it for himself. Eventually he decided it was, but I'd have supported him one hundred per cent either way."

"That's me, too. Public service is what the Forresters do and always have done. A political career for me was a given, probably from birth, but certainly from the age of ten or eleven, once I'd demonstrated that I wasn't completely stupid. It was taken for granted, so I accepted my destiny and embraced it: politics became my passion and my ambition. Simple as that. Like your Seb. The question is, am I doing it for myself or for other people, notably my father?"

"And have you found your answer yet?"

"Not finally – but I think I know what it's going to be. I want out of this job, and eventually of the Commons too."

"Christ, Dan, that's a big shift. What's brought that on?"

"Several things. Meeting you, seeing how settled and happy you are in your marriage. Seeing Luke again. I'd spent the last fifteen years convinced that I was better off on my own and staying single was the safest way to achieve my ambitions."

"That's so sad."

"I agree. And, of course, I'd already thrown away my chance with the one man with whom I could form a bond. But suddenly, out of the blue, there he is again and I get another go."

"That's enough to rock anybody's world."

"Exactly, but my life gets in the way *again*. My ambition, my drive for power, pretty near fucks it up before it even gets going."

Jeremy thought for a little before he replied. "Possibly – though maybe not. Nevertheless, I understand where you're coming from."

"But there's one other thing in the mix, just to make life a bit more complicated. My father said over dinner the other week that he wouldn't blame me if I gave up politics."

"That's a bit of a stunner! You didn't mention that before."

"No. I was so taken up with the news about my uncle that it got shoved onto the back burner."

"So how do you feel about it now?"

"I don't know. I suppose it almost gives me a 'get out of jail free' card if I want it."

"You mean you've got his gracious permission to do what you want with your life?"

Despite myself, I laughed.

Jeremy looked a bit abashed. "Sorry, that was a bit strong."

"There's a lot of truth in it. Trouble is, I haven't the faintest idea what I want to do, and that also scares the shit out of me."

"No idea at all?"

"Not beyond the fact that I very much want Luke to be a part of my life, no. I fancy this online work that Glyn Pargiter talked about, but I've no idea whether it will come to anything."

"It would be a start."

"But it doesn't make me into much of a catch, does it? 'Unemployed ex-politician. No profession, no ambition, no prospects. Seeks partner for a life of penury'."

"You left some things out, Dan. How about 'funny, bright, compassionate, intelligent and good-looking'."

"Thanks." I blushed. "You could add, 'likes furry animals and small children'."

"What? To eat?"

We both laughed, which reduced the tension and shifted my mood a little. As the amusement subsided, Jeremy fixed me with a look. "So, what's the plan?"

"I need to decide, don't I? I know we're away all week, and I've agreed to stay with Glyn for a couple of nights next weekend, but I've got to find some time to think. I'll give myself till tomorrow week. Can we find a gap in the schedule for me to meet Luke next Monday evening?"

Jeremy checked the diary. "If it's at the House, yes."

"Okay, let's do that. I'll get this red box done while you make the arrangements, then I'll give him a call."

Governing Passions

Chapter Fifty-Eight

Luke

Dan telephoned a few minutes before three o'clock on Sunday afternoon.

Josh had arrived at my place at ten, waking me up long enough to let him in. He'd taken one look at me and insisted I go back to bed and get some more sleep. The extra rest did me the world of good, because I awoke at noon feeling much brighter. Shaved and showered, I felt almost civilised as I went downstairs. Josh greeted me with coffee and said that brunch was on the way – he'd nipped round to the corner shop for supplies while I'd been asleep. A few minutes later, a plate of bacon, eggs, sausages and mushrooms was put before me, with a side order of toast.

"God, the man plays the piano, sings, writes and cooks a brilliant full English. No wonder his husband loves him."

Josh gave a small curtsey. "We aim to please."

"Seriously, though, thanks a million for this and ... just being here."

"No problem. Once realised what had happened last night, we were worried about you. Steve would've

437

been here as well, but he's got that report to finish by tomorrow."

"Oh, the Lancashire Traction job?"

"Yeah, that's the one. Anyway, it's good to be out of the house while he's working. Talk about bears with sore heads."

I grinned. "I thought he was a woolly lamb these days. That's what he told me on your wedding day."

Josh snorted. "Hmm. A woolly lamb with fangs sometimes." He paused. "Bless him."

I suppressed the pang of jealousy I felt at the closeness of their relationship. "How did you know what happened?"

"You were filmed running off. It's all over the web."

My mood plummeted and I pushed away my plate. "Oh, fucking hell. I'm such a bloody idiot."

"No, you're not. Now, come on, finish your food and then we'll talk properly. You'll feel better for it. Trust Uncle Josh."

Reluctantly I returned to my meal, trying to tune out my anxiety. When I'd finished, Josh poured us both more coffee and we moved into the sitting room.

"So tell me the worst. Have people been really nasty?" I asked.

"Put it this way, you've got your own hashtag – #DansDasher."

I couldn't stop the laugh that escaped me, despite my revulsion. "Surely that should be Dan's ex-Dasher."

"Oh? And why would that be?"

"He won't want me now, will he? He comes out for me, puts his life and career on the line, and I betray him within twenty-four hours. Hardly the basis for a strong relationship, is it?"

Josh sighed. "Number one, he didn't come out for you, he came out for himself. Ultimately, we all do. I accept that he probably would have stayed in the closet if he hadn't met you again, but he decided that he wanted a relationship with you and that he needed to be open and transparent in order to do that. He did it for himself."

"I see what you mean, Josh, but even then..."

"No buts, Luke. You did *not* betray him, okay? You panicked. Most of us would have done the same in those circumstances. You were tired, emotional, frightened – I could see that when we were at Jeremy's. I'd be astonished if Dan is sitting at home this afternoon feeling betrayed."

"But I'm no good for him, Josh. Surely you can see that. I can't cope with all the media intrusion as it is. What if he got promoted and went into the Cabinet? I'd be a millstone round his neck. He deserves somebody better."

A flash of anger crossed Josh's face, but he controlled himself quickly. When he spoke again, he was calm and patient. "Please stop talking yourself down, Luke. From what I've seen, you're perfect for each other. Of course, life in the public gaze isn't easy, but you can live with it, provided you don't fight it all the time. You need to do it on your own terms, keep giving them little pieces of material that you control. Most media people respect that – after all, they're only trying to do their jobs."

"I know." I sighed. "I suppose part of it is reaction against my mother. She's always craved attention and reacted badly when she didn't get it. I've spent my life trying to be exactly the opposite."

"Mine is a bit the same. But what about your dad?"

"He's quite good at it, in a modest sort of way. But he has to be – it's his job. Preaching from the pulpit every week, being seen as a community leader."

"Isn't that the model for you? Doing your job as Dan's partner in a modest sort of way?"

"I suppose it is. That's actually a very good way of thinking about it. Thanks, Josh."

He gave me a big grin back. "My pleasure. Now, are you feeling better? Up to a film, perhaps?"

"Sounds great. A musical?"

"Yeah, great. How about *Guys & Dolls*? Haven't watched it for ... oh ... three weeks?"

"Fine with me. Shouldn't we do a new version called *Guys and Guys* though?"

Josh giggled. "Who would you like to take to Cuba for the day?"

"Hmm, There's a promising Junior Minister I know..."

At that point my phone started to ring and Dan's face flashed up on the screen. I stared at it in horror for a moment, but fortunately instinct took over and I went into the kitchen to accept the call.

"Hey," Dan said in a neutral tone.

"How are you?"

"Been better. Jeremy's been keeping me company. You?"

"Same. But Josh is here."

"Good."

"Listen. About last night – I'm so sorry. I feel as if I let you down."

"It's not a problem. We were both exhausted and fairly pissed off with the world. Hardly the best of moods in which to be ambushed by the press."

"No, I suppose not. But I still think I let you down and I'd be bound to do it again if I stayed around."

"Luke..."

I cut him off. I had to do this, to get the words out before my throat seized up completely with emotion. "No, hear me out, please. I'm going to hold you back in your career. I really think we should stop this ... whatever it is between us ... before we invest too much in it."

"Luke, please..."

Governing Passions

Chapter Fifty-Nine

Dan

"I really think we should stop this ... whatever it is between us ... before we invest too much in it." As Luke uttered those words, I felt a curious sensation in my stomach as if the whole world were trying to push through it.

I closed my eyes, squeezing them shut to keep out the light. "Luke, please..."

"I've thought about it a lot, and..."

"Yeah, too much, I think. Please don't do this, not today. It's too soon to make any big decisions..."

"But..."

"Luke, please. You did *not* let me down last night. We were tired and unprepared, okay?"

"Okay."

"And you know I love you, don't you?"

"I'm not good enough..."

"Luke, stop saying that!' I felt my temper slipping away as the fear of losing him loomed large, and I fought to get myself back under control. I was convinced that I had to stop him saying the actual words that would break us up.

"I know we need to talk, to think some more about what's happening to us. But I'm away most of this week, as you know, plus there's this weekend thing, so we're not going to get to do that for a few days, right?"

"Yeah."

"So let's not say any more until we've both recovered a bit and had chance to think things through. Jeremy and I have worked out that we can meet next Monday night at the House. Is that all right?"

There was a pause, then he sighed. "All right."

"Good. What are you doing now?"

"Josh and I were about to watch a film. *Guys and Dolls.*"

"Go and enjoy that – think of Jeremy and I flogging up to Newcastle later, though, won't you?"

"I always think about you, Dan. I'm so worried though." Luke was on the edge of tears.

"Me too – I think about you too, all the time. Let's use these next few days to calm ourselves. I'll see you a week tomorrow. All right?"

"Yes, all right. Bye, Dan."

"Okay. Love you. Bye."

I ended the call and breathed a huge sigh of relief. At least we'd established contact, and he wasn't completely freaked out by what had happened. At the same time, I knew he'd been intent on calling a halt to what was developing between us, if not breaking up completely. I was determined that was not going to happen – at least not without a fight.

I got up from the sofa and moved into the bedroom. Jeremy had nipped home to get his bags ready, and would pick me up at about four o'clock for our flight north. In many ways, the timing of this trip couldn't have been worse. I'd be away from London, from the centre of events, unable to influence what was going on. Worse, I'd be away from Luke at a time when we needed mutual affection and support.

Politically, the press stories also devalued the visit; there could be no avoiding the sense that I was "damaged goods". I might easily be on my way out of office, and therefore my ability to influence decisions or help with problems would be diminished. On the other hand, it would be good for me to be outside the Westminster bubble for a few days. By the time I got back, hopefully the media would have moved on to something else.

Perhaps our enforced parting might do Luke and me good, and help get the events of Saturday night into some sort of proportion. That was the logical part of my brain speaking; the emotional part craved his company, the feeling of holding him in my arms. What if that never happened again? Emotions once more threatened to get the better of me.

I took my luggage into the bedroom to pack but spent the next fifteen minutes rooted to the spot, unable to decide what I needed to take. My brain was focused on the future and creating a series of increasingly depressing scenarios. No job, no career, aimless and broke – and lonely. No Luke, Jeremy moved on, no Helena. Forced to sell the cottage, then the flat – a spiral of decline. I had a sense that I had no future to look forward to. My eyes filled again, and my head went into my hands.

I was brought out of my reverie by the noise of the key in the front door. Surely not Jeremy already? I glanced at my watch – ten to four. Christ! "Hi, Jeremy," I called out. "Just packing. Won't be a mo."

I forced my brain into action. Underwear and socks for five days, two suits, half a dozen shirts, several ties. I closed the case, zipped up the suit carrier and went into the hall with my cases. "Sorry. I'm ready now."

Jeremy's face was a picture. "Er, hi. Travelling casual, are we? Might be a bit chilly though."

I looked down at myself. I was dressed in tatty sweatpants and a battered old T-shirt. I might have managed to pack, but I hadn't remembered to change. I burst into laughter and was on the verge of becoming hysterical before I got hold of myself. "Right. I'll be with you in thirty seconds."

***

"How did your chat with Luke go?" We were in the car on the way to Heathrow.

"It was a bit difficult. He was okay, but he seems to have made up his mind that he's not good enough for me."

"Where on earth did he get that idea?"

"He's convinced that he let me down last night – he even used the word 'betrayed' – and that he'd do so again."

"Oh, dear."

"I managed to calm him down a little and persuade him not to say any more until we meet up next week. I'm hoping he'll get it into proportion by then."

"And you'll have made your decision, as well?"

"That's the general idea."

Jeremy turned his head and smiled. "Okay. Should be an interesting evening next Monday."

Chapter Sixty

Luke

Josh insisted on staying over on Sunday night, to make sure I was all right, he said. I resisted at first, but in the end I was glad of his company. Steve joined us and brought some takeaway with him. While he and Josh tucked into some excellent Chinese food, I'd toyed with mine. It was only after a great deal of cajoling that I managed to force down anything at all.

I felt hollow, almost zombie like. I could wash, dress, make hot drinks and polite conversation, but I felt detached from reality and I performed these tasks like an automaton.

I insisted on going into work on Monday morning, despite Steve's offer of time off. I managed to get some work done by tuning out all thoughts apart from the task in hand. After an hour or so, I made it known via Barbara that I was very grateful for everybody's sympathy and good wishes, but would they please stop coming to tell me.

In some ways it was good that Dan would be up north for the rest of the week. Part of me could pretend that him being away was routine, and things would get back to normal when he returned. But part of me knew that was nonsense: for a start, we hadn't been together long enough to have established what "normal" might be. And secondly, the ache in my heart at his absence was too powerful to ignore.

The fact that I'd put the ache there in the first place by trying to push him away didn't make it any easier. My conviction that I was doing the right thing remained intact, but it was proving much harder than I'd expected.

I reached rock bottom on Tuesday night when I began to wonder whether there was any way I could live without him. I might have survived on my own for the last fifteen years, but *survive* was the operative word. For the last few weeks, I had done so more than that. I had *lived*.

Everything had seemed sharper, brighter, more exciting since Dan and I had got together; having somebody else in my life, even for these few weeks, had changed me completely. For a start, I'd become a cuddle junkie, totally addicted to the warmth, reassurance and joy that being held in my boyfriend's arms gave me. I missed the silly domestic moments, especially down at the cottage: the jokes, shared chores, watching TV together. How could I go back to a solitary existence?

Then there was the added layer of uncertainty over the *London Figaro* story and the hints about corruption. Everybody at the office was being very supportive, but I couldn't shake the belief that had overtaken me during the meeting on Saturday night that I would be the sacrificial lamb. I would be blamed for trying to exercise undue influence over Dan on the one hand, and for ruining

Pearson Frazer's reputation on the other. My career as a consultant would be over.

I went to bed early feeling dog tired but only ended up replaying the same thoughts and regrets, like a playlist on endless repeat. Eventually I gave up trying to sleep and went downstairs to make some tea. I put the heating on and sat at the kitchen table to drink it. It was no good, I had to get a grip.

"The simple answer is that you'll survive all this because you have to," I told myself. Not only was there my betrayal on Saturday night, but also my insecurities and the harsh words I'd used. Dan didn't have the time or the capacity for that sort of thing. It wasn't fair to expect him to cope with me and my fears of media exposure.

But then I remembered the reassurances he'd uttered and the way he'd refused to let me say anything irrevocable during our call on Sunday afternoon. They were not the words or deeds of somebody who was prepared give up and walk away.

I told myself that made no difference. If he wasn't strong enough to recognise the truth and accept the futility of carrying on with our relationship, I would have to do it for him.

Another voice within me argued with that, though, pointing out that Dan was an independent human being, capable, intelligent and successful. Why didn't he get a say in his own future? I had no right to make decisions for him. Surely the best thing to do was to wait this out, to do as he'd suggested on Sunday: use this week as a cooling-off period and talk again when he got back to London.

Eventually I stilled all the voices in my brain. Back

upstairs, I manage to drop off to sleep.

When I got into the office on Wednesday morning, I still felt adrift, but better than I had done. I managed to summon up the energy to fake a smile and a joke. Both Steve and Barbara commented on how improved I seemed, and even young Matt Somerville managed to crack a joke with me instead of running away from me like a frightened rabbit.

It was a brilliantly sunny morning, and that may have helped too. The November gloom had rolled away and been replaced by the pin-sharp light of a frosty winter's day. It was bloody freezing, but it was worth the cold to see the brilliant blue sky.

Chapter Sixty-One

Dan

The schedule for the four-day visit was hectic. A day in Newcastle with two visits and three meetings came first, then it was on to Durham for dinner and overnight at the university. Tuesday saw me talking air quality in Teesside and lunching with politicians in Darlington, before more plant visits and an early evening discussion on environmentally friendly farming in Teesdale.

The first two days were enough to convince me that nowhere was enough being done to develop the economy in the region, and I began to understand why the people had voted so heavily for Brexit. If this was all that forty-odd years of EU membership could do for the region, who wouldn't want to try something else?

It was now Wednesday morning and we were en route to East Lancashire. This was not a part of the country I'd visited before, and I was impressed by how green and attractive much of the area was despite its industrial past. Like the North East, this too was an area of high unemployment and low expectations. I worried how we were ever going to help these places without the money and trade that the EU had provided. We might be on the way to controlling our own destiny, but what if the only outcome was that we had the freedom to get poorer?

When I listened to Jeremy's briefing about everything that governments had done over the years to foster economic growth, I was reminded about how powerless ministers often were in the face of intractable problems. Politicians made policies and passed laws but almost never had the ability to oversee their implementation. It all helped to inform my thoughts about my own future – not that there was much time in the schedule for reflection.

As we arrived in Burnley, my phone buzzed with an e-mail notification. Jeremy's followed a few seconds later. I thought at first that the same message was being sent simultaneously to both of us, but I was wrong: mine was from Jim Hayden, whereas Jeremy's was from a colleague back at the office.

Jim's message told me that Sean Andrews had resigned that morning from his post as a SPAD to the Secretary of State. Adam had recognised Sean Andrews's picture, identified him as having been a client on the day his phone had been stolen and let the Chief Whip's office know.

Jim had confronted Andrews, who'd blustered at first but eventually admitted to being the author of the plot. Apparently, he'd developed a real hatred for me during our time in Portcullis House. I'd snubbed him repeatedly, apparently, and been contemptuous of him. He'd decided that he could kill two birds with one stone: destabilise the government and, with luck, destroy my career.

That could have been the end of the matter. However,

Jim had been worried what Sean might do if he was fired. "I'd prefer to have him inside the tent pissing out than the other way round," he wrote. As a result, God knows how, he had prevailed on one of the leading Eurosceptic think-tanks to hire Andrews as a senior researcher – on condition that he ceased all attempts to undermine members of the government. Further, Andrews was obliged to admit that there was no foundation to the allegations about Pearson Frazer or Luke personally. He'd written a confession about stealing Adam's phone, which would be held under lock and key but could be released to the authorities if there was any transgression of those terms. It was a stunningly clever solution.

"Brilliant!" I exclaimed, making Jeremy jump.

"Is this Griffin House?" he asked.

"No, Sean Andrews. He's gone."

"Now that is seriously good news. What happened?"

I passed my phone over so that Jeremy could read the message for himself. "Wow. I wonder how many favours Jim had to call in to get that sorted."

"More than a few, I guess. But it's a big relief all round."

Jeremy beamed with pleasure. "Certainly is. God, this is turning into quite a red-letter day."

"How do you mean? Did you mention Griffin House just now?"

"Yep. Apparently, Sir John's hand-picked working party has turned on him and recommended that we maintain the project."

"Holy Moses! That's a real turn-up, isn't it?"

"Absolutely. I bet he wasn't expecting that – I certainly wasn't."

"So what now?"

"It's got to go back to the management group and on to the Secretary of State for approval, so we're not home and dry yet. But, having commissioned the review, Sir John would find it difficult to overrule the result."

Our conversation was cut short as we arrived at our destination for the first visit of the day. Neither of us had had time to process all the news, but I left the car in a much better mood than I'd entered it.

Chapter Sixty-Two

Luke

At the office, our mood was brightened considerably by an e-mail from our contract manager at DECRA. It seemed that the departmental working party set up as part of the spending review had come down strongly in favour of renewing and extending the Griffin House project for another three years. This apparently ringing endorsement of the scheme had come as a something of a surprise, our source told us. Sir John Radford, having been forced into convening the group to review the scheme, had proceeded to pack the working party with his own placemen.

We sat in Steve's office discussing the implications of the news. We were not out of the woods yet – the recommendation had still to be approved. Even if it that happened, we'd have to go through a re-tendering exercise in the New Year for the start of a new contract in April. Nevertheless, the fact that the department was not going to cancel the scheme of its own volition without a fight felt like a victory.

"That's terrific news!" I exclaimed. "Jeremy will be

455

pleased. He did all the spade work, going round and talking to colleagues. That's what seemed to stop abolitionists in their tracks."

"It was good work," agreed Steve. "Though he may not have done much for his promotion prospects with Sir John."

"I think he knew that when he went into this fight. At least, that's what Dan says. He's got a lot of time for Jeremy."

"So have I," Steve said. "If things worked out, you know, he might be a very good fit here."

"Hey," interrupted Andy. "We've got to win the bloody contract back before we start hiring again."

"Yeah, I know, Andy ... only speculation at this stage. After all, we don't even know whether he wants to leave the service yet."

Our discussion was interrupted when Steve's mobile started to vibrate. He glanced at the screen. "Sorry, guys. I'd better take this. It's the lawyers."

Steve stepped back into the meeting room after his chat with the lawyers with the biggest beaming smile on his face that I'd ever seen.

"Do you have news?" Andy asked, spotting the width of his smile.

"I do indeed. You'll be pleased to know that there's been a complete retraction."

"What?"

Steve nodded vigorously. "I kid you not. It appears

that between them, Jeremy's cousin and the government Chief Whip have achieved a miracle. That guy Andrews has left DECRA and issued a complete retraction of all the allegations concerning Pearson Frazer, admitting that there was no truth in any of the stories that he gave to *London Figaro*. They will be issuing a retraction in this week's issue and their cheque is in the post."

I was stunned. To be exonerated like that without going through the sort of inquiry we'd been discussing on Saturday night was one of the greatest surprises of my life. "Crikey. That's a huge turn up for the book," I said as I was flooded with feelings of relief and pleasure.

"You're not kidding," added Andy. "How do you think they managed it?"

"A combination of the carrot and the stick, by the sound of it. Apparently, Andrews has been offered a plumb job with some Eurosceptic think-tank."

"Oh, very clever," said Barbara. "You get him out of harms' way without losing the talent." She nodded. "It serves everybody's interests – including ours – to get him out of DECRA. But give him the carrot of another job and you get him to keep quiet as well."

"Dan and Jeremey will be pleased," Steve remarked. "I don't think Messrs Forrester and Andrews will ever be bosom buddies."

"That's certainly true," I laughed.

The meeting broke up shortly after that and I returned to my desk feeling two tonnes lighter. The rest of the day passed in a haze of goodwill and relief, not only for me but for everybody in the firm.

I was packing up for the day when Steve put his head

round the door. "I'm off," he said. "But Josh said that you'd be welcome for supper later. Thought you might appreciate the company with Dan still being away."

"Oh, great. Thanks, that would be lovely."

"About eight?"

"See you then."

I left the office shortly after Steve and enjoyed a relaxing bath before getting ready to join them for supper. It was only a few minutes' walk up the hill to their flat.

Josh let me in and welcomed me with a hug. "How are you doing? Still okay?" His eyes were full of concern.

"I'm fine, thanks. Missing him, but over the worst, I think. I didn't thank you properly for your company on Sunday. You made such a difference, Josh."

"My pleasure. I'm glad you're okay, though. Saturday was a totally shitty day, wasn't it?"

"Certainly was. Dan's thing was bad enough, but all the other thing about us and Griffin House... I still can't grasp the fact that it's all over."

We went into their lounge and, as ever, the view bowled me over. It was a clear, frosty night, so the lights from the buildings in central London seemed to be twinkling.

My attention was diverted when Steve handed me a large glass of wine. "To celebrate the end of our persecution," he explained. We toasted everybody concerned, but especially Jim Hayden, the Chief Whip.

"Actually, I can't decide whether the Andrews retraction or Griffin House was the better news this morning." Steve remarked.

"The Griffin House news is great, but it's not a done deal, is it?" I asked.

"By no means. Still a lot of hoops between us and a new three-year contract," he replied.

"On the other hand, it's a hugely better than straight abolition," Josh pointed out. "That'd have left us feeling that we'd been wasting our time for the last three years."

"True," said Steve. "At least there might be a contract to compete for now."

"And we must stand a good chance of winning again, mustn't we?" I commented.

"Yeah, especially if I write the bid again," Josh added, polishing his nails on his lapel and grinning at us.

"I don't think anybody would argue with that," Steve commented dryly.

"It's a deal," replied his husband. "But to go back to your earlier question, Steve. I think it was the retraction that made the real difference."

"How so?" I asked.

"First of all, those allegations were so very damaging. They threatened to destroy our reputation, and they didn't do much for morale in the office, either."

"You're right. Everybody's been on edge for the last couple of weeks," Josh remarked.

"It really got to me," I added. "The business about Dan was pretty devastating. The idea that I'd might have seduced him simply to gain influence was so bloody offensive."

"I can well understand that, old love," Steve responded. "It must have been awful – I could see how it made you squirm on Saturday night."

"Me too," Josh added. "And they were so casual about it."

"You know, I think it was that, as much as the media ambush, that made me panic."

"I'm not surprised," Josh replied. "I know Dan laughed when the allegation came up, but..."

"Yeah," I interrupted, "But what if he hadn't? Once an idea like that had been planted in his head, there'd always be that little voice within him that wondered."

"Maybe, but Dan knows you, Luke. He knows what you two have got is special."

"Anyway," Steve said, "that's all over now. It's clear to everybody that it was all lies."

"Yep, all over now," Josh said brightly. "We can forget the whole lot and just enjoy the fabulous casserole I've made."

"Sounds a good plan to me," I remarked, getting up and following Josh to the table. So much baggage had been cleared out of the way, leaving us all free to get on with our lives.

After dinner, we were sitting around chatting about the prospects for the future when Josh fixed me with a look. "You seem more together tonight, Luke. No more thoughts of pushing Dan away 'for his own good'?" He punctuated the last four words by using his fingers to make air quotes.

"I gave myself a good talking to overnight. I suddenly realised that I had no right to make Dan's decisions for him. If he doesn't want to pursue whatever there is between us, then I'll understand – and I honestly couldn't blame him. On the other hand, he might want to take the risk that I'll be able to cope with something like that in future. But it is his decision to make, not mine."

"Amen to that," said Steve raising his glass.

Josh followed suit, but added with a twinkle in his eye, "After the way he stood up for you in that meeting on Saturday night, I'm pretty sure which way Dan will jump."

Governing Passions

Chapter Sixty-Three

Dan

It was Friday, and I was sitting with my hosts Glyn and Matt over the remains of an excellent dinner for the second evening in a row. Jeremy had arranged for a car to take me from my last visit on the previous afternoon to Glyn's house and to collect me from there after lunch on Sunday. We'd stopped at York station to drop him so that he could get back to London. This weekend with Glyn and Matt was a private visit, and I had no need of a private secretary to hold my hand.

My hosts lived in an historic manor house on the outskirts of a village in the Vale of York, to the east of the city. It was not an area I knew well, but I could see during the drive how beautiful it was – totally different from the wildness of the Dales or the Moors, of which we'd seen more on our travels this week.

The land was smoother and more fertile, and the countryside was full of prosperous-looking farms. I knew enough from the agricultural side of the department's portfolio that the prosperity was somewhat illusory, and was now hedged by the uncertainty of life outside the EU Common Agricultural Policy. But I wasn't going to worry about that today; I was here to enjoy myself and possibly to forge a plan "B" for my future. I felt drained after an exhausting few weeks, but also excited about what the next couple of days might have in store for me.

We'd spent Thursday evening talking about what the business was currently doing and how they envisaged the future. On the face of it, a politics website sounded dull and unexciting, but the material they were providing had won the respect of key players in the public affairs business; the combination of Glyn's rigour as a journalist and Jerry's flair for presentation and style was delivering a genuinely high-quality product. The service was inevitably heavy on data, and there was a great deal to watch and assimilate. Speed and fast turnaround of news and information were key, and they'd managed to do that very successfully.

The next step was to up their game in video, which was why Glyn had approached me. I continued to protest that I was unused to TV or video work and had no experience in presenting or interviewing. However, they were adamant that they'd seen a spark in me and wanted to test it out.

I'd found myself in a small recording studio after breakfast, working with them on a dummy interview. Glyn was my subject and we went through the preparation, research and scriptwriting before recording a ten-minute "as live" interview. After lunch, we worked on an op-ed directly to camera using an old script of Glyn's that we adapted to my speaking style. The next day, they planned to have me chair a discussion session using a couple of their knowledgeable editorial staff as guinea pigs, again going through the stages of research, preparation and recording. It had been a fantastic experience and I'd loved every minute of it, even if I was now dog-tired. I was so looking forward to the next day's session.

"That was a fantastic dinner, Matt. Thank you so much."

He beamed with pleasure. He was a delightful man. Slim and lithe, he moved with all the grace of the dancer he had once been. Whereas Glyn was a couple of years older than me, Matt was about my age but he wore his years lightly, dressing fashionably in tight shirts and skinny jeans that showed off his figure to perfection. A career in show business, which had now morphed into the wider media, had given him a certain devil-may-care approach to life. His manner was slightly outrageous, and he wore some quite subtle make-up. His sense of humour was sharp and he was also, judging by the two dinners he'd cooked so far, a brilliant cook.

"Thanks, lovey. It's always nice to be appreciated." He gave a slight glare at his husband, who had been so busy chatting about work that he hadn't said a word about the food.

"What? Oh, yes. Sorry. It was fab, darling," Glyn remarked absently, before resuming his enthusiastic monologue about the exciting possibilities we were exploring.

Matt smirked and rolled his eyes at me. "I'll go and get dessert. I've heard him rehearsing this bit already. If you don't watch it, he'll have you on three TV programmes at once, all while juggling half a dozen plates."

"That's so unfair!' Glyn exclaimed. "But you've got to admit that he's bloody good, sweetheart."

Matt faced his husband, hands on hips. "I know he is, sweetie pie. We've spent all day proving it. But the poor love's exhausted, so you ought to give it a rest."

I laughed. "I am here, you know. You'll be discussing whether I take sugar next."

"Oh, you're much too sweet for that," Matt shot back. "Sorry, but you do look pretty tired, love."

"You're right, I am, but I wouldn't have missed today for all the tea in China."

"Right, now Auntie Matty prescribes lots of syllabub, a nice cup of camomile tea and bed for us all." Noticing Glyn brighten at the mention of bed, Matt glared at him. "To sleep, Mr Pargiter. To sleep."

Glyn and I laughed, and Matt disappeared off to the kitchen.

I looked Glyn in the eye. "I hope you appreciate him properly. He's a joy."

He snorted with laughter. "A bit high maintenance on occasion, but who isn't? But you're right. He's made such a difference to my life – I'm a different person to the grump you worked for ten years ago."

"I had noticed."

"And what about you? I expect last weekend was a bit of a nightmare, wasn't it?"

"You're not kidding."

"And how's your boy after all that? Luke, isn't it?"

I nodded. "He's okay, I think. We spoke on Sunday but agreed on a cooling-off period this week. Anyway, I've been away, and he's busy at work. He was worried that he'd betrayed me by running off, so I had to calm him down, but I think I convinced him that he hadn't, that I understood."

"Good. Anybody who hasn't been through the media mill has no idea what it's like. Being thrown in the deep end must have seemed like absolute hell."

Matt came back with a tray full of sundae dishes overflowing with syllabub, whilst Glyn got up from the table and fetched three small glasses and a bottle.

"That looks spectacular," I said.

He grinned at me. "You can come again, Dan. I do love an appreciative audience."

"We'd noticed," Glyn remarked with a smirk.

Matt poked his tongue out at his husband.

"Anybody who produces food like this deserves a standing ovation every night," I said, winking at Matt.

"Many more compliments like that and you can move in, darling."

"Good excuse to open some pudding wine too," Glyn added, filling my glass.

"With this hospitality I will move in, I think – though Luke might have something to say about that."

"Oh, bring him too, sweetie. The more the merrier!"

The room went quiet while we ate our desert, conversation restricting to making appreciative humming noises.

"Well?" asked Matt anxiously.

"Fantastic," I remarked. "Perfect. Exactly the right sharpness and so light. A perfect way to end the meal."

"Creep," accused Glyn, only to receive a slap on the back of the head. He burst out laughing. "Matt, it was divine. In fact, the whole meal was stunning, sweetheart. Thanks."

Matt preened himself. "I must say, I thought it was one

of my better efforts."

"A toast to the chef," I said, raising my glass. Glyn joined me, and Matt positively purred with pleasure. It was good to see, and offered a lesson for my own relationship.

Glyn raised his glass. "And here's to our future together as a team." We clinked glasses this time, before he reached to top them up.

I was touched by their enthusiasm after today's efforts. "You think I've got a future in all this, then?"

Matt spoke first. "From a show-bizzy point of view, I'd say you were a natural. You drew me in and made me want to keep watching. All the women will love you, Dan. You'll be fighting them off."

I groaned.

"He's right," said Glyn. "And from a journalistic point of view, the scripts you put together were crisp and logical. You looked authoritative, calm and knew your subject. Looking at the rushes, I think it was even better than I expected."

"Thank you, guys." I found myself blushing. "That's ... er ... really kind," I stammered, always unsure how to take compliments.

Glyn gave Matt a small smile, as if to say "I told you so", then turned to me. "And what about you? How did it feel to you?"

"That's the crazy part. Once I relaxed a little, it felt the most natural thing in the world. Even doing the op-ed, which was a big surprise."

"Yeah, I could see that. Tell me, who were you thinking of when you spoke?"

I laughed. "Luke, actually. I imagined that I was chatting

to him."

Matt laughed and clapped his hands. "A natural! Told you."

I frowned, puzzled by his reaction. "The secret of success in broadcasting – and this dates all the way back to FDR's fireside chats in the thirties – is to make the audience believe that you're talking directly to them, having a conversation."

"Like Alastair Cooke?"

"Got it one," replied Glyn. "Did you listen to *Letter from America*?"

"Oh, yes, as often as I could. I first heard one at school and was a fan right through until the end. He packed up while we were working together, didn't he?"

"At the beginning of 2004. He was a master, but it wasn't off the cuff, you know. He prepared his scripts very carefully."

"Yes, I remember them saying. And knowing when to pause is so important, isn't it? Otherwise you go through it like a train."

"Either that, or it's full of 'ums' and 'ers' which bore the audience to death," Matt remarked.

"So, about tomorrow's session, Dan, I thought..."

Matt harrumphed and turned to wink at me. "Oh, gawd, he's off. I'll go and make the tea."

We worked for most of Saturday with Glyn's staffers on the dummy discussion programme, eventually making a recording around four in the afternoon. I had the time of my life. Anna and Jimmy, were seriously bright – lively, intelligent and articulate. They knew their subject and we had a blast.

Dinner on Saturday night was in a local restaurant to give Matt a night off from cooking and to get us out of the house, which we hadn't left since my arrival at teatime on Thursday. We had a great time laughing and joking our way through a superb meal in the delightful surroundings of an eighteenth-century coaching inn.

As the coffee arrived, the conversation turned more serious. "Anyway, the thing is," said Matt, cutting to the chase, "do you want in or not?"

I thought for a moment. It was true that I had loved every minute of the two days and my gut instinct was to say yes. But there was a lot to think about. I'd have to resign as a Minister, and possibly even as an MP, though I'd probably be able to stay until the next election. Above all, I needed to talk to Luke: he barely knew anything about this. If we were going to build a life together, I couldn't go about making life-changing decisions on my own. I decided to be open about my feelings.

"To be honest, I don't know. Have I loved every minute of this visit? Definitely. Did I feel at home in the studio? You bet. Did I enjoy working with you guys? Absolutely. Am I ready to commit, here and now?" I shook my head. "No. For a start, it's a hell of a leap in the dark away from something I've known and worked towards all my life. Plus I need to talk to Luke about how it would affect us, if there is an 'us', that is. And finally, I need time to think, to have a few moments to myself to work out what I want to do with the rest of my life."

Spotting my hesitation, Glyn had made an impatient gesture but Matt reached out and grabbed his wrist to stop him. Glyn looked up and Matt gave the smallest shake of the head. "How long do you need, Dan?" he asked.

"When do you need an answer?"

Glyn sighed. "How long is a piece of string? If you say yes, we can start talking to funders and potential sponsors straight away. Matt can edit together a demonstration disk using footage we've shot over the past two days, and we could go for a launch early in the New Year. That would be my ideal scenario. If not, we'd have to find somebody else, in which case we wait to kick off the launch process until we've found them."

"When would you need my decision in order to stick to that timetable?"

"Next Friday."

I nodded. "It'll be sooner than that, Glyn. Get me a formal proposal and we can get something signed by then."

Glyn and Matt high-fived each other. "Told you," Glyn said to his husband.

"Whoa, I haven't said yes yet, you know!' I exclaimed.

"No, but you're going to, darling, aren't you?" Matt asked.

I grinned at him. "Probably."

Governing Passions

Chapter Sixty-Four

Luke

The drive to Harchester that Sunday was an easy one for once. It being early December, there was no holiday or day-trip traffic to contend with, and I was too early to get involved with people heading for the shops.

I'd ducked out of spending the weekend on the grounds of exhaustion after the last couple of weeks, but I'd promised to go down for a wedding anniversary lunch. My parents were marking thirty-six years since they'd married, somewhat hurriedly it seems – propelled towards the altar by my appearance in my mother's womb.

The fact that it was Advent Sunday provided an added incentive for my visit. It was always a special occasion in the Cathedral, and I loved the service that marked the start of the run-up to Christmas. This year, I'd hoped to bring Dan too, but he'd accepted the invitation from the internet guys before I'd had the chance to raise the subject. In the light of the events of the previous weekend, it was probably as well.

My mother had promised me faithfully that Edward

Bickerstaff would not be one of the guests this time but that Pru and Bishop Geoffrey would be there. I hadn't seen them since my "coming out".

As I neared my destination, I couldn't help reflecting on how things had changed, even in the space of a few weeks. Last time I was here, I'd been brimming with optimism for a future with Dan, and determined to be open with my family about myself for the first time ever. Now I was full of doubts.

I still felt so guilty about letting Dan down so badly, and I remained convinced that I was not the man for him. The chances were that he'd always be a public figure, whether he stayed in politics or not. For that reason he needed a partner he could rely on, not some wimp who panicked and ran away at the first sign of a flashbulb. Whatever happened, I would be haunted by last Saturday night and my fear that I'd let him down. But the thought of a future without him ... that was even worse.

I tried to force my mind back to the road. That was absolute nonsense. I'd been independent and content before I'd met Dan again, and I could be that way again. And yet... I grimaced at the familiar turn of phrase and completed Alan Jay Lerner's words out loud. "I've grown accustomed to his face." I fought back a tear and managed another smile. How Josh would have laughed if he'd known that I'd brought a song from a musical like *My Fair Lady* into the equation.

An hour and a half later, I pulled into the Deanery's small car park. The bishop's car was already there, but there was also another smaller one that I didn't recognise. I reached for my jacket from the back seat, straightened my tie, and grabbed the flowers I'd brought for my mother from the back seat.

In contrast to the birthday lunch, this event was a delight. My mother had not tried to turn it into a county social event, restricting the invitations to other members of the Cathedral Chapter and their wives, all of whom I'd met before. The only one I didn't recognise was introduced to me by my father: it was Gregory Allen, the clergyman who'd resigned over the church's attitude to homosexuality.

He was a shy and diffident young man, not yet thirty. He wore slim gold spectacles, which gave him an owlish look, and he seemed to be a deeply serious person. But he smiled when we were introduced, and it lit up his whole face. We had the opportunity for a chat over sherry. He told me that he'd got a fellowship at his old Oxford college and was enjoying the academic life.

"Do you miss the Church?" I asked him.

He shook his head. "Not really. I suppose I'm fortunate compared with many in that I haven't lost my faith, despite my anger with the church authorities. I always got on well with my college chaplain, so I'm happy with that side of my life. And I love my research, too, so I've been very lucky."

"What are you researching?"

"I'm doing a PhD on religious attitudes to homosexuality."

"Wow. Isn't that a bit depressing?"

He looked wistful for a moment as he considered his reply. "A bit at times, but I hope that my thesis might make a contribution at some point in the future. Airing the nuances and differences can sometimes help, especially when you can show that there is no scriptural basis for some of the things that are said. It won't stop prejudice, of course, but robbing people of their intellectual justification is a good start."

I smiled. "Like my father, I suppose."

"Indeed. Yes, his change of heart was very gratifying. Fortunately, he was intellectually honest enough to listen and then wrestle with his conscience. That's a rare gift, Luke. You should be proud of him."

"I was certainly relieved and grateful. I'd always held back from coming out because it seemed easier not to make waves. And, yes, I suppose I was proud of him that day for standing up to Edward Bickerstaff."

"He told me about that. I gather he almost caused a by-election by giving the man apoplexy."

I laughed. "It certainly made for an entertaining lunch."

Gregory's eyes sparkled with amusement, but his face turned serious. "You know, Luke, I suspect that deep down a lot of gay people feel a residual guilt about what they are."

"I think that's true. I know I struggled with it for a long time."

"But no longer?"

"I don't think so. I might have a problem coping with constant media exposure, but I don't think that's the reason."

"The media is bloody difficult at times. I experienced some of it after my resignation here, particularly with the local media, but nothing on the scale of what you and Dan had to put up with last weekend. That must have been awful."

I nodded. "It was, but the worst aspect is this feeling that I let my boyfriend down."

"You must be careful not to be too hard on yourself, Luke..."

I wasn't destined to find out more because we were summoned into lunch and directed to opposite ends of the table. When I took my seat, I was delighted to see that I'd been put next to Aunty P. That guaranteed an entertaining couple of hours.

The conversation with my godmother proved more challenging than I'd expected. It didn't happen over lunch, though; conversation round the table was entertaining and amusing, and the content was conventional and decidedly not personal.

As the others moved into the lounge for coffee, Pru fixed me with her eyes. "I need some fresh air for a few minutes, Luke. Come and walk with me – we'll take a turn round the close."

Refusal was out of the question, so I got my coat and borrowed one of my father's scarves and off we set.

"How are things, young man?"

"I like the young. Thank you."

She smiled back but was not going to be deflected. "And?"

I couldn't help the sigh. "We're having a cooling-off period after last week. But I think it's probably over."

"Oh, Luke, I am sorry, darling. Why?"

"I'm no good for him. I betrayed him last Saturday night, Aunty P. I panicked and ran because I couldn't cope. If I stay around, I'll only hold him back."

"So you totally are Dan's Dasher?"

I winced. "Aunty P, that's cruel."

She laughed. "At least I have a godson who's famous enough to earn his own hashtag."

"True, I suppose," I replied, trying to muster a laugh.

"Have you given him a chance to talk about this?"

"Not really, no. I tried to on Sunday, but he wouldn't let me say the words. Kept saying that it was too soon."

"A sign, surely, that he doesn't agree?"

"Maybe. I don't know. I'm not going to force the issue – I can't walk away from him. But if he doesn't want to take a chance on me then I'll understand. I don't think I'm up to being partner to a senior politician."

"I simply cannot accept that you're not up to the job, sweetheart. You're a successful young man with great future. Don't undersell yourself."

I harrumphed, though secretly a little knot of gratification took root inside me. But I was still convinced I was right. "How would I cope? If Dan stays in politics and gets into the Cabinet one day, how could I be the partner, maybe even husband, of a Cabinet Minister? I couldn't go to all those posh dinners – God, even to Buckingham Palace!"

My godmother stopped walking and fixed me with another of her stares. "How do you think I coped?"

I stared back with amazement. "What do you mean?"

"When I met Geoffrey, I was a poor, working-class girl from Westmoreland. My dad was a bus driver and I

not forget the cruelties that the Churches had inflicted on countless millions over the centuries, people of other faiths and no faith, those deemed to be witches or heretics – and, of course, LGBT people. That was a persecution carried on today; churches and religious zealots were still at the forefront of attacks on people of my own kind. Much as I loved this building and many of its traditions, I couldn't be starry-eyed about everything Christianity did or stood for.

Inevitably those thoughts took my mind to the two conversations that I'd had today: Gregory telling me not to be too hard on myself, and Pru cautioning me against throwing away Dan's love.

Perhaps Gregory was right: maybe I did have a residual feeling of guilt about being gay. Was that what all this was about? Surely not. But then again, Pru was also right – I was a successful, educated and highly qualified man. And I was out and proud. Why should I think myself inadequate in any way? It was illogical but, in the context of Dan's life and career, I did. So, could it be true? Was it because I expected people to look down on me because of who I loved?

Pru's words echoed in my brain. "Dan Forrester should be proud to call you his boyfriend. And I bet he is, too." Was that true? I realised how much I hoped it was. I didn't have long to wait, though: I'd know by the end of the next day.

Governing Passions

Chapter Sixty-Five

Dan

I got back to my flat about four on Sunday afternoon. After being empty for almost a week, it seemed cold and damp, even though the heating had been on for some time every day. Whereas I normally thought of the place as cosy and familiar, it now seemed more than a little shabby; at the very least, it needed of a coat of paint. A new colour scheme and some fresh soft furnishings wouldn't go amiss either.

I sighed. It would be nice to have the time to think about such matters, as well as having somebody in my life to share things like that – picking out the colours, wandering round the shops together browsing. I couldn't actually remember the last time I'd gone into a shop somewhere simply to browse. Maybe one of the bonuses of switching career could be that I'd have time to take an interest in life outside Westminster and Whitehall again.

Jeremy had dropped off a couple of red boxes with some urgent papers in them, so that was my task for the next few hours. Never mind the decoration, feel the paperwork.

Before turning in, I checked my e-mail and there was one from Glyn, sending me a first edit of the material we'd shot on Friday. The addition of some music and graphics made a terrific difference and the programme looked totally professional. The edited versions of the interviews came across – to me at least, though admittedly I was a little biased – as sharp and incisive. Matt had spliced the op-ed piece up with some graphics and film so it wasn't just a talking head. It made the talk come alive.

I wasn't normally one to blow my own trumpet, but I'd done enough media work to know whether somebody was any good or not. I understood now that Glyn had been entirely honest when he said I was a natural. I'd felt it during the recordings, and now I could see the evidence of it with my own eyes. Crikey.

When I eventually got to bed, sleep proved impossible. Even though my body told me I was tired, my brain simply refused to accept the idea. Instead, it flicked from one topic to another without ever allowing me a space for rational thought about anything. Talk about a random access memory. I felt on edge, full of deep anxiety about my future, about Luke and indeed about pretty much every aspect of my life

I sat up, shaking my head to try and clear it. Eventually I got out of bed. Sleep was out of the question; I had either to think things through, or get my mind to focus on something, anything. How about the future? Now there was an interesting subject.

I knew that the basic question was the same one that had been flitting in and out of my brain ever since I'd got this job at DECRA: what the hell I was going to do with the rest of my life?

It was no good wallowing, with thoughts and ideas cropping up almost at random when I had the odd idle moment because all that happened was that I pushed them away again. On some occasions, the thoughts were so radical that I became too frightened of their possible consequences and pushed them away; on others, my thinking time simply ran out and I had to switch off and focus elsewhere.

It was vital to go through this logically. That's what I'd told Jeremy I was going to do a week ago, and I still hadn't done it. I now had less than twenty-four hours left before meeting up with Luke again, by which time my decision about the future had to be made. There could be no more havering or whingeing. It was time to face up to the issues.

I poured myself a drink and sat at my desk, drawing a note pad and pen across in front of me. I wrote three headings on the sheet: politics, personal life, future career. They were inter-linked, but maybe if I focussed on them one at a time I could make some sort of sense out of them.

Politics: did I want to pursue a career as a politician? Answer: No. Tick. Simple.

I almost reeled from the shock of my instinctive response. I had lost my enthusiasm for the business of politics. Importantly, my father had lifted the burden of family tradition from my shoulders.

Personal life: did I want to build a future with Luke, ideally for the rest of my life? You bet. Big tick. Also simple.

Any lingering doubts after last weekend's events had been blown away by how much I'd missed him over the past week. He'd become integral to my life. End of.

Future career: could I see myself building an alternative career in journalism and broadcasting? Here, my views had changed radically. Whereas a few weeks ago, returning to journalism had seemed like a backward step, now it seemed like a route to the future. I already knew I could write; I'd made a good living at it for nine years before entering Parliament and my father's praise for my work ten days ago had meant a lot.

I knew now that I could make a pretty good fist of broadcasting, too. It wouldn't pay as much as I was getting now, at least not immediately, but what was I doing with my money anyway? Storing it away somewhere because I never had time to spend it. I had few obligations – I owned my flat outright and had a small mortgage on the cottage, but once I'd stood down from Parliament, it wouldn't matter if I had to sell that anyway. I'd be sorry, because I loved it down there, but needs must, etcetera.

I put my head back and sighed. "There you are," I said to myself. "All sorted." Now all I had to do was implement it.

I put my first list on one side and started on a second: a list of tasks. Number one was to tell Luke I loved him. Second was to resign from the government. That was top priority, and I would do that first thing tomorrow. Everything else could follow, because once I'd done that I would have time to breathe. My third task was to tell Luke that I loved him again. Number four was to tell the constituency people that I would be standing down at the next General Election. That would make the chairman's week; Anthony Burton and his cronies would be able to choose a nice compliant Brexiteer to feed their own prejudices. Number five was to talk to Luke about numbers one and three above. Number six was to tell Glyn and Matt that I wanted "in" on their video streaming venture. And number seven was to talk to my old newspaper about whether they'd take some articles from me. As for number eight, I thought I might possibly need to talk to Luke again...

I put down my pen and yawned prodigiously. Time for bed, and this time I thought I might sleep.

I was right; the next thing I knew the alarm on my phone was going.

Governing Passions

Chapter Sixty-Six

Luke

When I was woken by my phone on Monday morning, I reached out to turn the alarm off but realised that the ringtone meant there was an incoming call. I blinked myself awake and grabbed the handset, only to see Dan's name and picture up on the screen.

I beamed as I accepted the call. "Hey, Dan. Is there something wrong?"

He laughed. "No, nothing wrong. Sorry it's so early."

I glanced at my clock – seven-twenty. What the hell? That was at least forty minutes before my usual wake-up time. I'd never been a morning person and sleeping a bit later was one of the many advantages of living just down the hill from the office. "No problem. It's good to hear your voice."

"Mmm. Yours too. Listen, I know we're supposed to be meeting tonight, but is there any chance of seeing you earlier?"

"Yeah, okay. I think so – nothing much on today. What time?"

"Er … now?"

"Christ, Dan. Where's the fire?"

He laughed. God, he hadn't sounded this relaxed for weeks. What was going on?

"Only here's the thing. I've been doing a lot of thinking and I've made some decisions, but I want to talk to you about them before anything happens."

"Oh?"

"Yeah, I've got a list of tasks to do today. And … let me see … numbers one, three, five and eight concern you."

"Four of them? Concerning me?"

"That's right. Mind you, it's all the same task. First and foremost, I have to tell you that I love you. That's number one, and everything else follows from that."

My whole being came alive again, in a way that it hadn't been since that fateful Saturday night. "That sounds really … erm… interesting, Dan. Shall I come over to you?"

"That would be good. I'll sort out some breakfast for us."

"Fine. I'll organise an Uber and be with you as soon as I can. Oh, and Dan?"

"Yes?"

"Just for the record, I love you too."

Altogether, it took me about an hour to get over to Dan's place. I saved a bit of time by getting dressed while waiting for the car, but it was morning rush hour on a wet December Monday morning, so the traffic was hell. Fortunately, the driver was not a chatty soul, so that left me free to speculate on what was going on. Meanwhile, he bore the hassle of the journey in stoic silence, with a bland popular music station playing low in the background.

Eventually we reached Kensington and the entrance to Dan's building. As I got out of the car, I glanced across the road, remembering with a shudder the gaggle of reporters and photographers that had awaited us that Saturday night. Fortunately, the only people on the pavement today were commuters walking quickly to work, hunched against the cold.

I rang his doorbell and Dan buzzed the front door open for me. As I got out of the lift, he was waiting, a big smile on his face and his arms open in welcome. God, he looked so wonderful standing there, still in his T-shirt and an old pair of jeans.

I almost fell into his arms, and found myself in the biggest, tightest hug I'd ever had in my life. A feeling of relief, joy and comfort washed over me and I couldn't stop my eyes from filling and a tear trickling down my cheek. We fitted so well together, and when our lips met I felt an explosion of sensation and emotion. The kiss started gently but quickly turned passionate. As if by instinct, our bodies moved closer together. I could feel Dan's arousal grinding against mine, and it felt absolutely wonderful.

Eventually, Dan held me at arm's length and beamed at me. We were both breathing heavily, but he managed to speak. "Good morning, young Mr Carter," he said.

I swallowed my emotions, gulped in some air, and managed to croak a response. "And a very good morning to you, Mr Forrester."

I tilted my head ready for another kiss, but he moved away with a rueful grin. "Sorry, but if we carry on like that we'll end up back in bed, and Jeremy will have my guts for garters if I'm late. Besides, breakfast arrived a few minutes ago and I'm starving. It's keeping hot in the kitchen. Come through. Sorry about the early start."

"Doesn't matter at all. It was so wonderful to hear your voice this morning. And seeing you again now? I can't begin to say how good it feels, Dan."

"I take it you missed me?" he asked, his grin widening.

"Maybe a little." I took a deep breath. "Dan, I'm sorry – both about Saturday night and for the things I said on Sunday. I panicked, then freaked out. I felt so guilty. I wanted to run away and hide."

"There's no need to apologise," he replied firmly. "It was a horrible evening, that Saturday. We were tired, hungry and stressed out." He must have seen the slightly sceptical look on my face, because his tone become more urgent. "Luke, you mustn't worry about it. Anyway, it's over now and we're here together. That's what matters."

"You sure?"

"Absolutely positive. Now, I'm starving. Come and have some breakfast and I'll tell you what's going on."

Chapter Sixty-Seven

Dan

Any doubts I might have had about my decisions – and there were precious few – were swept away by the sight of Luke getting out of the lift that Monday morning.

He looked gorgeous, and the smile on his face as he came into my arms was something to behold. I couldn't believe how good the hug felt. I found myself starting to cry, and I could sense that Luke was too. And as for that kiss...

I served the breakfast I'd had delivered, and we sat at the kitchen table. It felt comfortable and we were silent for a while, both occupied with condiments and buttering our toast. After I'd swallowed the first mouthful, I could see that Luke was bursting with curiosity. Even so, not knowing what to expect, his expression turned serious as I began to speak.

"First of all, I had an absolute blast with Glyn and Matt – you'll love them, I'm sure. The material we did together in their studio was amazing. I loved being in front of the camera, and they said I was a natural."

As I spoke, Luke's smile returned tentatively. "That's

terrific, Dan."

"They sent me a video late last night. That's what started me on my big think."

"I'd like to see it."

"No problem. So, before I left they offered me a job."

"Brilliant! I wasn't expecting that."

"Neither was I, to be honest, but there we are. They're planning to start slowly, with some YouTube videos and postings on their own website. But they think the audience will build. If it does, they might sell the show to a streaming service or even one of the big networks."

"When?"

"New Year, probably. They've still got some funding to sort out, but Glyn's confident that if I get on board that'll be no problem."

"Okay... That sounds a bit less certain, but..."

"Yeah, I get that. But in one way, it's no big deal if it doesn't come off because what the offer did was to force me into a decision about the whole of my future."

Luke's eyes widened. "Gosh, you have been busy. Go on."

"The big question is whether I want to stay in the Commons. It's been building up for the last few weeks, but my father lit the fuse the other night. His words, and the story about Uncle Archie... well, it was like having a weight lifted from my shoulders. Suddenly, all the expectations and obligations I'd felt all these years vanished. I was free to think about what I wanted for a change – and there was Dad, virtually egging me on to do something else."

Luke's tentative smile widened. "That's good, Dan."

I took a deep breath and carried on. "That Saturday night

was pretty much the straw that broke the camel's back. I realised that if I stayed in politics and maybe joined the Cabinet at some point, most of my life would be like that. Constant media scrutiny, cameras everywhere, journalists shouting stupid questions, invasive personal security. I can't be doing with it, Luke and I'm sure you can't."

He shuddered. "No, you're right."

"When I'd watched the video from the boys and I couldn't sleep last night, I decided it was time to face up to it all and make some decisions." I paused for a moment and met Luke's eyes. He was anxious, I could tell, but I could also read the kindness in them.

"The first decision is to say again that I very much want a future with you. I know we've talked about that before, but it's always been hedged round with ifs and buts to do with my career and coming out. Now that's all cleared away."

"I want that too, Dan. More than you can possibly know."

"Good, because pretty much everything else depends on it."

"Oh?"

"I don't want to give you the impression that I'm doing all this for your sake, because that isn't true. You don't bear any responsibility for my decisions. I'm doing it because meeting you again opened my mind to the possibility of a life outside the bubble. I hope that makes sense."

Luke nodded. "I think so. From all that you've said, I think you felt trapped, pushed into politics by others' expectations. And I guess you didn't fight it because you hadn't got a viable alternative."

"Spot on," I replied, relieved that he seemed to

understand what I was saying. "And now I have one. You are my alternative, Luke."

He huffed a little. "Still sounds like a responsibility to me."

"Oh, yes, I am a very responsible job," I replied with a chuckle.

He looked at me as if he were astounded that I could make a joke at a moment like this. But then he laughed and the tension in the room lifted a little. He recovered first. "Seriously, Dan, I do get it. It's terrific. I feel honoured that I could play a role as some sort of catalyst."

"That's the perfect word, Luke. I can certainly go with catalyst."

"So, what now? How do we get from here to there?"

"First thing is to resign from the government. At the same time, I'll announce that I won't be standing at the next election. I can combine staying in the House with some media work for the time being, and the last thing anybody needs right now is a by-election. Then I tell Glyn and Matt that I'm game for their new venture and I start to sell myself as a freelance journalist again."

"Gosh, Dan, that's brilliant. Are you sure? *Absolutely* sure?"

I nodded, smiling. "Absolutely sure, Luke."

He paused for a moment, as if weighing my words. Then he nodded. "Yes, I think you are sure. And incredibly sane and sensible and very, very brave ... and I love you to bits."

He came round the table to hug me, moving so quickly that I didn't get chance to rise from my chair. Instead, he grasped me my shoulders and held my head to his tummy. I rested there, feeling warm and comfortable and, above all, safe. It was like coming home. It was magical.

"And when does all this happen?" he asked eventually.

"Today. I'm resigning today, with immediate effect. There's no point in waiting."

"But won't people in the tabloids think they've forced you out because of the stories about Adam? Another scalp for the press?"

I shrugged. "To be honest, I don't care. They can think what they like. Besides, in the great scheme of things, it hardly matters a twopenny damn," I told him. "God, you've no idea how liberating it is to say that."

"I'm sure you're doing the right thing, and for the right reasons. You're doing it for *you*." Luke gave me a big grin. "So, there we are, Mr Forrester."

"Yes, Mr Carter."

"Welcome to the rest of your life."

I left Luke about ten and set off for my office for the last time. I had a letter of resignation to draft and no doubt there would be other paperwork to complete before I could be free. I was greeted by a grim-faced Jeremy; indeed, he looked so unhappy that I thought word of my decision must have reached somebody, though I couldn't imagine how.

"Morning, Jeremy. You look glum. What's happened?"

"Today is my last day with you, Dan. I've been moved."

"What?"

He nodded. "Yup. After I left you in York on Thursday, I came into the office on Friday morning only to be summoned to see the HR people. Apparently it has been decided that my experience needs to be widened, so I'm being sent to run a new agricultural liaison office."

"What the hell's that?"

"It seems we're setting up a network of new offices to work with farmers in the post-Brexit era. I am to run one of the local offices."

"Where?"

"Ambleside."

"Ambleside?" I echoed incredulously. "Do you mean Ambleside as in the Lake District?"

He nodded. "The same."

"Bloody hell, Jeremy. You really did blot your copybook, didn't you?"

He gave a small smile. "Interesting that you should say that. Technically, it's a promotion – one grade up, more money on the basic, though without the London Weighting, of course. On the other hand, everybody knows that being sent out of the way to a regional office means that I'm no longer considered a potential high-flyer to be fast-tracked up the ladder."

I nodded, "I assumed that would be the case. Like sending people to DVLA in Swansea or the DHSS in Newcastle in the old days."

"Quite. I mean, don't get me wrong, I love the Lake District. In many ways, it would be a great place to live. But as a career move it's a disaster – and we both know why. Crossing Sir John over Griffin House. I might have got away with arguing back, but actually inflicting a defeat... It's my own fault, I suppose. I should have seen it coming."

"Would it have made any difference? If you'd thought about the possible consequences?"

"I wish I could say no, but I don't know. I wouldn't have stayed here in the private office for much longer anyway, but hints had been dropped about a move upwards to work for a Cabinet Minister, which would have been a fantastic experience. I'm sorry that I'll miss out on that – but how I can I regret making a stand about something I believed in?"

"I suppose they would say that's the point. As a civil servant, you're not supposed to believe in things."

"I've no doubt that's what they *would* say. But in this case, I don't think it stacks up. There is no policy question at stake here – the disagreement was about means more than ends. I happened to think that Griffin House was – is – an excellent means of delivering policy objectives."

"I can see that. And I agree. But where does that leave you now?"

"Looking for a job. I thought about it over the weekend and submitted my resignation this morning as soon as I got in."

"Well fuck, Jeremy, I'm staggered. That's an amazing turn of events. I never thought..."

"Me neither. But there we are. I couldn't stay after they'd done that to me. If there isn't room for honest disagreement in the service, I don't have a future in it. It's that simple. Now, enough about me. I'll cope. Seb thinks I'm doing the right thing, so we'll survive."

"Good. For what it's worth, so do I. And I'm glad you've got recent experience of writing letters of resignation because you can help me draft mine."

His eyes went wide. "Er... what? Dan, what the hell...? What provoked this?"

"All sorts of things. As you know, I've been wondering about quitting politics and this weekend showed me how I could do it. I decided last night that it's time to do something about it." I couldn't resist a small chuckle at my next thought. "To 'take back control', to coin a phrase."

Jeremy guffawed at my stealing the Brexiteers' mantra. "God, I shall miss you," he said.

"I need to give whatever's happening with Luke a proper chance, and to pursue a career I might love as opposed to one I chose out of duty."

"I'm a bit taken aback – I know you've mentioned it before, but even so it seems very sudden. Are you leaving the Commons, too?"

"Not until the next election. I decided that I owe at least some loyalty to the local party. Plunging them into a by-election right now would risk chaos, I think."

"I can see that. That means that the only question is when."

"No time like the present, Jeremy. I know it's only been two and a half months, but I've had enough. I want out, and the sooner the better."

"And I thought I was being impulsive, giving a month's notice. We'd better get drafting."

Jeremy and I finished my resignation letter reasonably quickly. We had a bit of a debate on the explanation I would give; simply citing "personal reasons" would be like giving victory to the tabloids on a platter. But in many ways, it didn't matter. If I said something else, nobody would believe me anyway. If my time in politics had taught me anything, it was that perception was everything.

Jeremy was concerned about setting the record straight; after all, I wasn't planning to disappear completely. I acknowledged the point, and I was pleased with the result in the end. It mentioned my growing concern about the direction of the government, worries about the future of politics, and the change in my personal circumstances. It was honest, open and – crucially – verifiable. Nobody could go digging and speculate about the real reason for my decision.

The letter was sent across to Downing Street by e-mail and copied to my own Secretary of State and the Chief Whip. After that the resignation took immediate effect, so I handed over everything and said my goodbyes. George, the Secretary of State and my immediate boss, was his usual affable self and thanked me for my hard work. Sir John Radford was stiff and formal; our conversation was brief, the handshake at the end perfunctory and cold. That left Jeremy, the only person in the building for whom I'd formed any regard and whom I would miss. We'd worked well together and become very close. His resignation would make it easier to maintain our friendship and we swore to do so. We hugged before I left the building. Thus ended my short ministerial career.

I would miss some aspects, and I was glad that I'd had the experience, but I couldn't regret the fact that it was now over. As I walked from the department's offices past Westminster Abbey and into Parliament Square, I felt an enormous sense of relief and freedom. From now on, I would be living my life the way I wanted to, not because of the expectations foisted on me by other people's expectations. It felt liberating.

Epilogue

Dan, November 2019

The Palace of Westminster was surprisingly quiet: few visitors, virtually no media. Even though it was the last day of the Parliament, the focus was already on the General Election campaign that would begin in earnest the following day.

The dissolution meant that this was my last day as a Member of Parliament and that soon my career as a professional politician would be over. I couldn't feel anything other than relief; once I'd taken the decision on that December night two years earlier to focus elsewhere, my continued membership had seemed a bit like a hangover.

From a journalistic point of view, it had been a fascinating period. The political events surrounding our departure from the EU had got steadily more bizarre. The levels of abuse we received via social media and e-mail continued unabated; if anything, they got nastier. In my case, I had homophobia to contend over as well as the Brexit controversy. It had made the lives of my teams in

Westminster and in the constituency seriously unpleasant, and we lost a couple of part-timers who were worn down by the extreme language and threats.

The new venture with Glyn and Matt had started on schedule and was going to plan. The stats for the YouTube videos were good, and the revenue was starting to flow. Visitor numbers to the original website had also increased thanks in part to the videos, but also to some top-notch editorial content from the guys and their staff. I'd contributed some articles, as well as selling some to my old paper and various magazines. My income so far was never going to make me rich, but it was enough; importantly, it was growing. The crunch would come over the next few months after my Parliamentary salary stopped, though I would have more time to devote to developing my other ventures.

Luke and I had agreed to move in together, so I spent most of the time at his house in Crystal Palace. The Kensington flat was on the market; though I would be sorry to see it go after all those years, it was time to move on. The plan was to sell his house too, and buy something together that would be ours. The proceeds of the flat sale would enable me to make a sizeable contribution towards a new place and clear the mortgage off the cottage: both of us loved the place, the site of our first real tryst, and we were determined to keep it if we possibly could. Apart from anything else, that would mean we could stay in touch with the many friends I still had in the constituency, especially Helena.

This morning, I'd finished packing up my belongings at Westminster and said farewell to my team in the office. It had been a sad occasion, and I was sorry to see them go. They'd all probably get jobs with somebody in the new Parliament when it was called into session in six or seven weeks' time, but it was a difficult period of uncertainty for them.

After I'd finished packing, I sat in the chamber for the last time, listening to the adjournment debate which, as so often on such occasions, was light-hearted and generous despite all the bad blood that had existed for the last few months. I'd made my final intervention in the Commons a few days earlier during DECRA questions. Now, though, I wanted to wander, so I left the Chamber after bowing to the Speaker for the last time, and went towards for my favourite part of the complex, Westminster Hall.

This is the oldest building on the site, having by some miracle survived both the great fire of 1834 and the Blitz of May 1941, when the entire Commons chamber had been destroyed. I'd been fascinated by the place ever since my father had brought me here as a boy. Not only was there the beauty of Richard II's spectacular timber roof but also the hall's crucial role in our long history – 900 years of it, back to the reign of King William II. It had been the site of coronation banquets, the trial of King Charles I at the end of the English Civil War, and the lying-in state of monarchs and other major figures such as Sir Winston Churchill.

My father, already an MP by the time of Churchill's funeral, had told me of that occasion. Thousands of ordinary people had queued for hours in the cold January weather to pay their own tributes to the great man, shuffling silently past the coffin, heads bowed and many shedding tears. From where I now stood on the steps at the southern end of the hall, I could see the brass plaque in the stone floor marking the spot where the catafalque had stood.

Dad had been in the Commons at the same time as Sir Winston, who hadn't relinquished his seat until 1964, a few months before his death. Within weeks of Dad's retirement after fifty-one years, I had arrived here. Though I was relieved to be leaving, I felt immensely honoured to have served in this place for nine years and been a member of the oldest Parliament on the planet, the cradle of freedom and democracy throughout the world.

It may have sounded trite, and the cynics could scoff, but it was all true and it did matter. As a gay man, I could also be proud of the fact that members in this building had enacted the legislation that had helped to turn my community from despised and criminalised outcasts into accepted citizens with rights. If only other countries – including so many members of the Commonwealth – would follow suit.

As to what was would happen now – we would see. I would not be participating but I would be involved, reporting and commentating on the upcoming campaign and covering the events that would lead to the formation of a new government.

I was awoken from my reverie by a vibration from my phone. Glancing down, I saw a text from Luke saying he was on his way and he'd meet me by the Commons exit. We were heading for a dinner with our friends to mark the end of my Westminster career – my liberation, as Luke called it. I would have preferred to go home and cuddle up with my boyfriend, but needs must; I might no longer be an MP, but I still had a media image to burnish. And I was learning that, in some respects, the two lives were not all that different.

Suddenly a cry echoed down from the central lobby through St Stephens to my place at the top of the steps. "Who Goes Home?" the stentorian voice asked, signalling that the Speaker had left the chair. Business was at an end and Parliament dissolved. As of that moment I ceased to be a Member of the House of Commons and my political career was over. I smiled to myself and continued towards the exit, ready to get on with the rest of my life.

Luke stood by the exit with a big smile on his face, his arms open for a hug. "You ready for this, then?" he asked.

"Yes, let's go. Time to move on."

Acknowledgements

My grateful thanks to all the people who've worked so hard to help me bring this book to fruition: my editor Karen Holmes, beta readers Kirsten Waite and Jill Wexler, and cover designer Garrett Leigh at Black Jazz Designs.
My deepest thanks also to my husband Michael Anderson and to all my friends for their help and encouragement over many years.

About the Author

Chris Cheek was born and brought up in South London. He has strong family ties with northern England and is a graduate of Lancaster University. He and his husband, Michael, have been together for over forty years and moved to the Sussex Coast in 2018 after many years in the Yorkshire Dales.

This is Chris's fourth novel. His first book, *The Stamp of Nature*, was published in June 2018. The second, *A Year of Awakening*, followed in October 2018 - it was the first book in the *Love in a Changing Climate* series, of which this is the second. His third book, *Veering Off Course* was published in February 2019 - it is the first of a planned series under the title *The Navigation Quartet*.

He writes a regular blog which can be found at www.chrischeek.me.

"Fantastic, poignant, powerful, bittersweet, emotional, gripping, and grab-you-by-the-feels"

Reviewers' verdicts on Chris Cheek's third novel, published in February 2019.

"A fantastic story filled with intriguing and entertaining characters"

Meeting up after six years, old friends David and Alan rekindle their friendship. Bus driver David and advertising executive Alan have grown apart – but quickly recognise the strength of their feelings for each other. David is now married with two sons, though: can they really contemplate a life together?

"A wonderful story. It has your heart on an emotional roller coaster".

"The story sucked me in on page 1 and kept me wrapped up in it till I was finished with the book."

Available in print and ebook format

See **www.chrischeek.me** for more details

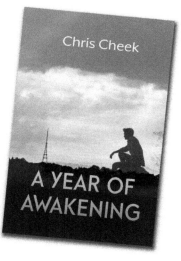